HIDDEN DEPTHS

Carla Vermaat

Also by Carla Vermaat

Tregunna

What every body is saying

Cover the lies

HIDDEN DEPTHS

Carla Vermaat

First published in Great Britain in 2019
by Carmichael Publishers, Cornwall
Copyright © Carla Vermaat 2019

A CIP catalogue record for this book
is available from the British Library

ISBN 978-0-9933339-6-5

Typeset in the UK by C. Vermaat
Cover Image © Carla Vermaat – Design by Carla Vermaat
Printed and bound in Great Britain by
TJ International, Padstow, Cornwall

MIX
Paper from
responsible sources
FSC® C013056

www.carmichaelpublishers.com

For my grandchildren

PROLOGUE

Its engine humming softly, the car was driving fast. Too fast to open the door and get out, curl herself into a ball and roll over the tarmac onto the grass verge, so that she could get up and run and hide in the woods beside the road. Admitting defeat, the girl pressed her head against the window and sobbed quietly.

The easy listening music on the radio was interrupted by the vaguely familiar tones of classical music on a mobile phone. Beside her, the driver cursed softly, quickly pressing a button to disconnect.

The girl swallowed with the feeling that this might have been her last chance. And she had missed it. If the call had come through, she could have screamed and yelled, banged on the dashboard, anything to attract the attention of the caller.

Ten seconds later, the unknown caller tried again. In front of them, a car suddenly pulled out from behind a lorry on a dark lay-by and the driver had to brake. Concentrating on the road and swearing under their breath, it was too late for the driver to cut off the high-pitched voice of a woman that crashed into the silence in the car.

'Where are you?' Angry, but somehow also lonely. Hurt. 'Is everything alright?'

A hand slammed on the buttons. Disconnected.

'She'll try again,' the girl said bravely, despite her precarious situation with a hint of sarcasm.

'Oh no, she won't!'

The car slowed down and bumped over the uneven hard shoulder, the crisp sound of grit crushing beneath the tyres. They came to a halt. The girl shifted in her seat, startled by the new situation and the unexpected opportunity that was opening up to her so suddenly that she could hardly believe her luck. She stared at the driver's hands that were now holding the mobile phone, tapping rapidly at the buttons. It must be a trick. They couldn't just have stopped to give her this chance …

She didn't hesitate. As slowly and quietly as she could, she unlocked the seatbelt, letting it wind-up gently, almost without making a sound. Then one click and she was out of the car, stumbling into a shallow ditch beside the road, her shoes slipping and sliding on the wet grass and rotting leaves.

She scrambled to her feet. She stood still for a moment, uncertain, instinctively inspecting her hands and knees. Her tights were torn and one of her knees was bleeding. There were smudges of mud on her skirt. No doubt she'd receive a reprimand from her mother about it, but that was currently the least of her worries. She peered into a pitch-black wood that stretched out in front of her. It wasn't appealing at all.

A bitter, frustrated curse erupted behind her. The shock of her own bravery was replaced with the fear that she was wasting time. Perhaps this was her last chance to escape. Panicking, she looked around. The road was deserted. Dark, wet tarmac, only a few cat's eyes in the middle of the road, lit up by the car's headlights. Dense trees and bushes on both sides of the road. In the distance, she could just make out a pair of oncoming headlights, but they were too far away still. She couldn't wait, she couldn't take the risk.

Behind her, the car engine spluttered. Then died.

As the girl quickly stepped into the ditch, she caught the expression on the driver's face as it was illuminated by the interior light. Pale and fraught with anger and frustration.

A hand quickly turned off the light, which, somehow, was more threatening. Taking a sharp intake of breath, she looked around in a last desperate attempt to find help, somewhere to hide, something to defend herself with. Nothing. Nowhere.

Then, a single click that sounded like a gunshot in the darkness. The driver's door was opened and the girl could hear the scraping of shoes on the gravel.

'Come on, girl, come back.'

She hesitated, wrapping her arms around her upper body. It sounded genuine. Sensible. The night was cold, it felt like the temperature was dropping below zero. But it wasn't the cold that made her shiver: it was the memory of hands pulling at her skirt, hot breath in her face.

'No!'

'Don't be so silly!'

She turned her head, panicking as she realised how close the voice was. Too close. Hearing it again, a cold sensation settled in her chest, as if her body had suddenly been exposed to a freezing blizzard.

'Darling, come back. I won't hurt you. I promise.'

Promise? How could she trust that promise ... after everything that happened in the car? What sort of promise would that be?

'No!' She smothered the single word behind her hand, realising how stupid it would be to get dragged into a discussion.

She had to get away. Promises were only hollow words. Some people kept their promises forever, others discarded them when it suited them.

Taking a deep breath, she stepped into the bushes. Her foot slipped on something soggy. Dog poo, perhaps. She stifled a nervous giggle. The ground sloped downwards and she continued to slip and slide on mud and leaf-mould. Too quickly, the wood seemed to be closing in on her. All she could see were trees, the slope of the hill obscuring any possible human life. Suddenly, her right foot slid from under her and she couldn't rebalance quickly enough. Falling, she tumbled down the hill, rolling through wet grass and bracken, and eventually she banged her shoulder hard against a tree that broke her fall. Breathing hard, she lay on her side for a moment, staring up at the hillside above her, expecting to see the face of her pursuer to appear above her.

She struggled to her feet. Trying to grab something, her fingers found a fence post. The weathered wood was wet and dirty beneath her fingers. Her hand grasped it, moving upwards finding rusty barbed wire that scratched her fingers. She gasped, sitting for a moment, putting her fingers in her mouth to suck away the blood and traces of dirt and rust, while her eyes adjusted to the darkness. She could see the fence now, the two strands of barbed wire. If she hadn't tumbled down, if the tree hadn't stopped her, she would have run straight into it.

Someone was calling her name, urging her to come back. But there was also a threat hidden behind the words. Frantically, she crouched down on her knees and scooped away the dead branches, the rotting leaves and wet soil, until she could slide underneath the rusty wires. Glancing over her shoulder, she couldn't see anyone following her but she could hear the distant voice. Threatening. Pleading. Begging.

Was it only her imagination that the voice sounded louder, closer? She clawed at the earth and roots of trees, trying to pull herself forward, under the wire, towards what she hoped would lead to safety. She was on her back for a moment, one cheek on wet leaves, her heart pounding and breathing heavily, sucking the air into her lungs. The sky was clear, moonless; the *temperature dropping.*

She scrambled up and started running again, fighting her way through the dense wood, branches that whipped at her face and brambles that clung to her clothes, her arms and legs. Every so often, her skirt snagged on something sharp and she heard it tear, digging into the flesh on her hips and thighs.

And then, all of a sudden, the trees and bushes opened up and she was on a narrow farm track, weeds and grasses growing in the middle of the cracked tarmac. Potholes and puddles, overgrown walls on both sides. She stood, listened. Which way to go? Left or right? Her head said right, her gut feeling told her to go left. It didn't really matter. Every road, however little used, leads from somewhere to somewhere. To another road, to a house, cars. People. Help.

But she was also out in the open. Visible. And she'd be trapped if a car appeared and all she'd be able to do was run like a rabbit caught in the headlights.

To the left the track sloped downhill, which made sense.

A distant whirr of an engine. She stopped and listened, but her breathing was heavy and her heart was pounding, so she couldn't make out whether it was a vehicle on the farm track with its lights turned off, or something further away, on the main road.

The wind was strengthening and it felt much colder. Her fingers and toes were getting numb. A line of tyre tracks in the mud crackled under her feet as she stepped on them. Frozen.

The wall on one side seemed to be getting a bit lower here, the trees behind it getting thinner. Then there was an opening in the wall, wide enough for tractors to go through, into the field beyond. Peering into the darkness, she looked across the field that sloped down the hillside. She knew now what the whirring sound was that she had heard earlier. A wind turbine, red warning light at the top. A bit further away, she could just make out the outline of a building silhouetted against the sky. Yellow and red lights were flashing and it took a while before she realised that treetops were obscuring the full view as they swayed in the wind in front of the lights.

Lights mean people. Warmth. Safety.

A petrol station.

1

A thick layer of mist hangs over the landscape. It is prematurely darkening. The air is thick with moisture, almost rain. Miserable. Cold and wet. Diffused headlights flash by, briefly followed by the glow of rear lights.

Concentrating, he leans over the steering wheel, eyes peering into the mist that seems to get thicker every minute. He curses himself for not thinking things through more thoroughly when he decided what the perfect place would be. Or at least he could have checked the weather conditions.

Tense and impatient, he doesn't want to miss the turning. He'd missed it once before. On one of those rare, pitch dark nights, he had ended up in a muddy farmyard, sheep gazing at him from behind a rusty gate. It had cost him nearly forty minutes, and three twenty pound notes to the farmer who had only agreed to pull his car out of the field when he'd promised him fifty pounds; it was even more annoying that he only had twenty pound notes in his wallet. Not to mention the cost of a pair of new leather brogues; his expensive Italian designer shoes had been completely ruined in the mud.

Closer to the coast, the mist is lifting gradually. All of a sudden, there are breaks in the clouds, casting a white light so bright that it almost looks fluorescent. However, the wind is gathering strength here. He can feel it battering the side of his car when he reaches the top of a hill. Every now and then, when there is a small gap in the hedges he can see the intermittent beam of a lighthouse. Godrevy Lighthouse. He remembers. They used to walk up the hill to the cliffs to watch the colony of seals on the shingle beach below, beaming excitedly when one of the seals slowly waddled towards the water.

Recognising with a hint of relief the dark shape of a church in front of him, he slows down until the hedges on one side of the road open up and he can see the familiar narrow lane, grasses and weeds in the middle and potholes on either side where the original tarmac has cracked long ago. It leads to a cluster of old cottages, some refurbished by new owners, and a few farm buildings. Whitewashed walls and old stonework. Slate roofs, some new and shiny, others old and overgrown with mosses and lichen. A disused shed with a rusty corrugated roof and a door that has lost one of its hinges.

The track is even narrower further down the hillside. His mind drifts off. Memories of running feet and laughter, the sun on their shoulders, the barking of a dog - he can't remember which one, there was always one -, a woman calling that tea is ready.

His throat tightens and he shakes his head, clenching his fingers around the wheel. Not far now. Another hundred yards. He stops where the lane is wide enough to make a sharp turn onto a short drive. As he gets out into the gloomy, grey evening, he feels the dampness in the air on his face. Mizzle. Another memory. They'd found a kitten stuck between the brambles, its fur an extra-ordinary light shade of grey. The people from the nearby farm didn't know whose kitten it was - or so they claimed - and Mizzle ended up in a box in the back of their car, carsick and scared. The smell had still been in the car weeks after they got back home.

Too many memories. Perhaps he shouldn't have come here.

Barely visible from the road, the cottage nestles in the cleft of the hillside, surrounded by an old stone wall that is now overgrown with ivy and brambles, and with bent rowan trees and conifers that have been deformed by the prevailing winds. The small windows look out across the valley, and a few miles away, to the sea.

The path is littered with slippery clods of wet leaves. Stepping carefully between them, drops of drizzle nestle in his hair. The padlock on the gate is heavy and cold. He tries to remember the six numbers which open it, but he can't concentrate. Memories are flooding over him like the thick mud of a swamp. His eyes are wet; the drops that wriggle down his face through his stubble taste salty when they reach his mouth.

All of a sudden, this feels wrong. He shouldn't have come here. He shouldn't have chosen this place. But it is too late now. There isn't a way back. He dropped the letter in a mailbox. A first-class stamp on it. It should arrive the following day. It means that there is no time left to reconsider the options and possibilities and find another place for his plans.

The padlock. He turns the digit dials and presses the button. Nothing happens. Then he remembers. They'd changed the number because there'd been a break-in just before Christmas. As far as anyone could tell, nothing had been stolen, but there were signs that one of the beds had been slept in. Collectively horrified, the women had insisted they'd change the padlock number, but then they had all joked about it: whoever had known the six digits of their father's birthday, would, in all probability, also know the six digits of their mother's.

Weighing the now unlocked padlock in his hand, he stands there for a few long moments, staring at the dark windows. Amazingly, he can see the small crack in the glass where his nephew had nearly broken it with the kick of his football. Was that only last summer? No, it must have been the year before because last year the boy had struggled with a broken leg, sulking about the beautiful weather that had drawn them all to the beach and onto their surf boards.

He shakes off the memories. Going back in his tracks to his car, he drives it through the open gate and closes it behind him. He considers changing the numbers of the padlock again, but realises that would only make things more difficult for the others. It'll be difficult enough for whoever comes here tomorrow.

For some unfathomable reason, he thinks about his mother. Poor woman. She's had so much on her plate already, things she has now forgotten. Events that are now locked in unreachable pockets in her brain. His father ... As if it was yesterday, he can picture him: a quiet proud man, strong enough to carry the world on his shoulders. His world. Theirs. Until it collapsed and he collapsed with it. Daisy's death changed him the most.

He shivers, not wanting to recall the memories of that tiny body, her face bluish pale as they pulled her out of the pond. *What have you done? Nothing. I did nothing.* And afterwards, *I know what you did ...*

The sentence has forever stuck in his mind. It wasn't true. He knew it. His father knew it, but he could always see the accusation in the man's eyes.

He takes a deep breath. His wife ... the thought of her almost makes him choke. She's usually quite laid-back and easy going, but she can also be stubborn. If only he knew for certain that she would follow his instructions exactly as he'd written them. Otherwise ... he just doesn't know what will happen ...

But he can't be bothered with that anymore now. His instructions are clear. If she chooses not to follow them ...

He unlocks the front door and pushes it open, stepping in with the awkward feeling that he is trespassing. The cottage is cold and damp. Closing the door behind him, he stands dripping in the hallway, eyes adjusting to the darkness. He knows there is an electricity meter above the window in the corner, with a tin of old pound coins next to it, but he has already decided not to turn it on. What would be the point anyway?

There is an unidentifiable smell that has penetrated the walls and the carpets and curtains; the vague pine scent of a fresh Christmas tree and the many scented candles his mother used to bring. It seems like a very long time ago.

'Hello?' The sound of his voice piercing the darkness is swallowed up in the silence of the cottage. Although it is unlikely that someone is here, he feels that he has to be certain. After all, someone had once slept in one of the double beds, so he has to be prepared to encounter an uninvited visitor.

'Hello?' He tries again, opens the door to the kitchen. As though his limbs are paralysed, his feet frozen to the spot, he stands on the threshold for several long moments, taking it all in. The cupboard doors so carefully painted by his father, light beige with a touch of yellow that, despite there only being one small window above the sink, somehow made everything look warm and sunny. The watercolour paintings are still in their identical frames. Seascapes by a local artist. The fruit bowl on the table is empty. Beside it, is a small notebook his mother used to scribble her shopping list in - and then forgot to take the list when she went to the supermarket. He stares at her neat, round handwriting. There is one word written on the top page. Bleach.

He turns and swallows, his throat thick with fear. The cottage is different somehow. Perhaps because he has never been here on his own. First as a child, with his parents, later with his own family, or all of them together. He feels as though he doesn't belong here anymore. As if the boy of all those years ago, has passed away. Already. He shivers, shocked by his own thoughts.

One last look and he walks out, closing the door behind him with a firm click.

He enters the study. A side room with an old wooden desk in front of the small window that overlooks the garden behind the cottage, sheltered by old drystone walls and one big windbreak with glass panels overlooking the view. The walls are lined with bookcases. A collection of crime thrillers, romances and children's books. He swallows when he sees the framed photographs on the otherwise empty desk, and all of a sudden, he feels the tears pricking in his eyes. The filing cabinet with the key bent in the lock. The remains of a yellow smiley sticker on the side, stuck on it, he remembers, by his little sister.

One of the framed photos catches his eyes. It has a brown leather frame with two small gold-coloured lines around the edges. He knows the photo in it so well, yet, he realises with a pang of guilt that he hasn't looked at it for a long time.

Picking it up with an unsteady hand, he stares at the woman in the middle. The dress she's wearing was one of her favourites, red cotton printed with yellow and white daisies. The swelling of her belly is barely visible. Her dark hair is tied back, earrings dangling beside her cheeks. There is a smile on her face, but it isn't reflected in her eyes and the dimple in her left cheek seems to have vanished. At the moment the photo was taken, the boy on her right side was just about to escape her hand that rests loosely on his shoulder, but the knuckles of her hand are white as she firmly holds him in position. His eyes are twinkling mischievously and his cheeky grin shows the gap where, just two days earlier, he had lost one of his front teeth. To the other side of the woman is a little girl in a white dress with a smile that would soften any stone-cold heart.

He swallows a few times, then, on an impulse, he removes

the photo and puts the empty frame back where it stood. Holding the photo in his hand, considering whether to put it in his breast pocket, he goes back to the hallway.

The last door opens onto the family room. The walls are painted a rich cream above polished mahogany panelling. Three identical sofas covered with an orangy-red corduroy, arranged in a U-shape around a log burner. Above it, a large watercolour painting of a field full of daisies and, near the top, a small figure barefoot on the grass. Daisy.

More paintings, not as delicate as the watercolour, but vibrant oils by different artists, each of them capturing sparkles of light on the sea. He sits down, stares blankly at the large watercolour painting, numb with fear and regret. Daisy. He remembers her soft young skin. Her chubby hands so faithfully thrust in his, the sweet scent of her soft blonde hair.

It is close to nine when he sits up with a start. He must have fallen asleep. It's completely dark. His hands and fingers are numb with cold. His breathing is loud and his heart is pounding. Something has woken him. He doesn't know who or what it was, but he knows it's there, watching, laughing, waiting.

He looks at his watch; there is still nearly half an hour to go. He picks up his holdall. It isn't heavy, it only holds a rope, a plastic sheet and his mobile phone. He leaves the room without looking back. His footsteps are soft on the carpeted staircase. To his own surprise, he automatically avoids the left side of the third step, the one that always had a creak. He shakes his head and wipes off yet more memories.

On the narrow landing, all four doors are closed. He opens the first door to the left. Daisy's room. He can almost see the outline of her small body under the blankets, her thin blonde hair spread out on the pillow. Her thumb dropped out of her mouth, her hand close to her face. A dried tear in the corner of her nose.

He stops and stares, thinking how bizarre life can be. Looking back at all the twists and turns, the coincidences and bad luck, the mistakes and misunderstandings, he doesn't feel angry. Not even bitter. This was triggered for all the wrong reasons, yet he knows that what he is going to do now is unavoidable.

He empties his holdall on the end of the bed. Spreads the plastic sheet on the floor; he'd hate to make a mess on the pristine beige carpet. His heartbeat is increasing. His eyes are blurred. Wet. He remembers the photo and retrieves it from his pocket. Briefly, he thinks about pressing his lips on the cool shiny paper, but it is difficult to make a choice who to kiss first. The mother or the girl. Not the boy. Definitely not the boy.

As if the paper is burning in his hand, he drops the photo on the floor.

Then he picks up the rope.

2

There is a torn open plastic shopping bag lying on the car park. A dozen seagulls are tearing it open, pecking at its contents to find something to eat. Fighting greedily. Sharing nothing. I stare out the window and cut the engine. The pale blue sky is dotted with clouds that drift in from the Atlantic, casting shadows on the water. They look like cottonwool balls, gradually getting bigger as they cluster together further inland.

It has been three years since I was diagnosed with cancer. Unknown to me, my body had welcomed and nurtured a couple of cells that invaded my bowels and battled against my own, planting seeds that grew like Japanese knotweed. By the time their roots had eaten their way into my tissue, it was too late. The surgeon had to remove certain vital parts of me, replaced them with artificial ones and I had to get used to living with a colostomy, a stoma to the layman. Which, I must admit, isn't as horrifying as I thought in the beginning.

I lock my car and enter the police station. As the door closes behind me, all sounds from traffic and seagulls seem to evaporate. Three of the chairs in the station foyer are taken by two girls and a woman who seems to think she must do all the talking as if the girls can only speak and understand some foreign language. They are about thirteen years old, with long skinny limbs, their bodies only just starting to fill out into a womanly shape. They appear to be the same height, but that is where the resemblance stops. One has thin, dark blonde hair that hangs straight down beside her narrow face as if she needs to hide behind it when she feels exposed to the rest of the world. The other girl has dark brown hair that dances loosely onto her shoulders, a fringe that is just short enough not to irritate her big brown eyes.

The woman's face has a frustrated look that must be the cause of her flushed cheeks and probably high blood pressure. She clutches her handbag against her chest as though she's protecting the family jewellery.

I step forward and the desk officer can't suppress a sigh of relief. By the look on her face, the woman has given her a hard time already.

'This is Detective Inspector Tregunna,' Anita Barron says quickly, begging me with her eyes not to disappear. I give her a brief encouraging nod. We had a less than friendly start when she came to work at the station in the role of desk officer, but somewhere down the line we have come to a mutual understanding, and somewhere even lurks the beginning of a solid friendship.

'Mr Tregunna will handle your … case, Mrs Quayle,' the desk officer says, lips curling into what looks to me like a badly hidden grin.

Mrs Quayle turns her head round and examines me from top to toe. She reminds me of Hyacinth Bucket, but younger and slimmer. Apparently, what she sees doesn't meet her expectations. Or her approval. She raises the left corner of her pale lipsticked mouth and her left eyebrow at the same time as though she's trying to surprise me. I'm not impressed. I've seen one of the newsreaders on TV doing a much better act.

'The girls are reporting a suspicious … find,' Anita Barron says helpfully, not only adding information for my benefit, but also adding to the woman's annoyance. 'Virginia Quayle and Roberta Ferguson.' She studies her notes and adds, as an afterthought, 'And Mrs Quayle.'

I look at the girls, trying to work out which one is Mrs Quayle's daughter. Neither of them shows much resemblance to the woman. Their body language tells me that they are highly uncomfortable with the whole situation. Avoiding my eyes, the blonde girl stares ahead blankly and the other examines her fingernail with undue interest.

'We would like to make a statement,' says Mrs Quayle pompously.

'In short, what would be the nature of the statement?' I ask curtly.

The woman blinks with pale blue eyes. The red patches on her cheeks turn a deep crimson. She looks at me for a long time, her nostrils flaring and her lips curled up as though she's thinking of swallowing me in one go. Unconsciously, she pulls at the sides of the short jacket that matches her skirt. She isn't as confident as she wants me to believe. I hold her gaze. Her mouth opens and closes. She doesn't speak now. Her mind is weighing up the possibilities. She finds none.

The momentarily frozen pantomime is interrupted when the door behind us opens and a man comes in. Perhaps sensing the tension in the air, he shrugs briefly and takes a seat in the waiting area, crossing his arms in front of his chest.

Mrs Quayle recovers and finds her voice. 'Erm … I'd rather discuss that in private.'

The dark-haired girl moves, as if she's considering running out of the building. The other girl takes a packet of chewing gum from her jeans pocket, popping a bright blue piece in her mouth before offering one to the other girl, ignoring the rest of us.

'It is a rather … delicate matter,' Mrs Quayle continues, her voice already returning to what I guess is her normal tone.

Anita Barron winks at me, immediately diminishing the

sound of the alarm bells in my head that the three females have come to report a case of sexual assault.

'Of course,' I say gently.

'Interview room …,' Anita starts with a straight face, but stops abruptly when, as if on cue, the door bangs open and another man, heavily bearded and in dishevelled clothes stumbles in, almost falling as he trips over one of his loose shoelaces.

'Oh no.' I hear her mutter as she glances at the man. 'Not that vagrant again.'

The seated man looks round from under bushy grey eyebrows and decides immediately to ignore everyone present in the entrance hall.

'I've been robbed!' the vagrant exclaims, apparently addressing no one in particular. 'I want to report a criminal offence.'

There is a brief uneasy silence. Even Mrs Quayle seems put off-balance by the disturbance. Then she turns her permed head and looks at the newcomer disdainfully. Her nostrils flare up as they sense a smell of grime and stale alcohol.

'You will have to wait,' she says arrogantly. 'We were here first.'

I see the desk officer stifle a grin behind her hand. The two girls look embarrassed and horrified at the same time, but I'm not sure if it's because of the man's behaviour or the woman's.

'Mum, maybe it wasn't what we thought,' the blonde girl interrupts suddenly, head hanging down and looking shyly from between the straight strands of hair flopping over her face.

'Certainly not!'

'Maybe we need to see it again,' the dark-haired girl adds bravely.

'I. Said. No!' Mrs Quayle's voice sounds as if a two-year-old child has just grabbed a trumpet and started playing it loudly. The result is a voice echoing in my ears, hitting my eardrums harshly. Even the vagrant steps back involuntarily before he remembers he has no intention of being ignored.

'I've been a victim of robbery,' he repeats, his voice suddenly adopting a posh accent in an attempt to match, and mock, Mrs Quayle's.

'I don't care,' she responds grandly, lifting her chin, eyes blazing. 'This is a matter of life and death.'

'Exactly.' Despite his earlier exclamation about being robbed, the vagrant's eyes are twinkling and he seems to be finding the situation very amusing. 'I could have been killed if I had caught the man in the act!'

I stare at the blonde girl who, every so often, exchanges glances with the other girl, in unspoken mutual under-standing. They are clearly wishing that they were miles away.

'Interview room 2 is vacant, Detective Inspector.' Anita Barron is pulling a straight face, eyes avoiding mine. I stare at her stoically. We both know that room 2 is barely used; everyone avoids it as it's a dark and gloomy room where several unidentifiable smells have penetrated the walls and carpets, perhaps even the ceiling. DC Jennette Penrose once claimed to know for sure that a builder with a grudge against the police who came to refurbish the station a decade ago hid a dead rat between the walls.

'Thank you, Anita. We'd better go into interview room 2 then, Mrs Quayle,' I say in an affected gentle manner, turning and gesturing as I open the door that has a sign saying 2 on it. By way of a joke, someone has tried to remove the sign, with the result that it hangs on the one screw that can't be unscrewed and now sticks out of the black metal sign. Someone else has already declared it a health-and-safety risk, but that suggestion has been dismissed by DCI Guthrie as 'bullshit'.

'Shall we?' I say gallantly, retrieving my phone to use it to make preliminary notes until we have established that a formal complaint has to be made.

'Perfect,' the vagrant says happily. 'Now, I want to declare that I've been robbed.'

But Mrs Quayle can't leave it at that. As the girls reluctantly enter the interview room, she turns and makes a gesture towards the first man who has been sitting in the waiting area, patiently waiting for his turn. 'You will have to wait,' she says to the vagrant, pointing with her index finger as though she wants to stick it into his chest. 'That gentleman over there was first.'

I stare at her with a mixture of loathing and contempt. The woman has the hide of an elephant and I know that, whatever I say or do, she will disagree and object. She's just that sort of person.

3

All down the road from St Eval to the coast road the wind batters my car from the northwest, finding free rein on the barren plain on my left where once the airfield of St Eval was situated. Now all that is left are some concrete gun shelters and a vast expanse of cracked tarmac, partially overgrown with grass but also home to the still operational MoD high frequency transmitter station, and some grazing sheep. In the distance, I can see the flashing lights of a commercial aeroplane making a turn over the sea in preparation for landing at the modern airport of Newquay.

St Eval church stands alone, a square church tower that can be seen from miles away. A weathered signpost indicates the turn to Treburrick, a settlement rather than a village that hugs both sides of the road. The coast road curves and gently drops towards the cliff edges where the fierce Atlantic gales batter the rugged coastline. In the distance, waves break on the rocky island outcrops, every so often caught in white spray as the sea crashes onto them.

I have driven here several times before, past half a dozen houses on either side of the road; a holiday home with ample parking for big family cars. A weathered, bluish shed where a local mechanic fixes cars in the old-fashioned way by listening to discrepancies in the roar of the engines, stubbornly refusing to use computer technology. Alongside the road is a makeshift wooden cabinet on rusty legs with a glass top, holding a mouth-watering collection of home-made cakes and pies, sheltered on sunny days by a parasol that turns around with the wind. Fields run parallel, planted with various crops, sometimes producing the intrusive smell of cabbage, while sheep and cows nibble the stalks after the migrant workers have picked the harvest. Smaller fields, surrounded by the inevitable overgrown walls and hedges, shelter grazing horses. At the edge of the village is a campsite where city children can stay to experience rural life, where they can touch and feed goats and sheep, chicken and rabbits, ride the donkeys, or stare at the occasional land turtle taken in by people who got bored with it. Next to the camp, built probably to serve a wider community, is a soulless village hall which the local parish council uses for its meetings.

I slow down and pull in between two cars parked alongside the road. The door to a workshop cum garage is open; I can hear soft music and the sharp tone of an electric tool. It stops abruptly as I approach. A man in grubby overalls is leaning over the engine of a small red car, ducking beneath the open bonnet. He looks up as I walk in, a mixture of expectancy and annoyance on his face.

He pushes what look more like goggles than safety glasses onto his forehead, holding an electric hand-tool in one hand, wiping the other hand on trousers that are covered in oil stains and streaks of rust. He looks to be in his sixties, with a mop of thick dark hair speckled with silver and bright hazel eyes. His movements are slow and slightly odd.

I put my hand in my pocket to retrieve my ID card and introduce myself, but on second thoughts, take out a yellow post-it note instead, folded, where I have written a name.

'I hope you can help me. I'm looking for Mr Cawley.'

He raises bushy eyebrows. 'Cawley? There's Nathan, Boris, James, Harry. Or Rich?'

'I'm not sure. J. Cawley. I suppose that must be James.'

'Or Nathan.' He nods seriously. 'That'll be Jonathan.'

'Oh. I see.' I feel clumsy and inadequate, half grateful that I didn't tell him that I am a Detective Inspector of Devon and Cornwall police.

'What is it about?' he asks brusquely.

'I'm not in a position to say.'

He casts me a cautious look. 'Well, either way …'. He offers a slow grin and motions towards a point behind me. 'They live almost next to each other. Can't miss it. At the end of the lane. Nathan's door is yellow. I doubt he'll be in though.'

He points and I follow his oily finger to the gap between his garage doors, where I can see part of a white gate in front of a short drive next to a bungalow. I can't see the front door, but I'm sure I would have noticed if it had been painted yellow.

'Where are you parked?' He shakes his head as if he's speaking in a foreign language I don't understand. Not waiting for my reply, he shuffles to the door and without hesitation spots my car. 'Turn round and take the next lane left. You see the mirror? Right there.'

Half obscured by brambles and ivy is a round convex mirror to help drivers coming out of a narrow lane to see if there is any traffic coming.

I thank him and he nods, offering a small grin. 'Nice car. Good make.'

'I hope so. It's brand new.'

He nods, unconsciously picking up a hammer and weighing it in his hand. 'Good luck with the Cawleys.'

I wonder if his last words are meant as a warning when I turn into a narrow lane that is covered with chunks of mud and tractor tyre tracks. It leads to a cluster of old cottages and refurbished modernised houses. Whitewashed walls and old stonework. Slate roofs, some new and shiny, others old and overgrown with mosses and lichen.

None of the houses have a yellow door. I drive further to where the lane is wide enough to park. I climb out into the crisp, blustery morning. My hair whips around my head as though some invisible electric force is playing havoc with it. Dodging chunks of mud, I follow the road to where it ends, then I go back on my tracks to another lane, to a house that looks like a barn conversion. The lower part of the building is made of stone while the upper part has natural wood cladding and windows with solid wood frames rather than the now common PVC ones. Three steps and a wrought iron handrail with a metal letterbox attached to it lead to a yellow front door.

As I climb the steps, a dog starts barking. A net curtain moves behind a window, a glimpse of a hand. I knock on the door and wait patiently as someone inside fumbles with a bunch of keys and unlocks the door, opening it no wider than three inches.

'Yes?'

Between her legs under a dark skirt, the snout of a dog is frantically trying to get sight of me. Or more, judging by the look in its eyes when it manages to see me.

'I'm looking for Mr Cawley.' I show the woman my ID card but, small eyes narrowed, she barely looks at it.

'Oh. Police. Wait two seconds, please.'

The door is closed, not locked. I can hear the woman's voice and the muted barks of the dog. Then she's back, opening the door to let me in, an apologetic smile across a pale, round face. She is barely five foot tall with narrow shoulders and dark short-cropped hair. Her eyes are small and slightly slanting upwards, suggesting some Asian origin.

'I'm Jinny Cawley,' she says softly. 'You'll want to speak to Nathan.'

She hasn't asked the purpose of my visit, so I presume I have come to the right Mr J Cawley.

'It's all very … unfortunate,' she mutters over her shoulder, leading me through a square hall that is laid with big slate tiles and a huge rug with white flowers on a burgundy background. The walls are lined, waist-high, with vertical wooden panelling and, above it, paintings in plain bronze-coloured frames, nearly all of them depicting horses.

'I just made a brew for my husband,' she says, opening a dark wooden door and stepping aside politely as though she is a humble servant. 'Can I get you a cup of tea? Or would you prefer coffee?'

'Coffee would be lovely, Mrs Cawley.'

She pushes open the door and simply says, 'Nathan', before disappearing.

The first thing I notice is a huge TV screen on the wall showing a football match, the sound muted, but the scoreboard at the bottom which was flashing 0-0 changes to 0-1. A figure rises from a deep leather chair. A tall man with broad shoulders and a long, rather weather-beaten face, with red cheeks veined from too much exposure to the elements, or excessive alcohol. His hair is shaven to a silver stubble, a salt-and-pepper moustache curls upwards on its orange-tinged ends, suggesting he was a redhead when he was young, which seems probable with the pale blue colour of his eyes. He gazes over a pair of rimless glasses pulled down to the middle of his large, bulbous nose.

'Are you alone?' he asks, making it sound like we are involved in some kind of conspiracy.

'Yes. Sorry, I'm Tregunna. Detective Inspector.'

'Nathan Cawley.'

In three strides he comes forward, reaching out to shake my hand, and his big, calloused hand nearly crushes mine. He doesn't seem to be aware of it and I successfully hide my aching fingers.

'Good of you to come.' He motions towards the TV screen, picking up a remote control from one of the small side tables. The room is, so it seems, solely meant for watching TV. The screen dominates the room that has three linked brown leather sofas arranged in a semicircle facing it. Small side tables are placed at each end of the sofas with a pile of newspapers and magazines balancing on one of them.

'Mr Cawley, you called the station.'

'Yes.' He frowns, clearly not used to someone else taking the lead. 'Has my wife offered you a cup of tea? Or coffee perhaps?'

'She has.'

As if on cue, his wife opens the door pushing the handle down with her elbow as she carries in a tray of cups and saucers. Her eyes flash in my direction and she bites her bottom lip nervously as she places my coffee on the nearest side table. 'Carrot cake?'

I open my mouth to say that I'm trying to lose weight, but there is something in her eyes that makes me say, 'Yes. That's lovely. Thank you, Mrs Cawley.'

'Okay. Now take a seat, please, Mr Tregunna.' Cawley's gesture involves all of the seats. I choose a seat opposite him.

He sits down, pressing buttons on the remote to freeze the TV screen. Football players, in opposing teams, are dressed either in blue or red shirts and smudged white shorts. Three players hang motionless in mid-air, looking up to the ball, faces distorted, as they're each frozen in a jump to head the ball in different directions.

'Are you a football fan, Mr Tregunna?'

'Not really,' I reply earnestly and I see how this adds to his opinion of me. A disappointment.

I take a small notebook from my breast pocket and click the end of my pen. 'How can I help you, Mr Cawley?'

'A letter.' He seems a man of few words. Reaching for the pile of newspapers beside him, he lifts a magazine and finds a brown envelope the size of half an A4, torn open on one side. 'This is what I received yesterday.'

He opens the envelope and takes out a white sheet of paper, unfolding it. 'If you're worried about fingerprints, Mr Tregunna, then don't. Not necessary. I know who sent it.'

The letter is not signed. It is a short note, typed and printed in a standard font, although the size is larger than normal.

'*You will regret it when you go on with your plans. Or an accident may happen.*'

'You said you know who sent this, Mr Cawley.'

'I do.' He speaks without hesitation. 'My nephew. James Cawley.'

'And you received it yesterday?' He sees the question, 'why didn't you call us the day before?' in my eyes and quickly continues, 'I found it in our mailbox outside when my wife and I came home from our weekly shopping. I didn't check the mailbox before we went, so it is possible that the letter was put in it the night before.' He pulls his mouth into a forceful grin. 'Which may well be plausible, knowing my family, Inspector. He wouldn't dare deliver a letter like that when there is a chance of being spotted by me or my wife.'

'Do you believe it is a serious threat?'

'I'm not sure, to be honest, Mr Tregunna. I was inclined to chuck the letter in the bin, but my wife insisted on keeping it, and after I'd given it some thought, I decided that it wouldn't hurt to let the police know about it. Just in case.'

I stare at the letter. And at him. A bulk of a man. Strong, even at his age. The eyes of a bully. It doesn't make sense.

'What plans are being referred to in the letter, Mr Cawley?'

He shrugs. 'Well, I suppose this has to do with the meadow. It's a piece of land I own. I'm planning to build on it and there is a meeting about it tonight.'

'People object?'

He shrugs dismissively. 'I don't see the problem. It's my land. I can do with it what I want.'

'If you're taking this letter seriously, Mr Cawley, I'll need to know who objects to your plans.'

He places his elbows on the armrests of his chair, lacing his fingers. 'Now there's a problem, Inspector. Nearly everyone here is against my plans.'

'You mentioned your nephew?'

'My brother's son. James, acting on behalf of his father who, I must admit, has more common sense than fighting against me.'

'And what can I do for you?'

He grins sardonically. 'Nothing. I'm aware that I'm wasting your time, Inspector. I wouldn't have called at all if my wife hadn't insisted. She thinks the letter is a serious threat.'

I pick up a plate with a generous piece of carrot cake. It looks good but it is rather dry.

'And you don't?' I take a sip of coffee to wash the cake down.

He grins arrogantly. 'There's nothing they can do. I have powerful support behind me.'

4

'I can't believe there is nowhere to park,' Jennette Penrose mutters under her breath, casting a hopeful glance sideways at the man in the passenger seat. Refusing to wear his seatbelt because for most of his life there weren't any, he sits rigidly beside her. His back and shoulders straight, he is staring in front of him, holding a walking stick between his bony knees, rheumy hands folded over the top.

'There is always somewhere to park,' he insists with the almost childish stubbornness he has developed since he suffered a mild stroke.

'Yes, father, but that will be further along this road.' She has to make an effort to sound gentle and patient. 'This car park is full and people are now parking on the road.'

'I can see that. I may be old, but I'm not blind,' he scoffs, banging his walking stick on the floor as if to emphasise his point.

'I expected you earlier,' he continues sulkily, clearly unaware that they had that same conversation several times already.

'Yes, father.' Jennette clenches her teeth to keep her lips from forming an angry retort. There is really no point in going against him, she knows. If anything, she knew from the start that it wasn't a good idea to bring him here and she wishes she'd had more willpower to overrule his demands, or, in a more subtle manner, distract him with a story about her work. She can tell him anything about an investigation because he's forgotten about it ten minutes later, though he enjoys sharing her anecdotes and secrets.

'If I can't find a place to park, we'll have to go back home, I'm afraid,' she says eventually, hoping she doesn't sound as hopeful and threatening as she feels.

He bangs the walking stick on the floor again, then stamps his feet like a rebellious child, crushing lumps of mud into the carpet.

'There is always something or somewhere.' He glares at her angrily and accusingly. 'There must be.'

'Hmm.' She knows better than to respond. The short silence fills with muted voices from people walking along the side of the road, all heading for the village hall that stands solitary beside the country road, overlooking fields on all sides.

Her father frowns as if he's trying to remember where he is or what they are doing here and, for a fleeting moment, she wonders what will happen if she just takes the next turning and drives back home. Would he notice?

But the void in his memory seems to have cleared and he knocks on the side window with a white knuckle, saying hopefully, 'Maybe people are already going home.'

'I doubt that, father, people have just arrived for the meeting,' she answers wryly, slowing the car to let a couple cross the road in front of them.

'I'm sure that bloody councillor will have found a space near the door.'

'He's bound to if he is the one who's organising the whole thing.'

'She is the biggest liar on the planet,' he says but he doesn't explain that any further.

'She?' Jennette queries.

He grunts. 'Don't tell me you've never heard of her. Iris Spencer. She's in business and she's also a councillor. To me, those two jobs don't go hand in hand.'

Jennette stares at him again questioningly, but, seeing the angry look on his face, decides not to react.

'Look, father, these people are all parked at the end of this road. We can park there too, but you can't walk all the way to the village hall. I think it's better to go home. Your vote, if it'll ever come to that, will make no difference anyway.'

'Two votes.'

She shakes her head vigourously. 'I told you from the beginning, I'm not going in.'

'But I need you to find me a seat.'

She suppresses a sigh, glancing at her mobile phone in the holder on the dashboard as if she's willing it to ring. Even if DCI Guthrie rang her now and asked her to catch a loose cow on the road, she would happily oblige rather than go to the meeting with her father.

'We could have got a parking space near to the entrance of the village hall. We could have got you a seat on the front row if you hadn't been so damned ... slow.'

As soon as the angry words come out, she already regrets them. It is unfair to blame him for something he can't do anything about. He is a frail old man, and slow, but it wasn't his fault that she came home later than expected. Yet, he could have put his shoes and coat on ready, and found the keys that always seem to get lost and appear in the most extraordinary and unexpected places, and made sure he'd got the right pair of glasses on his nose.

'I'm sure there are parking spaces for Blue Badge Holders. They must be very close to the entrance of the Hall,' he lisps, optimistically all of a sudden.

'You don't have a Blue Badge, father.'

'Maybe not, but I'm entitled to one.'

She purses her lips. 'You don't even have a car.'

'Exactly. And whose fault is that? Yours! You took my car away and sold it because you thought I wasn't able to drive anymore.'

'Because you weren't. You aren't, father.'

'I've never had an accident. Never.'

'You caused one, father, but you didn't even notice. You just drove on when another car had to swing to the other side of the road to avoid crashing into you, and then that car hit an oncoming car.'

'That wasn't my fault! They should have paid more attention!'

Jennette sighs, stopping the car and putting it into reverse in order to turn onto a little lane.

'Why are we stopping here?'

'I'm turning the car round.'

He bangs the walking stick on the floor. 'We're not going home.'

'No father.' She sighs, knowing that she will have to stop as close to the entrance of the village hall as she can, and then help him all the way inside, as he undoubtedly will want a seat on the front row. Whether they're already taken or not.

'There!' He points, his hand shaking.

An expensive looking silver car is parked beside an equally impressive looking black Jaguar leaving a space on the grass in front of the entrance to the steps to the village hall.

'I can't park there father, it's too narrow.'

'Of course you can. Look at the tyre tracks. There has been another car there.'

'But it isn't even a parking space.'

She blushes when she sees someone waving at her. Reluctantly, she gives a small nod. Kim Naylor, the reporter from *The Cornish Gazette*. To Penrose, every reporter should be kept at a considerable distance. To her annoyance, Tregunna seems to make an exception for Kim, whom he always regards with a mixture of fondness and admiration. However much Penrose dislikes the other woman, it might be a good sign that the press is here tonight.

'Who is that?' Her father demands to know about everything. 'Someone I know.'

She tightens her lips, wondering if she can still pull out of this time-wasting expedition without making him too angry and act like a sulking toddler for about a week. But as usual, it will be much easier to give in to his wishes than to resist.

It isn't a surprise to her that he is right. There are tyre tracks in the trodden grass beside the silver car; it wouldn't be difficult to squeeze in her little red Clio.

'Okay, I will try, but we are definitely going home if this doesn't work.' She is aware how unconvincing she sounds. She's almost disgusted with herself. She is a push-over, especially when dealing with her father. Always choosing the easy options, always giving in to save herself the hassle. How many times has she told herself the same things already? And what did she do to change things? Nothing.

She kills the engine and stares out of the window in front of her for a moment, preparing herself not to take the bait when he'll gloat that he was right. But for once, he is quiet and says, much to her surprise, 'You've done that very well, love.' He opens the door and it almost swings open, caught by a gust of wind. Miraculously, he holds onto the handle.

'Careful!' Thoughts about damaging the car next to them make her shiver. It'll cost her a fortune, and then she won't even have the damage repaired on her own car. 'Wait, father, I'll help you out.'

She runs around the car, just in time to see him open the door for a second time. Her feet sink in the muddy grass and she thinks about her shoes and what state they will be in when they get home. Too late to think about that now.

She shrugs, casting a glance at the other car. There is a bunch of flowers wrapped in cellophane on the passenger seat. Red roses. A bit late for Valentine's day. Perhaps it is a belated gift for Mothering Sunday, which was the previous day.

'Take my walking stick!' her father snaps.

Leaning heavily on the side of the other car, she helps him to his feet and supports him as he shuffles up the two steps and into the crowded village hall. People recognise them and someone from the front row waves, pointing at an empty seat. Gwyn Penrose, who albeit a nuisance to his daughter, still seems to be a popular man within the community where he has lived all his life.

5

I'm woken by the sound of my mobile phone vibrating against
the stem of an empty glass on the coffee table. Opening my
eyes, it takes me a few seconds to recognise my surroundings.
I have fallen asleep on the sofa. The heating has switched itself
off and the room is cold. An open-mouthed news reporter is
frozen on the TV screen at the point where the recording I
was watching has finished. I remember the film: a woman was
trapped in a house with no doors or windows. I can't remember
how she managed to escape.

I pick up my mobile and press the green button.

'Sorry to wake you, sir,' says Anita Barron. Her voice is soft
and subdued as though she doesn't want me to recognise it.

'I wasn't asleep.' Some lies are too easy.

A brief silence. 'Oh. Well, I'm sorry anyway.'

Through the open door to my bedroom, I stare at the alarm
clock on the bedside table. The red digits are flashing 12:00.
There must have been a power cut.

'What's the time?'

'Ehm, just past one, sir.'

'At night?'

'It's dark outside, sir, so … yes.' Irony in her tone.

'Oh.' I scratch my head, rub my fingertips over my nose and
eyes. 'What's so urgent?'

'We've had a call from one of our colleagues. About a
suspicious death.'

'Can't they handle it themselves?'

She hesitates momentarily. 'It's complicated.'

'A suspicious death is always complicated, Annie.' Unconsciously, I'm calling her Annie again. When she came to work at the station, I was too preoccupied, possibly too self-absorbed to make an effort to remember her name. 'Sorry. Anita.'

'I suppose you're still sleepy,' she responds wryly.

'Perhaps you will always be Annie to me.'

'Are you flirting with me?'

'No!' After a wearisome start, we're now getting on well.

'But seriously, can I tell you about the call?'

'I'm listening.'

'They received a call from Mrs Charlotte Lynham.' She pauses as though she's expecting an instant response, continuing when none comes. 'On Sundays, Mrs Lynham and her husband often drive to see her mother in Gloucester for lunch. This weekend, Mr Lynham had a lot of work to do and his wife went alone. It was Mothering Sunday. Her mother wasn't feeling very well and she called her husband to let him know that she would be staying the night in Gloucester. On Monday, she was still not sure about leaving her mother on her own and she tried to call her husband but there was no reply. She called his office but his secretary told her that he'd taken the day off. His wife thought it was rather strange, because he had told her it was so busy at work. She worried about him and after she had tea with her mother, she decided to go home. Her husband wasn't there. According to the officer who took the call, she was then seriously concerned that something might have happened to him.' Anita Barron pauses. 'Her husband is Edward Lynham.'

I pinch the bridge of my nose. 'You sound like I should know him.'

'Yes. He's been in the news lately.'

'I don't ... wait a minute. Ed Lynham? The politician?'

'That's him.'

'He's been under a lot of scrutiny about alleged sexual harassment.'

'According to his wife, he found it difficult to deal with all the allegations and what the press said about him. Apparently, there were accusations against him, but he wasn't told who made the claims. Privacy. Human Rights. Or victim protection. You name it. Anyway, he's been in the press for a while now. They're all over him. That's why his wife got so worried.' A brief silence. 'She came home around ten o'clock, last night. The house was dark. They're quite friendly with their neighbours and, seeing they were still awake, she went round to see them to find out if they'd seen her husband. They hadn't. They'd assumed he'd gone with her to Gloucester. Like he usually did.'

'Go on.' I'm not sure where the story is going and why Anita Barron thinks it is urgent enough to call me in the middle of the night, but I'm not doubting her judgement.

'When she returned home again about half an hour later, she used the front door rather than going round the back through their garage. And then she found his letter.'

'Telling her that he'd left her for his younger girlfriend?'

'Hardly that. He'd written that he couldn't handle it anymore, saying he was sorry, but he didn't see any other way.'

'Suicide?'

'Sounds like it. He also told her in the letter where he could be found. In a holiday cottage he and his sister inherited from their parents. His instructions were to call the police in the morning, not earlier, and let them enter the cottage with her. He didn't want her to find his body.'

I'm holding my breath. 'And the reason for your call?'

'Initially, Mrs Lynham decided to ignore her husband's instructions. She couldn't believe he was doing that to her. But, whether it is true or not, she doesn't want the press to know about it. He's had so much negative publicity of late and if this turns out to be someone else's sick joke, which she hopes it is, she fears it will drag him even deeper in the mud.'

I stifle a yawn and stumble to the kitchen. Fill the coffee machine. It sounds as though I'll need a strong coffee.

She's still talking.

'Mrs Lynham got in her car to go to the holiday cottage. But as she was driving, she had a good rethink and she started to believe that the letter might be genuine after all. And she thinks that it may be better not to enter the holiday property by herself. As her husband told her.'

'Sensible.' I sigh. 'I take it you have the address of the holiday cottage?'

'I have.' She hesitates. 'She said she would wait for the police to arrive, but I have a feeling that she won't be able to stop herself if she finds the waiting too long.'

'Okay. Can you text the address to me?'

The coffee machine works overtime while I get dressed. Munching a handful of biscuits, I take a few sips of coffee and pour the rest into a thermos flask. As it has become second nature, I check my stoma bag, and the battery of my mobile phone and put my arms in my jacket.

It will be a long night.

6

At this time of night, the A30 is almost deserted. I pass the odd lorry with supplies for the supermarkets in the southwest, various other delivery vans and a handful of cars.

It is a pitch dark night. Clouds are hanging low, threatening to rain. There's no moon. Fifty minutes later, I exit the dual carriageway and take the road towards the coast, feeling the wind increasing. Southwesterly gales are expected, along with heavy rainfall, and flooding in the usual areas.

It takes me a while to realise that I'm following a light, medium-sized car. As far as I can see, there is only the driver. Checking the maps app on my phone, I follow it, keeping just enough distance away not to blind the driver in the rear view mirror but not losing it in the darkness all the same. The road dips and rises, the sharp bends and in places almost U-turns, making me feel like I'm driving in a labyrinth where they've obscured both the centre and the exit. Every now and then, I can see the glow of the lights of Hayle and St Ives at one end of the bay and Godrevy lighthouse at the other. Yet somehow I don't seem to get any closer to the address Anita gave me.

Google maps also seems to be calling it a day. The map freezes on the screen, the arrow to tell me where I am is still there, but not moving.

I'm in the middle of nowhere. Online maps can be very helpful, but you don't get anywhere without a signal. This is Cornwall. I should have got used to having no reception by now, but it annoys me still, especially at moments like this. I'm tapping the screen to make it work, but to no avail. Meanwhile, without noticing, I'm slowing down and suddenly I realise that the car in front of me has disappeared. I curse myself for not paying more attention.

I am hopelessly lost. I must have missed a turning so carry on until the road descends gently through a village. I see signs that will take me back to the coast road. Somewhere to my right is the intermittent beam of Godrevy lighthouse watching over the bay and the estuary, but somehow my instinct tells me it isn't the right way.

On the driveway of what looks like a holiday let, vacant now, I turn the car and head back the way I came, making another wrong turn that takes me to the end of a lane and onto a farmyard.

As the road rises to a hilltop, I'm even more exposed, the wind battering the car. It has started to rain. Big drops wash relentlessly across the windscreen. I have to hold the steering wheel in both hands now, leaning forward as far as I can, straining to see in the darkness what lies ahead of me. Fortunately, Google begins to pick up a faint signal.

I almost miss the turning again. There is a small white sign that says 'Lavender Barns' and I find myself on a potholed track that dips and curves, past a sleepy hamlet, and fields with sheep and smallish trees that have bent in the wind.

A red light reflects momentarily in my peripheral vision. I stop abruptly at a short drive beside a darkened house. There are two cars parked on the drive. One is close to the house, also in darkness. The other car has stopped halfway through the gate, still with its lights turned on, the engine running. The driver's door is open and a woman's foot is sticking out, unmoving.

I get out. Using the torch on my phone to guide me as I make my way to the car.

'Mrs Lynham?' I say, trying to sound casual so as not to frighten her. 'Hi. I'm Andy, Devon and Cornwall Police.'

The woman doesn't move. Her head rests on the steering wheel, long dark hair hiding her face. She is sobbing, her shoulders shaking uncontrollably, her hands clutching at the wheel as though it is the only thing that can save her from drowning in despair.

'Mrs Lynham?'

For a brief moment she stops sobbing then she shakes her head and starts again.

'Mrs Lynham, is that your husband's car?'

'Hmm, yes. That's why …' Sobs again. Hopeless. Fear. Shaking her head in disbelief.

'Do you mind if I have a look?'

She lifts her head a few inches and wipes strands of hair from her face, staring at me. 'Are you a police officer?'

'Yes.' I retrieve my warrant card, but she shakes her head.

'Do you have a key to the house, Mrs Lynham?'

'The key … is under the flowerpot in the porch.' She hesitates. 'That's what the letter says. He's left it there.'

'Do you want to wait here or would you like to come with me?'

It is cold and wet. Raindrops fall off her shoe. I don't want to leave her here on her own.

'I don't know. I need to see him … for myself … but I'm so … I'm scared.' She shakes her head again, finding a paper tissue in her lap. She blows her nose loudly. 'But I'm also scared here, in the dark.'

I put my hand on her shoulder. Through the fabric of her short jacket, I can feel how cold she is.

'I must admit that I'm not looking forward to this either,' I say gently. 'Perhaps we can go in together?'

'I ... I ... I don't know.'

I gesture towards my car. 'There is a flask with some coffee in my car. Shall I fetch it for you?'

She shakes her head. 'Thank you, officer, but no, I don't drink coffee.' A thought occurs to her. She stares at the cottage, momentarily forgetting why we're here. 'I can make some tea, I suppose.'

'That's a great idea.' I smile at her. 'To be honest, I think the coffee will be cold by now.'

'Have you come far?'

'Not far. I'm from Newquay.'

'Oh.' She's lost interest, but her sobbing has stopped and she straightens up, leaning backwards in the seat, taking deep breaths to calm down. Finding a clip in one of her pockets she ties her dark hair in a ponytail. She looks as if her whole demeanour has changed. She seems older and more balanced somehow, more in control of the situation. Without thinking, she checks her make-up in the rearview mirror. Then she realises what she's doing and she gives a wry sad smile.

'Do you have the letter your husband sent to you?'

'It's in my bag.'

'Can I see it?'

A thought crosses her mind. 'Should I not have touched it? For fingerprints or something?'

'If necessary, we can eliminate your prints.'

'Erm ... thanks ...' She shakes her head, confused. Frantically she digs in a brown leather designer handbag that is delicately decorated with small brass chains. Amongst packets of tissues, lipsticks, hair clips, crumpled receipts and loyalty cards, wallets and folded shopping bags, she finds a white envelope with her name on it in what could be a man's handwriting.

It is a hurtingly short note from a husband telling his wife that he is going to end his life because he can't cope with the situation any longer. His last, rather intimate words bring a lump to my throat. '*So sorry, my love.*'

Silently, I fold the letter and she slides it back into the envelope, keeping her head down.

'Shall we …?'

She looks up quickly. 'Sorry, what is your name again?'

'Andy. Andy Tregunna.'

'Ehm … you go first, please Andy. I'll follow you.'

She stumbles out of her car, automatically reaching for a dark grey umbrella that has slipped onto the floor beneath the passenger seat. I wait patiently and then loosely take her elbow as we make our way over the gravelled drive to the front door. She smells vaguely of Indian food and wine. I don't ask how much she drank. I lift a flowerpot with a geranium that is still trying hard to survive the winter. I pick up a single key and hold it in my hand.

'I'll check the house while you make the tea.' I say gently. 'I'm here to help you, Mrs Lynham.'

'Thank you.' Her voice is softer than a whisper.

The hallway is dark but she knows the place well enough to find the light switch without stumbling over thresholds or bumping into hall tables or other obstacles. Slowly, she opens a door and enters the kitchen, sighing with a mixture of relief and more concern as she finds it empty.

'I'm afraid I haven't got any milk,' she says distractedly. Opening cupboard doors and finding cups and saucers and jars, she is momentarily caught up with domestic matters.

'I don't take milk.'

She's back to reality. 'He … he wrote that he would be upstairs.'

'Yes. I'll check now.'

She nods and as she stares at me from the doorway, I climb the stairs with a feeling of dread.

'It'll be the first door to the left.' Her voice is barely audible.

'Okay.'

I open the door. The smell of death hits me instantly and I am grateful that Charlotte Lynham didn't come here on her own. I stare into the empty eyes of a man who has recently been in the papers and on the local news with accusations of sexual assault. A man condemned by the press, guilty even before he was properly charged. A man desperate enough to take his own life.

7

Although it is almost mid-March, the country is recovering from an Arctic blast that disrupted normal life for a couple of days. The Met Office initially issued an amber warning, then changed it to a red warning, urging people to stay at home unless it is really necessary to go out. Cars are stranded on roads, schools are closed, rural communities are snowed in. Supermarket shelves are almost bare as a result of logistic problems on the southwest-bound motorways and, consequently, people are panic-buying.

'Imagine what it'll be like in Iceland.' Harradine Curtis sniffs, shaking his head disapprovingly.

'Iceland?'

He shrugs. 'Norway, Sweden, Canada, you name it. They have snow and freezing temperatures all winter. Every year. Do you ever hear that those countries come to a complete standstill for a bit of snow like we have now?'

Retrieving my gloves from my pocket, I watch him clear the windscreen of his car, wondering why he even bothers because he won't be driving today anyway.

My neighbour is a man of principles. He has a strict regime and lives by it to the letter. Friday used to be the only day he would use his car to drive to his job at Newquay Town Council, because on that day he does his weekly shopping after work.

'Are you driving today?' I ask curiously.

He wipes his headlights although there isn't much snow on them.

'Huh. I'm going to a reading group.'

'Reading group?'

'You know. A Book Club.'

'I didn't know you were such an avid reader, Mr Curtis.'

He frowns, eyeing me suspiciously. 'Are you taking the Mickey?'

'No.' I pull a straight face. 'Of course not.'

He's not convinced, but gives me the information nevertheless. 'One of my female colleagues tricked me into going to this Book Club because I said I know everything about Tolkien's books.'

'And do you?'

'I read the books when I was a teenager and I've seen the films on TV.'

'The first to triumph is the first to fall. Fall from grace.'

'Very funny.'

'How did she trick you?'

He shakes his head vigorously. 'Women can be so wicked!'

'Don't tell me about it.'

He ignores the humour and offers me his windscreen scraper. 'When I took her home the first time, she offered me a cup of tea.'

'Single lady?'

'Appears to be, but, honestly, Tregunna, I didn't know that. I thought she was married. Well, maybe I accepted the invitation because I was curious about her husband. I couldn't see why he didn't take her to work.' He sees me smile and interrupts himself. 'I don't think that is funny at all, Tregunna.'

'I think it is.'

'Are you going to work?'

'I am.'

He shakes his head, changing the subject, I'm sure just to annoy me in return. 'I really don't know why you bother,

Tregunna.'

'I love my work.'

'I'll be happy when I can retire.'

He hates his job at the town council. He has to give financial support to residents living on the poverty line, which he willingly does, but he is always very suspicious about being conned. He knows it is his duty to help those who are really in need and to try to rule out those who are trying to claim benefits when they have undeclared income from other undisclosed sources. It's made him a cynical bastard.

'Are you working on an interesting case?' he asks.

'Not really.'

'Were you involved in … the police search on Bodmin Moor?' Trying hard to keep a straight face, he fails completely.

'No. Why do you ask?'

'It was on the local news this morning.'

'I didn't see the news.'

'You've missed it! What a joke!' He grins widely. 'What an embarrassment for the police force.'

'You're making me curious, Mr Curtis.'

'Am I? Don't you really know what was going on yesterday?' Seeing my expression, he continues, stamping his feet in the snow and rubbing his hands together. 'I tell you what, Tregunna, it could well have been a scene from Candid Camera. Or something similar. Can you imagine dozens of police officers gathering at a farm on Bodmin Moor after they were notified that a lion had been seen in a barn?'

'A lion?'

He inclines his head. 'A lion. In a barn. Whoever found it must have had the scare of their life! The police were notified. And the police reacted. Oh boy, did they react! Snipers, people from the zoo, vets, the lot! Poor animal wouldn't have stood a chance against all that display of power.'

'But what …' Then it dawns on me. Virginia Quayle and her stepsister Robbie Ferguson, were visiting Roberta's grandparents near Helstone on the edge of Bodmin Moor. They were shocked when they discovered a young lion sunbathing under a hedge. When they dared look again, it had disappeared into one of the barns.

I hadn't followed it up when they came to the police station because I had my doubts whether it was true. I was going to call the farmer and check if the beast was still there and ask if I could come over and see it before I alerted anyone. But I was sent to see Nathan Cawley and totally forgot about it.

'The police are supposed to protect the citizens of this country, Tregunna. And they did! They stormed the barn to capture a dangerous animal. Ha!'

Still grinning, he pulls up his sleeve and checks his watch. 'I'll be late for work. Ehm, are you going to the police station? Any chance you can drop me off in town?'

'Of course,' I say, not bothering to remind him that he's just wiped snow off his car.

I am already opening a news page on my mobile phone, reading the headline with a feeling of dread: '*Armed police in escaped lion alert find … a cuddly toy.*'

I can't help grinning when I read that DCI Guthrie, never shy of attention from the press, is named and shamed as the instigator of the police action, and ridiculed for wasting taxpayers' money. I can almost sense his barely suppressed anger when he said in a statement that, unusual as it may have seemed, any call reporting a potential danger to the public has to be taken seriously. Until it is clear what the situation is, every option has to be considered.

The last line of the article quotes one of the attending

officers. He saw the funny side of it and announced publicly that they would take the cuddly lion cub to the police station and keep it as a mascot. I doubt if Guthrie will be pleased.

'Like I said,' Curtis says, clicking his tongue. 'I don't understand why you bother. Let's face it, who'd want to work for, and with, a bunch of idiots?'

8

DCI Jason Guthrie sounds stressed when he summons me to his office. Urgently. With the incident which was headlined in the papers as a '*False attempt to make the police force look like fools*' in mind, I replace the phone and get up. Although the majority of the officers can now laugh about it, I'm pretty sure Guthrie won't be able to let it go so easily. Unfortunately, he posed for the camera of a newspaper photographer before the assembled policemen went up to Bodmin Moor to capture the alleged dangerous big cat. Guthrie's photo then appeared in the newspapers next to that of a cuddly lion cub toy. The action was instigated after he found on his desk my interview notes I had scribbled down when Mrs Quayle's daughter and step-daughter reported the sighting to me. Assuming that it had to be a joke, I had more or less dismissed the sighting as highly unlikely, with the intention of checking it out before taking proper action. I have a suspicion about who might have accidentally put the notes on Guthrie's desk, knowing very well that he would panic and overreact. He is now probably looking for a scapegoat and, as my name is on the notes, I am the most likely person to pick on for the position.

Looking at his face, at the contempt in his eyes, I wonder why I even bothered coming to the police station this morning. I've spent most of the night in Hayle, acting like a family liaison officer between my colleagues and Charlotte Lynham, who obviously was in pieces by the suicide of her husband. I can easily justify going home right now and taking the rest of the day off. Even Guthrie won't mind, as he's made it clear several times in the past that he would rather see the back of me. We have nothing in common except for our mutual wish that my future as a part-time police officer will come to an end sooner rather than later. I want to go back to work full time, he wants me out of his hair. Permanently.

Although he will never admit it, I am sure he has made several attempts to get rid of me through official channels. As many times, perhaps, as I have tried to get back full time on the payroll again. But for whatever reasons, the people at the HR department have still not decided what to do with me. Other people in my situation might have already suggested and accepted a generous financial settlement for a permanent exit from the police force, but that is not what I want. As a teenager, I knew that I wanted to be a policeman and I will not have that taken away from me just because I was diagnosed with bowel cancer and I have a stoma. People who don't know anything about stomas seem to think I am severely disabled and have to be treated accordingly. Perhaps in some cases, patients with my condition are indeed worse off than me, but as far as I am concerned I know I can function perfectly well. Almost as a normal healthy person.

DCI Guthrie, sadly, even goes a step further and thinks more along the lines that I am both physically and mentally disabled. A while ago, he came up with the idea that I needed counselling to 'be able to cope with my … thing', words he had to retract when I reminded him quite subtly that I felt like a victim of abuse and discrimination.

Sometimes, in my darker moments, I think he is right and it may be in my own best interest to give in. The tasks he's given me are hardly what I thought my job would involve when I signed up with the police force. Only when a complicated case comes up and they're running out of time and options, or when they are short staffed for other reasons, I get involved, but only from the sidelines, ending up with jobs nobody in their right mind would want.

Except sad and desperate Tregunna.

Fortunately, the DCI doesn't think very highly of the role of an intelligence officer, otherwise he would never have chosen me for the job. In fairness, I had my doubts too but, since I've been doing it more often, I find it can be quite intriguing and inspiring to read the statements of an investigation thoroughly, sifting through the pages and finding discrepancies, lies and similarities. The fact that I am still working part time also means that I have time to check the details and search for additional information when I come across something that attracts my attention. As Guthrie is not really interested in what I am doing, he isn't aware of the work I do after I finish my paid hours.

However, DI Maloney, who took over my job when I went into hospital for the operation, feels more or less the same about me as he did before I was ill. He also finds it useful to pick my brains occasionally when he needs a fresh pair of eyes and ears. He seems quite happy to use me as a replacement whenever he feels like it. Sadly, I am still keen enough to be happy with the crumbs of work I get offered. I don't mind either way. Without being arrogant, I know that without me, Maloney wouldn't have as many good results as he is claiming.

The door to DCI Guthrie's office is ajar. I knock on it as I push it open wider. 'You asked for me, sir?'

He is standing behind his desk, sorting papers in preparation for heading off. In fact, to my knowledge, he wasn't supposed to come in at all today. He looks up briefly, his eyes wandering to the clock on the wall. 'Yes, Tregunna, a few minutes and I'll be off.' He runs a hand through his hair and smiles in a failed attempt to appear to be friendly. 'The wife made me an appointment at the hairdressers. So I have a few moments to talk to you about a few things. Ehm … I'm going on holiday tomorrow.'

The lion cub seems to have disappeared to the back of his mind. The holiday is more important.

'Sir.'

Maloney has told me that the DCI and his wife will soon be on their way to one of London's international airports to catch a flight to South Africa where they are going on a safari holiday. I grin inwardly, wondering whether he realises the irony of it, wondering if he was thinking about his holiday when he decided to capture the alleged lion on Bodmin Moor.

'Tregunna, I'd like you to keep everything low profile while I'm away.'

'Low profile, sir?'

'Yes. Exactly. I'm sure I don't have to tell you that it was very unfortunate that Mr Lynham chose to hang himself in one of Cornwall's most important tourist areas.'

By which he means Hayle, a stone's throw away from St Ives, the coastal town that has become famous for its light, attracting numerous artists, as well as thousands of tourists each year.

'Yes sir.'

'We can't, of course, keep a lid on it. And I don't think that's necessary in this case.'

'Why not, sir?'

'Mr Lynham is a rapist, Tregunna,' he states bluntly. 'I know I'm not in the position to say it, but the simple fact that the coward has committed suicide proves that he is guilty.'

I shrug, not wanting to be pulled into an argument about morals, crime and punishment, which, doubtlessly, will be won by Guthrie. Anyone with a grain of sense will always tell him he is right.

Nevertheless, after spending most of the night with Lynham's widow, I feel the need to object. 'Ed Lynham was released on bail, pending further investigations, sir.'

'He was sacked by his own party.'

'Everyone is innocent until proven guilty.'

'Bollocks.'

'He was dismissed by the party before the inquest even got started. He wasn't even given the benefit of the doubt.'

He narrows his eyes. I can see annoyance grow in them and I know I might already have said too much. The fact that he'll be going on holiday tomorrow seemed to have softened him a bit but it isn't in anyone's interest to anger him now.

'Who told you this?'

'Mrs Lynham.'

'Clearly, you're impressed by pretty little Mrs Lynham,' he sneers.

'She believed in her husband.'

'Yes, well, she's bound to, isn't she?'

'If you say so, sir.'

'Anyway, his political party has decided that they will be handling the press and issue press releases if and when possible or needed. That takes the pressure away from us.' He rubs his hands and licks his lips as though he is looking forward to opening his best and most expensive bottle of wine.

'Clearly, they don't want their party to be damaged and they are looking for a way to take advantage of the situation,' I say, against my better judgement.

Before he can lash out to me with his sneers, the mobile phone on his desk rings, the wooden top enhancing the vibrations. He stares at the caller and directs the call to his answerphone.

'Well, Tregunna, as you may be aware, we have a new investigation on our hands. An as yet unidentified woman has been found dead on Goss Moor. From what I've heard so far, it is a suspected murder investigation. It's too soon for any details yet, but I'm sure you'll understand that DI Maloney will be in charge of this new case, and of course of everything else during my absence.'

'Yes sir.'

'I've suggested to him to give you a couple of old cases to look at, things we haven't been able to follow up or cases that haven't been closed properly. It seems to have become the fashion to pick up old cases from the dusty shelves nowadays and have our forensic departments do what they weren't technically able to do years ago.' He pauses and gives a tiny little smile by way of encouragement. 'You'll be good at that.'

With which he means that I'm thoroughly boring. And so are, no doubt, the old cases. In fact, I like the idea of re-opening an old case and studying all the material again, hoping to find a fresh clue, or let forensics have a go at the evidence and find things with the new methods and knowledge that might have been impossible in the past.

'Right then.' He glances at the clock again. 'As soon as you've wrapped this suicide up, ask Maloney and he'll have a few old case files ready for you.'

'Sir, I'm not sure that Lynham …'

'You've heard me,' he interrupts brusquely. 'The man committed suicide. We can't afford to treat it any other way. He is a public figure. It's bad enough that he did what he did, but it's in nobody's interest to stir things up.' He is patting his trouser pockets to check if his keys, or whatever else, is still there.

'Yes sir,' I mumble politely.

'Perfect.'

I can see his eyes wander from my face down to the side of my belly, to the bulge of the stoma bag under my shirt. I know it is empty, because I always make a point of making sure I have changed it before I come to the station, but he sniffs like a police dog trained to pick up the tiniest of smells of a suspect on the run.

'Well, I hope you have a lovely holiday, sir.' I put my hands on the armrests to rise to my feet.

'Yes. Thank you.' Surprise flashes over his face. 'Oh, one other thing, Tregunna.'

I slump back in the chair. 'Sir?'

His smile is tight and I can't see the expression in his eyes. 'It was very good that you made notes of the sighting of the alleged lion so that when DS Reed saw them, he took immediate action. Although we were initially in the limelight as a couple of fools, I have managed to turn things round to our advantage. You'll see in tomorrow's papers that the public is grateful that the police acted so quickly and correctly. After all, if a dangerous animal had really escaped from a zoo somewhere, it could have been much worse.'

'Of course, sir.'

'We couldn't afford to take chances, Tregunna. I'm sure you've heard about the Beast of Bodmin? It was a while ago, in the eighties. There had been several sightings of what appeared to be a black panther. There were occasional reports of mutilated livestock. It wasn't like everyone had mobile phones and other gadgets on hand to record the sightings, so people panicked. And with all those stories the animal seemed to grow in size by the minute.' He shakes his head. 'I'm glad we've won some Brownie points from the public for this one, Tregunna.'

'Yes sir.'

'Only, next time, bring me up to date straight away, will you?' With Guthrie, there is always a sting in the tail.

'I thought I'd investigate it first, sir.'

'I mean, Tregunna, next time, you'd better leave the thinking and decision-making to me.' His voice has an edge as hard as titanium. 'Clearly you didn't understand the impact of this case. If a lion was on the loose on Bodmin Moor, then we'd have to act immediately. Lions get hungry, Tregunna, they aren't interested in a bowl of dog food. They are hunters and it doesn't matter to them if they catch a rabbit or a hare or a human being.'

'According to the girls, it was a rather small animal, sir.'

He pulls his face in a grimace. Smirks. 'Ask ten people about the size of something they saw briefly. One will say it is the size of a mouse, another will say it is as big as an elephant. Or anything inbetween.'

I open my mouth to remind him that Virginia Quayle and Roberta Ferguson had definitely spoken about a lion cub, but I know better than to go against him. He is fighting for the remains of his dignity. I'd best leave him be.

His mobile phone rings again. This time he answers it, waving at me to let me know that our conversation has come to an end and I can go, so I happily oblige.

'Oh, Tregunna?'

I turn in the doorway. He holds his mobile phone against his shoulder. 'Go and see Maloney. He will give you some of those old case files.'

'Yes sir. Enjoy your holiday, sir.'

I briefly contemplate adding a warning not to get too close to lion cubs. Maybe that isn't a good idea.

9

One of the things Jennette Penrose likes about Tregunna is that he doesn't speak for the sake of hearing his own voice. If he has nothing to offer, he doesn't feel the need to fill the space with irritable noise or useless information. He talks only when he has something sensible to say.

Occasionally, he just wants to think out loud, but it is always about a case they're working on or, at least, it is about something related to work. Very rarely he opens up with information about himself and, if he does, it's mostly about facts, never about his feelings.

Silences between them have always been comfortable and easy. Lately, however, there has been a subtle change in his attitude towards her. Sometimes he looks at her with an indecipherable expression on his face that makes her wonder about his opinion of her.

She finds him sitting at a desk, staring at a stack of paperwork with the enthusiasm of a magician watching a colleague pulling a rabbit from a hat. His face is pale and his eyes are tired, not surprising after he'd found local politician Edward Lynham had hanged himself in one of the bedrooms of his parent's holiday home near Hayle.

She sits down at her desk and brings the computer to life. Looking around, she says unenthusiastically, 'Where is everybody?'

'They found a body.'

'Oh.' She feels so depressed that she can't even be bothered hearing about someone's death, which, in itself, is a bad sign.

She is a policewoman, she is supposed to be there for the community. Instead, her only concern is currently for her father who makes her life a miserable mess.

'Everything all right, Jennette?' Tregunna looks at her with those piercing eyes of his, reading, it seems, what is going on in her head.

'Sure.' Not wanting to meet his scrutinising gaze, she keeps her eyes on her screen, uncomfortably aware that he has noticed that her hand holding the mouse is trembling.

'At home?'

'Yes,' she replies firmly, but she can't hide a tremor in her voice.

Unconsciously adding to her distress, he presses on. 'Your father is in good health?'

His voice sounds perceptively casual, almost as if he isn't really interested.

'Ehm … I suppose.' She purses her lips, clenching her teeth, wishing she hadn't told him that she too had missed the morning briefing because of her father.

Looking up, she finds sympathy and compassion in his eyes. She would like to tell him about the ordeal of living with and caring for her father, but she doesn't know where to start. How to start. But she has to. She needs to talk to someone, and he is the only person she can think of who will make her feel better afterwards, who will look at her situation in all honesty and not come up with cliches and platitudes that everything will be alright. Because it won't. Her father's condition won't change, won't improve.

'It's personal,' she erupts, suddenly curt and to the point, like him, not wasting time with unnecessary pleasantries.

'Okay.'

She isn't sure if she's only imagined the sigh in his voice.

Immediately defensively, she feels she ought to explain herself before she gives him the chance to pull out of this. Which is ridiculous in a way.

She helped him out once, when he needed it, now it is his turn to help her. After his operation, when he was definitely unfit for work, she kept him informed about a case he had been working on. She provided him with statements she'd secretly copied and met him in cafes with new information, handing over the papers like they were both spies in a badly scripted movie.

'If there's anything ...'

'No.'

'Okay,' he says, not giving an immediate response to her outburst. Instead, he keeps quiet, waiting, although the expression on his face reveals his curiosity. She suppresses a wry smile. She knows him well enough to realise what he is doing: he's giving her time to get back on track before she launches into a tirade of complaints and insults about everything and everyone. She knows he hates that. He would never tell her to her face, but he's let slip once that he thinks that part of her frustration is based on her belief that life has cheated on her, physically and professionally. She's certain she isn't pretty or attractive or that she has any form of charm or charisma. She thinks of herself as plain, unattractive and undesirable. He once told her that beauty comes from inside, but even that she can't believe.

'What can I do for you, Jennette? My time is unlimited, as you know.'

She gazes at him, trying to read what lies behind his words. Sometimes she isn't sure whether he's joking or completely serious. Like now. She decides it is better not to respond at all.

'There's a new cafe a bit further up the road.' He points

vaguely. 'Do you fancy a coffee?'

'Tea.' She suppresses a wry smile, slightly annoyed because he still doesn't know that she prefers tea, or he is mocking her with what, in his opinion, is her lack of good taste. She shrugs. 'Yeah, why not?'

They drive in silence until he points to where to pull in and the car jumps back and forth on a car park of grit and granite that hasn't been levelled properly. As she sees him wincing, she wonders briefly whether he might still be suffering from his operation.

There is a recently opened cafe as part of a group of buildings that houses some modern arty businesses. She's noticed them before but could never work out whether they're worth a visit or a waste of time. She can't help looking around disapprovingly at the dull grey facade, but she is pleasantly surprised to enter the cafe to find a decking floor that stretches out onto a large area outside, sheltered by glass panels, fit for summer days.

The cafe is decorated with tables of polished wood and comfortable chairs. Leather settees with a variety of coloured cushions on each of them. Framed prints of old railway posters are lined up on small shelves on the walls. The soft background music adds to a sense of homeliness.

Penrose chooses a seat at the table furthest from the entrance door and gazes out of the window, trying not to feel like she's on a date. This is just work, for heaven's sake.

Two other tables are taken. At one of them are three young women, chatting and giggling away. By the look of the amount of empty cups on their table, they've already been there for a while. At the other table is a couple in their late fifties, talking and gesturing enthusiastically, like they haven't seen each other for a long time.

As Tregunna takes the seat opposite her, she notices that

he's putting his hand over the side of his belly. Hiding his stoma bag has already become a natural action for him. She wonders briefly how it must be to live with something like that, but then pushes the thought away.

He leans back. 'How can I help, Jennette?'

She looks down at her hands and opens her mouth, but a waitress appears at their table, clutching a plastic tray under her elbow and holding in her hand a device that looks like a mobile phone.

'Hi folks, what can I get you? Tea or coffee?'

Penrose scratches her wrists, annoyed by the interruption.

'Filter coffee for me, thank you. Black.' Tregunna gives a friendly smile to the woman. 'And a pot of tea for the lady.'

Penrose blushes, keeping her eyes down not to meet his, glaring at her mobile phone on the table in front of her, willing it to ring or to ping with a message. Anything.

'Okay. Cool. Anything else? Cake?'

'No,' Penrose says stiffly.

'Okay. Cool. Thanks.'

Penrose stares at her as the waitress makes her way back to the counter. There is a line of coffee machines and a row of cake stands overflowing with cakes. Perhaps she can order a slice of chocolate cake when the woman comes back with their drinks.

The door opens and Penrose is quickly distracted. A young couple enters the cafe. The man has a baby strapped to his chest. The cold breeze has coloured the young mother's face and her blue eyes are sparkling with life. For some reason, Penrose feels a pang of envy.

'Nice place.' Tregunna leans back. Waiting patiently.

'Yeah.' She shrugs off her discomfort. 'Thanks for coming, sir. I really appreciate this.'

She meets his eyes. He has asked her to call him Andy,

especially when they're not at work, but somehow she can't. However, now, all of a sudden, in this case, it seems ridiculous to hold on to her principles. 'Andy.'

He is staring at her with compassion in his eyes. And something else. Pity, maybe.

'Perhaps you'd better tell me what is really bothering you.'

'Well, yes … you may have guessed …'

'Here you are, folks.' The waitress grins companionably, placing a tray on their table. 'Cool. R'you sure you don't want any cakes?'

'Yes, we're sure.'

As the waitress leaves them with another, 'okay cool', Tregunna smiles faintly. A picture of patience, Penrose observes. If it was the other way round, she'd be drumming her fingertips on the edge of the table now, barely controlling her impatience. Not Tregunna. He is simply waiting.

'It's my father,' she says, rather miserably.

She has let slip snippets of information about her personal life before, unconscious outbursts of anger and frustration and she thinks that Tregunna already knows that her father is suffering from memory loss. Whether it is dementia or Alzheimer's or something similar, is irrelevant. Point is that he can be aggressive towards her in a rather bullying way. Sometimes she receives a phone call that puts her on edge or makes her mumble an excuse to go home quickly but, so far, she thinks she's been very good at hiding her troubles from her work colleagues. Tregunna is probably the only one who knows that life is not always easy for her.

'Is he getting worse?' he asks gently.

She doesn't even bother to look surprised, yet she prefers to answer his question directly.

'I don't know how he orchestrated it, but he made me take

him to a parish council meeting last night. When we came home, he was restless and jumpy. Confused. He wouldn't go to bed. He kept going on about councillors, calling them names and accusing them of all sorts of things. I don't know. I didn't really listen to him. I was hoping he would soon forget his train of thought, as he usually does. But last night he didn't. I could hardly persuade him to go to bed. He wanted to go out and see someone, I think, but he wasn't even aware that it was late at night at that stage. When I woke up this morning, he was gone.'

'Is he missing?'

'Not anymore,' she stretches her lips over her teeth. 'I hardly noticed he was gone, to be honest. I woke up at about seven, had a shower and got dressed and went to the kitchen to make him a cuppa. Then I found his bed empty. It had been slept in, but he was gone. Luckily, I didn't have much time to be worried and think about what to do. Soon as I put my coat on, the doorbell rang and there he was. Someone had found him waiting for the Post Office to open. The man thought it was rather early for the Post Office to be open. Then he discovered that my father couldn't remember what he was doing there.' She pauses. 'He was kind enough to bring him home.'

'So your father did remember his home address?'

'I've attached a label to the back of his collar with his name and address on it.' She smiles ruefully. 'It works.'

'You mean he goes out on his own quite often and gets confused and someone has to take him home?'

'What else can I do?' she reacts defiantly. 'I have a full-time job and there is no one else to look after him.'

'I thought you had a brother?'

'Yes. He lives up near Middlesborough. He comes here three or four times a year. He takes our father out for lunch and that's it. He says there is nothing wrong with him and that

I'm creating problems where there aren't any.'

'I'm sure you'd be able to get some help. There are all sorts of volunteers.'

'I know. We have a few neighbours looking out for him, but he can be very rude and aggressive. I can't blame them if they turn around as soon as he treats them like that.'

'Can't you ask Guthrie for compassionate leave or something? I'm sure …'

'And what then?' Her voice trembles. 'Stay at home with him? All day and all night?'

'There has to be a solution, Jennette.'

'I don't know where to find it.'

'There are places for people like him. There are … '

'Put him in a care home? No, sir, I won't do that! I can't bear the idea that …'

'The people who work in care homes know best how to deal with people like your father. It is their job. He will be safe and you can …'

'No,' she interrupts bluntly. 'His sister had the same problem. My cousin couldn't handle her anymore and she took her mother to one of those care homes. My cousin thought it would be good, because it was close to their home and it would be easy for her to visit her mother every day.'

She pauses to sip her tea. Then she pulls a face, wipes a hand over her eyes and straightens her back. 'The bottom line is that, within six weeks, my aunt died. In a way it was a relief for the family, but it was clear that the poor soul hadn't been happy at all. She was often dirty and smelly, they didn't pay attention to what she ate and drank and, in the end, she died of malnutrition and dehydration.' Once more she shakes her head. 'I'm not putting my father in a place like that.'

'They're not all like that.'

'Maybe not, but … my father has always been good to me. Him and my mother. He isn't being nasty because he chooses to be. He can't help it and I'm not going to punish him for this … illness by sending him to one of those … prisons.'

'I'm sure you'll …'

'Oh, there are some homes you only read good things about. But they are expensive. We can't afford that.'

She shakes her head again and stares into her mug, finding no answer or solution in it.

'Where is he now?'

'At home.' She shrugs disdainfully. 'He hadn't slept at all last night and he was exhausted.' She stops and smiles wryly. 'I gave him a sleeping pill. Even if he wakes up, he'll be dozy and he will certainly not be in a state to go out and get lost again.'

'I don't know what to say, Jennette, I would like to help, obviously, but I don't know how.'

She offers a faint smile. 'It is good to be able to talk about it.'

'Let me know if there is anything I can do, Jennette.'

She nods, avoiding his eyes. 'Last night was … horrible. He insisted on going to the parish council meeting. As soon as we got into the village hall and he saw the councillor, he started shouting and swearing. He accused her of stealing and lying and all sorts of things.' She looks down, swallows hard, on the brink of tears. 'Things got out of hand, then, and very politely, we were asked to leave.' Her face is flushed with the memory of the embarrassment and humiliation. 'In a way, it was a relief that we had to leave, but everyone was looking at us.'

'You must have felt awful.'

'I did.' She sits staring straight ahead, her hands clasped in her lap, fingers interlocked. She's lost in her thoughts for a while until Tregunna clears his throat. The silence broken, she looks up at him, half hoping he will come up with a solution, knowing there isn't one. Eyes full of pity, he covers her hands with his in a simple gesture of sympathy. She feels some of the tension slip away from her shoulders and then, to her horror, she feels tears running down her cheeks.

10

Goss Moor is a typical open moorland landscape with a maze of heather, bracken and boggy marshes. Water trickles and gathers into small streams that eventually form the river Fal, finding the open sea at Falmouth on the south coast of Cornwall. The name Goss is believed to derive from the Celtic word 'cors' meaning a marshy or boggy place.

It certainly is wet.

A line of police cars is parked on a muddy lay-by, along with a white van from the forensic department. Blue and white crime scene barrier tape flutters in the wind, stretched across the road between the posts of a cattle-grid entrance gate. The air is wet with soft rain and the ground is soggy, sucking at my shoes as soon as I get out of my car. The unlucky officer who has the task of monitoring everyone who enters the peripheral crime scene, is PC Danielle Champion. Thin as a rake, with hunched shoulders and so short she barely reaches to my chest, she looks like a push-over, but that is deceptive. Although she's one of the youngest recruits on the force, she has already stood her ground. I like her because she is averse to all of the nonsense that goes on.

She is sitting in the car with the door open, blue lights still flashing, one foot outside. Startled by my approach, she scrambles to her feet. Strains of reggae music drift out from behind her. Her face flushed red, she runs her hand across her head. I'm not bothered by the fact that she has decided to sit in a police car rather than spend the day standing in the rain with her clipboard.

The sky is a leaden purple-black, threatening more rain. A man is standing by the side of the cattle grid. Half hidden behind shrubs that are speckled with yellow flowers, he is looking at us suspiciously. A small black-and-white dog stands beside him. Alerted, it has stopped whipping its tail.

'Good morning Danielle,' I say, good-humouredly.

'Morning, sir; through there, sir.' A big raindrop lands on the tip of her nose. She wipes it off with the back of her hand.

'It has been dry for five minutes,' she says sombrely, reaching inside the car. The reggae music is turned down. She unfolds an umbrella and hands me a forensic kit.

'You'll need this, sir.'

I wrestle myself into a forensic suit and crouch to pull on a pair of overshoes.

An almost monochrome landscape stretches out in front of us. Bleak. Various shades of grey. The peculiar shapes of Cornwall's 'alps' are only vaguely visible in the distance. Water is trickling down forming a small rivulet beside the road.

A woman's body was found by a cyclist this morning. Maloney has sent me out to get a statement from the poor man, but I decided to get a feel for the crime scene first.

A white plastic tent has been erected behind the bushes to protect the victim from the poor weather conditions and prying eyes. Forensic specialists are examining the surrounding area, taking photographs and impressions of foot prints and tyre marks, working with pairs of tweezers to scrutinise every piece of debris, carefully placing anything of interest in evidence bags and scribbling notes on them.

An officer in a yellow reflective vest over his uniform is standing on one of the metal sheets that are laid out in front of the tent to form a secure path to the site and prevent disturbing any possible vital evidence. His hands folded behind his back, he seems oblivious to the wet weather. A pigeon flies out of the bushes in a clatter of wings, startling me. The officer doesn't move an inch. Giving me a serious nod of acknowledgement, he steps aside to let me pass.

Inside the tent, pathologist David Jamieson is issuing instructions to a photographer who is kneeling down, obscuring my view of the corpse. In one of the corners, forensic scientist Andrea Burke is holding her phone to her mouth with a gloved hand, speaking, rather than writing down her forensic findings.

'Hello Andy.'

Jamieson is carrying out the cursory examination of the corpse before it will be taken to the mortuary in Truro. Pulling his face mask down to his chin, he places his gloved hands on his hips and sways from side to side as though he's preparing for a hula hoop session at the gym. Beside him, the photographer stands up, adjusting something on his camera, and moves to a different angle.

The corpse of a woman is laid out on muddy grass dotted with multiple tyre tracks. She looks to be in her mid forties, with thick greying hair. The wet mud from beneath her has soaked her skirt and matching jacket, light with black decorative trim. A thin black blouse underneath. A thick gold chain necklace and matching earrings, a bracelet on one wrist, a gold watch on the other. Dried blood from wounds on her belly have stained the front of her suit jacket and the waistband of her skirt. The skin of her legs is white where her tights have been ripped open. Her skirt is pulled up around her waist, and a lacy pair of black pants is pulled halfway down her thighs. The most extraordinary sight, however, are the flowers. Red roses are scattered over her body and around her in the mud. One sticks out from between her legs.

'That one is stuck in her vagina,' the pathologist says, following the direction of my eyes.

'In it?' I ask incredulously.

'As far as I can see, yes.' His lips tighten. 'One. I don't know if that is significant, but I can see how it may be some sort of a sign.'

'Do we have an ID?'

'Nope. No wedding ring. Her handbag is missing. No keys. No mobile phone either.'

'Stabbed? Once? Twice?'

'As far as I can see, only once, but the blade has been twisted, which caused quite a bit of damage to her insides.'

'Any further clothes? A coat?'

'We've found a black scarf in the hedges.' Andrea Burke rubs her hands together as though she's been digging in the sand. 'We're not sure though if it is hers.' She gives a tight smile. 'And no. No coat.'

The officer standing outside by the entrance of the tent sticks his head in. 'There is a car, sir. It's parked a bit further down the road. We didn't pay attention to it earlier because we assumed it belonged to one of the residents.'

'Okay, thank you. We'll have a look.'

'I'm finished here,' Andrea Burke says. A strand of her red hair pops out of the hood of her protective suit. She used to dye her hair a ruby red colour, now it looks more like a carrot dipped in beetroot water.

'I'll come with you, Tregunna,' she says stiffly.

A silver-grey Audi is parked at the end of a small car park that is mainly used by the residents of a cluster of residential houses and farm sheds. Vicky Talland is waiting for us at the entrance, hands on her hips as though she's about to tell us off for being late.

'I've been waiting for you lot to show up,' she snaps disapprovingly, gazing at the white forensic suit Andrea Burke hasn't bothered to take off. 'I've got better things to do than this, you know.'

I open my mouth for a polite, apologetic reply, but Andrea just shrugs and Vicky turns her back on me, clearly deciding that Andrea is the person to talk to.

'That car wasn't here last night when I got home,' Vicky states and then answers unspoken questions. 'That was between ten and half past. My shift ended at ten. I had one drink with my colleague and it took me ten minutes to get here.' She senses I'm going to say something and adds, 'I work at the fuel station in Roche. I know this place. I know everyone here and I know all of the other cars that were parked here when I arrived. But not that one.'

She pauses as if she's expecting a reaction. Then she points over her shoulder with her thumb.

'My son went to work this morning. Normal time.' She speaks in staccato, hurrying up. 'Left at ten past seven. As usual. Two minutes later, he was back.' She twists her lips in disapproval. 'Forgot his phone. These days, nobody can survive without their mobile, hey? Any road, he said there was a strange car in our car park. He said, he wondered whose it was. He said it wasn't even locked. He said he knows someone who can start a car without the keys. Said he wouldn't mind having a ride in it. I says no, of course you can't. He'd have done it, though, if he'd had the time. So, my hubby went out later. Just to check, you know? And he says, 'Yes, it's a strange car.' She pauses, gesturing vaguely around with her head. 'He said, clearly it wasn't one of ours.'

We walk past a small blue car and a rusty old truck in

various shades of green and grey. The front wheels have been taken off and the axle is placed on two wooden crates. Between the truck and a battered muddy Volvo, I can see why the Audi immediately attracted attention: with its shiny silver body, chrome strips and alloy wheels, it is completely out of place here.

'We'll take it from here, Mrs Talland,' Andrea Burke announces blankly. 'Thanks for your help.'

'Is that it? Is this all you can say, after I've been waiting so long for you?'

Andrea raises her eyebrows as if she's about to reply brusquely, but thinks better of it.

'Can I take your details, Mrs Talland? We might need to speak to you later,' I ask and, while I type her details into my mobile phone, I watch Andrea Burke peering into the silver car through the window on the passenger side. She slips her hands into a fresh pair of latex gloves and opens the door. Her red clothes shine through her white suit as she kneels and bends over to reach under the passenger seat and picks up a black leather handbag smartly decorated with stitched lilies. She unfastens it and rummages inside. 'We've got an ID, sir.'

All of a sudden, Vicky Talland doesn't seem to be in such a hurry anymore. She stands beside me, waiting for any further information which she'll no doubt pass onto friends and family later, but Andrea Burke keeps quiet. She has dropped a shiny black purse into a plastic evidence bag, after opening it and showing me a pink plastic card. Looking over her shoulder, I see the name on the driver's license and realise I know who the victim is.

11

'Andy? Andy Tregunna?'
'Speaking.'
'I … I need your help.'
'What's your name?'
'Oh … I'm sorry. It's Chaz. Charlotte Lynham.'

Chaz Lynham, the woman who had to deal with the death of her husband and the fact that he couldn't handle the injustice of being accused of something he didn't do. At least so he claimed. The widow of a politician who was so devoted to his political role that he couldn't live with the accusations that undermined his integrity. The woman who feels guilty that she didn't support him enough, and that she hadn't noticed how deep his depression was. The woman who has to live on, knowing that her husband didn't love her enough to want to live. For her. With her.

'No problem, Mrs Lynham.'
'Oh … call me Chaz, please.'
'Okay Chaz, I'm Andy. How are you?'

A stupid question. Of course she isn't okay. Of course she's feeling miserable and sad. Angry and betrayed. She may even be thinking about doing the same as her husband.

There are a lot of people who come to a point wondering what life is all about and why it is worth living. I know the feeling. I stood on the edge of the cliffs three times, convinced that it was the only solution. When I walked back the third time, I promised myself I would never consider it again. There aren't many people who actually have the courage to do what Edward Lynham did. I know I hadn't. Or perhaps, somewhere deep down, there was, and there still is, a reason for me to want to live.

'I'm not as bad as I thought I'd be.' There is a nervous giggle in her voice. She's been drinking.

'That's good to hear.'

'One of my sisters is coming here tonight.' She told me she has five sisters. No brothers. One sister lives in New York, the other four live in the South West.

'What can I do for you, Chaz?'

She takes a deep breath. 'It may sound silly, but I'm sorting things out. At home. Ed's stuff. Ehm … I don't know what else to do, really.'

A tough woman. A survivor. Sorting his business papers won't have as much impact on her as dealing with his clothes and personal belongings.

'Some people chuck out everything that belonged to the deceased straight away; other people cling on to it for years. Decades even, sometimes,' I say smoothly.

I think of Mr Grose. Perhaps I can tell her about how he sculpted his deceased wife's face in clay; how he fabricated a frame for her body, put it in a dress and sat her down at the kitchen table, at the exact spot where she'd died. He needed the company.

Perhaps it will bring a little smile to Chaz's face when I tell her. Not now. Later.

'There is some stuff that the political party might like to keep, although, in all honesty, I can't be bothered with those bastards! They sent him over the edge and I …' She stops. Lets out a sob. Then she clears her throat, gathering herself.

'Maybe you could ask them to come and take everything

away?' I suggest.

'I don't want to see them! And I certainly don't want them in my house, smiling and apologising and feeling sorry for me. Anything to keep me quiet because they don't want me to speak to the press and blame them for his death.' Anger has replaced her tears. 'I don't want to see those ... hypocrites. And I'm certainly not going to invite them to the funeral!'

How do you keep people away from a funeral? There will always be people you don't recognise, or you might not even have seen before. It doesn't mean they're not grieving for the deceased. Avoiding unwanted visitors can only be managed by keeping the date and time a secret, which won't be possible in this case. Ed Lynham was a public figure.

'I suppose it is entirely up to you who you would like to be present.'

'Exactly ... ehm, sorry.' She lets out a deep long sigh, trying to compose herself. 'There is something I would like to discuss with you.'

'I'm listening.'

She hesitates. 'Are you at work?'

'No.'

I look at an elderly woman, struggling to walk a straight line, a small shopping bag dangling on one arm. She's approaching a zebra crossing, waiting and looking to both sides of the road. No driver stops for her. On the other side of the pavement, three youths in jeans and hooded sweaters emerge. Talking, gesturing, laughing. I'm not sure if it's their normal behaviour; they may well have had an argument about something. As they come closer towards the elderly woman, they don't seem to be aware of her and she has to step back, struggling to keep her balance.

I clench my teeth, but before I can get out of the car and

interfere, remind the three guys of their upbringing and manners, one has stopped, saying something to the woman. Am I prejudiced, thinking that he may rob her of her purse and pension money?

But the woman smiles and nods, and he takes her arm and helps her to the other side of the road, his mates waiting patiently. When he gets back to his friends, their conversation continues and they disappear around the corner.

'Are you still there?'

'Yes. I'm in my car.'

'Oh, I'm sorry, I didn't want to interrupt … whatever you were doing.'

'I'm parked. Go on, please.'

'Is anyone with you?'

'No.' I hesitate. 'Would you rather talk … in private?'

A long silence. Then a sigh. 'I would prefer that.'

'Okay.'

I was on my way back to the station, but my position is such that nobody will notice if I'm not there. They're used to me coming and going as I please and, after all, everyone knows that I only work part time.

'Where would you like to meet?'

'I'd rather not go out. I can't bear seeing anyone at the moment.' She pauses. 'I'm at home.'

Chaz Lynham lives in a Victorian semi-detached house just outside Wadebridge. Steps lead up to a small garden lined with pale yellow and pink primroses. The front door has recently been painted. The colour of honey.

I ring the doorbell. She opens almost immediately.

She's dressed in grey tracksuit bottoms and a pink T-shirt that says: 'I run for Cancer.' Her hair is tied up in a mess on top of her head. Her face is blotchy and red from crying but she has applied mascara, green eye shadow and pale pink lipstick.

'There is a reporter hanging about over the road.'

'I haven't seen anyone.'

She looks at me with a touch of pity.

'There.'

She points over my shoulder and I follow her line of vision. A small red car is parked on the other side of the road. I can't see the driver's face because he's holding up a camera with a telescopic lens.

'I didn't realise …'

Chaz giggles nervously. 'They may think that you are my secret lover and that our affair is the reason for Ed's …'

'Let them think what they want,' I say, quickly closing the door behind me.

'I try to ignore them. Tea? Coffee? Beer?'

'Coffee would be fine thanks. Black. No sugar.'

'Something to eat?' I follow her into a kitchen that has pale wooden cabinet doors and turquoise blue accents. It smells of burned toast.

'No thank you.'

The window looks out over the street. The driver of the red car is getting out, camera ready. Chaz sees him too. She shrugs, motioning me to follow her. 'Maybe we'd better go into the lounge.'

The lounge faces a fenced garden. In the middle is a rotary washing line with dark socks and underwear blowing in the breeze. Men's.

She follows my gaze. 'I've emptied the laundry bin. For some stupid reason, I can't throw dirty clothes in the waste bin.'

A dark blue leather settee dominates the room that is gloomy with mahogany wood panelling on the walls. There are several glass vases with bright yellow daffodils.

She sits in the bulky chair, pulling up her knees and hugging them with both her arms, resting her chin in the gap between them.

'I found a letter.'

I wait for her to continue, but she seems lost in her thoughts.

There has been a trend in fiction lately. Women's fiction, stories about husbands dying unexpectedly and widows finding out that their husband had a secret affair, a lover, a child, sometimes even a whole secret family. I hope for her sake that she hasn't come across a letter that reveals a scenario like that. For now, she has enough on her plate with her husband's suicide.

'I don't know what to make of it,' she says slowly, not getting up to show the letter to me.

'Do you have it here?'

'In Ed's study.' She points with her head at a door by the fireplace. I don't know if she wants me to get up and get it.

'I thought of tearing it into pieces, destroying it in the paper shredder, but … I don't know.'

She's silent for a long time.

'Can I see it?'

She looks at me. Debating. Then she gives a sad smile. 'I guess I asked you to come here because I wanted your advice. You are … warm and understanding. I feel I can trust you. You don't seem to be an ordinary policeman, but nevertheless, you are.'

'Not in my spare time.'

'Oh.' Tears fill her eyes. 'Thank you.'

She's silent for a long time. Then she slips from her seat and opens the door. Cold air comes through the doorway as I hear her flicking through papers.

She comes back with an A4 sheet and drops it into my hand before sitting down again, eyes downcast. She picks up her tea and watches me closely as I take my eyes off her and look at the letter. It is a simple white photocopied sheet. The writing is in letters that are cut out from a newspaper.

'*I know what you did. Wait for instructions*.'

'Was there an envelope?'

'I didn't find one.'

'Any idea what it means?'

'No.'

'Or who has sent it?'

'No.'

'Where did you find it?'

'In a pile of papers on his desk. From his work.' She shakes her head. 'I don't know what to think of it. I thought maybe …' She stops and swallows, taking a deep breath. 'I had this strange thought … That's why I called you.' Not waiting for my response, she continues. 'Suppose he didn't agree with the instructions in the letter. Suppose he was blackmailed but he couldn't pay them or he didn't want to pay them? I thought, if that is the case, it might not have been suicide after all. Perhaps it was staged like a suicide, to prevent the police from starting an investigation.'

Her eyes are pleading. I feel sorry for her. Desperately seeking comfort, she's clinging on to the idea that her husband didn't leave her voluntarily. A tiny comfort, maybe, but it doesn't alter the fact that he is dead.

'I didn't know what to do with it. Should I tell the police about it?'

'That is entirely up to you.'

'But what would it mean? Will there be an investigation?'

'That's feasible.'

'But … suppose he did something bad, something that he wanted to hide and therefore he chose to die? Suppose an investigation would reveal everything and his name will be in the papers and … It will be even worse than it was.'

'You will have to ask yourself the question, Chaz. If it would appear that he didn't take his own life, but that there was someone who killed him and made it look like suicide, would you want his killer to walk free?'

'Of course not, but everything has a price, hasn't it? What would be that price? For all I know now, Ed might have done something bad. Really bad. He might have been a fraud or a killer.' She shakes her head. Plucks at her nails. 'I'm not sure if I want to know that. Or want anyone else to know that.'

'If the letter did mean that he was hiding something …' I stop. 'Did you check his bank account? Has he taken a sum of money out that seems strange to you?'

'No. I mean, yes, I checked, but he didn't take any money out in the last couple of weeks. He never used cash. If he needed anything, he'd ask me. But he didn't.'

I don't remind her that it isn't likely that he'd have asked her for cash if he had something to hide.

'The letter wasn't folded,' I say thoughtfully. 'Normally when you send someone a letter you'd fold it in three or four, depending on the size of the envelope. It looks like a copy. Do you know where the original is?'

'I haven't found it.'

'Any idea when he could have received it?'

'He didn't tell me about it, that's for sure,' she replies dryly.

'I guess not.'

'Andy, would you… can you help me find out?'

Although I am intrigued, I'm not sure whether I'm being played here. It occurs to me that this is why she asked me to see her today. She needs my help. She knows that it is a long shot but she wants me to investigate whether her husband's suicide wasn't a covered-up murder. She doesn't want to be the one to find out. It will postpone her decision whether she'll want to know the truth or not.

12

Heavy rain and hailstones the size of small conkers hammer the windscreen when I hit the A39 on my way back to Newquay. Water gushes over the tarmac, filling potholes and slowing traffic. I get stuck behind a tractor pulling a long trailer with rolls of hay wrapped in black plastic. It is at the front of the queue, the driver stubbornly refusing to pull into a lay-by to let traffic overtake him. I can't blame him. He is sitting in an open cab exposed to the weather and he obviously wants to get to his destination as soon as possible.

My mobile is vibrating on the passenger seat beside me. Maloney's name appears on the dashboard screen. My first instinct is to ignore the call. I'm driving. But I can't dismiss him. I press a button to take the call.

'Tregunna?' He sounds tired already. 'Where are you?'

I didn't tell him I was going to visit Chaz Lynham. Let alone why.

'I'm on the A39 near Winnards Perch.' I say evenly, knowing very well that the A39 isn't the most logical of roads when you drive from Roche to Newquay. 'I am on my way back from Roche where I got a statement from the cyclist who found the body.'

'That was two hours ago!'

I'm about to remind him that I have done my hours for today already, but I don't say it. After all, Maloney isn't a bad person and it isn't his fault that Guthrie is so reluctant to let me work full time.

'We've got an ID on the body.' Maloney says. He has no

time for apologies or explanations, however unnecessary they would be. I can hear him pacing in his office. Voices and ringing phones in the background. 'Iris Spencer.'

I don't tell him that I already knew the victim's name. He isn't in the right mood to hear that I went to the crime scene without his permission, even without letting him know.

'The councillor?' I ask

A silence.

'I hope you're joking?' he asks incredulously.

'I'm not.'

I hear him holding his breath. 'Are you sure? Nobody said anything about a councillor. Let me check.' Fingers tap on a keyboard. A muffled curse. 'Iris Spencer. Let's see if it is really you.'

I can sense what is going on in his mind. He hopes that the victim isn't the councillor, but someone who happens to have the same name. He taps his keyboard and shouts to someone who seems to have the courage to stick their head around the door.

'Not now!'

Thirty seconds later and he has found what he was looking for. 'Have you been at the crime scene, Tregunna?'

'Ehm … I have.'

'And you've seen the victim.'

It isn't a question. 'Yes.'

He sighs. 'I have a recent picture of her right in front of me on my screen. She is 44, she has short grey or very blonde hair.'

'Sounds like her.'

He curses. Iris Spencer. Local councillor and business woman. I'm not sure what the nature of her business is, but I do know that she is renowned for her bold statements and decisions that aren't always popular. From what I've heard and read, she doesn't appear to be an easy woman to work for or to deal with.

'Why does it always have to be me?' Maloney whines rhetorically, sounding as if he's been deprived of his last reserves.

The tractor with the hay bales in front of me is slowing even more, the engine battling with the gentle slope of a hill.

'Right. Are you still there, Tregunna? I'll give you Iris Spencer's address, could you go to her family?' He knows better than to wait for a reaction. 'Right. She lives with … A niece, I believe it is. Since you are on the road you'd better go to the address and deliver the message.'

It's the least favourite task of every policeman to be the messenger of bad news. Telling someone that his or her loved-one is dead is something we all try to avoid. I wish now I had ignored Maloney's call.

I hear his phone beeping.

'Wait a sec, Tregunna, I've got another call coming in. Let me get that.'

I wait. The tractor has finally pulled into a lay-by. Drivers pass, thankfully lifting their hands with relief or making obscene gestures. The farmer is stoically waiting until the road is clear. I wave to thank him; I don't know if he can interpret my gesture correctly.

Two minutes later and Maloney is back on the line, his voice echoing through my car.

'I don't know how or what, but the circus is already running overtime,' he says cynically. 'I just had a call from Kim Naylor from *The Cornish Gazette*. She asked me if it is true that councillor Spencer has been murdered. How the hell can she know that?'

'Bad news travels fast.'

'Looks like it! Well, you'd better get yourself to the family before the press delivers the message.'

'If they haven't already done that,' I reply cynically. Kim Naylor is a keen and intelligent reporter. She knows how to use her imagination and intuition.

Maloney is still talking. 'You will be speaking to Matilda Disley. Apparently she is Iris Spencer's niece. Or so they claim.'

'Claim? What is that supposed to mean?'

'Something Naylor said. She's heard stories that Iris Spencer is a lesbian, something Iris has always strongly denied. Personally I don't care about her sexual preferences, but who am I to say?'

He doesn't expect an answer.

'Well, I'll see you later, Tregunna. Get me the statement from the cyclist as soon as you can, will you? And obviously from Matilda Disley and establish her whereabouts at the time Mrs Spencer was murdered.'

'Do we know when she was killed? Jamieson said we had to wait for the official autopsy.'

'No need. In one way, the conversation with Miss Naylor was rather useful. She could tell me that there was a meeting last night. Iris Spencer was there also. I have just double-checked it. It was last night in St Eval. The meeting ended just after half past ten.' He pauses. 'St Eval. Isn't that where Penrose lives?'

'Yes.'

I'll have to ask Penrose more about that meeting. She will never forgive me if I tell Maloney that her father had to be removed from the meeting because he couldn't behave himself.

'I'll see you later, Tregunna,' Maloney says, probably relieved that he managed to avoid having to do the worse part of the job. He's decent enough to add, 'To be honest, I don't envy you.'

Then the line goes dead.

13

Clearly, Matilda Disley has already been informed about the death of Iris Spencer. Her eyes are swollen and she's pressing a ball of wet tissues against her running nose. Her hair is a tangle of dark curls, eye make-up smeared around her upper face, mascara clinging to her lashes in coagulated lumps.

In her twenties, she's dressed in black trousers and a bright pink blouse but the dishevelled nature of her clothes suggests that she hasn't undressed since the previous day.

'Come in.' Barely looking at my ID card, she opens the door and stands back to let me in. Her eyes are staring blankly at a point behind me as though she's expecting more people to arrive.

I walk into the stale warmness of a living room where the TV is showing a decades-old comedy that programmers seem to consider as popular with today's viewers. Or perhaps they can't find anything else to broadcast that is cheap enough to make up for the huge amounts of money spent on shows, period dramas and sports events.

'Is there … any news?' Her voice is trembling. A thought flares up in her eyes: hopeful that I'm here to tell her that there has been a terrible mistake, that it wasn't Iris who died, but someone else.

'No, Miss Disley, I'm afraid not. But I do have some questions, if you don't mind?'

'Questions?'

'I know, but this is really necessary. I'm sure you wouldn't want the person who did this to Iris to stay free.'

Her eyes open wide. Astonished. 'The person who did this to her? What are you saying? I thought … they said she was with her car when she … when it happened. I thought it was a road accident.'

'I'm sorry.'

She stares at me in horror and disbelief. 'You mean she was … killed?'

'I can't say much more than this, Miss Disley, but I can say that we are treating her death as suspicious.'

'But that is … horrible! How could anyone do that? And why?'

'That's exactly why I'm here. It would help our investigation if we knew more about her latest whereabouts and her personal life.'

'But I wasn't there. I don't know anything about it. In fact,' she pauses, inhales deeply and adds, 'You know more than I do.' She ends with a sob.

'Can I make you a cup of tea?' Tea is still renowned for producing some sort of comfort; probably only just because of the sweetness of sugar and milk. Nevertheless, in many cases, it seems to work.

Before she can refuse, I find my way to the kitchen. She follows me like a faithful dog.

'Can you explain the nature of your relationship with Iris?' I ask, filling the kettle as she watches me closely from the doorway. I open drawers and cupboards in search of tea bags and mugs, and take the milk from the fridge.

'She is … she was my friend. That's all.' Confusion and embarrassment colour her cheeks. Her denial to a question not yet spoken is too obvious.

'Were you in a relationship, Miss Disley?'

'Oh!' She is trying hard to look horrified. 'Who told you

this?'

I can't tell her that DI Maloney told me that it was common knowledge that Iris Spencer was a lesbian.

'What was the nature of your relationship?'

'Nature? Oh, I see. Well, we were friends. I just told you. I was her friend. I looked after her, if you can say that nowadays. Like a … housekeeper.'

The kettle comes to the boil. Steam rises up. Matilda Disley seems to wake up from her hypnotic state, rummaging in a cupboard for a packet of chocolate biscuits which she places, unopened, on a plate in the middle of the kitchen table. Automatically, she sits down. I place a steaming mug of tea in front of her and she starts stirring it, adding milk and four spoonfuls of sugar.

'I wasn't paid. It was just …' She stops. Tears are forming in her eyes again, but she blows her nose and composes herself. 'Aren't you having anything?'

'No, I'm alright.'

She doesn't appear to hear me. 'Iris was my mother's best friend. They grew up together on the Scillies. Iris left the islands to go to uni, but my mum stayed there. She could never leave the islands, you see. She loved the Scillies. Even one day to Penzance to do her shopping made her feel homesick.'

She is silent for a while. She seems to have forgotten my presence.

'How long have you lived here with Iris, Matilda?'

'Tilda.' She corrects me automatically. 'When I was sixteen, my mum got ill and she died. Iris came to the funeral and she offered me help. She gave me her card, just in case I needed something. After a few months I contacted her. The island … as much as I love the Scillies … it wasn't the same without mum. Iris understood that and said I could stay with her for a while until I decided what I wanted to do.'

'And this was … when?'

'Nearly ten years ago.' She gives a small ironic smile. 'Iris used to joke that I'd overstayed my welcome, but it wasn't like that. It was okay. We got on very well and when, at some point, I said I should find somewhere else to live, she said she'd be happy if I stayed.' She hesitates. 'She dreaded living on her own.'

I nod, making a mental note to check Matilda Disley's background.

'Can you tell me about yesterday?'

Tilda swallows. 'She went to work in the morning, as usual. Of course you'll need to talk to her secretary about that. She came home after work. Normal time, just before five. We had a drink.' She swallows, overtaken by memories. 'We both like a glass of sherry before we have our tea, although it doesn't seem to be very fashionable nowadays. I'd cooked a green Thai curry. The way Iris likes it. Liked it. She left at about seven. Maybe five or ten to. There was a council meeting.'

'In St Eval?'

'I believe so.'

'Are those meetings always in the evening?'

'That depends. This one wasn't scheduled as usual. It had something to do with future planning. I don't know exactly. I'm sure there are other people who will be able to tell you the details.'

'What time did you expect her to come home?'

'Not before ten, but really, it depends on the agenda. Sometimes they stay a bit longer for a discussion or they have a drink afterwards. But she would only have one drink. Never more than one.'

I stare at my phone, reading the few details Maloney has emailed to me.

'When was the last time you saw her?'

She swallows hard. 'That's what I'm telling you. Yesterday. After we had our tea.'

'She didn't come home last night?'

'No.'

'Did you call the police when she hadn't come home?'

She moves awkwardly on her seat. 'She called me at about twenty past nine to say that the meeting was still going on. That must have been during a break, otherwise she wouldn't have been able to call. She said she would probably be late and, if I didn't want to, I needn't wait up for her.'

'Did you always wait up for her?'

'Most times, yes. She liked to wind down a bit after meetings. We would have a drink and talk about what was going on.'

'But you didn't wait for her last night.'

'No. I watched a film on TV and when it was finished, I went to bed.'

'What time was that?'

'After the 10 o'clock news.'

'Weren't you alarmed when you noticed that she didn't come home at all?'

She stares at her hands. Avoiding my eyes. Like people do when they are telling lies. 'I'm a deep sleeper. I don't even hear the alarm in the morning.' She points at the ceiling. 'My bedroom is at the back of the house. I never hear her park the car.'

'And where is Iris's bedroom?'

'At the front of the house.'

'What happened this morning when you got up?'

'She … she wasn't there. I didn't see her shoes or her coat or her handbag. Usually, she kicks off her shoes in the hallway and she drops her handbag and her keys on the little hall table. When I didn't see those, I went upstairs and knocked on her door. When there was no reply, I found that she hadn't been home all night. Her bed hadn't been slept in.'

'Can anyone vouch for that?'

She looks up. Confused. Angry. 'Don't you believe me?'

'It may be helpful if you had someone who can confirm what you just told me.'

'Well, I can't. I was on my own all evening. And all night!'

'I don't mean to upset you, Tilda; these are questions to eliminate you from our enquiry.'

'Oh.' She deflates slowly, like a loose balloon that has hit the rusty point of some barbed wire.

'Do you know what time … it happened?'

'We have no further information yet. Some time between the meeting and this morning, when her body was found.'

'Oh.' Her thoughts are expressed on her face. Guilt. Regret. She wonders if it would have made a difference if she'd stayed up and waited.

'Did Iris have any enemies?'

'Enemies?'

'Is there someone that you can think of who could have done her … harm? Was there someone who hated her so much and who would rather see her dead?'

She shakes her head and says miserably, 'She had a lot of enemies but not that kind of enemy, inspector. I'd rather say they were opponents. People who didn't agree with the decisions she made.'

'In her job?'

'And as a councillor.'

'Was there something bothering her?'

'If there was, she didn't tell me. You'll have to ask her secretary. Or her business partner. The office is in Truro.'

'Was she seeing someone?'

'Like …' Horror replaces grief. 'Like she had a date, you mean?'

I shrug. Tears are brimming in her eyes again. She's denied that she and Iris were in a relationship, but she isn't able to stick to that lie.

'No, she didn't have a date, Inspector. Why would she? She was perfectly happy with me!'

I wait until her sobbing ebbs.

'Did you share a bedroom?' I ask softly.

'Ehm … we did, but … Iris didn't want people to know. People can be funny, you know, even these days. She wanted to avoid possible problems with her position as a councillor. That's all.'

'Where did you sleep last night, Tilda? In your own room?'

'I … I never use that back room. It's just for … it's fake. To convince other people. But it is a lie.'

'Let's make this clear, Tilda. You watched a film last night. You went to bed after the ten o'clock news. To the bed you shared with Iris. When did you notice that she hadn't come home? Not in the morning, I presume?'

'No.' She is whispering now. 'I went to bed, but I couldn't sleep. I waited for her. I waited. And I waited and I waited.'

'You didn't call the police? Or anyone else?'

'No.'

'Why not?'

'I … I don't know.' Horror flashes over her face. 'Do you think she'd be alive if I had called the police?'

'I don't think so, Tilda. I think she must have met her murderer after she left the meeting.'

'But then … who …?'

I shake my head. 'I hope we'll find out soon, Tilda. Meanwhile, is there someone you can call? A friend? Family?'

'I … I don't know. I have to think.'

'It's best not to be alone now,' I say gently. 'We will assign a Family Liaison Officer to be with you for a while. She will help you through the first period, but it might be a good idea if you could call a friend too. Someone you trust.'

'I don't know, Detective Inspector,' she says miserably. 'Iris was my best friend. My only friend.'

14

It is just gone four when I leave Tilda Disley in the hands of a young woman she knows from her gym classes. It has stopped raining but the temperature has dropped significantly. The sky is slate grey and large snowflakes are drifting slowly down.

I hurry to my car, noticing that Fistral Beach is already covered in a thin white layer of snow. Two surfers are brave enough to be running to the sea, joining a couple of others. I had left my phone in my car before I rang the doorbell of the modern white bungalow where Iris Spencer lived with Tilda Disley. It wasn't a conversation to be interrupted by phone calls. As I pull the seat belt across me and turn the phone on, the screen tells me that I have half a dozen missed calls. One is my mother's. The rest are all from the same number. I don't recognise it. I start the car and turn the heating on. Press a button to return the calls.

My mother picks up almost immediately. She sounds breathless. 'Andy, love, sorry to call you at work.'

'No problem, mother.'

'It is ... he is ...' Her voice breaks into tears.

I swallow. Is this the call every son or daughter is dreading? 'Is it ... father?'

'No, no, I didn't mean to upset you. No, your father is alright. It is ... I just had a call from the care home. It's Mr Grose. He passed away.'

'Oh.'

Mr Grose. Archibald Grose. My mother used to visit him regularly as part of her volunteer job for a charity that aimed to assist the elderly and less gifted people, helping with odd jobs in and around their homes and giving them general support. On one or two occasions, she'd taken me to his house during school holidays. He was a strange man and for some reason, he intrigued me. I wasn't even aware of the fact that he was still alive, when she asked me not so long ago to see him after his first stroke. As a result, I was more or less adopted as the one person who took care of him. He didn't seem to have any relatives and I guess I felt I owed him something after he'd shared his big odd secret with me.

'I would have thought they'd call you.'

'They've only got my landline.'

'Oh. I see. Anyway, the funeral's this week. Your father's got something else to do and I wondered … would you come with me?'

'Eh …'

Hearing the reluctance in my voice, she hesitates. 'There will probably be no one else. Maybe one or two of the nurses in his care home, but that'll be all, sadly.'

'No family?'

'I don't know. I'm pretty sure he had a brother, but I don't think there was any contact.'

'Oh.' I sigh inwardly.

'I feel so sorry for him, Andy. It's very sad to have a funeral with nobody there.'

'No. Alright, mother. Let me know when and where and I'll come with you.'

Half wishing I hadn't returned her call, we talk for a few more minutes about an aunt I barely remember and a niece who's finally divorcing an abusive husband.

'Hello?' A woman who tried to call me five times answers.
'You called me.'

'I did.' A short silence. 'Tregunna?'

'Who is this?'

'Sorry. It's Andrea Burke.'

'Oh … hi.'

She is on the periphery of my work environment and I would prefer to keep it that way. It seems, the only time we meet is when we're dealing with a corpse. She only calls me when she is facing some sort of problem related to her work as a forensic specialist. I hate to admit it, even to myself, but she always makes me feel uncomfortable, incompetent, a target for her rather weird sense of humour. Other people may not have a problem with her, but I do.

'Tregunna, are you still there?'

I hesitate. She thinks the line has gone dead. 'Yes.'

'Are you alone?'

'I am.'

I look up and see Tilda Disley standing by the window, staring out, not seeing me. A figure of misery and despair. She has refused to be assigned to a Family Liaison Officer but, seeing the state she's in, I make a mental note to send someone to see her anyway.

A blue van stops and parks in front of me. Two young men get out and open the back doors. Without paying attention if anyone is watching, they pull off their jeans, jumpers and trainers, and wrestle themselves into their wetsuits. I can't suppress a shiver.

The driver of a passing car hoots. The surfers reply with gestures that only they seem to understand.

'Where are you?' Burke asks bluntly.

'I'm stuck in traffic.'

'When will you be at the police station?'

I stare at the dashboard clock. It is already getting dark. 'Tomorrow morning. I'm on my way home.'

The snow is falling heavily now. Traffic is slowing down. I pull out and follow a small blue car with a nervous driver who brakes every ten yards, not realising that it is better to keep driving than braking on slippery roads; front-wheel drive engines, like that car has, will propel the car sideways.

Andrea Burke is speaking again. 'I have something to share with you.' She seems in a strange mood. Chatty but impatient.

'What is it?'

'I would like to talk to you in private.'

'When?'

'Now?'

'I can't.'

She makes a noise in the back of her throat that sounds like a combination of a chuckle and a giggle. 'Ehm ... Do you have a date or something?'

'I'm just tired.'

'Oh.' She falls silent. I can almost hear her brain ticking over while she makes up her mind. 'Everything alright, Tregunna?'

'I'm not sleeping very well.' I don't know why I'm telling her this. I imagine that she'll share a joke at my expense with a colleague as soon as I put down the phone.

'Oh. Sorry to hear that.' All of a sudden, her tone is that of genuine concern.

'It's not your problem,' I reply curtly.

'No.' A brief silence. 'Of course not.'

The car in front of me has stopped to let a gritter lorry go first. Rock salt sprinkles on the tarmac.

I can hear shouting and screaming before I see a group of school children appear around the corner. Sliding on the already slippery pavement, they laugh and giggle, scraping up snow to make snowballs with red hands. One ball lands on the bonnet of my car. They chuckle and run.

The traffic is moving again. Slow motion. People want to get home before they get stuck in their cars especially on the hilly roads. Newquay is beginning to grind to a halt in what are, for Cornwall, unusual weather conditions.

'I really want to talk about this,' Andrea Burke presses on. 'I need your opinion.'

'Okay, but the weather isn't looking good.' I feel a pang of guilt as I use the weather conditions as an excuse to avoid making arrangements to meet her.

'I'm already in Newquay,' she says dryly.

A local bus is parked alongside the road. The driver is standing on the pavement, talking on his phone, his face dark with concern. He looks like he isn't going anywhere today.

'Okay, I'll come to the station.'

Turning left from Mount Wise, instead of going home, I drive to the police station where the car park is almost deserted. The gritters have left a trail of now dirty rock salt, and the snow is already melting in patches.

'I have a match for a set of the fingerprints,' Andrea Burke says abruptly.

'That was quick.'

'Yes, it was …'

The line goes dead as I step out of my car. I'm halfway across the car park when I see a red flash out of the corner of my eyes. Angela Burke is waiting beside a red sports car with a soft top. It is easy to imagine her driving fast on the motorway in the summer: a flash of bright red.

'Do you always walk so fast?' she asks neutrally.

'It's cold.'

She laughs, making me feel like a fool. 'I have news for you, Tregunna.'

'Good or bad?'

'That depends on your viewpoint.'

I don't react.

She shrugs. 'The fingerprints on Iris Spencer's car.'

I wait. Given the fact that it is only eight hours ago that Iris Spencer's car was found, this must be important.

'We have a match.'

'You could have emailed it to me instead of driving all the way from Truro.'

She shrugs and I realise I don't know where she lives. 'I could. But I didn't.'

We stare at each other. There is an unspoken conversation going on between us. Neither of us is willing to make the next move. I wish I hadn't given in to her. I'm cold and tired and I want to go home.

Andrea Burke seems reluctant to let me go. 'Listen Tregunna. I'd like to discuss this with you before it goes public.'

I've never seen her so hesitant and uneasy. Eyes down, she's tugging at the sleeves of her long red coat. 'Shall we go somewhere and ...?'

A lorry kills the sound of her voice. A gust of wind and snowflakes land on her face and her red hair. The silence hangs between us.

Then she lifts her chin, making up her mind. Pushing aside her discomfort, she looks straight in my face, her expression unreadable. 'I'm cold and I'm starving. What about if we get something to eat and we'll talk then?'

My surprise must have been written all over my face, because she grins, her eyes crinkling behind her red-rimmed glasses. I notice her eyes are green and she has applied green eye shadow. Green, the complementary colour to red.

She cocks her head, red lips smiling with a hint of mischief. She's challenging me. 'Unless you have other … commitments?'

'Not today.'

She nods and takes the lead. 'It's a bit early, but I know a place nearby where we can eat early. Right now.'

I don't ask where. For some reason, I'm sure she doesn't mean a chippy.

I follow the red sports car until she drives into a parking area in front of a building with blackened windows. I can't make out whether it is a pub in a very modern disguise or a boarded-up derelict listed building. I'm none the wiser when she steers me inside, heading straight towards a table with two tall bar stools. The ceiling is high and, apart from the black marble floor and bar counter, everything else is stainless steel and white. Soft easy-listening music hums in the background, along with the voices of a dozen other early customers.

'I like this place,' she announces, climbing the bar stool as she picks up the menu. Matt and black, the menu is printed in white letters.

'There's nothing red in here.'

She grins. 'That's why I like it. I stand out more.'

The man behind the bar knows her. He brings a large glass of red wine to our table and smiles politely, asking me what I would like to drink. 'On the house,' he adds casually.

'Soda water, please, no ice.'

'It's too cold outside for ice cubes.' He grins and looks at me questioningly. 'I haven't seen you here before.'

'That's right.' I look around and try to find words to express that I am positively impressed with the place. I can't find any and he lifts one shoulder, turning his back to me to let me know that I have disappointed him.

'Are you a regular customer here?' I ask Andrea Burke.

She inclines her head, not taking her eyes off me. 'My brother owns this place.'

'Was he …?'

'No, I'll introduce you later.' She smiles smugly and waves her hands towards the menu. 'What do you fancy? My treat.'

All of a sudden, I feel uncomfortable. Her smile is mildly sardonic, making me feel like I'm a schoolboy who's been taken out into the dangerous world of adults. I'm about to decline the offer, lie that I have remembered that I have a meal prepared in my fridge, when a gentle smell from the kitchen drifts in with a waitress carrying two plates.

I change my mind. 'I'll have what you have.'

She laughs. 'Are you sure?'

'I will probably regret it afterwards, but yes, I'm sure.'

As the waitress brings a bottle of sparkling water of a rather expensive brand, I hear Andrea Burke place her order and I decide not to ask if I've actually heard her mention crocodile croquettes and kangaroo steak. Or the other way round.

'About the fingerprints,' she says, sipping her wine. 'I'm sure there'll be a completely logical and innocent explanation, but it is not up to me to investigate that. As you know, our department is primarily there to do the research and provide evidential proof. We don't speculate, we deal with facts only.'

She pauses. I have a feeling that I don't want to hear the rest.

Opening her handbag, she retrieves a yellow folder and withdraws a forensic report. 'As you know, our department undertakes a range of the techniques to identify fingerprints comparing them with those on our database or suspects in a case.'

I wait, wondering why she has started with an unnecessary explanation that sounds like an apology. As if she expected me to question her professionalism.

'Why are you telling me this?'

'Look for yourself.' She slips the report in my direction. Waits. I'm aware that she's staring at me intently while I read the report. Cutting through the legalities, I stare at a series of black fingerprints at the bottom of the first page. I'm none the wiser. The second sheet has more fingerprints. Red dots and lines indicating the one important word: match. Eyes skimming the short, explanatory text, I am looking for a name.

I gasp when I find it.

15

The landscape is covered in a thin layer of snow. Around midnight, the wind changed direction and milder air is already pushing the cold away. As soon as the sun gains in strength, there will only be a slurry of dirty snow on the roads and in the verges.

Penrose has had her morning shower and is dressed in her working clothes when there is a knock on the door. She hesitates, half inclined to ignore it. In the narrow hallway, she stands still, uncomfortably aware of the smell of last night's spicy Indian food and laundry drying on the rack above the staircase.

There is another knock. Whoever it is, they have noticed that her car is still parked in front of the house. They know she hasn't gone to work yet. Through the frosted glass in the door panel, she can see the shape of a figure that looks vaguely familiar.

It can't be, can it? She hesitates. Horrified. Curious. Reaching out for the door handle, she becomes suddenly aware of another smell. Urine.

'Do I hear someone knocking on the door?'

Her father is standing in the doorway to the kitchen. He's wearing a greyed vest under a blue checked shirt that is hanging loose. He stares at her blankly and she suspects he's wondering who she is. He isn't at his best in the mornings.

'Come on, woman, why don't you answer the door? It may be important.'

She swallows and wipes clammy hands on her hips. Woman, he's called her. He's confusing her with her mother again, who he used to call 'woman' when he was annoyed, while she was his 'honeybee' when he was in a brighter mood.

She opens her mouth to remind him that it is only half-past seven in the morning, and that a visitor at this time of day probably means trouble.

Instead, she hisses, 'Go inside, father. Look at yourself! You're barely dressed and there is … '

She stops abruptly, not able to mention the large dark stain spreading from his groin. He may not even realise what he's done. No need to make him upset. She hates it when he cries like a child.

'Well?'

He is confused. He can see the shape of their visitor and he doesn't understand why she isn't opening the door.

'I'll deal with it, father.' Gently she pushes him back into the kitchen, closing the door behind him. Then, taking a deep breath, she wipes over her eyes with the back of her hand, rubs the slightly sticky moisture off her fingers.

They don't normally have visitors knocking on the front door. When she's working, neighbours keep an eye on her father, but they always use the back door. The only people who will knock and come to their front door are the couple from across the road. Shona is a nursery teacher, good with children but shy and hesitant when dealing with adults. Sam works in Newquay hospital as a cleaner.

Perhaps she was mistaken when, for one moment, she thought she recognised the visitor. No. It must be Sam. Occasionally, he brings them plasters and bandages, disposable mattress covers and adult nappies. For some reason, their neighbourhood isn't as affluent as other villages so close to the coast. There was a time in her teenage years when she even felt ashamed and embarrassed to live there, to be part of a community of people like themselves, people who had too few chances in life. Maybe she's doing them an injustice in thinking that the neighbours are only helpful because she's a police officer. She knows all about the people who don't declare that they have a job when they are claiming benefits, and the people who buy and sell stuff from dodgy sources. Those people trust her to keep quiet. She shouldn't, but she isn't always completely honest herself either. For example, she accepts Sam's gifts of nappies and bandages when she knows, although she's never actually asked him, where they have come from. In return, Sam happily accepts the odd banknote from her; not offered to him often as the policewoman in her doesn't want to encourage him.

Deciding that the visitor has to be Sam, she pulls open the door.

'Oh!' Startled, she tries to pull back as she recognises the man on the doorstep. She knows she has to close the door quickly, before it's too late. But she doesn't move. She can't.

'Jennette?' His face is tight and serious, concern in his dark eyes.

She's frozen on the doormat. 'Sir?'

Equally uncomfortable, Tregunna stares down at a carpet roll in the front garden, lifting the edge with the tip of his shoe as though he is expecting to find something valuable underneath. Penrose swallows hard.

It's the carpet she was supposed to take to the tip three months ago. Now it lies dormant on the strip of weeds and grass her mother once so proudly called their garden. It was a proper front garden then, with flowers grown from seeds her mother used to take from old plants in other people's gardens. Penrose feels a tiny pang of guilt when she thinks about it now. She should have made an effort to keep mum's garden tidier.

And the small vegetable garden at the back too. Maybe she could grow carrots and beans again this summer.

'What are you doing here?' she asks stiffly, still not believing her eyes.

'There is something I need to speak to you about.' Tregunna looks like he's regretting the impulse in coming here. 'I'm sorry. I shouldn't have turned up like this, without calling first. But I was ... I happened to be in the area and I thought ... you might be home.'

She doesn't move. He happened to be in the area? Where? Doing what? This early in the morning? She doesn't know what to do or say. Is it very rude not to let him in? How can she let him in while she's cooking breakfast for her father, who hasn't even got changed and dressed properly?

'Can't it wait?'

'Ehm ... I don't think so, no.'

'What is it about?'

'Ehm ...' He looks around, clearly very uncomfortable. In a neighbourhood like this, good or bad, people have eyes and ears. 'Ehm ... you're busy. I should have realised that.'

'No, it's alright, but ...'

'What are you doing, woman?' Her father gives a shout from inside the house. He opens the kitchen door and a terrible smell drifts out. He's wearing a black apron dotted with images of plates and cutlery and with the words, *Chefs don't cook, they create*. He is waving frantically with a long wooden spoon.

Penrose freezes. The porridge.

The pan already forgotten on the stove, her father is staring past her with big round eyes. Clearly realising that he recognises their visitor, but not remembering his name, or who he is. Confusion appears in his eyes, his mouth trembles.

'Do we have a visitor, honeybee?'

'No father, it's … it's my boss.'

As her words dissolve into nothing, realisation sets in. The veil over her father's brain lifts and then he is as bright and keen as he was when he was younger, when he was the handsome, vibrant young man she remembers from her childhood. The man who worked so hard to make his family a decent living, to help her and her brother with their education, to be able to buy them a house. This house, her mother's pride and joy.

'Do come in, sir.' To her horror, her father gestures jovially at Tregunna. 'Jen, make us a cup of tea! Join us, Mr Jen's-boss. Sorry, I forgot your name, but join us, please, by all means, you are very welcome to share our humble food with us.'

'Thank you, Mr Penrose, but I'm afraid I can't stay,' Tregunna says, and his refusal hits her like a brutal blow.

Anger makes her cheeks turn red. How dare he treat her father as an idiot? How dare he show up here, out of the blue, and yet be so uncomfortable and embarrassed with the situation? A situation of his own creation? Sure, their house isn't exactly up to modern standards. It hasn't got bare white walls, shiny laminated floors and the fashionable settees that you can only sit on for so long before your bottom goes numb and your toes tingle. But everything is clean. And after all, being poor is not something to be ashamed of.

'We're just having … breakfast. Aren't we, Jen?'

'No really, I have no time.' Tregunna tries hard to make his smile look polite and apologetic. 'Work,' he adds, retrieving his mobile phone from his pocket as if someone is trying to contact him.

'No, I insist! Jen always speaks so highly of you. We'd be honoured with your presence, wouldn't we, Jen?'

She doesn't know where these over-the-top polite words of

her father are coming from. It feels like she's entered a theatre where some hilarious comedy is being performed. A ripple rises in her stomach and she has to suppress a nervous giggle.

'Yes father,' she replies automatically, more for his benefit than anything else. Then she sees the smoke behind him, wondering vaguely why the smoke detector isn't beeping. She'd better check the batteries … She rushes to the kitchen and quickly takes the pan with burnt porridge off the stove, flapping at the thick smoke with her other hand.

She is hardly aware that the front door has closed and Tregunna emerges in the kitchen. His eyes take in the situation as though he's observing a crime scene, missing no detail. His nostrils flare as he picks up the smell of burnt milk and oats, the stale smell of beer left in bottles that are lined up next to the back door, ready for the bin collectors. And probably the smell of urine …

'Is there anything I can do, Jennette?' he asks softly.

'No, just … just go, please!'

She's close to tears. Wiping them away vigorously, she's trying to hide them. But there is no doubt that he's seen them.

'You can't speak to your superior like that, Jen,' her father butts in.

Tregunna gestures reassuringly. 'Sit down, please, Jennette. I'll make us a cup of tea.'

'I … I can make toast.' She shakes her head wearily. 'We have some home-made marmalade from our neighbour. There's a loaf of bread in the freezer.'

He nods seriously, clearly relieved that the situation is in hand. 'Sounds perfect to me, Jennette.'

Twenty minutes later, she has installed her father in the lounge to watch a replay of a football cup final. He doesn't realise that the match is from years ago. Tregunna sits at the kitchen table hunched over a mug of coffee. Somehow she'd remembered she had a handful of espresso sachets somewhere in a jar, glad to be able to offer him something remotely decent.

'Jennette, there is something I'd like to discuss,' he says gently.

Nervously, she looks round for something to do. He didn't just come here to disturb their morning ritual or have breakfast with them. He's here for a reason. And by the serious look on his face, she doesn't want to hear that reason.

'Sit down, please, Jennette.'

She swallows and sits opposite him. Waiting. For several long moments, the silence stretches out between them. Again she remembers that one of the things she likes about him is that he talks only when he has something sensible to say. Now, she realises that he's searching for words, which makes the waiting even more uncomfortable.

Suddenly impatiently, she stretches her shoulders and lifts her chin. She's done nothing wrong. 'Okay, guv, what's up?'

He stares at her, his expression unreadable, but she sees the tension in his shoulders.

'You told me you took your father to a council meeting.'

For a moment she's perplexed. Her mouth falls open. Then she recovers quickly, focusing her thoughts on the council meeting to avoid hearing what he really came for. But surely, he isn't here to discuss a council meeting?

'Oh!' She lets out a nervous laugh that sounds more like a screech. 'Well, I don't know how he orchestrated it, but my father made me take him to a parish council meeting. As soon as we got into the village hall and he saw that councillor, he started shouting and swearing. He more or less accused her of stealing and lying and all sorts of things. Well, things got a bit out of hand, and we were very politely asked to leave.' Her face is flushed with the memory of the humiliation. 'In a way, it was a relief that we could just go home..'

He nods briefly. 'You must have felt awful.'

She gazes at him, surprised, but the tension is still noticeable in the slump of her shoulders. He doesn't meet her eyes.

'I spoke to Andrea Burke last night,' Tregunna says slowly, in a matter-of-fact manner.

She sighs with an odd sense of foreboding. He's finally coming to the point.

'Burke told me that they have identified the fingerprints they found on Iris Spencer's car.'

'And?'

He avoids her gaze. 'They are yours, DC Penrose.'

16

The sun casts a bright glow over the coast as if the head of the tourist board has staged it himself to attract visitors and photographers. The sky is clear and blue, the waves sparkling against the darker mix of the blues and greens of the sea. I'm on the coast road, negotiating the narrow bridge in Mawgan Porth and, further towards Newquay, looking out at the surfing fanatics in Watergate Bay.

Penrose's explanation of how her fingerprints appeared on Iris Spencer's car is credible enough to me, but I'm not so sure if Maloney will share my opinion. Or the team. To me, the idea that Penrose may have had something to do with Iris's death, let alone played an active role in it, is too absurd to even consider. Yet, I have to acknowledge that there was a brief moment of doubt in my mind when I read Andrea Burke's report. Police work involves a lot of speculation and imagination, but in the end it all comes down to facts. And the fact is that Penrose's fingerprints have been found in relation to a murder investigation. Her explanation could only be confirmed by her father but, due to the nature of his mental state, his statement wouldn't hold.

As I turn round a sharp hairpin bend and drive up the hill, a car hoots behind me. A dark-coloured BMW is clinging to the back of my car, the driver frustrated by a speed I consider safe on this stretch of road. I look in the rear-view mirror and see a bully of a driver leaning forward over his steering wheel, his frame stiff with anger and impatience. It would only take a split second of recklessness for him to crash into me.

On top of the hill, I pass the remains of the demolished equipment from the time when the airport was operated by the MoD. I pull into the small lay-by and the BMW shoots past, the driver glaring sideways at me for too long that he almost drives into a double-decker bus coming around the corner. The loud engine of the car fades into the distance along with the rock music pounding from its radio.

I'm parked on a strip of tarmac opposite a field that stretches to the cliff edge. Sheep are now grazing here, early baby lambs running along happily as the ewes follow their antics with caring eyes. In August, this area around Newquay is transformed when the Boardmasters Festival is on a four-day event that combines surfing and skateboarding competitions with live music. In the first few years, it was chaotic, but now it seems to be better organised and local residents and businesses don't complain so much.

I stare at the ewes who have followed the curious lambs to have a peek at me. I pick up my mobile as it rings for the second time, thinking it might be Penrose asking me to tone down my concerns about her. She's going to come clean to Maloney this morning and she's refused my support.

'Tregunna? It's Kim Naylor. *The Cornish Gazette.*' Her voice is high and bright and it sounds so loud that I can't help looking over my shoulder, half expecting to find her sitting behind me.

'Kim. What can I do for you?'

'I might have some information for you.'

Dealing with reporters is always the tricky bit. While the police have much more information about an investigation than they want to tell the public, reporters usually have their own sources. Sometimes they know more than the police do and they can even, up to a point, determine in which direction

119

an investigation goes. Although it can be beneficial talking to a reporter, it is like walking in a minefield where both parties have hidden their own explosives.

Kim Naylor is an intelligent young woman and I know from experience that one single careless word can trigger her undue attention. And then she'll be a terrier, not letting go of the bait.

'Yes?' I say cautiously.

'Are you interested or not?' She sounds impatient.

'That depends.'

'I have something, Tregunna. I'd like your comments before it goes to press.'

'And if I don't comment?'

'You know me. If I decide it is important enough, it'll still be published. With or without your consent.'

'Perhaps you should talk to DI Maloney then. He's handling the case. I'm not in the position to act as a spokesman.'

She chuckles. 'Careful as usual, aren't you, Andy?'

'Talking to you? Yes.'

Another chuckle. 'DI Maloney won't speak or listen to me. He has announced a press conference but that might be too late for my deadline.' She stops for breath. 'I'm sure he's doing it on purpose.'

'I doubt it.' Maloney has much more on his plate than to think about press conferences and deadlines and keeping reporters satisfied with whatever information they choose to release.

'You won't regret it, Tregunna. What do you say? Shall we meet?'

'Okay.' It can't hurt to avoid the police station for an hour or so until the morning briefing is over and Penrose has spoken to Maloney and the team.

'Where are you?'

'I'm watching some mad surfers at Watergate Bay.'

'Oh. Do you mind meeting me in Fowey? I'll be there in ten minutes.'

I hesitate. It'll take me about forty minutes to drive to Fowey on the south coast. On the other hand, Kim has proven to be a useful and reliable source of information and it never hurts listening to her.

Kim is talking again. Explaining why she is in the vicinity of an undisclosed meeting point where she'll be interviewing an author who has recently published a rather controversial novel about his involvement in a secret operation in the Middle East. The general opinion about the author seems to lie somewhere in the middle. With some people believing that everything in his book is true, or others convinced that he is a liar with a great imagination who has watched too many James Bond films. Typically, Kim is persistent in getting to the bottom of the story.

She disconnects the call after we've arranged where and when we'll meet and, as I stare out of the window, I realise she hasn't asked me the latest about the Spencer murder case.

The river Fowey rises from a well near Brown Willy, the highest point on Bodmin Moor, and in Cornwall as a whole. It curves and curls across the county until it reaches the English Channel at Fowey on the Uzell estuary. Uzell is derived from the Cornish word for 'howling place'. I've never heard any howling, but I'm sure there will be people who claim they have.

This time of year, the car park at the ferry from Fowey to Bodinnick is almost deserted. Kim Naylor's car, white with a red top, is clearly not there yet and I wander to the water's edge. Herring gulls swoop over the water, always looking for food with their piercing golden-yellow eyes. I watch the car ferry coming in, engines pounding to operate the big rattling chains that pull it across the river and help keep the flat vessel on course in the strong tides. Across the water, I recognise the house where Daphne du Maurier once lived and which inspired her first published novel.

Kim's Mini is on the next ferry crossing over from Bodinnick. I see her leaning against her car, speaking on her mobile phone, gesturing like she's talking to a deaf person. She waves at me as if she's seen a long lost friend.

A couple of minutes later and she's smiling sweetly with a cute pair of dimples in her cheeks, thrusting her car keys into the pocket of her jeans. Tall and sexy, full breasts and curved hips, the proportions accentuated, she is undoubtedly a very attractive young woman. She's dressed in blue jeans and a light blue sailing jacket with a big navy blue number 26 sewn across the back, as if the fabric has been cut out of a discarded sail.

'I'm starving,' she declares good-naturedly and points in the direction of the centre of the village. 'Shall we find a pasty somewhere?'

'That won't be too difficult,' I reply mockingly.

We both know that tourist places like Fowey are usually overcrowded with Cornish pasty shops.

'I hope my favourite pasty shop is already open,' she says, not disclosing which one it is.

She is slightly out of breath when we walk through the narrow street where, occasionally, we have to step aside into doorways of houses to let vehicles pass.

'Have you spoken to the author?' I ask casually.

She pulls a face. 'He called me to delay the meeting. Again. Latest is that I'll see him after lunch time. At least I hope so. I'm not so sure if he'll see me at all.'

'He's probably suffering the stress of having become a celebrity so suddenly.'

She nods thoughtfully. 'Hmm. That's why I couldn't meet you in Newquay. He keeps changing the date and time and I don't want to be in the position that he agrees to see me within a few minutes when I'm miles away.'

'He can't be that important, Kim. If he doesn't want to talk, then perhaps you should leave it and use your own imagination and knowledge.'

'That is exactly what I told him this morning, when he changed the time again. He wasn't impressed.'

We dart into the doorway of a small tourist shop and let a delivery van struggle through the narrow street. 'In fact, he is arrogant enough to say he will take me to court if he doesn't approve of my article. My boss won't like that.'

'What's his real name?'

She grins, her eyes sparkling. 'Do you really expect me to tell you that?'

'I won't tell anyone.'

'I'm sure you won't,' she says sardonically but the subject is closed.

She finds her favourite pasty shop and we sit at a table in the window, watching passing tourists wrapped in winter coats and woollen hats and scarves. By contrast, the driver of another delivery van that has stopped in the middle of the road is wearing shorts and a black polo shirt.

'Why did you want to meet me, Kim?'

She hesitates, uncertain all of a sudden. 'I'm not sure, to be honest.'

'That is rather unusual for you.'

A fleeting smile passes over her face. 'It is, isn't it?' She shrugs and continues. 'I guess I wanted to pick your brain.' Seeing the expression on my face, she chuckles with unease. 'I need to make up my mind. There is too much stuff going on in my life currently.'

'Such as?'

'My boyfriend.'

A confession about her personal life is the last thing I expected. 'I didn't know you had one.'

'It is early days but … it feels good, you know.'

'Anyone I know? One of your colleagues?'

'I don't think so.' She smiles almost apologetically. 'He works for a bank.'

'Oh.'

'I can't help it.'

'Did I say anything?'

'Your face speaks volumes.' Then she is serious again, dimples gone. 'The one thing I'm not so sure about is our difference of opinion about money. I don't care about money as long as I have enough for a few pints of beer at the weekend and a holiday in a warm country in the winter.'

'He doesn't agree?'

'Not really, no. He thinks I'm a damned good reporter and I should go freelance and sell my stories to the highest bidder.'

'That'll only work well if there are stories to tell.'

'Exactly. He's in London, I'm in Cornwall. How often does a good story come up here in Cornwall or Devon? How often is a story big enough to sell to a national newspaper?'

'I really don't know, Kim. I don't know how these things work.' I start wondering where the conversation is leading to.

She nods thoughtfully, wiping flakes of pastry off her chin. 'I was lucky with that one story. That's when I met him, so he thinks there are more stories like that. And if there aren't any more in Cornwall, I'd better move away, go where the action is.'

'And you don't want to leave Cornwall?'

'No.'

The silence stretches out but it isn't uncomfortable.

'Which story were you so lucky with that this guy put these ideas about big money in your head?' I ask.

She shrugs. 'About the charity night.'

'You've lost me there.'

'Oh, come on, Tregunna, I'm sure you've heard about it. How could you have missed it? It was everywhere on the news, papers, TV, questions in Parliament even.' She sees the expression on my face and shakes her head incredulously. 'A couple of weeks ago there was a big charity night in one of the biggest hotels in Cornwall. They do it every year and it raises a lot of money for several charities.'

'The so called 'men-only' night?'

'That's the one.'

Then it dawns on me. 'Were you the whistle-blower? The undercover reporter who wrote about it all in the newspapers?'

'That was me, yes.' There is no triumph or arrogance in her voice.

I remember the story that shocked the nation. A charity night for businessmen. Invitees are only men, wealthy and influential men. A night organised to raise money. A yearly event in December.

Until it went horribly wrong and the event was condemned in the press.

Kim talks in a neutral voice. 'It was common practise that female partners and wives weren't welcome at those parties. I never thought anything of it, until I found out that there would be women after all. But only young women from a special agency. I wouldn't go as far as saying that they were from an escort service, but I'm sure I'm not far off there. These young women had to be of a certain age, a certain size and they had to wear short black dresses supplied by the agency. And preferably black lacy lingerie.'

Kim stops briefly to study my face. Then she continues.

'I heard about it from a friend of mine whose girlfriend used to work for this agency. She was asked if she wanted to earn a couple of hundred pounds. She said yes, of course, but she had doubts afterwards. She didn't trust it. She told me about it and I went in her place.' She stops to grin sheepishly. 'I didn't fit into the little black dress provided, so I used my own.'

I stare at her. 'What about your underwear?'

'Andy Tregunna, how dare you!' Wide-eyed, open-mouthed, she holds up her hands as if in surrender. But her eyes are sparkling. She's living and working in modern society, not in a sheltered narrow-minded environment. And she certainly isn't one of those women who weighs up every word in search of something remotely offensive. I know some women who take offence at a wolf whistle or a flirtatious look, saying it's sexual harassment. I know other women who just laugh and shrug off a pat on their bottom. I even know a woman who finds it normal to return the gesture.

'I hope you are aware that questions about my underwear can be seen as sexual harassment these days? It could get you in serious trouble if I go to the police.'

'I am the police. And you started talking about black lacy lingerie yourself.'

She grins, not the least offended. 'Well, to be totally honest, I did wear that stuff that night. I had to buy it all, though, I didn't have it in my wardrobe.'

'Your new boyfriend must have been pleased.'

'That's none of your business.'

'Okay.' I hold up my hands in mock defeat. 'Go on, please, Kim.'

She nods. Earnestly. 'We arrived at the hotel in small groups. We were each given an envelope with half of the promised money. We would get the rest if they were pleased with our performance.'

'Did they use those words?'

'Words to that effect.' She rubs her nose. 'The beginning of the evening was pleasant enough. I really enjoyed myself and I met a few interesting guys. But as the evening progressed, people got tipsy, or really drunk from excessive alcohol and drugs even... Some of the men wanted to take girls to their rooms. Some of the girls did go, for some extra pocket money I suppose, others blankly refused.'

'And you?'

I'm intrigued now. After it all came out, the story had a big effect on charity donations. Some charities even returned donations raised during these particular events.

'I was too busy making videos on my phone and recording conversations.'

'You were spying on them?'

'My integrity and the morality of the whole event wasn't really my concern, Tregunna, and besides, I had to keep the recordings for reference, and for evidence in case no one would believe me.' She pauses briefly, frowning. 'It was just a good story and it got a lot of publicity. And money. I sold the longer version of the story to one of the national newspapers and to one of those gossip magazines. I am not really proud of it but, hey, my bank account looks healthy for the time being.'

'I still don't understand why you are telling me this.'

Surprisingly, the question in my voice makes her uncomfortable. She's shifting in her seat, looking around for an escape route.

'I didn't realise it at the time, but now ... it might have a possible follow-up.'

'How?'

She hesitates for a long time. 'One of the men I saw there was Edward Lynham.'

'What?'

She nods. 'The man who hanged himself. It's crossed my mind that what happened that evening might be related to his death.'

I'm on my guard now. I'm not sure if she hopes to hear something from me. 'What makes you say that, Kim?'

'I don't know, but it seems too much of a coincidence.' She pauses. 'Don't you think?'

'Hm.'

I'm still not sure why she asked me to meet her. Does she want information about the circumstances of Edward Lynham's death? Or is there, as she seems to think, more to his death than meets the eye?

'What do you know that I don't, Kim?' I ask her slowly.

She hunches her shoulders, staring into her mug of green tea. 'Ed Lynham resigned from his position in his political party, or rather, he had to. He had no choice. Apparently, nobody cared to explain the actual reason, not even to Lynham himself.'

'If you know something, you'll have to tell me, Kim.'

'The whole story stinks, Tregunna. This is just the tip of the iceberg. It isn't just about a political disagreement, as the party wants us to believe. And I'm not entirely convinced that Lynham killed himself.'

'He left a suicide note.'

She ignores me, thinking out loud. 'What if someone helped him a bit with that? What if it wasn't suicide but murder?'

'Kim, he left instructions to his wife where his body could be found. It was in the press release, you know that.'

'But did you really believe it was suicide, Tregunna? You were there, I know you were. Are you sure it was suicide? Or has his death been covered up like it was his own doing?'

'I can't tell you any more about it, Kim. Sorry.'

'It would make a damned good story and I can probably get a lot of money for it.'

'Is that fair to a man who can't defend himself?'

She doesn't respond and I shrug, disappointed by her attitude. She knows it.

'What I need is some back-up, Tregunna. Your permission, if you like, to do more research about Lynham and then I'll write my story. Or I won't.'

'You still haven't told me what you want from me.'

She pulls a wry smile. 'That's why I'm hesitating. I met Ed Lynham and his wife three months ago for an interview. A lovely couple. I wouldn't want to drag his name through the shit any more than it already has been. It isn't fair on him or his wife. It's only … if he was innocent, like he claimed …' She pauses for a while, clearly making up her mind. 'I have the name of a woman who claimed that he raped her that night.'

'Rape? Ed Lynham?'

She nods gravely. 'You haven't heard this from me, Tregunna, but that's what happened. The woman cried rape and although she didn't go to the police, Ed Lynham's political party got to hear about it and took action. They didn't even tell him who the woman was. He had no chance to defend himself.'

'And what …?'

'If this is true, Tregunna, I want to get to the bottom of it. But I have to be very careful about what I say or write.' She grins without humour. 'In my opinion, even if he actually committed suicide, I'd say his party, or rather its leader, is guilty of murder.'

'That is a very bold statement, Kim.'

'Maybe, but he's been treated unfairly and he didn't deserve that. And Tregunna, I would like to hear from you if there is any doubt in your mind about his death.'

17

A schoolboy is sitting on a bench in front of Newquay railway station. Looking down. Sulking. Swinging his legs as though he has nothing else on his mind. Across the road, other school children walk by, gazing at him. Giggling. Poking elbows. Pointing.

Penrose parks and turns off the ignition and stares out, thinking that the boy looks exactly how she feels: reluctant to do anything or go anywhere. The only difference is that he is probably just in trouble at school. For her, it is much more serious: her job is at risk.

A car backs into a space between two other vehicles with an ease that makes her envious and annoyed; she's always had trouble reversing.

It is Maloney. Her annoyance turns into unreasonable anger. She purses her lips and her hands grab the steering wheel. Clenching. She watches her superior as he gets out, pulling up the collar of his coat against the cold wind and opening the back door of his car to retrieve a flat black briefcase. He sticks a newspaper under his arm and strides over to the police station. The entrance door swings open as he approaches but, as if he feels intuitively that he is being watched, he stands in the doorway for a moment and looks over his shoulder. Penrose ducks. Then he is gone.

She takes a deep breath. The schoolboy gets up with an air of reluctance, but nevertheless he joins two other boys. They laugh, shoulders are patted. Whatever his problems or worries were, they seem to have dissipated. Hers haven't.

Reaching for her handbag and unplugging her phone, Penrose thinks about Tregunna's cautious advice. Be honest. Tell them before questions are asked. Attack is better than defence. A surprise attack gives a slight advantage.

The main thing is that he believes in her. It feels good, it feels safe.

Her eyes scan the car park. She can do with his support, but she can't find his car. She swallows hard, then she composes herself, lifting her chin and stretching her back and shoulders. Getting out of her car, she's in a rush suddenly, hurrying to the police station and heading straight to the incident room.

The briefing, Ollie Reed explains, is delayed by fifteen minutes. There has been a blip in the computer system. Email isn't working. Maloney is expecting forensic reports. Until they can get their hands on them, the investigation of Iris Spencer's death is more or less in limbo. There is only so much they can do without the hard facts gathered by the forensic analysts. And Maloney wants to move on quickly, pick up the murderer's trail while it's still fresh.

Penrose stands in the doorway, fists clenched and trying hard to slow down her breathing. Someone has brought a box of pastries. Even Danielle Champion, who usually seems to survive on lettuce leaves, cherry tomatoes and sticks of carrot and cucumber, is enthusiastically munching away on a pasty.

Penrose helps herself to a cup of tea and perches on the corner of a table near to where Ollie Reed and Danielle Champion are grinning and talking behind their hands. They stop abruptly as Penrose comes within earshot. Pursing her lips, she rummages in the box without looking.

'That one is a veggie,' Ollie says, mouth full.

'I don't mind.'

He shrugs good-naturedly. 'Just saying.'

She takes a deep breath. Tries to relax. Sipping her tea, she sneakily slips the veggie pasty back in the box, picking up a sausage roll instead.

Champion grins companionably and, despite her mood, Penrose smiles back.

'Right. Are we all done?' Maloney comes in with an amount of energy that makes her cringe. Rubbing his hands together as though he is preparing for a boxing match, he looks around, scanning faces. He glares in Penrose's direction, but doesn't say anything. She swallows; maybe he hasn't seen Burke's report yet.

'Are we all present?'

Tregunna isn't there. For a fleeting moment Penrose thinks she should mention his absence. Nobody else seems to notice.

Maloney moves on quickly. 'Right. For those with a weak stomach and who've just been eating that unhealthy stuff over there, I suggest you should stop eating for a moment and take a few deep breaths.' He grins devilishly, picking up a handful of photos from the table. 'Let's review what we know so far, shall we? A woman was found dead on Goss Moor by a cyclist who lives in St Columb Major and works at the industrial estate in Roche. His mobile phone had no signal and he decided that it was too early to alert the nearby residents. He carried on to work and he called the police as soon as he arrived there, about fifteen to twenty minutes later.'

He points at two photos on the whiteboard. One is a close-up of the victim's face when she was found dead, all sparkle gone. The other is a selfie from her Facebook page: alive and happy.

'The victim has been identified as Iris Spencer, 44 years old, from Pentire in Newquay. Divorced. She lives with a young woman, Matilda Disley. She has a business in Truro, but she is also a local councillor.'

He is silent for a few moments, then runs them quickly through the facts they've already discovered. Updating everyone. Adding new information to the whiteboard.

'The autopsy report tells us that the killer used a sharp knife. He or she cut Iris's carotid artery on the left-hand side of her neck. The murderer used his right hand. Based on blood spatter analysis, she was killed where she was found. The killer must have attacked her from behind. We don't know whether she knew what was coming or not, but there are no signs that she defended herself. Now, our number one priority is to find the murder weapon. We'll have to search a wider perimeter of the crime scene, if necessary with a dog handler and a metal detector, but I'm not hopeful that we'll find it. This killer chose the crime scene carefully, he knew what he was doing. I doubt he was stupid enough to chuck the knife in the bushes after he killed her. But even the most careful criminal makes a mistake. Let's hope

Carla Vermaat

he did.'

He pauses and looks over their heads.

'Was the killer a man?' one of the officers asks.

'We don't know.'

Penrose wipes her mouth with a paper napkin that has come with the pastries, wondering when will be the best moment to interrupt and divulge her information. Maybe now?

But Maloney is speaking again. 'We know Miss Spencer lives with Matilda Disley, who is the daughter of an old schoolfriend of hers. Now, whether this Matilda is or isn't Iris's secret lover, is immaterial to me.' He grins mischievously. 'Let's treat this politically correctly, shall we?' He pauses, perhaps hoping that someone will share his sense of humour. When none comes, he shrugs and continues.

'What does matter is that Matilda Disley has no alibi. She claims that she was at home all night. At about six o'clock, they had their tea. A green Thai curry, which has been confirmed in the autopsy report. Then Iris Spencer left for a meeting in St Eval and …'

Penrose raises a hand. 'Sir, about that meeting …'

'Later,' Maloney says, annoyed by the interruption.

'Disley stayed at home. A neighbour saw her opening the door to a Tesco delivery van. Groceries. That was about eight o'clock. After that, Matilda claims she was alone at home, watching TV. Now, if she killed Iris, her motive might be jealousy or revenge. A crime of passion. So we need to find out more about the love-life of Iris Spencer. If any. Right?'

He looks around expectantly as if he's waiting for someone to raise a hand and object.

'Now, about Iris's background. She married Lester Boyd when they were both 21 years old. They divorced six years later. Obviously, we need to talk to the ex-husband, we need to know if there is an old grudge simmering.'

'Iris, as we know, was a local councillor, which was why she attended that meeting in St Eval. We need to know who else was there that night. I've been told that those meetings aren't normally well attended by the public, but that night there were quite a few people.

One of the subjects on the agenda was a planning application to build houses on a piece of land in a nearby village. And as always, there are people in favour or against such plans. We need to know if, and how, Iris Spencer was involved. If this meeting was of any significance to her death, then we're particularly interested in the Cawley brothers, Nathan and Boris.'

His eyes wander over faces, finding Ollie Reed. 'DS Reed, perhaps you can tell us more about these Cain and Abel characters?'

Ollie rises, flushing with surprise. He explains.

'I have spoken to Boris Cawley, his brother Nathan wasn't available. The Cawley brothers are in a feud. Nasty accusations and threats. From both sides. Nathan Cawley is the owner of the piece of land that is up for planning permission and, obviously, he is in favour of the development. His brother Boris is a farmer who owns the fields adjacent to Nathan's plot. From Boris's point of view, access to his barns would be a lot more convenient if he could create a shortcut. He has previously applied for planning permission to knock down a derelict shed. The permission was denied because Nathan said the shed was housing bats. And bats are classified as endangered species. Boris claims that there are no bats and he says his brother is a liar.'

Maloney is getting impatient. He looks at his watch and taps the whiteboard with a wiper. Ollie speeds up.

'Nathan has previously blocked Boris's application and Boris is now returning the favour, as it were. Boris has the backing of most of the local residents and Nathan is now threatening that he will allow travellers to settle on the land if he doesn't get his way.'

Maloney takes over. 'The bottom line is that this seems to have been the main reason for the parish council meeting. It looks a bit far-fetched that there would be a motive for murder here, but we can't rule it out either.'

'There is something else, sir.'

Maloney looks at his watch again. 'Yes, DS Reed?'

'Nathan had a visit from a police officer a few days ago. It might be related to this case.'

'Who was this officer, and why was he visiting Nathan Cawley?'

'I don't know yet, sir.' Ollie shrugs and sits down.

'Okay, find that out.' Maloney rummages in his papers, finds the one he's looking for and pins it up on the side of the whiteboard. 'Gregory Newman is the caretaker of the village hall and we have his statement here. After the meeting, he stayed there to clean and lock up. He says that Iris Spencer was one of the last people who left the hall, at the same time as three other people. He only knew one of them. Mr Cawley; unfortunately, he didn't mention Mr Cawley's first name and I believe there are several Cawleys in that area. We need to talk to this Mr Cawley. Mr Newman didn't know the other two people, but I hope Mr Cawley will be able to tell us. Mr Newman remembers that Iris's car was parked right next to the entrance to the hall. The other three people muttered something to Iris like why did they have to walk in the rain and on the muddy road and she didn't. Mr Newman locked the door behind them to do a quick clean-up. He was going to come back with his wife the next day to do it properly. He is certain that Iris got into her car and that she drove off. He is also certain that she was alone.' He pauses. 'Do we already have a list of calls from and to her mobile phone?'

'We're still waiting for the mobile phone company to come back to us, sir.'

'Speed that up will you?'

'Yes sir.'

He puts his index finger on the picture of Iris's torso. 'The flowers. In my opinion, they indicate a personal motive. Fourteen red roses were scattered on and around her corpse, the fifteenth was planted in her vagina. One of the thorns made a scratch but that was post-mortem. The autopsy report tells us that if she had sexual intercourse it was consensual. No traces of semen. No bruises or cuts, no signs of defence.'

'It looks like a crime of passion, sir.'

'Yes, and that takes us back to Matilda Disley. We need to know where the roses were bought and by whom. Cellophane wrapping was found at the crime scene. See if the purchase was paid by card or, ideally, if there is any CCTV material.'

Once more, Maloney rummages in his papers on the desk. He finds a folder and withdraws a forensic report.

'We've just received the first forensic report on her car. We are still waiting for more on that because they are going through it again with a fine-tooth comb. For the time being, we …'

Penrose clears her throat. She can't wait any longer.

'Sir, I have information about that.' Not giving Maloney the chance to cut her off again, she comes forward and stands beside him in front of the whiteboard.

'Perhaps some of you here know that I live in St Eval,' she starts, voice trembling at first but gaining strength as she goes on. 'My father wanted to go to that meeting at the village hall. So I took him there. We arrived late. There were more people than I expected. My father has difficulty walking and I parked my car close to the entrance to the village hall. In fact, as I found out later, I parked next to Iris Spencer's car. There wasn't much room to park and I had to help my father out. Therefore, I think it's feasible that mine and my fathers fingerprints are on the driver side of her car.'

She pauses, looking around, expecting anger, accusation, mock and pity on their faces. Seeing only serious faces, she continues, 'I didn't pay much attention and as I said, at that time I didn't know whose car it was. Anyway, I do remember that I looked into the car. I saw the flowers. I remember it because I thought that it wouldn't do the flowers any good if they were laying in the car the whole evening. Without water. Therefore it is feasible that Iris bought the flowers herself.'

Maloney nods seriously. 'We can speculate about this for hours, but we need facts.'

Penrose stares at Maloney, relieved and surprised that he hasn't made any comment about her fingerprints. Tregunna was right, it would have looked much more serious if she hadn't told them now.

'My father … wasn't very well and we left early. That must have been around half past eight. We were back home in time to watch the end of his favourite programme on TV. So I don't have any further information about the time Iris Spencer left, I'm afraid. But I do know a lot of the people who were present at that meeting and I have started drawing up a list.'

'Thank you, Jennette. Well, I guess that's it for now. We'd better get started.' Gathering his papers, Maloney looks at his watch and starts issuing his orders. Then he says almost matter-of-factly, 'Let's be back here at ... shall we say at four?'

Penrose stares at his back as he disappears, wondering why she was so nervous when she entered the room less than half an hour ago.

18

I leave Kim Naylor at the quay from where she will get the ferry to Bodinnick. She's meeting the secret author in a pub in a quiet village further upstream on the river. As I watch her joining the short queue, I call Chaz Lynham.

Grieving is a highly individual experience; there's no right or wrong way to grieve. How you grieve depends on many factors, including your personality, your life experience, your faith, and how significant the loss is to you. Consequently, everyone grieves differently. Some people will wear their emotions on their sleeve and clearly show their feelings while others will internalise their grief showing no emotion, and may not even cry.

Experts say that there are five stages in grieving. Chaz Lynham sounds like she's going through them all at the same time.

I ask her for contact details of Aubrey Sinclair, the regional politician, the man who stopped supporting her husband and forced him to draw up his letter of resignation instead; the man who may even be partially responsible for Lynham's suicide because he let him down so drastically.

Mr Sinclair refuses to see me, I'm told by a brusque woman who seems to be acting as his spokesperson.

'Why?' I ask.

A short hesitation. I don't hear voices discussing an answer; the spokeswoman is just taking her time to think carefully about what to say next. 'Mr Sinclair doesn't want to muddy the waters any more than they already are.'

'You mean: than he already has done,' I correct her.

The line goes dead.

I call Chaz again.

'It doesn't surprise me at all. Sinclair is a bastard,' she says bitterly. 'But on second thoughts, it wasn't a good idea anyway. I think it is better if you talk to Monica, Ed's secretary. Monica Gibb. If there's anyone who knows what was going on behind the scenes, it is her.'

I hesitate, thinking about what Kim told me. 'You said earlier that you thought that something must have happened some time ago, because you noticed a change in Ed.'

'Yes.' She sounds hesitant. Cautious.

'Can you remember when that was?'

'It was about a few months ago. I'm not sure. I became aware of it all of a sudden, but it might have been going on for a while.'

'Before Christmas?' The charity night was the 10th December.

'Just around that time, yes.' She sounds surprised, but doesn't ask further. She doesn't want to know. She is shielding herself against further bad news.

'I'm sure you remember the commotion in the press about the charity evening?' I say cautiously.

'Of course I do.' She sounds angry. Hurt maybe.

'Was Ed there?'

'He left early.' A short, curt answer.

'Did he tell you about what happened that evening?'

'As I said, he left early. With a friend. He told me that they went to the friend's house. Played computer games.' She falls silent for a while. Not being able to see the expression on her face, I can't imagine what's going on in her head. 'Of course we heard about what happened in the hotel that night. How could we not? But Ed said that he left early and I believed my husband.'

There isn't any doubt in her mind.

'Are you coping, Chaz?'

'My sister is here with me.'

'Will she stay with you for a while?'

'Unless there's an emergency at her home, she'll stay until we have made arrangements for the funeral. After that … I don't know.' A short silence. 'They have four boys.'

'Okay. Take care, Chaz.'

Penrose calls to fill me in about the latest news on the investigation of Iris Spencer's death. If I had any guilty feelings about advising her to tell the team about her fingerprints on Iris's car without my backup, albeit dubiously, those feelings are wiped away quickly as I listen to her version of what was said at the meeting.

'So you haven't been downgraded to a desk job?' I ask half-jokingly.

'Not at all. Maloney didn't say anything about it. Probably because he's short staffed. He's given me the task of finding out where the red roses came from.'

I nod, not thinking about the fact that she can't see me.

'No doubt you'll crack that, Jennette,' I say optimistically.

'I'm not so sure,' she replies cautiously, but I can hear that she is pleased with the compliment.

'Are you coming to the station, sir? Next briefing is at 4 o'clock.'

'I'll try to be there in time.' I look at my watch. It's just gone twelve.

Monica Gibb doesn't want to meet me in her office, but when I explained to her that Aubrey Sinclair refused to see me and Chaz suggested I should contact her, she's willing to meet me at lunchtime. Truro. Cafe Nero. One o'clock. She sounds as though she'll be gone if I'm one minute too late.

About five foot tall and chubby, she's in her early sixties, with short, permed grey hair; a string of pearls around several folds of neck. A pair of pink-rimmed plastic glasses balances on a small nose. Her eyes are pale blue and watery and she has a crumpled tissue in her hand with which she wipes her nose as if she has a cold.

She smiles hesitantly as she sits down opposite me and carefully places a bulky handbag beside her chair. Having had a pasty with Kim Naylor for breakfast, I decline the offer of a sandwich. She opts for a healthy looking green smoothie and a multigrain roll with chicken salad. I order a medium cappuccino and a glass of water.

'Aubrey Sinclair doesn't want to speak to me,' I say, opening the conservation.

She nods but doesn't respond, waiting cautiously. 'Are you recording this conversation?' she asks, cocking her head to one side, checking her pearl earring with a chubby hand.

'No,' I reply earnestly.

'Sorry, but I have to be very careful.'

'I understand that. But I can assure you that I have no recording equipment on me.'

She's only half-convinced. 'My niece tells me that her son records the conversations she has with her new boyfriend.'

'Naughty.'

'I suppose he wants to know what's going on.' Her massive shoulders rise and fall in a gesture that says it all. 'A divorce is always difficult when there are children involved.'

Retrieving my phone from my pocket I lay it on the table between us. The screen is black.

'Chaz Lynham gave me your number. You worked for her husband?'

'I'm the general secretary for the local party. I didn't work only for Ed, but yes.'

'How was he to work for?'

The door opens and she looks over her shoulder instinctively, as if she's expecting Aubrey Sinclair to emerge.

She smiles sadly. 'Ed was a lovely man. Always very kind and friendly. Never raised his voice. Unlike …' she stops abruptly. 'I miss him.'

'When was the last time you saw him?'

'I suppose it was on his last day. Friday. It all started well. We had a good laugh at first. I can't remember what is was about now, but … yes, it was good. Until Aubrey arrived. Mr Sinclair. When he's there … the atmosphere is always different somehow. That's what Cilla says. Cilla Dixon is our communication's officer. She takes care of the press. She's all right. Not like Aubrey at all. Mind you, it is surprising that she's still with us, because she and Aubrey ….' She waves a hand in a gesture that says more than words. 'She must be good, otherwise he wouldn't keep her on, would he?'

'I guess not.' I've never taken much interest in politics, which is probably down to my parents and uninspiring politicians. Full of lies and empty promises, my mother used to say. I suppose you tend to value the ideas you grew up with.

Monica Gibb has lost her train of thought.

'Ed's last day?' I remind her.

'Oh, yes, I'm so sorry.' She clasps her hands together as if in prayer. 'Where was I? Oh yes, well. Everything was hunky-dory at first. Ed had some letters to write and I was with him for about an hour before I went to type them up on my computer. I made coffee for us all at about eleven. Aubrey had a video meeting with London. He never wants to be disturbed or interrupted when he does that, so I left him to it. Cilla came in just after that. I made her favourite herbal tea as she waited for Aubrey. She was with Ed then for a while; I could hear them laughing. Anyway, then, all of a sudden, Aubrey comes out. Furious. A walking thunderstorm. He sends Cilla away for the rest of the day. That was rather unusual for him, so that explains how serious it was. He storms into Ed's office and I could hear him, well, I could hear his voice but not what he said. Minutes later he comes out, followed by Ed. I'd never seen Ed like that. Face white. Ashen. He went into Aubrey's office but it was to no avail. Aubrey had made up his mind already. Next thing I know Ed comes to my office, asking if I had a box or a few plastic bags for him. I ask what it is for and he says he is going home and he won't be coming back.' She shakes her head, staring at the sandwich, still untouched, in front of her. 'And that was it. I offered to help him, but he didn't want me in there. I suppose he was so shocked by the turn of the events that he wished to be alone.'

'Do you know the reason? Did he tell you, or Aubrey?'

She purses her lips. 'They didn't say anything. All Ed said was that it was a bunch of lies, a setup to get rid of him, but he didn't give any further explanations. And of course Aubrey wouldn't disclose anything to me. After all, I am only the secretary.' She sounds cynical but not bitter. She's used to people's differences and opinions.

'How long have you worked for the local party office?'

'Nearly thirty years. I started working for Mr Gideon. When he left, I had the choice of going with him or staying. I stayed and Helena came, but she was here only three years.'

'Helena Fairfax?'

'That's the one.' She grins with a mixture of pride and regret. 'She wasn't an easy-going woman, but she was always fair and straight to the point. If she'd asked me to go with her, I would've done it. But she didn't.'

'And then there was Aubrey Sinclair?'

'Yes. By then, I had bought my own cottage here. If I hadn't had that, I would have left. Aubrey is … what he is. Cold. Arrogant. Ruthless. I suppose he is perfectly cut out for running for Prime Minister in a few year's time. A bit too big for local politics, I'd say.'

'Did Aubrey go to the charity night in Newquay in December?'

My question doesn't surprise her. 'He did. Believe it or not, he and Ed went together.' She rolls her eyes. 'Not the kind of thing Ed would happily go to, but I suppose he couldn't refuse. Aubrey said that there would be a lot of important local businessmen there. Good for funding for the party, he always says. As I said, it wasn't really Ed's thing. He didn't like the idea that Chaz wasn't allowed to go too. Very close, those two. Lovely girl, Chaz. Pity they never had children. Ed would have loved that, but … well, that's all history now, isn't it?' She wipes her eyes, silent for a while.

'Ehm, did anything happen on that charity night?'

She shifts awkwardly, hesitates, then she scoffs. 'I would think so. It's been all over the papers, hasn't it? Although I had no idea of the extent of what happened, it didn't surprise me at all. I mean, it was known as a men-only night. Any fool would understand what was going on there, wouldn't they?'

'Did Ed enjoy the evening?' I am carefully leading her towards what she knows about the evening without alerting her too much. I have a feeling that she will shut her mouth as soon as she learns anything bad about Edward Lynham, who she clearly doted on.

Suddenly remembering her lunch, she picks up her plate and

starts munching away. I drink my cappuccino, wondering if we will ever get to the subject I wanted to discuss in the first place.

'I was with Chaz when she found Ed,' I say casually.

'I'd gathered that.' Flakes of the crust spray from her mouth. 'Sorry, my mother always said we shouldn't eat and talk at the same time.' She wipes her lips, ready for the next bite.

'My mother says the same,' I confess.

'Good old-fashioned rules,' she comments. 'Everything wasn't better back then, but I do believe that it was better in the sense of family life. I spend a lot of time with my sister's family. I couldn't bear living with a family when everyone eats on their lap with the TV on and phones handy.'

'It's the new generation,' I say gently.

She nods. 'Anyway, where were we?'

'The charity night.'

'Oh yes.' Her face darkens.

'Chaz told me that Ed changed after that night. Not significantly, but … noticeable.'

'Indeed he did! I saw it too.'

'Do you have an idea why that was?'

'I guess it was because of that woman. Sylvia. At first I felt pity for her, but when I got to know how she really was … I'd warned Ed, but he wouldn't listen to me.'

'Sylvia?'

She nods vigorously, taking another bite and I have to wait until she's swallowed everything down. 'She'd been with us for a while. That was before the elections. Admin worker, she was. A temp from an employment agency. She wasn't very good, but she had a way, you know. All smiles and blinking and, of course, wearing short skirts and blouses with just that one button too many open, you know. Even Aubrey thought the world of her.'

'Ed too?' My thoughts go out to Chaz.

'My father used to say that a man can easily be blinded by a pair of beautiful legs or big boobs. I'm not sure how far she got with Aubrey, but that wouldn't have lasted very long anyway. Aubrey is a bachelor, Inspector, always has and always will be. He doesn't want to get tied up with some woman, that's for sure. Anyway, she'd set her mind on Ed. I'd told her that he was married, but she didn't care about that. I'm sure she was of the opinion that Ed would divorce Chaz for her. I warned Ed about her. I saw that she was obsessed with him. She'd come to the office every day after she left us. Waiting for him at the end of the day. Needing help at her home, like changing a light bulb, or putting a screw in something. Mind you, I'm sixty-three and I've never needed a man to fix any such things for me. And if I really need a handyman, I will pay for the job. But no, Sylvia was different. She played the helpless woman, needing two strong hands, and all that. And yes, Ed fell for it too, but he saw sense before it got out of hand. There was one night when we had a big storm and she claimed her house was falling apart. So he went there, good lad that he is … was, but there was nothing, was there? It was all in her mind. She said she wouldn't be able to sleep with all those weird sounds in and around the place. Ed couldn't find anything wrong there, he didn't even hear the sounds she was so scared of. But then she tried to get him into bed. I think that was the eye-opener, eventually. He told her he loved his wife and there was no way he would cheat on Chaz. So she went berserk, Sylvia did. She hit him, kicked him, scratched his face. She even tore her blouse to pieces and threatened she would tell everyone that he'd done that to her.'

'When was that?'

She rolls her eyes again, nodding firmly. 'A few days before the charity evening.'

'Did she know he would go there?'

'Oh yes, did she indeed! She'd joked to me about it, she said she would try to get one of the men to invite her. I suppose she was thinking of Aubrey, but they weren't to take their spouses or partners, were they?'

'Do you know what happened that night?'

'I don't know. I honestly don't.'

I hesitate. I would like to have a chat with Sylvia, but I don't want to draw too much attention in that direction. Monica is quite chatty. Clearly she doesn't know everything and I don't like the idea of making her any the wiser. But, surprisingly, she isn't interested.

'I'd rather not know about what happened, Inspector. I loved Edward and I want to keep remembering him as I knew him.' She grins sheepishly. 'Does that sound daft?'

19

Spencer & Kelly Consultancy is located on the bank of the River Fal just outside the city centre of Truro. It is a white, three-storey office building with black tinted windows. We push through double glass doors that have a scattering of white stars on them, probably to make visitors aware of the glass. The reception is an airy room. Round coffee tables and black-and-white couches covered in a pop-art pattern fabric that was very popular in the 1960s; a matching trio of Andy Warhol prints on the wall.

Penrose marches straight up to the long white reception desk and slaps on it with a flat hand.

The woman behind it looks up, clearly having difficulty taking her eyes off her mobile phone. She's wearing a fluorescent orange cardigan with white edges that looks suspiciously like a tracksuit top. The white vest beneath it only adds to that impression. Oddly enough, she doesn't look out of place. Her dyed black hair is tied in a ponytail that swings from shoulder to shoulder with every movement. A row of five piercings balancing on a henna pencil-thin line seems to have replaced one of her eyebrows; it makes her look like she's constantly amazed. A badge clipped on the edge of her vest tells us her name: Nadia.

She gives a cheery smile but her eyes are unwelcoming, if not hostile.

'Hi.' Her eyes dart from Penrose to me and back. She can't make up her mind who she should speak to.

Penrose raises her eyebrows. Her lips are tight and, from the way she looks at the receptionist, I know she's already formed a judgement of her. Which is clearly negative and dismissive.

'We would like to have a word with the manager,' Penrose says briskly, trying to keep up the image of having everything under control.

A short hesitation. 'Mr Kelly isn't here today. He's on a business trip.'

'His secretary?'

'Mr Kelly's secretary? She's called in sick this morning.' She smiles faintly, as if she's happy that she's won the first round of a fight. 'But Nigel is in. Nigel Sparks, though I'm not sure if he'll see anyone today,' she says hesitantly. 'Ehm … our other manager has been involved in an accident.'

Penrose nods sternly, putting her hand in her pocket to retrieve her ID card. 'Is that Mrs Iris Spencer?'

'Yes, but …' Nadia stops and stares at our cards, duly comparing the photos with our faces.

'We are investigating Mrs Spencer's … accident,' I say gently. If nobody bothered to tell her how Iris Spencer died, whatever reason they might have, I'm certainly not telling her either. 'Therefore we have some questions for her secretary.'

'Oh. I will let him know that you are here.' The unwelcoming attitude is barely changing, however there is now a slightly different look in her eyes: a subdued mixture of excitement and curiosity.

She picks up a mobile phone and speaks. 'Police are here, Nige.'

Listening to the response, she pinches the bridge of her nose with her thumb and index finger and closes her eyes as if she has difficulty concentrating.

'All right.' Her eyes snap open. 'He will see you straightaway.' Nadia points towards another set of glass doors. 'Lifts and stairs are to your right. It'll be on the third floor. Nigel will be waiting for you.'

Penrose takes a deep breath, annoyed by the suggestion that we ought to be grateful for the secretary's time. She opens her mouth for a snort but, thinking twice, she manages a sweet smile instead. She seems to be learning to hold back her impatience better now.

Nigel Sparks is in his early thirties with a mop of curly red hair, his skin, as far as we can see, is covered with freckles. His eyes are ice blue and with his dazzling smile he could easily be in a TV advert for toothpaste.

'Terrible. I still can't believe it,' he says, when we have introduced ourselves. He wipes his eyes with the back of his hand, but there is no real emotion in them. Whatever his motives, he tries hard to let us believe that he cared for his boss and that his grief is genuine.

His office is shrouded in semi-darkness, blinds down, shutting out the sunshine. There is a faint smell of coffee and pastry, but there is nothing on his desk apart from a small white Apple keyboard, an empty 'Out' tray and an 'In' tray that has only a handful of A4 print-outs. Otherwise, his desk is pristine. It certainly doesn't look like he has much to do.

'Sorry,' he mutters, pulling the blinds up and we blink out at the sparkling sandstone spires of Truro cathedral in the background.

Penrose narrows her eyes before giving a little shrug and then takes the lead. 'We have some questions for you, Mr Sparks.'

He nods quickly, pulling at the visitors chairs, re-arranging them, gesturing and wandering around like a nervous housewife who is suddenly confronted with unexpected guests.

'Do sit down, please. First I thought of meeting you in Iris's office but ... under the circumstances ... I think it would be rather inappropriate.'

'This office is fine, Mr Sparks,' I say, slowly sitting down on one of the offered chairs.

'Yes. Of course. Anything.' He pulls at the sleeves of his light blue shirt as though he's trying to cover his hands. 'I hope I can help you. Terrible thing. Poor, poor Iris.' Once more he wipes his dry eyes. 'I hope she didn't suffer.'

He doesn't wait for an answer.

'Can I get you coffee?' His eyes drift towards Penrose, weighing her up, then making the right judgment. 'Or tea?'

'No thank you, Mr Sparks.' Penrose shifts impatiently in her chair, the first straightforward question already on her lips. 'Can you tell us when you heard about her death?'

He sits behind his desk and pulls the 'In' tray towards him, glancing at the top sheet as though trying to find inspiration.

'Midday. We ... I'd been worried. It wasn't like Iris at all not to come to work without letting me know.'

'Who told you?'

'Nadia.' The receptionist.

'Did Iris have any enemies that you were aware of? Anyone who would want her dead?'

'No! Definitely not!'

'Iris and Hugh Kelly are equal partners in this business. How is the business doing?'

'All right, I suppose.'

'No financial troubles?'

'I don't think so, but you'd better to speak to Hugh Kelly about that.'

'We will, Mr Sparks, but, like the proverbial secretary who knows the boss better than the partner at home, I'm sure you know more about her than anyone else.'

He shakes his head vigorously. 'Not Iris. She kept her private life strictly private.'

'She never talked about, for instance, her friends or family?'

'No, never.'

'What about phone calls?'

'Private calls, you mean? No. She used her mobile phone for those things. And I had no access to her laptop. Whatever she decided I needed to know, she forwarded to me.'

I lean closer to him. 'Where is her laptop?'

'She always carries it with her.'

Penrose is about to react but, meeting my eyes, thinks better of it.

'Where were you on Monday evening, Mr Sparks?'

His eyes widen. 'Ehm … I was out with friends.'

'Can you write down their names and contact details, please Mr Sparks?'

'Is that really necessary? I … I don't want my friends to get involved in this.'

'It is either that, or we'll have to charge you because you have no alibi,' Penrose says bluntly.

'Oh.' He's slightly taken aback. 'Okay then.' He grabs a sheet of paper from the printer tray behind him and writes down three names, adding their phone numbers from the contact list in his mobile phone.

'Anything else?' he asks. His attitude has changed. Defensive. Almost aggressive.

'What can you tell us about Monday, Mr Sparks? Was Iris in her office? Did she have any appointments?'

He doesn't need to look in a diary. 'She was in Redruth and Camborne. She met the mayor of Redruth in the morning and, after that, she went for a lunch meeting in Camborne. I can pass the details on to you, if you wish.'

'That would be helpful, Mr Sparks. Was it a normal working day?'

'More or less, yes, however … with Iris … there were never what you could call normal working days. She is … was a very lively and vibrant woman. There were always … unexpected issues.'

'Was that the case on Monday?'

'Not during the day but there was the meeting, of course.' His attention seems to be drawn to the top sheet in the 'In' tray again. It looks like a printed email. Moving it slightly, he seems to be reading it. Frowning. Folding one of the corners, he places the sheet in the 'Out' tray.

'What can you tell us about Monday night's meeting, Mr Sparks?'

He shrugs. 'I wasn't there.'

'You were her secretary. You must know what went on.'

He shrugs, not meeting my eyes. 'I work for the business. Not for the council.'

'We've been told that you do the minutes of some of the council meetings for her, instead of someone else who is supposed to do the work for the councillors?'

'There is, yes. In fact, there was. Megan. But, well, I would never have told you if Iris was still alive, but … Iris and Megan had fallen out about something. I don't know why and it is probably something trivial, but they couldn't see eye to eye. It happened before I came to work for Iris anyway. My predecessor was already doing the minutes for her - if necessary, which wasn't always the case - and I more or less took over.'

'But not for last Monday's meeting.'

'No.' He blushes and shifts uneasily in his chair. 'I … I'd already arranged the meeting with my friends that night. Weeks ago, as it was one of my mate's birthday.' He hesitates, then takes a deep breath as though he's about to jump into deep water and explore the sea bed for unknown species.

'As you may know,' he starts arrogantly, 'the Government has recently launched plans for more affordable homes in the county. This is not always possible or it isn't what people want, sadly. Sometimes, local residents object to new developments and there can be … situations.' He stops for breath. Or perhaps he's giving us the opportunity to ask which 'situations' he's referring to. I don't respond. With an effort, I notice, Penrose bites her tongue.

'At the last regular meeting a few weeks ago, one of the points on the agenda was an application for a redevelopment plan in the parish of St Eval.' He pauses and gestures vaguely. 'St Eval is in the area between Newquay and Padstow.'

'We know where St Eval is, Mr Sparks.'

'Oh.' He shakes his head, slightly taken aback by Penrose's blunt interruption. 'Most of those meetings aren't very popular and the audience is normally limited to only a handful of residents. But it was quite different that time. The village hall was packed, there weren't even enough seats for everyone.'

Penrose nods, casting me a glance as if asking for my permission to go on with her enquiry. But before she can say something, Sparks already continues. 'Clearly, people were rather emotional and there was a long and lively discussion. Not everyone seemed to have the same opinion about the plans and it was concluded that the application would be on the agenda of the next meeting, so that everyone had the opportunity to study the case properly.' He stops, pulls a face and continues sarcastically, 'Generally, there is a limited time for people to object to applications and if the matter had been postponed to the next scheduled meeting, it would have been too late. One of the residents knew about that and demanded an earlier meeting. Which was the reason for the meeting, last Monday night.'

'What would have happened if it had been too late?'

His face twists in a cynical grimace. 'Iris was hoping for that, because then the application would have been approved and the residents would have no more opportunity to object.'

'And what was the result of Monday night's meeting?'

His expression is resigned. 'I understand that the majority was against the development.'

'I'm aware that this might not have to do with this company, Mr Sparks, but can you explain to us what Iris's role was in this matter?'

'Oh, she was very much in favour of the development, as were most of the councillors. It would have meant additional homes for the local community, the village wouldn't be a so-called ghost town anymore, and there would be work for the builders for at least one or two years. Plus a boost to the local economy.'

I lean forward, catching his eyes for the first time. 'Could this have been a motive for her death, Mr Sparks?'

'A motive for her death? I thought it was a car accident? '

'We are treating her death as suspicious.'

He swallows hard, eyes wide. 'Oh, I see. A motive? Ehm … no, I can't see that, but … I suppose you can never tell, can you?'

I see Penrose staring at him. Perhaps she isn't the right person for this; I know how passionately involved her father is in the future of their village. But it is too late for that now.

'I presume there are minutes of the two meetings, Mr Sparks? Do you know where we could find minutes of these meetings?'

He nods uncomfortably. 'Not last Monday's, I'm afraid. I can't even produce a transcript at this moment because Iris …'

'A transcript?' Penrose interrupts.

'Well, a while ago, I had a situation at home and I wasn't able to go to a meeting with Iris. A business meeting. Iris said not to bother. She would make a recording on her phone. I could print out a transcript and type the minutes later. It seemed to work fine and we've done it again like that.'

'Who was doing Monday night's minutes?' I ask, realising at the same time that I already know the answer.

'The recording will be on her phone.' He points at his keyboard, regaining his confidence as he is finding his feet on safer ground.

'We try to be a paper-free company,' he explains with a hint of pride. 'Everything is stored in computer clouds. We can all work from anywhere, you see. Like Hugh is currently in Scotland, but he can access any document he wants.'

'Are you saying that Iris recorded the meeting and she stored the recording in the cloud?'

'Or on her phone.' He stares at us. 'You need internet access to be able to access the cloud. I'm not sure if there is a connection at that village hall. But I can check.'

'How?'

'See if Iris stored the recording from her phone in the cloud.'

'Can you access her phone?'

'Oh no!' He smiles sarcastically. 'Iris was too private a person for that. We can only access documents etcetera in the cloud once she has copied it there.' He taps his keyboard rapidly, then shakes his head. 'No. She must have meant to do it later. From home.' He pauses. 'But I'm sure one of your technicians will be able to retrieve everything from her phone.'

'We'll see,' I say, not telling him that Iris's mobile phone is missing.

Nigel Sparks glances at his wrist watch. 'Is there anything else I can help you with?'

'Can you think of anyone who hated her enough to want her dead?'

'I don't know.' He hesitates. 'She was blunt and straightforward, Inspector, but I don't think there was anyone who disliked her enough to want to do her any harm. Let alone kill her.'

'Maybe not, Mr Sparks, but the fact is that she was killed by some-one.'

'Yes, of course.' He blushes again, embarrassed with himself.

I shake my head, smiling. 'That's it for now, Mr Sparks. Can we have a look at her office?'

He hesitates, shrugs. 'I don't think you'll find much there, Inspector, but by all means, go and have a look.'

He opens a door and we see an office the same as his, only the view is different. The river is sparkling in the sunshine, the sky a blue so pale I can almost feel the ice crystals in the air.

Iris's desk is bare. Not even trays for incoming and outgoing mail, or a keyboard for the modern screen that is pushed to one side. The drawers in her desk hold a few plastic folders with some papers and a variety of barely used stationery, a lipstick and a new pack of black tights.

'Thank you, Mr Sparks. I know you'll want us to find her killer, so, we might be back later if we have any more questions.'

'I have told you everything I know.'

'I'm sure you have.' I find a card in my pocket and place it on his desk. 'This is my card, with my phone number. Please don't hesitate to call me immediately if you think of something that might help us, Mr Sparks.'

He stares at it, pondering whether to tear it into pieces, but then he opens a drawer and places it beside a couple of ballpoint pens. Shuts the drawer with a firm bang.

'I had a schoolmate with red hair like that,' Penrose says later, getting in the car while briefly looking up at the building, sensing, rightly so, that Nigel Sparks is looking at us from his office. 'She used to complain about her eyebrows and lashes.'

I stare at her. 'I don't follow.'

'Nigel Sparks has black lashes.' As if that explains everything.

'And the relevance is?' I ask, getting slightly impatient as she seems to be speaking in a code I don't understand.

'He's used black mascara. Like my schoolfriend.'

'Oh.'

She grins. 'I know. There is no relevance. I was just stating a fact.' Holding her head in a cocky angle, she adds, 'You always want to know the details. The not-so-obvious. The layers under the surface.'

'Are you telling me that he is gay?'

'He definitely is, but that wasn't why I said that about his eyelashes.' She pauses. 'I'm not discriminating but he might be one of those men who sometimes dresses like a woman.'

I nod, feeling a bit silly and ignorant. Although people say that I can read body language, I hadn't detected this about Nigel Sparks.

'It has nothing to do with our investigation,' she says hastily. 'All I'm saying is that, if Nigel killed his boss, he might have been dressed like a woman.'

'Hm.' I look up at the building. Nigel Sparks is no longer standing at the window. 'Did you notice anything else?'

'Like what?' She fumbles with the car keys.

'He didn't seem surprised that Iris's death wasn't an accident.'

20

The road to Bodmin is a nightmare. An accident on the A30 has brought traffic to a standstill for almost an hour. Penrose's face looks as if it is going to explode any minute. She keeps stretching her neck to see what's happening in front of us, but a parcel van blocks most of her view. She has her hand on the door handle, perhaps contemplating getting out to have a look, but she just manages to keep herself under control. Or it might be the cold wind and a fine drizzle that has turned to rain that stops her losing it.

We pass a sign indicating Bodmin Jail as a tourist attraction. A partially restored prison that is now open daily to the public to wander through the cold dark cells or visit the fully restored Execution shed, a Victorian hanging pit, the site where the last man was executed in Cornwall at the beginning of the 20th century. The harshness of those times is in stark contrast to what prisoners have to endure nowadays. In those days they didn't only have to worry about their imprisonment and desolation, but also about endless days of cold, hunger and hard labour. Nowadays prison cells are warm and reasonably comfortable; even the worst criminals still have their human rights.

'Have you ever been in Bodmin Jail?'

'Yes,' Penrose replies hesitantly. 'I went just after we caught the murderer of … Jane Croft.'

Casting me a sideways glance, I realise she was going to say something else: the name of the killer who has had so much impact on my personal life. And, in a way, still has. One of the killer's victims, Becca, is still in hospital, deep in a coma, breathing but otherwise vegetating in a bed, oblivious to the fact that she's getting older but not living the life she should have.

'Prisoners must have had a hard time in there back then.'

She shakes her head, looking in her mirror before turning to the right. 'I have little sympathy for people who take another person's life.'

I nod, but keep quiet. Sometimes she can have an outspoken opinion about someone or something, forgetting that the world is not just black and white.

Lester Boyd lives on the edge of Bodmin in a two-story detached house. His next-door neighbours have recently installed new windows and a conservatory; Boyd's home looks a bit dated, but it has been cared for. On the drive is a tatty green Citroen C2 and a scooter that seems to be in a constant state of repair. Oil stains on the slate paving stones.

We park the car behind the scooter and walk to the front door. The sound of electrical sawing comes from somewhere at the back of the building. Penrose presses the doorbell, and we hear it ring through the house, followed by the sound of feet clattering down stairs. The door is pulled open by a man with a halo of fluffy grey hair that waves around his head like seaweed in shallow water. Lester Boyd, Iris Spencer's ex-husband, is in his mid-forties. His hazel eyes are alert and lively, but the rest of his body looks twice as old as he is. He is painfully thin and his bony shoulders are slumped.

'Lester Boyd?' Penrose asks bluntly, holding up her ID card.

He nods without looking at it. He is dressed in corduroy jeans that look two sizes too big for him, held up by a leather belt, a green checked shirt with the top button undone and a black quilted body warmer with the logo of a car repair company on the breast pocket. A pair of bright blue Crocs explains the noisy descent of the open staircase.

'My wife isn't here,' he says uncomfortably. 'She's a school administrator. I expect she'll be home within an hour.'

'We would like to have a word with you, Mr Boyd.'

'Oh.' He wipes grubby hands over his hips. 'I suppose you're here about Iris?'

'We are.'

'I won't shake your hand,' he says, holding his up by way of explanation and apology. 'I'm working in my greenhouse.' Hesitating, he casts a look over his shoulder. 'But I'm just about to have a tea break.' Another hesitation. 'You'd better come through.'

He takes off his blue Crocs and we follow him to the kitchen. Beech-wood doors, white walls, green floor and worktop. Everything is shiny and clean. It feels like we've entered a kitchen showroom and I half expect the tap to be just for display and not actually work.

He stops in the middle, confusion on his face. 'Ehm … can I see your identification again?'

'Of course.'

I take my ID out of my pocket and show it to him. He takes it between his thumb and middle finger and, holding it closer to his eyes, studies it carefully. With the other hand, he takes Penrose's card and repeats the action, eventually placing both cards beside one another on the green top of a breakfast bar.

'Tea? Coffee?'

We nod and he motions us to sit down at the breakfast bar. There are six bar stools on stainless steel poles with five legs each and a ring to support our feet. The seats are covered in shiny white plastic in the shape of a shell. They are surprisingly comfortable.

There are drawers under the worktops and he opens one, retrieving an electric kettle, and a cafetiere from the drawer below. He fills the kettle and plugs it in, opens cupboards above the worktop, finding something in each of them. A tin of tea bags in one. A glass jar with ground coffee in another, a bowl with sugar cubes in a third, and mugs for coffee and tea come from a different cupboard again. As he opens the doors, I can see neat rows of items placed in an order that seems only logical to him.

He grins faintly as he spoons coffee in the cafetiere, then rinses the spoon under a steaming hot tap. Perhaps he is doing it for our benefit, but somehow I think he isn't. When my mother makes tea, she uses the same spoon to stir in the milk and then to add the sugar, leaving lumps of wet sugar in the sugar bowl. The only thing she makes sure of is that she doesn't use the spoon for their tea after it has touched my coffee. I've never really noticed how other people do it, but I just assumed it is the same in every household.

Lester follows my stare at the contents of his cupboards. 'Our son has a mild form of Asperger's Syndrome,' he explains matter-of-factly. 'He gets frustrated when there is too much clutter around. He likes everything neat and tidy and in the right order.' He shrugs his shoulders. 'We've adapted to help him. It's not worth upsetting him.'

I see Penrose frown and look around carefully and I know it's not just my imagination that this household is a bit odd.

'When did you last see Iris, Mr Boyd?'

Slowly, Lester Boyd washes his hands with liquid soap from a dispenser on the wall beside the worktop, dries them with a paper towel from a roll next to it, but his nails are still dirty with soil from his greenhouse.

'I can't remember exactly, Inspector,' he replies finally. 'It must have been two, maybe three months ago. We're not in regular contact, I must say, sadly.'

He places our mugs on coasters and sits down, leaning his elbows on the worktop.

'Iris and I married when we were 21,' he continues as though he's been silently rehearsing the story while he made our drinks. 'We were both students and … and we became lovers. It was the first time for both of us.' He pauses briefly, shaking his head, his hair waving from one side to the other in slow motion. 'I guess it all got a bit out of hand. Her parents were much older than mine and she'd grown up in what seemed to be a Victorian environment. As soon as they found out that we were sleeping together, they insisted that we got married.'

He looks up at the ceiling where one of the bright tube lights has started flickering. It makes me wonder how the son will react to that.

'The marriage should never have happened. We drifted apart. Iris was much more ambitious than me. She tried to push me into a career but all I ever wanted was to be a teacher and start a family. She had no intention whatsoever of having a family.' He smiles cynically. 'At least not until she'd made enough money to pay for a nanny.'

'The divorce was by mutual agreement?'

'Oh yes, definitely. As I said, her parents more or less forced us into the marriage but it was never going to work. She …' he stops abruptly, frowning. 'Ehm, I guess it suited us both. Certainly for her, because her parents also wanted her to have a family and our marriage was good for Iris in the sense that she could escape from their constant interfering.'

'Did you become a teacher?' I ask, ignoring Penrose showing no interest in his history. She wants to move on quickly with our investigation.

Dark clouds seem to float across Lester Boyd's face. 'I always wanted to be a teacher. Iris couldn't understand it, but it was my passion. I knew I could teach the children so much. And I did.'

'You took early retirement?'

His face darkens even more. 'It wasn't by choice. Although I know now that it was for the best. I ... something happened ... I was involved in something which got out of hand.' He pauses, staring at his fingertips and frowning at the dirt under his nails. 'I've always been aware that I shouldn't get too involved with the students. You hear all kinds of stories about teachers and students and I've always been careful that it wouldn't happen to me. I've always tried to be honest and fair to everyone. Some of my colleagues were bullied by students. I saw it happening around me. There were a lot of tears shed in the staff room, Inspector, I hate to say. Tears of frustration mostly. I'd never really let the students get to me until that night. Two years ago.'

Penrose stirs beside me. She's been surprisingly quiet and patient, but clearly she thinks it is now time to move on. 'Mr Boyd, can I ask ...' she starts, but he doesn't seem to hear her. Oblivious to her agitated body language, Lester Boyd seems quite keen to explain himself.

'It was at the end of the school year when the students in their last year who are leaving school for good are always up to something ... naughty. That year, a group of fourteen girls locked themselves in the basement with enough food and drinks to stay for a fortnight, but it was of course only meant for the one night. The boys in that group found out about it and one of them got his hands on the key and made a copy. The girls had DVDs of horror and ghost movies, that sort of stuff, and when the boys found out that too, they decided to give the girls a good scare. They dressed in white sheets and entered the basement. There was total chaos, as you can imagine, but it was all one big joke. The girls had also brought candles and unfortunately, one of the sleeping bags caught fire. They managed to put it out, but the smoke alarm went off. Anyway, I was on call that night. I knew about the girls' plans and I had agreed to it. Obviously, I didn't know about the boys' plans, but it was all fairly innocent and harmless. Nothing happened apart from some burn marks on the sleeping bag. It was all laughs and giggles when the caretaker arrived in the morning. Everything was alright until they found the sleeping bag which was left behind because the girl didn't want her parents to find out. Then suddenly, everyone pointed their fingers at me. It could have been a lot worse, they said. The whole building could have gone up in flames, and thirty students could have been trapped in the building. And so on. I got blamed for everything that could have happened. Stupidly, I confessed that I'd known what the girls had planned and so it was decided that I was the one who'd acted irresponsibly, etcetera. I was politely asked to accept early retirement on the grounds that I was suffering from emotional and mental stress. Which wasn't unusual, as a lot of my colleagues had left for similar reasons. But in most of those cases it was true and in mine it wasn't.'

'Did you find another job?' I ask, ignoring Penrose's frown in my direction.

'I had one, but that didn't work for me. I was a driver for a bakery company. I hated it. My wife has a good job and our income was … is sufficient enough to survive.'

'Apart from your son, do you have any more children?'

'We have Caleb and our two daughters. Emily is fourteen and Lydia is twelve.'

'And Caleb?'

'He's eighteen.'

'How was your relationship with Iris after your divorce?'

He shrugs. 'You couldn't call it a relationship. We had contact, but it wasn't very often. We'd almost become strangers. There wasn't much we had in common. All Iris was ever interested in was work and making money. It was like she never had enough, you know. She never understood how I could live on a basic teacher's salary. She used to mock me because I always knew what I would get at the end of the month. She couldn't understand it.'

'How did she get on with your second wife?'

'I guess it was alright. My wife is quite laid-back. She accepted Iris for what she was, but again, we didn't see each other that often.'

'Did Iris have any enemies, that you knew about?'

'Iris? Enemies? I don't think so. She was a tough lady, but … enemies? No.'

'I suppose,' Penrose says slowly, 'there wasn't any jealousy between Iris and your wife?'

His eyes narrow and for the first time he seems uncomfortable. 'Of course there wasn't. She knew my marriage to Iris was a mistake from the beginning.'

'It was a mistake, wasn't it, Mr Boyd?' Penrose asks bluntly. 'Wasn't the real reason for your divorce the fact that Iris wasn't sexually interested?'

'How … what do you mean?'

'Was it because Iris preferred women?'

He flushes red, shrugging. 'I don't want to talk about that, if you don't mind. That was Iris's life, not mine.'

Penrose presses on. 'When did you find out that she was gay?'

He hesitates. 'She told me about eighteen months after we got married.'

'And how did you feel about that? Were you offended? Embarrassed? Humiliated?'

'No. Nothing like that. Yes, I must admit that I was disappointed at first when she refused me, but I understood when she explained. At that point, it was already clear that our marriage had come to an end. But it was … complicated. For a while, we still lived in the same house, but we led our lives separately, until eventually, we divorced.'

'Where were you last Monday, Mr Boyd?'

He smirks. 'I suppose I was at home. I am nearly always at home these days.'

'Monday evening between ten and twelve o'clock?'

'Last Monday? Yes, I was at home. With our children. Caleb was in his room all evening, like he usually is, playing games on his computer. I was in my greenhouse when the girls came home from a friend's house further down the road. That must have been … ehm, quarter to nine I think it was. Caleb came down and we had a cup of tea together, then the girls went to bed and Caleb went to his room again. My wife was out for her Zumba lessons and she came home at about ten. Quarter past ten, maybe. We had a glass of wine and she had a bath and went to bed. I don't know about Zumba, but she always seems exhausted. Anyway, I noticed I hadn't switched off the lights in my greenhouse and, when I got back inside, I didn't feel like going to bed yet so I watched something on the telly.'

'Alone?'

'Yes.'

'And your wife?'

'As I said, she was in bed.'

'What did you watch, Mr Boyd?' Penrose asks meaningfully.

'It wasn't exactly TV as such. It was a film I had recorded a while ago.'

Penrose is tapping frantically on her mobile phone; making notes on it rather than writing the details in her notebook.

'So you didn't go out at all? Or your son?' she asks with a frown of concentration.

'No.'

As if on cue, a door bangs shut and Lester Boyd looks up with a hint of surprise. His mouth opens and his lips move, but his words dissolve when a tall young man appears in the doorway, taking everything in with dark eyes in a pale face. He's wearing low-slung jeans and a dark green hoodie sweater, with the hood up and his hands in the pockets.

'This is Caleb,' Lester Boyd says, trying to sound casual. 'Caleb, these are Mr Tregunna and Ms Penrose. They are police officers.'

'My scooter was moved.'

I know that Caleb Boyd is eighteen, but he looks like a thirteen-year-old teenager and has the manners of a ten year old. He ignores us completely, staring at his father, not blinking.

'Caleb, why don't you say hello to our visitors and ...' Lester starts, with an embarrassed shrug to us.

His son just stares, lost in his own world. Taking one hand out of his pocket, he pulls at his earlobe as if he has trouble hearing us. But his father's voice seems just like background noise to him. He's concentrating on his own internal dialogue, one that doesn't involve any of us, or the current subject.

'You moved my scooter! Again!' Caleb's arms are now hanging motionless by his sides. It seems odd that his anger is not visible in his body language. 'I told you this morning ...'

Lester blinks, his eyes restless. 'That's right, son,' he says slowly, trying to keep his voice calm and reassuring. 'I had to move it to the side because I had to carry something to the garden.'

'I don't want you to move it!'

'I know, Caleb, and I'm sorry.'

The biscuit tin is still on the worktop. Caleb focuses on it. Arm across his chest, he pulls at his left earlobe with his right hand. Beads of perspiration gather on his forehead. Uncertain, he wipes the side of his hand over his face.

'I had to move it and wash it.'

'Caleb, I said I'm sorry!'

Caleb licks his lips, his eyes restlessly wandering through the kitchen. Lester grabs his tea mug. He has placed an empty saucer in the middle. For our spoons. Lester stirs his tea. Absent-mindedly, he puts his spoon down on the worktop.

'I don't want you to move my scooter, Dad. I don't like it when you touch it. I don't want it under the tree because of the birds.'

'Then you have to put a cover over it.'

'I don't want bird droppings on the cover.'

The issue seems to evolve into an endless cycle of accusation and denial.

'Would you like a cup of tea, Caleb,' I say softly.

Lester coughs, quickly putting down his mug. Relieved, he turns and presses the button on the kettle. Then, gazing at his son, he tries again. 'Caleb, these are police officers. Detective Inspector Tregunna and Detective Constable Penrose. They're not here because you've done something wrong.'

The young man nods but he avoids shaking our hands by thrusting his own into his jeans pockets. His eyes are fixed on the biscuit tin as if debating whether to open it and grab a handful of biscuits or simply take the whole tin.

'Po-police?' His breathing quickens and he seems to wake up from a doze. Nervously, he reaches for his ear. 'Why are they here? Is it because my scooter …'

'No, no son, nothing to do with you, honestly. They're here to have a quick word with me.'

Caleb Boyd turns his head in my direction but he looks straight through me. There's no light, no story, no smile in his eyes. No connection: Asperger's is a form of autism.

'Nothing to do with you, son.' Lester repeats, shaking his head to no one in particular. Behind him, the kettle comes to the boil. He opens drawers and cupboards. The ritual of finding the right items to make a cup of tea starts all over again. But Caleb can only stare at the drops of milky tea, clearly visible on the black marble top.

Lester pours water in a mug that says '*Best son in the world*'. Adds milk. Stirs and puts the spoon beside the saucer.

'It's routine Caleb,' I say gently, getting up. 'And we're done. Thanks for your time, Mr Boyd.'

I feel Penrose's eyes on me, but I ignore her. Clearly, she wants Caleb Boyd to confirm his father's alibi, but his body language tells me he is uncertain, if not uncooperative. Caleb focuses on the tiny puddle forming underneath the spoon. His shoulders move involuntarily.

'And thanks for the tea.'

Lester Boyd makes nervous movements to get up but I shake my head. 'We'll let ourselves out, Mr Boyd. Thank you.' I retrieve one of my business cards from my pocket and place it on the breakfast bar, where he put our ID cards earlier. He doesn't respond but, seeing Caleb's stare, he snatches up my card before the boy can even start thinking about picking it up. 'Give me a call if you remember something that can help our investigation, Mr Boyd.'

'I will, yes, of course I will, Inspector,' Lester says, casually taking the teaspoon and wiping the worktop clean with a paper towel.

Without a word, Caleb turns and tramps off, his footsteps loud on the staircase.

21

'Coffee?' Grinning sheepishly, my neighbour stands in front of my door, in his eyes the warning that he won't accept an excuse. Placing one foot over the threshold, he gazes at me expectantly, repeating, 'Coffee?'

He never waits for my reaction. He has the infuriating habit of inviting himself into my home. He doesn't seem to care if it is convenient for me or not. He doesn't even ask. He claims that he prefers the strong black coffee from my coffee machine, but then he adds so much milk to it that I doubt if he can actually taste the difference. Usually, he brings a pack of cheap biscuits that contain the most preservatives and E-numbers imaginable; today he steps in with a Celebrations tin tucked under his arm.

'Coffee, Mr Curtis, yes, why not?' My sarcasm is lost on him.

'Perfect.'

'But I only have half an hour,' I say, dragging up a list of plausible excuses in my mind.

'And then what?' He looks me up and down. I have just had a shower and I'm dressed in jeans, a T-shirt and a long-sleeved shirt, unbuttoned. I have started to wear a wide elastic girdle over the stoma bag lately, but it makes the bulge only a little less noticeable.

Curtis sniffs in the air like a police dog picking up the trail of a missing person.

'Meeting someone?'

'Ehm ... yes.' The easiest lie in the world.

'Someone I know?'

'No.'

He shrugs. Not so long ago, he tried hard to put my budding relationship with Lauren Gardiner, a young divorced woman with two boys, back on track, but he gave up when I made a mess of it. He's even given up on suggesting other women; I must be a complete failure to him.

'Do you know which was the shortest war Britain ever fought?' he blurts out.

I know him well enough that there is no point in wondering where this comes from. 'No.'

'It was between Britain and Zanzibar.'

'Oh.'

'Do you know how long it took?'

'No. Who won?'

'That is the most ridiculous response I've ever heard.' He sounds offended.

'I'm trying to work out the answer to your question.'

'Britain won.' He looks like a slowly deflating balloon. 'Zanzibar surrendered after 38 minutes.'

'Good to know if it ever comes up in a pub quiz,' I say, suppressing a smile.

'You never go to pub quizzes.'

'I might do in the future.'

He has to digest the information. He glares at me suspiciously, uncertain whether I'm serious. 'One of my colleagues has a niece called Mary.'

'From Zanzibar?'

'Very funny.' He grimaces. 'Is it so difficult for you to have a proper conversation?'

'I have difficulty following your train of thought, Mr Curtis. What is the relevance of the shortest war, Zanzibar and your colleague's niece?'

'Facts.'

'You've lost me now.'

'Fact one is what I told you about the shortest war. Fact two is also that two centuries ago, a quarter of the girls were called Mary.'

'And?'

'Facts can be very interesting.'

'True. But ... Mary?'

'Yes, well, I'm coming to that. Mary is my colleague's niece. She's recently divorced.'

'I see.' I sigh inwardly. He's convinced that I need someone to make my life complete. That I need a woman in my life. And he is also convinced that I need his help to find someone. Fortunately, his conviction that Lauren and I were meant for each other has dissipated since we're not in contact anymore.

'I really have no time for this, Mr Curtis.'

'Why not?'

'I told you, I'm going out in half an hour.'

He chuckles, entering my kitchen, sensing my objections and having answers before I can speak. 'You'd better get properly dressed then. You know what? You put your socks on and make yourself look handsome. Meanwhile I'll make the coffee.' Without waiting for my response, he adds, 'So, you've got a date?'

'It's work.'

He lifts his arm and studies his watch meaningfully. 'I thought you worked part time.'

'I do.'

'It is five o'clock. Are you getting paid for overtime?'

'My hours are flexible.'

He stares at my bare feet as if he's going to remind me that my toenails need a manicure. 'You'll need to wear a proper pair of trousers.'

'You sound like my mother,' I say, gritting my teeth.

'I think we have something in common. She and I would make a perfect couple.'

'She's married to my father.'

'You're changing the subject.' He grins almost triumphantly; he's always keen on having the last word. 'Where are you meeting?'

Digging myself deeper in lies. 'In Newquay.'

He's quick to make connections, albeit the wrong ones. 'A drink first and then dinner? And after that?'

'It is work,' I repeat, to deaf ears.

'Yeah and I am your grandfather.'

'I thought you fancied my mother, not my grandmother.'

He shrugs. 'Again, you are avoiding the question, Inspector.'

'And you are not listening to me, Mr Curtis. I'm telling you I'm meeting someone about work.'

'In Newquay?'

I sigh. He's like a stubborn terrier, not letting go of a bone.

He cocks his head to one side. 'You aren't on one of your private crusades again?'

'I can't talk about work, Mr Curtis.'

'I can remember …'

The coffee machine finishes with the usual spluttering noise, steaming in protest. Mr Curtis shakes his head and pours two coffees. The one for himself is the yellow mug with purple pansies which he bought and now lives in my cupboard as though to make sure there will be a next occasion. Reluctantly, I follow him to my living area, where he makes himself comfortable on the sofa. Pushing newspapers and magazines to one side, he grabs the remote control to turn on my TV. Having the TV on in the background, albeit with the sound muted, is one of his other annoying habits. At first, I turned it off immediately, but he declared he is used to having it on in the background as it makes him feel he isn't alone.

'I can remember that I once saved you from a precarious situation,' he recalls, referring to the occasion that I'd been kidnapped.

'Yes, but …'

'Perhaps you'd better take someone with you.'

'You watch too many crime dramas on TV.'

'I do, but that's your fault. As your neighbour, I need to keep up to date with your work.' He pauses. 'Perhaps it isn't such a bad idea.'

'What isn't?'

'Me being your backup.'

I suppress a smile. 'I don't think that would be a good idea, Mr Curtis,

'How old is the lady?'

I focus on the first person that comes to my mind. 'Late twenties.'

'Single?'

'I believe so.'

'Pretty?'

'I don't know.'

He stares at me as if he knows very well that I'm making things up. Then he opens the Celebrations tin and takes his time to chose two chocolates before he pushes it in my direction. 'Have one. They're nice.'

'Thanks.'

'I suppose you're investigating the death of Iris Spencer?'

I stare at him. A thought pops up. 'Did you know her?'

'Of course I knew her. She used to come to our office quite regularly.'

I recall again his work for Newquay Town Council where

he deals with benefit claims some of which are not legitimate. That's what he once told me in a despondent tone. Although he seemed to despise his work, he isn't the type to leave and try something else. In his work environment, I suspect he is a man who always wins an argument. Or, as with me, people just give up, worn down by stubbornness.

'How was Iris?' I ask carefully. He can be a valuable source of information, but he can also be an unreliable gossip.

'Can I call a bitch a bitch? Excuse my language?'

'So she wasn't popular?'

'Let's put it this way, Tregunna. In my opinion, it was never her intention to be popular. When she was nice to you, you always had to wonder what she was up to.'

'Did she have enemies?'

'In the sense of people wanting her dead? No, I don't think so. She was sneaky, always out for something that was for her own benefit. But she always kept her word. If she said she would do something, she did it, unlike most other people in politics.'

'Have you ever heard anything that might have caused this to happen to her?'

'I'd rather not speak ill of the dead, but ...' He pauses and stares at his watch. 'I'm sorry, I'm not holding you up, am I? You don't want your lady to be kept waiting for you.'

'It's not ...'

My phone rings. He nods graciously that I am allowed to answer it.

'Mr Tregunna?'

'Speaking.'

'Sorry to bother you so late, Mr Tregunna, but you have an appointment with Dr Bailey next Wednesday.'

I swallow. Dr Bailey is a nice enough chap, but he is also the oncologist who is keeping a close eye on me after his colleague removed the cancerous tumour from my bowels and placed the stoma in my belly. 'Yes?'

'Dr Bailey will be unavailable next week and we are rescheduling his appointments.'

I suppress a sigh. Like the proverbial ostrich, I'd do anything to postpone meetings with Dr Bailey.

'He won't be back until next month, Mr Tregunna, but we've …'

'No problem.'

'You haven't been to see him for a while,' she continues persistently. 'He thinks it's best if you see him before that, Mr Tregunna. I can book you a slot tomorrow, if that suits you?'

'Ehm …' I have no time to digest this. I can't find an excuse. 'I don't …'

I stare at Mr Curtis. He can't have heard the conversation, but he looks at me as though he's a schoolteacher sensing I am lying about my homework.

'Is that OK, Mr Tregunna?'

Holding the Celebrations tin under his arm, Curtis is making gestures to me. He looks like a marionette whose strings have been mixed up. He mimics something I don't understand. I nod anyway.

'Half past two?'

'Yes,' I say lamely, 'That's OK.'

Putting down my phone, I find that Curtis has gone back to his own flat.

22

PC Champion is leaning over Tregunna's desk answering his phone when Jennette Penrose barges into the room with a mug of tea in one hand, tapping on her mobile phone with the thumb of the other hand and a packet of chocolate biscuits tucked under her arm.

'Yes sir. No sir. Yes sir, it is. This is Detective Inspector Tregunna's phone, but he isn't at his desk at the moment. Can I take a message?'

Penrose stops at her own desk, putting everything down and cursing inwardly as the mug instantly forms a ring on a sheet of paper someone has put on her desk.

'Oh, I see.' Champion's eyes drift across the room, meeting Penrose's expectant stare.

'Oh, well, I can put you through to DC Penrose. She's the Inspector's right hand … so to speak. Wait a sec, please, Mr Sparks.'

Holding the receiver to her belly, Champion frowns at Penrose. 'This is Iris Spencer's secretary. He says that Tregunna has been to see him and left his card and …'

'I know,' Penrose interrupts crisply. 'I was with him. What does he want?'

'He says he needs to speak to Tregunna.'

'Thank you, Danielle, I'll speak to him.' She reaches out for the phone. 'Mr Sparks, this is DC Penrose, we have …'

'I need to speak to Inspector Tregunna.' He sounds agitated. Breathless, as though he's just come back from a long run.

'He's not here today,' Penrose says tight-lipped. 'But you can

…'

'He left his card with me and said to call him immediately if I remembered something.'

'I know, I was with him when he spoke to you, Mr Sparks.'

'Oh.'

A long pause. She tightens her lips. What a prick. Clearly, he doesn't remember her or he is of the opinion that she can't be trusted with his, undoubtedly, very important message.

She smiles angrily, making an effort to sound sweet. 'If it is not important, Mr Sparks, I can ask him to call you back as soon as he comes in. But I doubt if he'll be in today.'

'Of course it is important!' he mutters. 'I wouldn't be calling if it wasn't.'

'In that case you'll have to deal with me, Mr Sparks,' she says smugly. 'Have you remembered something?'

'I have indeed. Ehm … you'd better come up here,' he continues, quickly making up his mind. 'There is something I need to show you.'

She hesitates, but it would be unprofessional and petty to tell him to come to the station. And besides, there is something in his voice that makes her alert.

'Okay, Mr Sparks, are you at your office?'

'I am, yes. That's where I found it.'

'Found what?' She sighs, looking at PC Champion who's tearing open the biscuits.

'Ehm … I'd rather show it to you.'

She'll be wasting her time with Sparks if he is only trying to be self-important but just in case he has something of significance to show her, she doesn't want him delivering it to the desk officer to pass it onto Maloney. She can do with some Brownie points. If the rumours are true that DCI Guthrie is looking for someone to replace Tregunna, then she's going to make sure that her skills and abilities aren't ignored.

'I will come myself, Mr Sparks,' she says, sounding as if he should be grateful.

'I will wait for you then. I was going out but I can't leave this letter here unattended, can I? It is … it is very important. It is a bomb … ehm … Ms Penvose.'

'Penrose. DC Penrose,' she corrects him automatically. Then his last words sink in. 'What did you just say, Mr Sparks? About a letter? About a bomb? I hope you're not talking about a letter bomb?'

But the line is already dead.

'What was that all about?' PC Champion asks curiously. 'A letter bomb?'

'I don't know.' Penrose lowers herself on to her seat.

'Aren't you going to do something?'

'Like what?'

'If he really received a letter that might explode …'

'No, I don't think he meant it that literally.'

'But you're not sure.'

'No, not really.'

Champion nods and grabs her jacket from the backrest of her chair. 'Let's go and find out.'

'But Maloney …'

'He isn't here. Neither is Tregunna.' Champion grins sheepishly and rolls her eyes. 'We need to follow this up, but we don't want to get ourselves in a situation where they can take the Mickey out of us.'

'No, but …'

'We can't take the risk, Jen, can we?'

'But his office is in Truro.' She stares at Champion, who is raising her eyebrows. 'Okay then, let's go.'

'We'll call Maloney when we're on our way,' Champion says, but by silent, mutual agreement, neither of them makes the call as they drive to Iris Spencer's office, where Nigel Sparks is waiting for them.

'First I wasn't sure about the letter, but then … I think it may be very important.'

'Where is the letter, Mr Sparks?' Penrose asks bluntly, wondering if they should have alerted a bomb squad before entering the building.

'It's on my desk.'

He gestures and they follow him into his office. A single sheet of paper is on his otherwise bare desk.

'Where is the envelope?' Champion asks, pulling latex gloves on.

'There wasn't one.' Sparks looks guilty. 'That's why I hadn't given it much attention, I suppose. It has been hectic here, as you can imagine. Clients calling, wondering what's going to happen now that Iris is gone and … well, you know.'

His voice dissolves as Penrose pushes past him and looks at the letter, not touching it.

'When did this arrive?'

'I don't know, but … to be honest, I found it between other papers in the drawer.'

'In your drawer?'

'In Iris's desk.' He clears his throat. 'It was between other letters that arrived on the day she was … she died. I checked. We have a system. All incoming and outgoing mail is registered in a log. In the log, it says that Iris received a letter that was addressed to her personally. We don't open personal letters.'

'And this letter was received on the day she died?'

'No. Well, we can't be certain because we can't check if that was the letter that was in the envelope that was addressed to her. But assuming … the last personal letter was registered three weeks ago.'

Penrose frowns, but gives no comment. Instead, she reads the words in the letter out loud. Written in letters that are cut out from a newspaper and stuck onto a sheet of A4 paper, it says: '*I know what you did. Wait for instructions.*'

23

Once more I am one of the few people who has come on his own. I swallow hard as it reminds me of Lauren who came with me to the hospital on several occasions. To be my support, my second pair of ears, my objective rational ally. I know very well that I am too nervous to take in exactly what is being said about the tests, the scans and the results. People tend to have a very selective memory when it comes to bad news: you hear what you want to hear and you dismiss the bad bits. Not intentionally, but probably due to a sense of self-protection. Lauren used to remind me of the exact words, the implications they might or might not have on my future.

The waiting room is crowded. People are standing near the door, leaning against walls, or sitting in hospital wheelchairs at the entrance. I hear people muttering under their breath about how they needn't have worried so much about arriving on time for their appointment. The general thought is that Dr Bailey, the oncologist nearly half of the people here have an appointment with, has been held up in traffic; hopefully not due to an accident. But then someone whispers something behind her hand and the word spreads like a fire in a dry haystack: one of Dr Bailey's hospital patients deteriorated and died overnight. Apparently Dr Bailey was with the patient until relatives arrived and then stayed to comfort the family. If it is true, and I have no reason to think why it shouldn't be, I think even more highly of him. People might be of the opinion that it isn't a good thing for a doctor to be emotionally involved with their patients. But it shows that even doctors are ordinary human beings and not like in the old days, when they seemed cold and aloof and were put on pedestals and worshipped like gods.

The woman opposite me is staring blankly ahead, her eyes locked on a point on the wall behind me. Next to her, at the end of a row, is another woman who can only be her sister. They have the same broad face, the same large hazel eyes, and the same nose which is proportionately a bit too small. They appear to be in their early forties, but I can't work out which one of them is the elder sibling. For some reason, I don't think they are twins. However, they seem to have the same taste in clothing: blue jeans, black shoes, matted woollen red jackets over checked blouses. The woman who is staring over my head has brown shoulder-length hair held back from her face by tiny plastic clips, while the other woman has a ponytail and a fringe that is too long. She is flicking through the pages of a glossy magazine about horses, picked up from a pile beside her on the floor where someone has left it to use the small table as a seat. She looks nervous, checking her watch every other minute, licking her dry pale lips. I guess she is one of Dr Bailey's patients, awaiting some results and the prognosis for the future that she would rather not hear, yet knowing that it is inevitable, unavoidable, that she will have to listen to the dreaded diagnosis. The staring sister, I think rather accusingly, should be more supportive and understanding, speak to her with words of encouragement and hope. Or perhaps everything has been said already and they have found themselves trapped in a vacuum of despair.

Then the staring sister stops staring over my head and looks at me, her eyes full of annoyance. Perhaps she doesn't like being stared at, but what else is there to do in an overcrowded waiting room where time seems to have stopped altogether? Where people at their most vulnerable are waiting, half expecting to hear a death sentence?

Today, my mind has also stopped working. All that matters to any of us here is the next hour; if we're unlucky longer, until we hear what the doctor has to say and have time to digest it so that we can leave the dreaded hospital department and get on with our lives, like everyone else. Until the next time … I always try to think of a case I'm working on, but even that seems to be difficult today. Perhaps, if Lauren, or someone else, had been here with me now, we would have whispered, spoken small talk to each other to take away the tension.

I shake my head, aware that I have at least drawn the attention of both sisters. They may think I am mad. Or perhaps that I have a medical condition that causes me to make involuntary movements. Spasms.

I don't want to think of Lauren. I had hopes once, but they have withered like summer plants in winter. My neighbour, Mr Curtis thought I should take matters into my own hands, go and see her and tell her how I felt about her. Encouraged by a man who wasted half his life hesitating about contacting the woman of his dreams, the love of his life, until it was too late, I did as he suggested. I gathered my courage, pulled myself together and went to her house. And there she was, lovely, pretty, beautiful. Smiling, laughing, happy. But she was with another man.

I haven't seen her since that day. I have avoided the street where she lives, the supermarket where she does her shopping and, miraculously, I have never bumped into her anywhere else accidentally. Which is, I know, a relief and a disappointment at the same time.

'Sharon Deane?' A nurse is standing beside the reception desk, staring over the edge of her reading glasses at the top sheet of a bundle of paperwork. The two sisters fidget. The glossy magazine lands on the floor as the one with the ponytail bends to pick up a black handbag. The one with the staring eyes shifts her gaze from my face to that of the nurse, and then to all those other faces which are staring back at her, partially envious because at least for someone the wait is nearly over.

Much to my surprise, ponytail picks up her magazine and opens it again, while the one that was staring gets up. There isn't a word spoken between them, only a small nod of shared concern. Then the one I thought had come for company, the staring one, is following the nurse and disappears behind a wall of plants. There is no hesitation by the man who has been loitering by the entrance doors to the reception area to step in and take the woman's vacant seat. Then everyone returns to their magazines and newspapers and their own thoughts.

The fact that I had misjudged the two sisters completely, by assuming that ponytail, the nervous one with the magazine was the patient, and not the other staring one, makes me think of the death of Iris Spencer. It is so easy to make the wrong assumption, to let it grow in your mind until you have deliberately turned all the signs in the same direction.

We have nobody in custody yet for Iris Spencer's murder. We don't even have a suspect. All we have is thoughts and ideas, but nothing seems conclusive. Maloney asked us to concentrate on the roses. Who bought them for her? Where were they bought? How and why did the apparent romantic rendezvous end up in a murder? But we are back at the start when, after painstaking enquiries, we eventually discovered that it was Iris herself who bought the roses. We didn't find any lead to a possible get-together with someone after the council meeting, so we eventually settled on the thought that she bought them for Tilda Disley, her partner and lover. Not that it is her birthday, or their anniversary, or anything that could have been a reason for a celebration of sorts. Hours have been spent at monitors, watching CCTV images. The rural area where Iris Spencer was found is such that there isn't a camera in the vicinity useful enough to pinpoint someone. Nowhere near enough to attract our attention. Within a timescale of one hour before the end of the meeting and midnight, we ran PNC checks on the registered owner of every car that drove past the village hall in St Eval, and past Iris's home, and even her office in Truro. According to studies, nearly 44 per cent of victims are murdered by persons known to them, either by family members or others in close relationships. Some 12 per cent are murdered by strangers, but even then there appears to be some sort of connection. Only random killings, like on the street, don't show a connection between the murderer and the victim. I can't believe that Iris Spencer's murder falls into that last category.

Alibis have been checked and double checked, motives researched and dismissed. No other DNA was found on the outside of Iris's car than Penrose's and her father's fingerprints, and of her alleged partner Tilda Disley. A footprint was found in the mud, about twenty metres from where her body was found but, even if we find whose it is, it will be hard to prove that this person was actually there at the time of the murder.

We still have a lot of possible other leads to follow and check but the first hours that are so important for an investigation have gone by without telling us much.

If Iris Spencer had arranged a meeting with her murderer, she hadn't told anyone about it. So it must have been someone she trusted well enough to meet late in the evening. Where did they meet? Why so late, so secretive? Was it business or personal? Personal would be the obvious answer. You don't usually buy red roses for a business contact. Unless it was a woman, someone she fancied, which would make it personal again. But then, we don't know who she bought the roses for. Someone she was meeting? Or did she buy them to take home, for Tilda as we had thought?

Sharon Deane returns from her doctor's consultation, pressing a piece of white cotton against her arm, her sleeve rolled up, her handbag tucked under her arm. Her stare turns to the man who has taken her seat, trying to annihilate him with her eyes. He sits hidden behind a newspaper, reading every sentence that is printed in it.

'Please, take my seat.' Another man rises to his feet, looking rather relieved to have an excuse to escape from the waiting room. The windows are steamed up and the atmosphere is oppressive. I can't blame him for wanting to have some fresh air.

'Andy Tregunna!'

The nurse looks around as if she has decided that I am the least likely person to be the man she's called for.

'Yes?'

'Would you come with me, please?'

The man who had offered Sharon Deane his seat lowers himself into it again, a mixture of disappointment and embarrassment on his face as she takes my seat instead, her eyes cast downwards. I follow the nurse down the corridor past several small rooms equipped with all kinds of medical paraphernalia for examining patients. On the way, she explains that Dr Bailey is expected in half an hour and they are doing their best to see the patients as quickly as they can. 'For those patients who don't really need to see him, we suggest they see one of the other doctors who are available this morning,' she says lightly. 'Dr Bailey will need to see you today, Mr Tregunna, albeit a bit later than scheduled. I hope it causes no major problems for you?'

'No.' I try not to think of the murder investigation. Maloney is very capable of handling it. He doesn't need me. Nobody needs me. Even Penrose seems to be thriving without me. She's getting better at her job too. Her confidence is growing, slowly but steadily. She seems to be better at containing her prejudices and making instant judgements about the people she has to deal with. She's admitted to me lately that she was more likely to suspect a vagrant as a murderer, rather than someone in a suit and tie. She now realises how deceptive appearances can be. One day, she will be a good investigator. But it will take time.

Following the nurse, I enter one of the examination rooms and she gestures towards a seat. She leaves the door ajar and I can see people walking past; nurses, student doctors, patients.

'How are you, Mr Tregunna?' The nurse sits down behind a small desk, opening a folder with all sorts of papers clipped inside it. My name is written on the outside, TREG-A, followed by my date of birth and the names of Bailey and Cole, doctors who had, and still have, my life in their hands.

'How's the pain? Do you feel tired?'

She takes a syringe-full of my blood and tells me I should have brought samples of urine and faeces with me. I nod, not telling her that they didn't tell me that, and I promise I will do it later. As I reply to her questions, I have difficulty concentrating on them. Every time I blink, I see the white face of Iris Spencer appear in front of my eyes. Life and death, especially in this department of the hospital, are closely woven together.

Afterwards, I'm sent back to the waiting room to wait for my meeting with Dr Bailey. Volunteers are pushing a trolley, laden with free coffee, tea and biscuits, through the crowd. My seat is still taken by Sharon Deane and I go outside, inhaling the cold air deeply. Through the glass door, I stare at a notice board that is covered with various items offering health warnings, lifestyle advice, how to claim sickness benefits, guidance on flu-jabs, support from different charities, dates of sports events to raise money to support cancer research, MacMillan. I'm not sure about the appropriateness of the ones about funeral arrangements or making your will but I do agree with the importance of donor registration.

Have I made my will? I haven't. If I die before my parents, everything will go to them. If not, it is possible that all my worldly goods, such as they are, will be inherited by my ex-wife. I don't care. I haven't drawn up my last wishes because I don't want to think that I need to.

But it does make me wonder. Have we found out if Iris Spencer had made a will?

24

'Kim? Kim Naylor?'
'That's me.'

'Oh. Eh … my name is Penrose. DC Jennette Penrose. I work with Detective Inspector Tregunna.' Penrose speaks slowly, still not sure if talking to the reporter is a good idea and aware that Ollie Reed is still at the police station.

'Yes?'

'Is it possible to meet?'

A pause. 'Are you going to ask me for information or give me some?'

Penrose swallows. The image she has of Kim Naylor, cute, blonde, voluptuous, doesn't correspond with this business-like approach.

'Perhaps it can be of mutual benefit,' she says cautiously.

A chuckle. 'You work quite closely with Tregunna, right?'

'I suppose.'

'I'm sure you do. It is exactly the kind of thing he would say.'

'Oh.' Somehow Penrose thinks it sounds like a compliment.

'Hang on,' Kim says. 'I've got another call coming in. I'm sorry but I'll have to take this. I will call you back. Okay?'

'Right.' Penrose puts down the phone. Newspaper reporters don't usually speak to the police unless they want something in return. They don't like giving away any information or their sources, especially not to the police. For that reason, she doesn't expect Kim to cooperate. But it's worth a try.

'What's up, Jen?' Ollie Reed stops in front of the desk. 'You look like someone who has just discovered that your best friends drank a very expensive bottle of wine you saved for a special occasion.'

'I don't drink.'

'Yeah, well, I was just thinking …'

The phone rings. Penrose stares at the screen. She hadn't expected Kim to call her back so soon. Uncomfortably she looks at Ollie, hoping he will go to his own desk, wishing that she'd gone to a quiet place to make the call to Kim.

'You called me two minutes ago.' Kim says.

'Yes, I did. Thanks for calling me back.'

'When would you like to meet and where?' Kim doesn't beat about the bush.

'As soon as you can? I'll leave the location up to you.'

'You mean … now?'

'If that's possible.' She glances at her watch. Twenty past five. She'd dropped PC Champion at her home, rang Louisa Blake, her neighbour, to ask her to look in on her father and then came back to the station, hoping she'd be able to talk to Tregunna about the letter Nigel Sparks gave her. Tregunna wasn't at home and, though she should have known better, she half-hoped that he would be at the station. The obvious explanation for the letter is that Iris Spencer was being blackmailed, but for some reason, she isn't sure about that and she would like Tregunna's opinion before she hands the evidence bag with the letter to Maloney. Then she had another idea … Tregunna always accuses her of not being pro-active enough. He wants her to take more initiative.

'Can I ask what it is about?' Kim Naylor asks.

'Ehm …' Another glance towards Ollie Reed's desk, but he's gone. 'I can't say.'

'Okay. No worries. How about I see you in half an hour at the corner of the old train track? I'm parked at the supermarket opposite the railway station. I need to collect a parcel from the Post Office. I will have 90 minutes parking time. I suppose that will do?'

'Ehm … could it be somewhere else?' Penrose doesn't add it would be too close to the police station. Although it is highly unlikely that she will meet one of her colleagues in the company of Kim Naylor, stranger things happen and she doesn't want to be accused of leaking information to the press. Even if she doesn't say anything to Kim it doesn't mean other people won't think that she has.

'Listen.' Kim seems to sense her hesitation. 'It's either this or tonight after nine. But you wanted to meet as soon as possible.'

'I did. Okay I can meet you in half an hour.'

Kim is already waiting at the corner of the old train track, now a footpath, that used to run from Newquay Harbour to the railway station. She is dressed in a blue denim jacket over a green shirt, a short black leather skirt and green tights. Her blonde hair looks a mess, as if she hasn't brushed it after washing it. Penrose suspects it is all down to the image Kim wants to create of herself.

They don't shake hands, they just nod at one another, testing the water, weighing each other up. Suspicion and caution on both sides.

'How can I help you, Jennette?'

Penrose swallows. It had seemed a good idea when she asked Kim to meet her. 'You were at the last meeting with the local council in St Eval this week,' she starts, with a hint of authority as she notices Kim's suspicious expression. Perhaps she had forgotten that they had seen each other outside the village hall.

'I was yes.'

'And Tregunna told me that when you were at that charity do a couple of months ago you made some recordings on your phone.'

'And?' Caution in her voice.

'What do you normally do with those recordings? Do you keep them?'

'What are you after, Jennette? Has someone whispered in your ear that it's against the law to make recordings?'

'I don't know about that,' Penrose says slowly. 'And I'm not here to accuse you of any wrongdoing, Kim.'

'Talking about recordings … are you recording our conversation?'

'Of course not!'

Kim smiles vaguely. 'I didn't think so, but I had to make sure. Nowadays, in my job it's a minefield and I don't want to step on a hidden bomb.'

'I can assure you …'

'Even if you are recording this, Jennette, and you are lying about it, it won't look very good for you. So, tell me, why are we here?'

Penrose shrugs, feeling as though she's been out-manoeuvred before she's even got going. 'Ehm … I'm clutching at straws, to be honest.'

'Your investigation?'

'Ehm, yes.'

'Iris Spencer?'

Penrose hesitates, then makes a quick decision. 'I was hoping that you recorded everything that was said at that meeting in St Eval.'

Kim lets out a slow whistle, cocking her head to one side, concentrating. As if on cue, they stop at a few benches behind high metal gates through which they have a view over the bay.

'Shall we sit down here for a minute, Jennette?'

'If we must.'

Kim nods seriously. 'I think we need to be very honest and clear with each other, Jennette. This isn't as straight forward as you may think.'

Penrose shrugs.

'This is how I work, Jennette. I record interviews because reporters are often accused of writing something that might have been taken out of context. I always try to be as accurate as possible and I make recordings to make sure that I report exactly what has been said. That's for the benefit of myself and also the person I have interviewed. If in doubt, I might call him or her later to make sure I got it right.'

'You don't …'

'With an interview, I always ask the person's permission. Most times, they agree. But it is different with meetings. I can't ask everyone for their permission, so I ask the chairman before the meeting starts. Legally, I guess, it isn't right, because I quote speakers who aren't always aware of the recordings.'

'So you did record that meeting in the village hall in St Eval before Iris Spencer was killed?'

'What if I did?'

Penrose ignores the question. 'Do you still have that recording?'

'What if I have?'

Penrose takes a deep breath. 'I was wondering if there was something that was said that might have triggered someone's anger.'

'Angry enough to kill Iris Spencer, you mean?'

'Maybe.'

Kim narrows her eyes. 'Does this mean that the police still haven't got a clue about who murdered her and why?'

Penrose freezes, trying to hide the shock that she can be read so easily by this sharp, intelligent reporter. She pauses to compose herself and think of something to avoid giving too much away. 'I can't say anything about the investigation, Kim. I'm sorry. But this is more because that meeting was kind of personal to me.'

'Personal? Is that why you were there?'

Penrose can't help smiling cynically. Damned right that was why she was there. She knew Kim had seen her outside but didn't think she had seen her father's embarrassing outburst which had forced them both to leave the meeting.

'I was only there for the first part of …'

Kim interrupts quickly. 'Were you with the man who … ehm … who left early?'

'Who was politely but urgently asked to leave the meeting, you mean? Who was yelling loudly and making so much disturbance? Yes, that was my father.'

'How are you involved?'

'We live in St Eval. Although this planning application doesn't affect us directly, we're afraid that, if they do get their permission in this case, it will set a precedent and more houses will be built in the area. The obvious place would then mean more development in St Eval and then it would be right on our doorstep.' She pauses for breath. 'My father has got Alzheimer's. He can get so upset about these things. Which was why he was politely asked to leave the meeting.'

Kim nods understandingly, then frowns. 'I still don't understand what you want with my recordings?'

Penrose takes a deep breath. 'It's just so that I can reassure my father that nothing has been decided.'

'I'll see what I can do for you,' Kim says abruptly. 'But I can't promise. I have to check it with my editor.'

Penrose thanks her, avoiding her eyes, not sure if Kim Naylor has guessed the real reason why she has asked for the recording. The reporter isn't stupid; she senses that Penrose has other, more professional interests too.

Since they still haven't found Iris Spencer's mobile phone, on which she must have recorded the meeting in the absence of her secretary, it seemed like a good idea to use her personal reasons as an excuse to get her hands on another transcript of what had been said during the meeting. Hopefully, to find out if there was anyone present who had enough reason to follow Iris Spencer after the meeting and kill her. And if she is right, the motive for Iris Spencer's murder was blackmail.

25

The tension subsides after my meeting with Dr Bailey, but I leave Treliske Hospital with a feeling of exhaustion. If I'd go home to bed now, I would sleep for the next twenty-four hours. As usual, seeing the oncologist is such an anticlimax that I need a while to wind down. Sadly, I can only think of going to the police station.

Maloney is pacing up and down in his office, a perfect candidate for a heart attack or a stroke.

'Come in, Tregunna. We've got a problem.' He closes the door behind me. 'Guthrie has been on the phone.'

His words come out like an eruption of a volcano that has been lying dormant for centuries: unexpected, threatening, slowly coming to the boil. That and the fact that Guthrie has been in contact while he is away on his safari holiday in South Africa, makes me wary. It feels like DI Maloney is going to say something I won't want to hear.

He stops beside his desk, rolling his head around. He stretches his arms above his head, then runs his hands from the top of his head down to his face, covering it as if he is going to cry.

Uninvited, I sit down in the chair opposite his desk and say flippantly, 'I thought Guthrie was on holiday?'

'I thought so too.' He gives a faint, crooked smile, as though we're schoolboys sharing a secret about the teacher.

'I can remember the days when we went on holiday to places where we couldn't even buy an English newspaper. We were completely cut off from all the news from home. We had to use a phone box to call our parents to let them know we were safe and make sure they weren't ill or something. That has all changed now. Everyone has a mobile phone and you can see and hear your parents and children any time of day through Skype or FaceTime. You don't even need to buy a newspaper to hear about what's happening in the world or in the place where you live.'

He stops for breath. I nod, not knowing where this is coming from and where it's leading to.

'Now, clearly, Guthrie knows everything about the investigation. Not only from what he's read online in the local papers, but he has also been in contact with some of his pals.' The last words come out with a cynical grin. 'Buddies he plays golf with or bridge or what have you. People with power and influence.' He shakes his head vigorously. 'He asked me why we haven't got Iris Spencer's murderer behind bars yet.'

I open my mouth to say that Guthrie is, as usual, a pain in the backside, but perhaps that isn't a good idea. Maloney tends to be more on Guthrie's side than mine, albeit perhaps only to keep in his good books.. So instead I say, 'He only really knows what he has read online. He and his buddies won't know the full details of our investigation, Philip.'

'I know that, you know that, but he doesn't.' He is walking and talking. 'If one of those papers says how obvious it is who killed her, he will believe them. And as you know, every paper, every reporter will sensationalise a story to attract more readers. What they don't know, they make up. Nasty pieces of shit, thinking they know better, thinking that they can do our job for us.' He pauses for breath again, staring but not seeing me. 'And on top of that, his pals from his various clubs like the rotary, they all have their own agendas. Their own reasons for pointing the finger in a certain direction. They all have their fingers in a lot of pies and …'

'Philip,' I interrupt gently. 'Sit down and relax.'

'They all know better and know who to blame …' he stops abruptly. 'What?'

'I said, sit down and relax. Forget Guthrie, forget the newspapers, forget the reporters and forget all the other idiots.'

'You don't know what it's like to feel him breathing down my neck,' he says lamely. Nevertheless, he sits down obediently. Hands flat on his desk, palms up, fingers trembling, he stares at them as though he can't believe they're his. He must have had a really bad time on the phone with Guthrie.

'Guthrie wouldn't be any use even if he were here now,' I say bluntly.

'Those are your words, not mine,' he mutters.

I shake my head, hoping he won't relay this conversation to the man we're talking about. 'We both know it's true, Philip. His only concern is that he's missing out on appearing in the papers and on the TV.'

'You can't say that, Tregunna.'

I shrug. 'Maybe not, but you and I know that it's true.'

'DCI Guthrie isn't just anyone. He's had a brilliant career, which is why he is where he is now.'

'Perhaps, but he seems to have forgotten about real police work. How screwed up some investigations can get. It is so easy to stand on the sidelines and tell other people what they should do. Especially with hindsight. Compare it to football, where every fan is a better manager than the one they've got.'

'I could report you for this, Tregunna,' he half-jokes.

I shrug. 'Why am I listening to your moans and rants, Philip?'

Using his first name seems to do the trick. He is trying to relax.

'Why are you here?' He stares at me as it dawns on him that he's completely forgotten why he called me into the office. His face blushes again.

'It's about this bloody case. We're getting nowhere. Guthrie wants a result handed to him on a plate before he boards the plane to come back here, all ready for a press conference the next day. To show off his tan.' His eyes widen as he realises what he's saying.

'Let's hope he hasn't got eyes and ears in this office,' I say facetiously.

'Yeah ...' His shoulders drop in defeat. 'I can't see the wood for the trees any more. I have the feeling that Iris Spencer's murder has something to do with that last meeting she went to before she was killed. She must have ruffled someone's feathers. The problem we're having is that the people who were there are all sticking together, confirming their alibis and so on. They're forming a united front against the police.'

'I understood that they fall into two groups. One is in favour of the development of that plot of land, the other is strongly against it.'

He nods. 'And somehow, Iris was in the middle of all that, holding the key to the final solution, as it were.'

I shake my head. 'I believe it was decided that there was to be a referendum. Yes or No to the development.'

'Referendum? Bollocks. It sounds very democratic, but I'm afraid it doesn't work like that. The outcome is already clear, mark my words. Those houses will be built and everyone in that village knows it.' He casts me a wary glance. 'I know what I'm talking about, Tregunna, because I have checked it. And a significant detail is that Iris was the one who could make the final decision. Even though one percent of a referendum might be against the development, she could overrule the outcome with the snap of her fingers.'

'Are you saying you think it was a motive for killing her?'

'We can't rule anything out, can we?'

We are still going round in circles. He hasn't come to the real point of this conversation.

'Other key players are the Cawley brothers. Mind you, me and my brother don't get on very well, but we would never end up in a situation where we're shooting at each other.'

'Nathan Cawley?'

He nods. 'You spoke to him. Latest is that he fired a shotgun to chase his own brother away. Boris Cawley claims that his brother had the intention to kill him.'

'Why would Nathan try to kill his brother? What would he gain from his death?'

He shrugs. 'I don't know. Why did Cain and Abel fight? Anyway, my next problem is that one of the lovely brothers has been arrested.'

'Boris Cawley?' My mouth falls open. 'Why? Did he kill Iris Spencer?'

'I wish it were as simple as that, Tregunna. He certainly has a motive, because it wasn't a secret that Iris was in favour of the development of the plot his brother owns.'

'Wouldn't it have been more sensible to kill his brother?'

'Hm, good point. Anyway, his arrest is just one of those things that's muddying the water, making everything even more complicated for us.'

'Why has Boris Cawley been arrested?'

He shrugs dismissively. 'Illegal activities, apparently. I'm not sure about the exact charges yet, but it has something to do with illegal migrant workers.'

'I don't understand. What has this got to do with our murder investigation?'

He sighs, rubbing his forehead with the side of his hand. 'I don't understand it either. I would like to find out whether this is related to our case. But I would also like to keep this low-key. I don't want to stir things up with anything to do with illegal immigrants. Can you imagine what the press would have to say about it all then?'

'I wouldn't worry about the press, Philip.'

He smiles ruefully. 'Easier said than done, Tregunna. Mind you, we're already halfway through Guthrie's holiday. He can face the press himself.'

'But what …?'

'I need you to have a word with Boris Cawley, Tregunna.'

26

The car park of the police station in Bodmin is half full, the bushes around it littered with rubbish. An officer with a fluorescent yellow jacket has been assigned to the unsavoury job of clearing it all. Using a long-handled rubbish picker stick to grab the pieces without having to bend down every time, his body language tells me that he is still cross about being assigned this job.

He looks up. Nods reluctantly. 'Tregunna.'

His face is vaguely familiar but I can't remember his name. He remembers mine, which is embarrassing.

'You don't remember me?' He sighs with profound resignation. 'Constable Steve Granger. I worked for you in Newquay on a murder case. The woman who didn't fall down the cliffs.'

I nod. Jane Croft, again. Penrose inadvertently mentioned her when we were walking about Bodmin Jail. It was my first murder investigation, which was suddenly interrupted when they found cancer in my body and I had to hand the case over to DI Maloney.

'How's that girl?' Granger continues.

I hesitate, suppressing the urge to ignore his question and leave him to his litter. He means well. All he wants, probably, is a little chat to distract him from his boring job. But the thought of the Jane Croft case always brings a bitter taste to my mouth. As a result of my failings, Becca is still in a coma.

I visit her every so often, sitting next to her bed and staring at her white face. I talk to her. In fact, she knows more about my feelings, my worries and concerns, about my whole life, than anyone else. She's unable to respond. At one point she was taken off the life-support machine that kept her alive by breathing for her and everyone was prepared for her to die. Miraculously, she started breathing for herself. Since then there has been the occasional trembling of her eyelids and little spasms around her mouth, with excited nurses hoping she would wake up, but it has never happened. Sometimes I wonder if it would have been kinder to her if she hadn't been kept alive by the machine, or if she had died the day she was shot, or if the surgeon hadn't managed to operate on her and remove the bullet from her brain. The bullet that was meant for me …

'She's still in a coma?' Granger presses on.

'Sadly, yes.'

'Shame. Lovely girl.'

I smile faintly. 'She still is.'

He shrugs, uncertain whether to ask more or leave it.

'Not a very nice job to do,' I say, pointing at the rubbish bag in his hand and changing the subject before he can go on about Becca. 'Been windy here?'

'Bloody migrant workers,' he grunts. Then, seeing my expression, he corrects quickly. 'I have nothing against migrants or migrant workers, I promise. But they made a real mess here, as you can see.'

'What happened?' I have a vague recollection of an item on the local news but I fail to make the connection here.

'Protests against the arrest of their bosses.'

A ringtone of Queen's '*We are the Champions*' fills the silence and he leans his rubbish picking stick against his knee to retrieve his mobile phone. He seems to have forgotten me as he stares up at the building, expecting, maybe, to see a mocking colleague waving from behind a window.

Granger looks at the screen, half turning his back to me. 'Hi love ...'

I leave him in a discussion with his wife or girlfriend about who is doing the shopping and the cooking today and enter the police station. The officer at the reception desk tells me I need to speak to DS Mike Martin about the migrants. He speaks to DS Martin on the phone, gesturing me towards an interview room. 'Coffee machine is down the side. You'll need a pound coin for it.'

I follow his instructions and fill a plastic cup with something that is called black coffee but looks like tar. It tastes of neither.

DS Martin introduces himself. He is in his mid-thirties, with a round face and puffy blue eyes. His hair is neatly parted on the left and I can smell his deodorant. He grins sheepishly at the cup. 'I would have brought some down for you, but the coffee tastes only marginally better in the office.' He sits down at the other side of the table, placing a transparent blue plastic folder in front of him. 'Most of us have a kettle upstairs.' He shrugs and adds, by way of explanation or excuse, 'It's all down to financial cuts, I suppose. A cheap coffee machine in favour of one of us.' He gestures over his shoulder towards the entrance hall at a trio of flowerpots with half-dead plants in them. 'Even the plants don't seem to like it.' He opens the folder. 'You want to know about the migrant workers?'

'Yes please.'

'I suppose you've seen it on TV and in the papers?'

'I'm afraid I missed it.'

'No harm done.' He grins and takes out the top sheet. 'In short, we received an anonymous phone call that illegal immigrants were being held in a barn. Obviously, we went there immediately. Two men were arrested on suspicion of modern slavery offences at Trevarra Farm near St Eval.'

'Boris Cawley?'

'That was one of the men we held in custody. The other was his son. James Cawley.' He gestures at the window. 'You've seen the mess outside? That was after the arrest. About 100 migrant workers gathered outside the police station to protest against Cawley's arrest. The protesters said they were also angry because they had been portrayed as modern slaves after police raided the farm. They threatened us with discrimination and breach of their human rights as we closed the farm and they weren't able to work.' He shakes his head wearily. 'Complete cock-up. They more or less camped outside on the car park until we released James, the son. We had nothing on him, as the workers, who were mainly from Eastern Europe, are quite happy to live on the farm where they pick vegetables. They don't call themselves slaves, they have chosen to work on the farm, some of them have been there for several years, and they are quite happy living in the static caravans provided for them on the property, which allows them to send more money to their families back at home.'

'You just said that James Cawley was released?'

'That's right. His father remained in custody, pending further enquiries after he allegedly attacked one of the officers who raided the farm. But he claimed that the man tripped over his own feet, which was later confirmed by the officer himself. Which was after he'd been to A&E because he'd broken his foot.'

'Who made the initial call to report the migrants?'

'It was anonymous.'

'What did Boris have to say about it?'

'Oh, he accused his brother. He was furious. He claimed it had to do with the referendum and travellers and money laundering. To be honest, we were fed up with the whole case and we couldn't wait to see the back of the lot of them.'

'And they left a mess all over your car park.'

'Not deliberately, to be honest. Every so often a group of them went to collect food and drinks, all takeaways, mind you, and our bins were getting fuller until they overspilled. None of us here had the bright idea to have the bins emptied. Our own fault, to be honest. I believe there was even a request for bin bags, but nobody responded to that.'

'Has the call been checked? Whether is was Nathan Cawley who made the initial call?'

'We did. There was a lot of publicity and we wanted to do it properly, you know. Migrants are the underdogs and, basically, we'd made fools of ourselves by arresting people who weren't really to blame. We acted too quickly, I suppose, without checking properly first.'

'And the call was genuine? By brother Nathan?'

'Well, no. We weren't able to find any proof that it was his brother. Or anyone else.'

He chuckles and closes the file. 'I've made copies for you, if you want them. But there wasn't anything to it. Only that the two brothers don't seem to like each other.' He shakes his head. 'I suppose their parents are both dead. It would kill mine if me and my brother behaved like the Cawley brothers but, from our point of view, there was nothing we could do.'

27

Boris Cawley is three years younger than his brother Nathan, but he looks at least ten years older. Otherwise he is the spitting image of him, less the moustache. He sits in a faded burgundy chair in a kitchen where little seems to have changed in the past five or six decades. An enamel kettle sizzles on a stove that spreads heat over a small perimeter that barely seems to reach him. One of his three sons has let me in: young and skinny with a sulking expression on an acned face. He mutters something that I take for an excuse and disappears up a staircase with a threadbare striped carpet held on each tread with brass bars that need polishing.

Boris Cawley is drinking milky tea from a mug half the size of a jug.

'What do you want, son?' he asks quietly.

'A chat.'

'You're police.' Apparently, I don't need to introduce myself. 'Police don't chat. They act or sit on their hands.'

'My name is Detective Inspector Tregunna.' I stand in the doorway. 'I can sit on my hands if you like, but that doesn't prevent me from having a chat with you.'

'Huh.' He takes a long sip. 'Kettle's on the boil, if you want some tea.' It is as good as an invitation as any.

'Any chance of coffee instead?' I reply, not expecting a positive reply.

He nods and motions toward one of the cupboards. 'The wife is out with the horses. She won't mind.'

I open the cupboard and find a small electric espresso maker on the bottom shelf.

'For some reason, she always wanted to see Venice,' he says almost grudgingly.

I nod, waiting for him to reveal the relevance.

He's just returned from the police station, where he's been held and charged for allegedly keeping illegal immigrants on his property, employing them and housing them in circumstances that don't comply with health and safety regulations. All charges have been dropped except for one of verbal abuse against one of the officers when Boris was arrested while he was working in one of his fields, cutting cauliflowers from the stalks alongside his workers.

'I've never been across the border of Cornwall,' he says evenly. 'Why would I? My life is here, in this house, on my own land. But she kept nagging me about going to Venice and I let her go. That was three years ago. After she came back, she insisted on having her own coffee machine to make Italian coffee. Cost me an arm and a leg, but, hey, she's happy with it.' He shakes his head. 'I don't know head or tail of it, but be my guest if you want to give it a go.'

'Are you sure she won't mind?'

'I'm sure she'll be pleased that there is someone else who'll appreciate her precious coffee.'

He stares out of the window that overlooks a field with three horses nibbling at a hay bale. Behind the overgrown wall, I see the top of a double-decker bus pass by. The Newquay to Padstow route. Or vice versa. One of the horses looks up, whips his tail and continues his meal.

'Did your wife ever go back to Venice?' I ask casually.

He raises his eyebrows. 'Why? She saw it all the first time.'

I don't reply. He won't understand his wife's desire to go

and visit a different part of the world. Perhaps she was satisfied that she'd been to Venice. Seen it, been there; it may have been enough for her.

I make an espresso that is too strong for my taste and I empty the contents of the small cup in one of his jug-type mugs, adding hot water from the kettle.

'What are you here for, son? I've just seen the lot of you in Bodmin.'

'So I heard.'

He gestures towards the window. 'You see these horses? My brother wants to build houses on that field. Can you imagine what our view will be like?'

I don't answer. I hadn't realised that the disputed building plot is right on his doorstep. It will definitely spoil his view.

'Cornwall needs affordable homes. That's why the young people are leaving the county,' I say calmly.

'I agree, but …' He interrupts himself. 'Tregunna? Are you Cornish?'

'I'm afraid so. Born and bred.'

'Then maybe, you'll understand. You see, there won't be any affordable homes here. Nate and his mates have big plans for modern houses with big glass windows to make the most of the sea views.'

'Nate? Your brother Nathan?'

'He's got the land, but he's become a partner of some building company that they've set up specially for this development. And I'm sure nothing will stop them. They will build here, mark my words. It'll cost them peanuts, but the profit comes in diamonds.'

'Do you know the name of that company? Or who his partners are?' I ask, for no other reason than to encourage him to keep talking.

He shakes his head. 'They're hiding behind the facade of a limited company or something. I'm not a fool, son. I understand that people want to make money. I do too. But that doesn't mean I agree with everything. I'm a farmer. Other people here are farmers. We don't need rich people in glass houses with big cars that block our roads and who complain about mud.' He gestures vaguely. 'There is a field further down the road that is even bigger than this one. Why don't they build there?'

'I don't know the answer.'

'Simply because it doesn't offer a sea view, which will cut the price by half.' He chuckles without humour. 'But I suppose that isn't what you wanted to chat about?'

I smile faintly. 'I'm investigating the death of Iris Spencer.'

'And you've come to see me about that?' he asks, but there isn't a spark of surprise in his eyes.

'You had a few words with her on the evening of the last meeting.'

'I did. No sense in denying that, son.'

'What was it about?'

'The meeting was about that development. But it was all one big lie. Those people have the money and the power and they will do whatever they want.'

'Where were you after the meeting?'

His eyes narrow. 'You mean, you want to know my alibi?'

'If you have one.'

'Sure I have. I went to the meeting with two of my sons. Jamie and Harry. Richard, the youngest, you've just met him, wasn't interested. He's sixteen, still at school. He doesn't want to be a farmer. He's more like his mother, wants to see what lies beyond the boundaries of Cornwall. He … but you're not interested in my son's motives, are you? You can ask them, but Harry and Jamie will tell you pretty much the same, which is that we came home after the meeting. We had a cup of tea with the wife and Jamie left and we went to bed.'

'Jamie left?'

'Harry lives with us. Got married three years ago but his wife left him, so his mother said there will always be a bed for him here. Jamie lives further up, in one of the caravans, where the workers also live. Mind you, what's good for the workers is good for my son, huh?'

'The alleged illegal immigrants?'

'They're not illegal or immigrants to me, son. They're workers. I don't care where they come from as long as they understand what I'm saying and they do what I ask them to do. They're decent people, like you and me, only they happened to be born in a country where there is just a bit less of everything what we have here. They are free to come and go, and they're certainly not forced to do anything outside the law. I have a record of all of them. They work harder than you and I put together and I pay them decent wages. I don't see what the problem is, but, well, it's all quiet again.'

'Someone claimed that the … men who work for you were treated badly.'

He nods. 'My brother, I'm sure it was him. Coward. Didn't even give his own name when he called to report the situation to the police.'

'But I'm here for something else,' I say gently. 'You were seen having an argument with Iris Spencer in the hours before her death.'

He nods, not bothered. 'I don't deny that, son. I must confess I hated the woman. She's like a bulldozer, no regard for what other people think. All she's after is making even more money than she's already got.'

'How well do you know her, Mr Cawley?'

'I've had more dealings with her than I ever wanted to, son.'

'How?'

'She's had her fingers in too many pies for my taste.'

'Meaning?'

He shrugs. 'Nothing I can prove, sadly. But I know one thing. Years ago, she bought a cottage on the headland in Porthcothan. It belonged to my family and she bought it off our father for a pittance. Blinked her lashes at him, told him how lovely the cottage was, begged him to sell it to her. Our mother didn't agree, but he wouldn't listen to her. Next thing we knew the cottage was knocked down and they built a completely new house and sold it for a couple of million.'

'Iris Spencer did that?'

'Oh yes. That was even before she got involved in her council work. Or should I say that it was why she got involved in council work? Perks of the job?'

'That is quite an accusation, Mr Cawley. Are you saying she was corrupt?'

'As I said earlier, I can't prove it, son. All I wanted was to see the back of her. Let her spoil somebody else's view if they're stupid enough to trust her, but not me.'

'You said you hated her?'

'I did and I'm not going to take back my words. I'm sorry for her family that she's dead, but for her ... they say you get what you deserve and maybe that is exactly what she got.'

'You are aware, Mr Cawley that you are presenting me with a motive for her murder?'

'Maybe so, but I'm not so stupid that I'd have said that if I'd really killed her.'

I suppress a smile. 'Before the meeting, you followed her to the corridor where the toilets are. What did you talk about?'

'I told her that I knew what she was doing. That I knew

she was working her own deals behind everyone's back. I won't repeat this to anyone else, son, but I did say to her that I would talk to the press if she didn't make sure this plot of land would not be built on.'

'You blackmailed her?'

He shrugs. 'Technically, verbally, maybe, yes, but I didn't want it only for myself, but for the whole community. Nobody here wants those new houses built, son.'

'I understand there will be a local referendum.'

'That's what they say, but the outcome is already clear. The only people who were in favour of the development are my brother and Iris Spencer and her lot, and maybe a handful of people who live in the area and don't really care about what happens here or who still believe that their children have a chance of buying a house for a reasonable price.'

'What was her reply?'

He shakes his head, uncertain suddenly. 'That was kind of weird, son. At first, she said she wouldn't allow anyone to blackmail her or stand in her way, but I laughed in her face and I said it wasn't blackmail, but an insurance policy. You know? So, in terms of a motive for her death, Iris should have killed me, rather than you looking at me for being the killer.'

'And then?'

'Then she said that if I was to bring her down, she would also bring down my brother. Next thing I knew she referred to family honour and all that, but, I must confess, she had a point. I mean, Nathan and I have always had our differences and we will never be friends, but he is still my brother and I will never do anything to harm my own flesh and blood.'

'He fired a shotgun at you. You made an official complaint to the police.'

He chuckles. 'We're good shooters, son. If Nate had aimed

well, he would have hit and killed me.'

I take a moment to digest his words, realising that I can charge him for wasting police time.

'What did Iris mean when she said she'd bring Nathan down too?'

'I'm not sure but, about one year ago, I received a letter that wasn't meant for me. It was for Nathan. It does happen every now that we get the wrong mail, you see. Too many of us called Cawley living here and we all have the same postcode. Anyway, I didn't pay much attention until I opened the letter. It was something about a scheduled meeting with two other people. Stewart and Bingwell. They supposedly were shareholders of the company my brother was involved in. I didn't know what it was about and I closed the letter and sent it through to Nathan. But when all this about Nathan's plot of land came about and we all got letters about the plans they had and how we would all benefit from it, blah-blah-blah, I recognised the name on the letter.'

'Which one?'

'Bingwell, which was the name Iris Spencer used when she got her hands on my father's cottage. Later, I found out that Mrs Anna Bingwell her mother is.'

28

Penrose drives with her usual impatience, bent forward towards the windscreen as if she's trying to make the car go faster. She gestures with her head towards the glove compartment. 'I've got a new CD in there. Can you take it out for me?'

Obediently, I open it, finding what looks like the inside of a woman's handbag to me: full of items that aren't really necessary. On top is a clear box with a rewritable CD in it, the label blank.

'Rag'n Bone man,' she says, as if that explains everything.

'What?'

'The singer. Very popular at the moment.'

'What's his name?'

'Rag'n Bone man.'

'Like a tramp or a vagrant?'

'Have you never heard of him?'

'I'm probably glad I haven't.'

She grins. 'I didn't think you were such a fossil.'

Choosing not to answer to that, I slip the CD in the system, half expecting to hear the loud sounds of some heavy metal group. But somewhere along the line, her taste of music has changed. Her preference for heavy-metal rock has made way for more modern pop music. I even have to admit that, although I didn't know the singer's name, I do recognise the music. Not a bad change of taste.

We're on our way to speak to Hugh Kelly, Iris's business partner, who has returned from a business trip. We're picking up the tail end of the usually very busy traffic into the county capital. The short dual carriageway is crowded with slowly moving cars, delivery vans and lorries. There has been an accident on Chiverton Cross roundabout. Just between the exits to the A30 and to Truro, the outside lane is blocked by two vehicles. One of the drivers is standing beside a dark-coloured car, hands loosely in the pockets of his black trousers in a 'see-what-happens' pose. The other car was driven by a young woman, who is hunched over on the grass verge, looking flushed and agitated and trying to comfort herself and three crying young children at the same time.

Penrose curses but I'm spared her, no doubt, nasty comments on everything and everyone when my phone rings.

'Andy?' Andrea Burke's voice echoes through the inside of the car. Too late, I realise my phone had connected to the speakers when I plugged it in to charge the battery.

'Yes?'

'It's Andrea. It's about the letter.'

'What letter?' I look sideways at Penrose. She seems to be only half listening, concentrating on what is going on in front of us in the traffic.

'Lynham's letter?' I gave her the letter Chaz Lynham found in her husband's papers to see if there are any fingerprints or other forensic material on it.

'Well, not exactly, but I guess it's about that too.'

'You've lost me.'

I can hear her deep sigh. Penrose stirs beside me, frowning, opening and closing her mouth repeatedly, but she doesn't say anything.

'You gave me the letter Edward Lynham had in his possession,' Andrea Burke continues.

'Yes, but that case is now closed,' I say slowly. Perhaps I

should have let her know that Ed Lynham's death has been officially declared a suicide. 'There won't be an investigation. Sorry, Andrea.'

'I know that, Andy, but that isn't the end of it. The point is, Andy, I now have the original letter.'

'Original letter?'

'Yes.'

'Sorry, go on.'

'Can you stop saying sorry all the time and listen to me?'

'Yes. Ehm … sorry.' I can't suppress a smile and even Penrose smiles now, although I can see she's slightly annoyed, probably because she doesn't understand what the conversation is about.

'As I said, I have a letter here in front of me, right? This one has the cuttings from the newspapers actually stuck onto it, so I call this the original letter.'

'I wasn't aware there was an original.'

'All I know, and that's what matters to me, is that I have it on my desk. When I recognised it, I got onto it straight away.'

Penrose is pulling my arm, stabbing her index finger on her chest. 'That was me. I sent a letter with paper cuttings to Forensics.'

I don't understand what's happening here, but I sense Andrea Burke hasn't got the patience or the time to explain.

'Penrose says she gave you the letter.'

'Yes. There is a note attached. It was found in Iris Spencer's office. I did …'

'What? The same letter?'

'The original. Ed Lynham had a copy.'

I let out a whistle. Even Penrose looks astonished.

'So the cases are connected?'

'That's up to you to investigate, Andy; I'm just telling you the facts.'

'I can't believe it.'

'Well, there is always a possibility that they could have known each other. They're about the same age and Lynham was a politician and Spencer was a councillor.'

'Okay, we'll have to look into that.'

'Right. Well, the reason I'm calling you is that I have found a beautiful set of fingerprints on the original letter. I thought you'd like to know.'

'Whose fingerprints?'

'Let's start with the copy that you gave me. There are prints of Ed Lynham and his wife and of someone else. On the original letter, I found fingerprints of Iris Spencer and her secretary Nigel Sparks. Plus, again, someone else's. The same someone else.'

'Have you been able to identify them?'

She chuckles. 'You owe me another dinner for this, Andy. Same place?'

'That depends.'

Beside me, Penrose clenches her fists around the steering wheel, mouth tight. I'm not sure if it is about what Andrea Burke just said or the still unmoving traffic. We hear an ambulance approaching. Not a good sign.

'So you've been able to identify the other fingerprints? You've got a name?'

'Not yet. We're working hard on that, but you'll have to be patient.'

'Okay. Thank you, Andrea.'

'Dinner?' she repeats, a smile in her voice.

I glare sideways at Penrose. Her lips are pressed into a thin angry line. 'I'll call you later about that, Andrea. Thanks for the update.'

29

Hugh Kelly is sitting at his desk, propped forward on his elbows, staring at his computer screen, squeezing his eyes like a mole suddenly exposed to bright daylight. His jacket is hanging over the back of his chair. He has pulled his tie loose and unbuttoned the top of his white shirt, sleeves rolled up. His face is flushed due to constant high blood pressure or temporary excitement.

He gets up as we appear in the open door of his office, startled as if he's been caught red-handed in an illegal action, quickly pressing a few keys on the keyboard to hide whatever he was looking at, or just to save a document before his computer falls asleep.

'It's such a mess,' he declares theatrically, shaking my hand as though he is clutching desperately onto the stern of a lifeboat. His hand is warm and sweaty. Late last night he returned from a business trip to Aberdeen, which, he had decided, he had to go to despite what had happened to his business partner.

'I am a mess myself.' He shakes his head, staring at Penrose for sympathy. 'I don't know what I'm doing.'

He is in his forties with thinning grey-blond hair. One of his front teeth seems almost twice as big as the others, his bottom lip forced over them, which gives his face an expression as if he is constantly amused.

'You are both here to talk about Iris, I suppose,' he says, not waiting for an answer but interrupting himself and saying, 'Have you been offered coffee or tea?'

'We have, thank you.'

He pulls up two visitors chairs for us and sits down behind his desk, drumming his fingers on the armrests as if he can't wait for this conversation to be over.

'We understand you were on a business trip, Mr Kelly?'

'What? Yes, I was. To be totally honest with you, it did cross my mind whether it would have made any difference if I hadn't been away. With Iris, I mean.'

Penrose ignores his last words. 'Where were you Monday night, Mr Kelly?'

'I was in Aberdeen.' He stops, eyes wide open. 'I hope you're not thinking I murdered my own business partner?'

'At this stage, we are keeping an open mind, Mr Kelly. We are interviewing everyone and checking everything.'

He nods, frowning, lost in his own thoughts.

'Terrible, terrible,' he says slowly, wiping an imaginary tear from the corner of his eye. 'I hope you will catch this killer sooner rather than later.'

'We're doing our best,' I say warmly, 'But it's early days. The investigation has only just started.'

He nods gravely. 'If there is anything I can do, please ask.'

I smile encouragingly. 'We have some questions, if you don't mind, Mr Kelly.'

'Fire away.' His eyes sweep from Penrose to me and back again.

'Where were you last Monday between 10 and 12 pm?'

He frowns. 'Like I said, I was in Aberdeen. I flew to Edinburgh on Monday and took the train to Inverness where I met a customer for dinner. I stayed in a hotel and the next day, I travelled to Aberdeen, where I was until this morning.'

'We will need your flight details and the name and address of the hotels where you were staying.'

'I can send you the details of my trip.'

'That would be very helpful, Mr Kelly.'

'No problem.' He reaches for the pocket of his jacket and retrieves a series of business cards, flicking through them and making two small piles, shoving one of the piles in Penrose's direction. 'Those cards are from the hotels and three of the people I met with there. My secretary will give you the details of the fourth person.'

Penrose collects the cards, spreading them out between her fingers as though she's inspecting her hand in a poker game.

'Do you know Edward Lynham?'

'No. I … isn't that the politician who killed himself?'

'Do you know him?'

'I've heard of him, of course. In the papers. On the radio. But I can't think I've ever met him.'

'Did Iris have any enemies that you are aware of?'

'Enemies?' He almost sounds offended as if I have personally accused him. 'We run a business, Detective Inspector and, as always when there is money involved, you come across people who don't always agree with what you're doing. Just as we don't always agree with other peoples' decisions. That's human nature. But I can't say that any of those disputes or disagreements could have led to a despicable act like this.' He shakes his head disapprovingly. 'Someone's life is more important than money.'

'We would still like a list of the people you have been dealing with in the last three months,' Penrose persists.

'Of course. I'll make sure my secretary sends you the details.'

'Has anything happened recently, that struck you as odd? Something out of the ordinary?' I ask.

He has to think about this. 'No, I can't think of anything. Honestly.'

'Has Iris been threatened by anyone?'

He frowns. 'If she was threatened, she didn't tell me.'

'Blackmail?'

'Blackmail? Good grief, Inspector, this isn't some sort of a conspiracy theory, I hope?' He grins uncomfortably, sensing that I am serious.

'Did Iris have any unexpected visitors?'

'Not that I know of, but you might want to ask her secretary. He knows more about her appointments than I do.'

'We have already spoken to Mr Sparks,' Penrose says crisply.

'You could also check with my secretary. When Nigel has the day off, my secretary takes over. And vice versa.' He stops abruptly. 'Wait a minute, since you ask, there was something … There was someone … No, I'm sorry. I thought there was something, but … no.'

'Mr Kelly, please, it may be important. Clearly, you were thinking of someone or something. You may think it might be irrelevant but the police will make that judgement for you.'

He shrugs. 'Well it has nothing to do with anything, I think, but there was something odd. Last week. Or perhaps it might have been the week before last.' He rises to his feet and starts pacing around behind his desk, wiping a hand over his forehead, thinking. I'm not sure if he regrets now that he mentioned the subject and is trying to think of a way out of this self-created problem. Or if he is just trying to remember exactly what it was, seeking his own solution before sharing it with us.

'There was a young woman last week who came to see me. Cathryn, she said her name was. My secretary will be able to tell you the exact day she was here. I didn't know her, I mean, I didn't recognise her name before she came in and gave me her full name and explained who she was. Penhallow. I hadn't seen her since she was a teenager. I remember she used to help out in the office in her school holidays to earn some pocket money.

Last time I heard something about her was when Arthur told me that his ex-wife was going to Australia, taking their only daughter.'

'And Arthur is?'

'Yes, well, let me start at the beginning, that would make more sense. When Iris and I started this business about twenty years ago, we had a third partner. Arthur Penhallow. He was older than us and had experience in running a business. Although we were equal partners, he was more the investor than working alongside Iris and me, but that didn't matter. I must say, from the start, we were very successful. Apparently, we hit the right note and we were able to grow and expand the business quickly. When his marriage went on the rocks, Arthur lost interest. The divorce hit him hard, especially when his wife took their daughter with her when she went to Australia. We parted company with him. No hard feelings. He sold his shares to Iris and me equally, but he kept two per cent himself. I've never really understood why but, for some reason, he didn't keep in contact. We tried though, but he seemed to withdraw himself from the company and from us. We sent his dividends to his bankaccount and that was it. I am sure our accountancy department can show you where the money went, if that might be of any relevance to you. We heard about his death about three or four months ago. Apparently he had been ill for a while but, obviously, we didn't know that.'

'As I said, Arthur had only one daughter and she was living in Australia. After his death, she inherited everything, including the two per cent shares in our company.' He pauses, frowning. 'Out of the blue, Arthur's daughter came to the office last week. I didn't recognise her name and to be honest, I still can't get my head around it. She said she was Cathryn Penhallow, but for some reason I didn't make the connection. Anyway, she wanted to sell her shares to me and … no, let me rephrase that. She asked if it would be convenient for me to have her two per cent shares. She knew of course that I already had forty nine per cent, as did Iris, and she thought I might be interested in having fifty one per cent of the business, which would give me the majority shareholding.'

He pauses and shakes his head. 'Iris and I have built this company successfully and I can say that we do that in good harmony. Of course we don't agree all the time but eventually, we always come to a solution or compromise that we can both live with. I explained this to Arthur's daughter and told her that I was happy to keep the arrangement going but, if she preferred to opt out completely, she would have to sell the two per cent shares to Iris and me equally.'

'Why were you not interested in having the majority of the shares?'

'Iris and I decided on equal shares years ago and I didn't think we should change that.' He pauses, looking sombre, no doubt thinking back at working with his business partner.

'What about Iris?'

'What about her?

'Do you reckon that Penhallow's daughter met Iris for the same reason?'

'I don't know.'

'Didn't you discuss it with Iris?'

'I think I mentioned it to her, yes, but I can't remember what she said.'

'Would you think it could be a motive for her murder?'

'I can't see how, to be honest. As I said, Iris and I run this business quite successfully, so why would we change things? I'm sure Iris feels … felt exactly the same.'

I nod in agreement. I don't think any of this is even remotely connected to her death, but I don't like loose ends until I know for sure that it is just that. Every case has its loose ends, but I need to be certain there isn't the thinnest, invisible thread.

Hugh Kelly introduces us to his secretary, Gina, a rather young girl with dark hair and purple glasses. Matching lipstick and nail polish. While Penrose waits as the girl writes down the required details, I walk into Iris Spencer's secretary's office.

'Mr Sparks, Mr Kelly told us that he had a meeting with a young woman called Cathryn Penhallow last week. Do you know if she also met Iris?'

'I don't think so, but … let me have a look.' He eyes me as though he is doubting my sanity, flicking through the diary on his desk with such speed that I'm not sure if he can be reading anything. I'm surprised that he doesn't use a digital diary.

'Do you use only a paper diary?' I ask for no particular reason.

He shrugs almost defiantly. 'That was what the lady wanted,' he replies philosophically. 'Iris didn't like those digital gadgets. Didn't trust them. I only did as I was told. Not very efficient, but that is how Iris works. Worked.'

Eventually, he finds a page and runs down a list of scribbled notes with his fingertip. 'Right. Ms Penhallow. Here she is.' He frowns and looks up, staring blankly. 'I remember the call now. She told me she had an appointment with Hugh … Mr Kelly, as well, and she wanted to see Iris right after that. I told her that Iris wouldn't be in the office on Thursday. I said I could arrange a meeting with them both together for another day if she could explain what it was about, but either she didn't want to disclose that to me, or she preferred to see Iris and Hugh in two separate meetings. She said she had to be somewhere else and that she would contact Iris again later.'

'Did she explain the nature of her business to you?'

'No, it was private, she said.'

'Private?' I think of what Hugh Kelly explained about the shares. It didn't sound like a private matter to me.

Sparks shrugs. 'That's what she said, which I found a bit strange, as I could see in the system that she was seeing Hugh about shares.'

'Can you describe her?'

'No I can't, I'm afraid. You'll have to ask Hugh or Gin, because I wasn't here on Thursday when she came to see Hugh.'

'And she didn't contact you again to make an appointment with Iris?'

'No. She had told me it was private, so I assumed that she'd called Iris at home and maybe made an arrangement to meet her somewhere else.'

Returning to the desk of Hugh Kelly's secretary, I don't feel any the wiser. Gina gives me an English mobile phone number which she got from Cathryn Penhallow, but the line goes dead.

I doubt that Maloney will find all this to be significant information, but I make a last attempt.

'Can you describe this Ms Penhallow for me, Gina?'

She checks the dates on her screen. Unlike Iris, Hugh Kelly has his diary on the computer system. 'No sorry, I didn't see her. She must have arrived when I was out for my lunch break.'

Briefly I contemplate going back to Hugh to ask him, but she purses her lips primly and tells me that Hugh is already in a meeting and I'll have to wait until he comes out, which won't be in the next hour. Beside me, Penrose frowns, checking her watch. I shrug and decide it isn't worth waiting. As we walk back to the car, I try the mobile number Gina gave me again, but the operator tells me that there is no response.

30

Even on a safari trip in tents surrounded by elephants, giraffes and lions, DCI Guthrie is managing to keep an eye on the investigation. At least that is what Maloney claims when he urges the team to follow leads that would normally be discarded as ridiculous and time-wasting. But the case seems to have come to a dead end. Even Penrose is convinced that they're dealing with a murderer who seems to know everything about forensic evidence and how to leave the crime scene without a trace. It didn't help that the rain had possibly washed away important clues that might have led them to Iris Spencer's murderer, and that cattle had trampled in the mud where they might have been able to find footprints or tyre tracks.

Maloney is clutching at straws, hoping that something will crop up eventually. He isn't the only one who has DCI Guthrie on his back. Someone has placed a cuddly toy elephant beside the lion cub that was rescued by Guthrie from the barn on Bodmin Moor. Penrose doesn't think adding the elephant is funny, but she must admit that it has lifted the atmosphere.

In a desperate attempt to keep the case afloat, Maloney accepts no excuses to skip the briefings, but there is little news to be added and all they will be doing is repeating the same facts and sharing the same ideas and opinions.

This morning, Maloney is standing in front of the whiteboard. He has sweat stains under his armpits and he's staring at the whiteboard as if he hopes someone has added vital information while he was asleep. Turning, his gaze drifts over their faces.

'Where is DS Reed?'

'He's on the phone, sir.'

Penrose shifts in her seat, aware of the empty chair beside her. Tregunna isn't here yet. Briefly, she wonders if he and Ollie Reed are on to something. She always feels a slight pang of envy when those two are together. There seems to be a sense of friendship, a mutual understanding between them that doesn't need a single word to be spoken. It's like what she used to have with Tregunna herself, but lately she feels something has changed between them and the camaraderie between them seems to have evaporated.

'Shall we start?' Maloney frowns. He's been frowning since he came in half an hour ago. 'Any more sightings on CCTV?'

'We've picked up her trail from where Mrs Spencer bought the roses,' someone says, but the tone of his voice already tells them not to be too hopeful. 'At 6.17pm she bought the flowers at a petrol station on Trevemper Road in Newquay. From there, she drove back to the roundabout and turned right, past the boating lake and under the railway viaduct, past Newquay Zoo. She drove on to Cliff Road and Henver Road and took the coast road to Porth.'

'Which was pretty obvious if she was going to the meeting in St Eval,' Maloney says cynically.

'It confirms what we already thought, sir,' the same voice admits.

'I'm more interested in CCTV after the meeting.'

'Nothing yet, sir.' A hesitation. 'Not much luck there so far, sir. There aren't many cameras on the roads in and around St Eval. But we're working on it, sir, chasing up private cameras.'

'Right. Thanks. Any news about her mobile phone? Andrews?'

'We haven't been able to find it, sir. Wherever it is, it is switched off. We're waiting for the phone company to give us a list of calls she made and were made to her.'

'Speed that up, will you?'

'Yes sir.'

'Anything on her financial status?' Maloney moves to the next subject on the list but, before anyone can answer, the door swings open and DS Ollie Reed comes in, holding a large brown envelope against his chest, torn open in haste, with the papers he's pulled out in his hand. His face is flushed and his eyes are sparkling with excitement. Even Penrose finds herself holding her breath when Ollie confidently walks straight towards the white board.

'What have you got for us, Ollie? Maloney asks, his voice thin with suppressed hope.

'This has just arrived sir.' Ollie smiles. 'I haven't had time to copy it and I only gave it a quick glance, but … it gives us something to get our teeth into.'

'What is it?' Maloney barks impatiently.

Ollie glances at Maloney and blushes to the roots of his ginger hair. 'It's a copy of Iris Spencer's will, sir.'

'I thought Tilda told us that there wasn't a will,' Penrose says sharply, annoyed with herself that she didn't double-check it.

'Even her business partner thought that, but we … to be fair, Tregunna said we still had to investigate it, sir, and he was right.'

'What does it say?'

'Yes, well, skipping the formalities, I have found a list of several beneficiaries, which gives them all a motive, I suppose.'

The whiteboard is already covered with scribbled notes and arrows, A4 printouts and post-it notes. Ollie pulls a metal easel with a large pad of paper on it to the middle of the room and finds a green marker pen.

'Okay. First of all, Iris Spencer appears to have had more money than we thought. In fact, she is, or was, quite a wealthy woman.'

'We'll have to get hold of all her bank accounts ASAP,' Maloney says, nodding at Ollie. 'Go on.' He looks around. There is a new sense of optimism and enthusiasm. The team is slowly waking up from its apathy.

Ollie starts writing down a list of names. Company and family names followed by first names and initials, adding monetary amounts after each name that stun them all.

'Most of these companies are part-owned by Iris,' Ollie explains, his back to the team while he's writing. 'And as far as I can see, she'll leave most of her company shares to her business partners or the shareholders.'

'We'll have to check them all,' Maloney says, as if nobody has come up with the thought.

'But the main beneficiaries are more important,' Ollie continues, building up the excitement like a skilled screenwriter of thriller movies. 'Tilda Disley is the first on the list. She'll inherit the house she lived in with Iris and there is a trust in her name that'll allow her to live comfortably for the rest of her life.'

Ollie scribbles as he speaks. 'There is the sum of one million pounds for someone called C.C. Ashton. Half a million goes to B. Connolly. The same amount goes to C. Ennis and there is a trust for A.A. Bingwell.'

Somebody lets out a long whistle.

'Then we have Lester Boyd, Iris's former husband. Although they were divorced, she owned half of the house he currently lives in with his family. He inherits her share in the house where he lives. Apparently, she owned half of it. On top of that, he'll immediately receive a sum that is enough to pay off the remainder of the mortgage on that house. And he will keep receiving the monthly sum of seven hundred pounds, with a five-yearly increase of five per cent to cover inflation. This will be transferred to his new wife if he dies before her.'

'Keep receiving?'

Ollie has to read it again. 'That's what it says.'

'All the more reason to get copies of her bank statements,' Maloney repeats but nobody listens. His face is flushed and his eyes are sparkling. The will opens a lot of new opportunities in finding Iris Spencer's murderer. They'll have to speak again to nearly everyone they have already spoken to, as most of them will benefit from her death.

'Right,' Maloney continues. 'Now, I would like to know two things for starters. First, why didn't we know that she's been paying seven hundred pounds to her former husband each month? Anyone?'

'We've made a request to the banks, sir, but there are accounts with more or less every bank in the high street and each request needs to be done separately. It is a very slow process, as not all the banks are cooperative.'

'Speed that up! This is important. If we don't get cooperation from the banks, then approach it from the other end. Ask Tilda Disley for copies of every bank account Iris held, ask Lester Boyd and Mr Kelly, everyone we can think of. Sooner rather than later.'

'Yes sir.'

'And, second, we need to know who Ashton, Bingwell, Connolly and Ennis are. As far as I know, we haven't come across any of those names yet.' Maloney looks around questioningly but, as there are only shrugs in response, he continues, issuing tasks as if he's presenting them with a big piece of cake. 'All right, all done? Let's start! I have a gut feeling that we're finally getting somewhere!'

Ollie is still flicking through the papers. 'Ehm, there is an addendum to the will, sir.' He interrupts quickly before everyone can disappear. 'In fact, there are two.'

'Not more surprises I hope?'

'You could say that, sir. The first addendum says that none of the beneficiaries is to know about the others.'

'I suspect that isn't really so extraordinary, given the fact that families sometimes fall out over a few pounds.'

'I'm just saying, sir.' Ollie clears his throat. 'The other addendum is about Caleb Boyd, sir. There is a trust held in his name to provide for housing and care, if necessary, for the rest of his life. He has ...'

'Caleb Boyd? Is that Lester Boyd's son?'

There is a brief moment of silence. 'Caleb Boyd is also Iris Spencer's son, sir.' Ollie looks round as though he's expecting applause, but all he gets is perplexed silence.

31

At the front desk in the entrance hall, Anita Barron is slumped over a copy of that day's *The Cornish Gazette* with a yellow pencil that has teeth marks on the end, tapping on a half-completed crossword with one fingertip. She looks up as Penrose approaches and grabs the edge of the reception desk.

'Have you heard from Tregunna?'

A Blank look. Then, frowning, 'Wait.'

Anita pulls out a notebook from under the newspaper and flicks through it, licking her thumb before she turns a page.

'I don't think …'

'Here.' Anita Barron nods at a hastily scribbled note. 'Thing is, I've just been called in for duty. Matt's supposed to be on duty today, but he has an emergency dental appointment.'

Penrose stifles a yawn, trying not to get annoyed. Tregunna is quite friendly with Anita Barron but she can't understand what the attraction is. She can't think of any other two people that have less in common than Barron and Tregunna.

'So you don't know where Tregunna is,' she concludes, tight-lipped.

'That's what I'm saying. Matt had a call earlier. For Tregunna. As soon as he came in, Matt gave him the message and he stomped off again immediately.'

Penrose frowns. 'What was the message? From whom?'

'Matt just told me to let DI Maloney know that Tregunna won't be back until the end of the day.'

'So you don't know where he is?'

'No.' Anita Barron closes the notebook and, for an instant, stares at the crossword. 'I was going to ask you the same question. I assumed you'd know.'

Penrose shrugs, not bothering to give the obvious reply.

'All I know is that Matt said that he hoped Tregunna wouldn't get caught in traffic.'

'Traffic?' Penrose asks. Puzzled.

'It was on the radio. A collision with several casualties on the M5.'

'M5?'

'Near Exeter. I'm not sure, but I think Matt was referring to that accident. Ehm … have you tried his mobile?'

'What a good idea,' Penrose replies sarcastically, quickly making her way out before she makes an offending comment. Walking to her car, she digs out her mobile and fiddles with the buttons while opening her car with the remote car key. Brilliant. How can she seriously think that she can unravel a murder when she can't even establish the whereabouts of her colleague?

A dark grey cloud is rolling in from the Atlantic which seems to pause above Newquay, discharging the bulk of its contents. She's adjusting her seat belt when the first hailstones batter the windscreen. Champion and Ollie Reed are running for their car, laughing, shaking the little white ice particles from their hair. For a moment, Penrose is distracted. She can't see why people laugh when they're caught in a hail shower, or any heavy shower, but she envies their companionship. The two have been paired up by Maloney to talk to Hugh Kelly and Nigel Sparks again, and ask them some more questions since they now know the contents of Iris Spencer's will. Penrose and Tregunna have initially been assigned to talk to Lester Boyd about the same subject. As Tregunna didn't show up at the morning briefing, Maloney is sending her on her own. She wishes Tregunna is coming with her. He is much better with people than she is. He can read between the lines, he can read body language. He listens to what people say but he also hears what's not being said. Lips sucked tight, she turns the key and the engine comes to life, sending a blast of cold air in her face. Ollie and Champion drive past her, the latter offering a small wave to accompany a smile.

Ignoring the wave, Penrose tries to concentrate. On her meeting with Lester Boyd and on the road. Rush hour is in full swing, the situation worsened by a heavy yellow lorry belatedly spreading a layer of rock salt on the roads. By the time Penrose turns onto the A30, the sun has broken through the dark sky and the road is dry.

The drive in front of Lester Boyd's home is empty. There are a few patches of oil mark where Caleb Boyd's scooter is usually parked. Cursing inwardly that she didn't check if Lester Boyd would be home before she drove up to Bodmin to see him, Penrose parks her car on the road, between Boyd's drive and the equally vacant one of his neighbours.

Debating what to do, she picks up her phone and checks her messages. Nothing from Tregunna. She ignores the other messages and stares out of the window. She is angry with herself because she has a sense of loneliness and vulnerability being without Tregunna. He always seems to know what to say, how to put the right tone in his voice. He is so quiet and patient. Thoughtful. Understanding. People rarely get angry with him. And they tell him things, she's sure, they would never tell her.

A knock on the window on the passenger side startles her. A long face with grey hair in a bob and a cheerful smile. 'Can I help you?'

Reluctantly, Penrose presses a button and lowers the window three inches. Cold and damp air comes in through the narrow opening.

'I'm waiting for Mr Boyd.'

The woman nods. She's in her late sixties with rosy cheeks and painted eyebrows the colour of charcoal. A drop of a misty substance hangs on the tip of her long nose.

'You're the police?'

'Detective Constable Penrose.' She can't help it that it sounds a bit pompous.

'You may as well come through.' Excitement grows in the woman's pale grey eyes. 'Lester will be here in about twenty minutes, I guess. No point waiting in the cold, is there?'

Penrose climbs out, checking her mobile before she puts it in her coat pocket. 'And you are?'

'I'm sorry. I'm Hazel Knowles. Rachel's mother.' She points across the garden at the front of the house. 'Rachel called me to ask if I can come in today as Lydia isn't feeling very well. She didn't go to school this morning.'

Penrose suppresses an uneasy giggle. Rachel, Hazel. Lydia. It feels like she has arrived at the wrong address. Perhaps this is how her father feels when he's forgotten who and where he is.

'Lydia?'

'My granddaughter.' The woman hesitates, fumbling in the pocket of her long aubergine winter coat and retrieving a key on a plastic keyring with a picture of a horse. Sensing Penrose's confusion, she explains, 'Lydia is Lester's and my daughter Rachel's second daughter.'

She opens the front door and shrugs off her coat, shouting from the bottom of the stairs, 'Lydia! Nan's here! Would you like a cup of tea?'

No answer.

Hazel Knowles takes off her short boots and slips her feet in a pair of purple fluffy slippers which she retrieves from her bag. 'I'd best put the kettle on and check on her.'

Shaking her head absent-mindedly, she seems to have forgotten Penrose's existence.

Penrose follows her into the pristine kitchen. The only item that seems out of place is a lunch box. Pink plastic with a scattering of cartoon stickers.

'Lydia's lunch,' Hazel Knowles mutters. 'Rachel always makes sure they take a proper lunchbox to school.' She shrugs as though she's still not convinced whether she agrees with her daughter's opinion or not. 'Rachel isn't a fan of the school meals.'

Penrose nods with a pang of guilt. Her own mother used similar words, she recalls. She too had a packed lunch most days, but she used to empty the healthy contents of the lunchbox into the nearest bin, in favour, when possible, of fish and chips offered by the school kitchen.

'Do sit down, officer, please. I'll nip upstairs to check on Lydia and then I'll make you a nice cup of tea. Lester will be here shortly.'

She's back within a minute. 'Poor girl's asleep.'

She opens cupboards and drawers, knowing exactly where to find everything.

'I suppose this is about Iris?' she asks in a matter-of-fact voice, but she's unable to hide the curiosity and excitement from her eyes.

'Yes.'

'Nasty business.'

'I'm afraid I can't talk about our investigation,' Penrose says, but the other woman doesn't seem to be listening.

'Poor woman. Murdered like that.'

Penrose swallows. 'Did you know Iris Spencer, Mrs Knowles?'

'Never met her. Lester was already divorced when he met Rachel.'

'Didn't Iris come here, every now and then?'

'Not that I know.'

'And Caleb?'

'Caleb? What about him?' A frown. Genuine surprise. Then, seeing Penrose's expression, she looks at the door, closes it softly and says in a lowered voice, 'I suppose you know that Caleb isn't my daughter's son? Biologically?'

'Yes, we are aware of that.'

She nods as if she's satisfied. 'I don't think Lester saw much of his ex-wife. They had nothing in common.'

'How was the relationship between Rachel and Iris? And with Caleb?'

'Relationship? Non-existent, I'd say.'

She busies herself with the kettle and tea bags. Finds mugs. Spoons. Milk. Penrose thinks it would drive her mad to have to open so many doors and drawers just to make a simple cup of tea.

'It wasn't like Rachel was involved in their divorce, you know. My Rachel would never do that. Get a man to cheat on his wife, I mean.'

'Of course not.'

'He never talks about it, but I think that Lester must have had a difficult marriage,' Hazel Knowles continues, frowning disapprovingly. 'Naturally I don't know the ins and outs, but I gather she was a difficult woman. Iris was. Very demanding. Lester is a soft and gentle man. I'd say he didn't have a chance against that woman.' She shakes her head vigorously. 'I don't think it was so long ago that Lester had a falling out with her.

Something to do with the boy, I presume. He's always been …'

An angry voice interrupts. 'What are you doing here?' The door opens and Lester Boyd appears on the doorstep, a shopping bag in both hands.

'Police officer Penrose is here to see you, Lester, she's …'

'I mean you.'

The tone is full of contempt. Penrose almost feels sympathy for the other woman.

'Rachel asked me to come and look after Lydia.'

'I'm quite capable of looking after my own daughter, Hazel, thank you very much,' he replies crisply, putting the shopping bags on the floor.

'Let me get that.' Apparently oblivious to his mood, she's on her feet already, reaching for the nearest shopping bag.

'No Hazel, I'll do that. I don't want Caleb to get upset when things aren't in the right place.'

'You are too soft on that boy, Lester,' she scoffs disapprovingly. 'Isn't it about time that he grew up? The way you treat him, he'll never be an independent adult.'

'Caleb is our son, Hazel, and Rachel and I are raising him in the best way we can.'

'Our son? Is that how Rachel sees it too? If it wasn't for the money …'

'That's enough!' Lester's face is red with anger, his fists clenching beside his body. 'Ms Penrose, I'm sorry about this. I think it'll be best if we have this conversation in my greenhouse.'

He glares angrily at his mother-in-law. 'It may be a little cold in the greenhouse, but at least we'll have privacy.'

Saying it is a bit cold in the greenhouse, is the understatement of the year. There are empty flowerpots with water frozen in the bottom. An icy wind rustles through openings in the glass window panes. There is a smell of rot and decay. Lester Boyd frowns and stares at an old bathtub outside. It is covered with weathered wooden planks, a collection of terra cotta flowerpots upside down on them.

Penrose follows his gaze.

'I must check the water butts,' he mumbles.

'I'm sorry?'

'The water butts.' He gestures with his thumb in the opposite direction. 'I collect rainwater. I must check that it isn't frozen.'

'Oh.'

'I'm sorry about my mother-in-law,' he continues apologetically, automatically unzipping his jacket and wiping clean hands down the sides. 'Give her a finger and she doesn't only take your hand, but your whole arm.'

'Let's make this quick, Mr Boyd.' Penrose pulls up her collar and wishes she'd taken her gloves and hat with her. Her warm, fur-lined boots. 'Did you know that Iris had made her will?'

He shrugs. 'She told me a while ago that she'd make sure that this house would be mine entirely and that I needn't worry about the future. I never thought much about it. I'd never expected her to pass away … so young.' He rubs the back of his hand fiercely across his face and in the gleam of light that filters through the dusty window panes, Penrose sees that his eyes are bright with tears. 'She was only forty-four.' Warily shaking his head, he picks up a pot with what looks suspiciously like a dead geranium. 'When Iris and I got married, we bought a house in St Austell but then we divorced and … well, neither of us wanted to stay there. So the house was sold and I found this. I couldn't afford the mortgage and she offered to help me financially.'

'That was very generous.' She can't stop a tone of cynicism creeping into her voice.

'It was.' He half-laughs to cover his embarrassment. 'She said I didn't even have to pay her back. She was alright about it as long as I paid my share and looked after the house. Of course …' He doesn't finish his sentence. Instead he says, 'She's always been good to me.'

Penrose arches an eyebrow and cocks her head to one side. There is something about him that makes her feel like she's missed a part of the conversation.

She takes a deep breath. 'She also mentioned your son Caleb in her will.'

He picks up a small shovel, inspects the handle and turns to lay it on the bench behind him, eyes cast down uncomfortably. 'What about it?'

'You never told us that Caleb is Iris's son.'

'You didn't ask.'

'You didn't think it might be relevant?'

'In connection with her death? Why would it? As far as me and my wife are concerned, he has always been our son. She … Iris never wanted him. She always said that she was forced to have him.'

'A nasty thing to say about your own flesh and blood, isn't it?'

'That's why we never talk about it. We've never told Caleb, because we didn't want him to know that his own mother didn't want him.'

Penrose frowns. 'Caleb doesn't know?'

'No. You've met him, haven't you? We always said that we would tell him when he'd grown up but, as the years went by, we realised he wouldn't be able to deal with it.'

'You've just said that Iris was forced to have him. What did you mean by that?'

'She'd always made it clear that she didn't want children. She didn't like them. She preferred to have a career. She didn't want to get stuck at home looking after a family. But your question about being forced ... to be honest, I have always wondered about why she said that. She could have had an abortion but, for some reason, she didn't. Now ... I've always been grateful that she didn't have an abortion and that we have him. I still am. I love him to bits.'

'And Rachel? Your wife?'

'Caleb was still a baby, not even a year old, when Iris and I divorced and I met Rachel. There had never been a doubt in her mind that we would give the boy a good life, even when we found out that he has Asperger's Syndrome. We love him as much as we love our two other children.'

'Iris clearly didn't forget him in her will.'

'Perhaps she felt guilty after all,' he says bitterly. 'It was easy for her to give her money away. She had plenty. She made four pounds out of each one she invested. Once you have money, Inspector, it becomes easier to get more. And Iris clearly knew how to do that.'

'You didn't tell us that you're getting a monthly allowance from Iris either.'

He shrugs. 'So what?'

'What is the money for, Mr Boyd?'

'To Iris, everything is about money. Money, money and more money,' he says rancorously. 'She also believes ... believed that everything can be bought. She paid me ... us ... for caring for Caleb.'

'But ...'

'Perhaps her real reason was a selfish one. If anyone ever found out that she had a son, she could always claim that she didn't abandon him.'

32

Penrose thinks it's a long shot and Maloney says it's a waste of time. They are probably both right. The team is building up files on all the beneficiaries of Iris Spencer's will. Everyone is hopeful that we will discover that one of these beneficiaries is behind the killing. I am too restless to spend the rest of the day behind the desk, sifting through the various statements and entering the details on the computer system. I volunteer to drive to Clevedon, in Somerset, where Anna Bingwell lives in Horizon View, a private care home.

It is early afternoon when I drive through the town and along the seafront, keeping one eye on my phone for directions. The wind has blown the rain away and is gathering in strength, bringing milder air. Over the sea, I can see the rain is still falling; above the land, the sky is slowly turning into a pale watery blue.

As the name suggests, Horizon View is located on one of the roads that zigzag along the coastline, offering a view over the Bristol Channel. It is a granite building surrounded by a gravelled car park and neatly maintained grounds. Trimmed bushes. Waste bins with dog poo bag dispensers beside the bright turquoise painted benches.

Two men are working in the garden, collecting dead leaves from the grass and dumping them into a wheelbarrow; half of them are blown away by the wind, but neither of the men seems to be bothered.

I get out of my car and as I walk to the front door, one of the men calls out to me. 'What are you doing here?'

Slightly taken aback, I smile politely and continue to the building.

'Who are you? What is your name?'

He follows me, stretching out a grubby hand in a vast attempt to stop me.

'What is your name?' Saliva drips from the left corner of his mouth. His lips tremble.

I stop. 'I'm Andy. And you are?'

He shakes his head as if my question is out of order, repeating, 'What are you doing here?'

'I'm visiting someone,' I say coolly.

'Are you visiting me?'

'I don't think so. Are you Anna?'

'No. I'm eh ... 'Leaning heavily on a spade, his gaze drifts off. He's searching his memory for something that has suddenly escaped him. A long minute passes before he finds an answer. 'I'm Oscar. What are you doing here?'

'I'm here to see Anna.'

'Anna? I don't know Anna.' He scratches his head with an expression of concern. Specks of dandruff flutter down. 'What's your name?'

'Andy.'

He stretches out his hand, dried mud on his fingers. He gives me a firm handshake. 'Hi Andy, I'm Oscar.' Rheumy grey eyes blink rapidly within a web of deep wrinkles that radiate outwards. He looks like he's laughed a lot through his life, but the blank stare that clouds his eyes now indicates that he's lost his sense of humour.

The other man comes forward, gently putting a hand on Oscar's shoulder. 'Come on, Bill, shall we leave this gentleman? We have work to do.'

Oscar, or Bill, nods earnestly, pointing at me. 'He's come

to visit.'

'Yes, Bill, but he's not here for you. Shall we go to the pond and see if the carps are still there? See if the heron has been at it again?'

He gives me an apologetic smile and they walk back to the wheelbarrow, where they continue scooping up the leaves. The carp in the pond are forgotten.

The glass front door is locked. I press the doorbell and say my name into the intercom system, explaining why I'm here. The door buzzes open and I am stopped by a friendly smiling receptionist behind a desk that has a big flower arrangement on it and a selection of perspex stands that advertise the cafe, an agenda for in-house craft courses and the opening times of the hair and beauty salon.

'Who are you visiting, sir?' In her late twenties, she has a pleasant open face and blue-grey honest eyes. Her forehead is hidden behind a long thick blonde fringe, a plaited ponytail swings on her shoulder.

'Mrs Anna Bingwell.'

She gives me a sheet on a clipboard; a ballpoint pen is attached to it with a red string. 'Will you please complete the form, sir? Your name, the resident you are visiting and the date and time of your arrival, please.' She meets my gaze. 'Security, I'm afraid. If, for some reason, the building has to be vacated and the residents evacuated, we need to know exactly who is in the building and who isn't.'

'Does Mrs Bingwell receive many visitors?' I ask casually.

'In general, we don't see as many visitors as we would like, sadly.'

I stare at the sheet. I'm today's fifth visitor. One of them hasn't signed out yet: J. J. Morris is still here. 'Do you keep these sheets?'

'We do.' Caution and curiosity.

'Can I see the pages for the last few weeks?'

She frowns. 'It is against our privacy rules to ...'

'Sorry. I'm a police officer.' I show her my ID card. The friendly smile is replaced by pursed lips. She feels misled. 'I don't know. I'll have to ask my boss.' She consults her wristwatch. 'She's out at the moment. She'll be back in an hour.'

'I'll see Mrs Bingwell first then.'

She nods, half-satisfied. Then she puts on her polite smile again and explains the simple rules for visitors. Every ward is locked and, at each entrance, I need to ring the bell and wait for a member of staff to open the door for me. Staff will also let me out, after which I'll have to come back to the reception desk to sign out. I'm not to take any of the residents out, not even for a walk around the building, unless I have written permission to do so, ideally applied for a few days in advance.

I tell her I have no intention of taking Mrs Bingwell out and she gestures towards the lift, adding, 'Stairs are at the end of the hall, but the lift is easier.'

Anna Bingwell lives on the second floor of the Marigold Ward with nine other residents. Some of them don't leave their rooms any more. Bedridden. On the brink of life and death. It makes me think of Becca, again, only the average age here is probably between eighty and ninety. Becca is only 23 years old.

The security door is opened by a young man with a broad face and a red beard. He introduces himself as Jakob. I ask him to take me to Mrs Bingwell and he frowns, but he says nothing, only nods.

I follow Jakob along a narrow corridor with strip lights on the ceiling. The walls are painted a sunny pale yellow and the blue Lino floor is speckled with yellow and white dots. We pass the closed doors of the residents' rooms. Photos of faces and first names are framed beside the doors. Robert. Betty. Eleanor. Bill. One of the doors is open. I look inside and see the end of a hospital bed with a pair of feet sticking up under a checked red blanket, not moving. Opposite is an antique chest of drawers with a clutter of framed photographs. A flat-screen TV is attached to the wall above it.

We come to a central area. There is an open kitchen with an oval-shaped counter opposite the dining area. The sitting room across the corridor has a fake fireplace and pink lampshades on brass poles. Comfortable recliner chairs and sofas are arranged in a semi-circle in front of a large TV screen that is showing Harry Potter as a young boy, probably the first film in the series. The only woman watching it sits bent forward, rocking slightly, her head repeatedly bumping onto the metal handrail of a Zimmer frame in front of her. She's either asleep or enjoying the sounds of the TV with closed eyes.

In a few words, I tell Jakob the reason for my visit. 'Her daughter died? Oh, how sad for Anna.' He says nothing about Iris. I ask if Iris is a regular visitor, but he either ignores the question or he hasn't heard me.

He asks me to take a seat while he gets Mrs Bingwell from her room. I want to say he needn't bother, but he's gone before I open my mouth.

I sit down and wait. The woman rocking on her frame doesn't seem to notice me. Or anything else, for that matter. Harry Potter's adventures come to a happy end. The woman isn't interested in the names as the closing titles appear. She's just enjoying the music.

Another woman emerges, pushing a blue trolley, a handbag in the basket. She has draped a green feather scarf around her neck. Bare feet in slippers with bulldog faces on the toes. Not paying attention to me or to the other woman, she sits down, rummages in the handbag and finds what she's looking for. Carelessly, she tears open a bag. Crisps are scattered around her feet as though she's feeding ducks in a park.

In the kitchen area are two care workers. Chatting, having a cup of tea, sharing a packet of biscuits. One of the male residents shuffles past me, looking at me suspiciously, before he disappears in the room next to Anna's.

I sigh, trying not to think too much. Although Horizon View looks like a friendly, well-managed care home, I find the state of the residents depressing. I can only hope I won't live long enough to end up in a place like this.

The endless list of people who worked on the Harry Potter film has come to an end. One of the female carers appears. She finds the remote control in the basket of the blue trolley and switches channels until she finds something that is arguably suitable for someone who seems to be asleep or audibly munching crisps and staring at the ceiling. An episode of a soap series about people who have moved to Spain and now seem to spend their life in the bar or swimming pool, gossiping about each other. Nobody seems interested in how the lives of these ex-pats have been reduced to menacing whispers and doubtful looks.

It feels as if life has paused here.

Jakob returns, walking slowly to adjust his pace to that of a tall, skinny elderly woman. Her head is held up with a mixture of arrogance and defiance. It dawns on me that this is how Iris Spencer would have looked had she been allowed to live to her late eighties.

'I've told Anna that her daughter has died, but you will probably need to tell her again. She forgets.' Jakob helps her to take a seat beside me, then introduces me.

'Anna, this is Mr Tregunna, he has come to talk to you.'

She clasps her hands together, a big smile on her face. 'Oh! How nice! Have you come all the way to see me?'

'I have.'

'Where from?'

'Cornwall.'

'Oh! That is a long way, isn't it?'

'Yes. Mrs Bingwell, Anna, I would like to …'

'What's your name?'

'Andy.'

'And you have come to see me? How nice! Where have you come from?'

It seems an endless circle. She is happy enough and laughs and giggles, but she keeps repeating the same questions. After a while, Jakob sits down next to her, taking her hand in his, stroking the weak trembling fingers. He doesn't know Iris Spencer very well, it appears. Although she visits her mother every week, they meet in Anna's room and Iris never stays long. She collects her mother's mail, Jakob tells me, although they have offered to send it through to her address, but she's ignored the offer.

'Mail?'

He nods seriously. 'Documents. Bank statements. Letters.'

'When was the last time Anna's daughter was here?'

'She comes every Thursday. Last Thursday, I presume. I was off last week.' There is question in his voice, which I choose to ignore.

'Has there been any mail since?' It seems odd that an old woman who is being looked after so well in this care home receives so much mail.

He hesitates. 'I can check, but I'm not sure if I can give it to you.'

'I understand.' I look at Mrs Bingwell. She looks like she's just performed an act on stage and is listening to the applause, a big smile on her face and her eyes sparkling, but the deeper expression in them is gone.

Jakob seems to feel sorry for me that I have come a long way to speak to a woman who is unresponsive. He invites me to share their lunch, which is prepared in the kitchen by carers with the assistance of the odd available resident. When I ask about her daughter, Anna Bingwell keeps replying that she hasn't got any children. She isn't even married. Giggles and winks at Jacob and the only male resident I have seen so far. Jakob laughs and the man just stares into the distance. Anna Bingwell insists on sitting next to me, behaving like I'm her long lost relative and lovingly pushing extra carrots and broccoli onto my plate. To my other side is the woman with the Zimmer frame, Elizabeth, dozing over her plate. Every so often another woman, called Bertha, pokes her in the side and she wakes just long enough to take the odd bite before falling asleep again. The pudding, a trifle, is surprisingly good, it reminds me vaguely of how my grandmother used to make it. They're all enjoying it. Even Elizabeth wakes up long enough to eat her portion and make sure none of the others snatch it away from her.

The whole event is rather moving and it makes me look at residents and carers in a completely different way.

The receptionist gets up as soon I emerge from the lift. Her eyes are staring cautiously at me from under the long fringe. 'I can't give you the details of our visitors,' she starts almost offensively. 'I will need the permission of the family. In this case, Mrs Bingwell's daughter.'

'I have just informed Mrs Bingwell that her daughter died last week.'

She lowers herself to her seat. Startled. Shocked. 'Oh! She

seemed in good health when she was here last time.'

'When was that?'

'That must have been last Thursday. I remember she was saying something about taking her mother into town in a few weeks' time. She said she would make a formal request to take her out.'

'Did she often do that?'

'Mrs Spencer? I don't know. Jakob was saying Mrs Bingwell was delighted because she kept saying she was going on holiday, but it would be only for a few hours. Maybe only for lunch or a walk in the park.' She pauses. 'What happened?'

'I can't reveal many details, I'm afraid. But we are treating her death as suspicious. I was hoping her mother would be able to help clarify some issues we've come across, but ....' I stop with a vague gesture.

She nods seriously. 'That is the problem. We communicate with our residents on a day-to-day basis. Food, weather, TV, that sort of thing. But the families usually find it hard to deal with their loved ones and don't talk to them much.'

'It would be very helpful if I could find out if there were any other visitors recently. Other than her daughter,' I say gently.

The situation has changed. She has to think about it. No mention now that she needs someone's permission. Making up her mind, she nods and turns to open a small filing cabinet. The shelves are lined with marbled grey lever-arch files.

'We keep the daily sheets of all our visitors here,' she explains. 'Each month they are digitised and every fact will be noted in our resident's personal files.'

'I would be grateful if I could have a look?'

'I'll have to write it down for you. There are also details of the other residents.' She sighs and shrugs. 'Rules. I'm sure you understand.'

'Of course. I'm only interested in Mrs Bingwell's visitors.'

'The daughter seems to have been a public figure,' she remembers, her tone slightly dismissive. 'She was always talking about important meetings.'

She opens a file and finds a page. 'Here is one. Iris Spencer. She was here every Thursday.'

'What about other visitors?'

'I don't think Mrs Bingwell ever had other visitors. Mrs Spencer was her only child.' She checks the page again. 'How did she die?'

'She was murdered.'

'Oh!' She turns a page, frowns, turns it back again. Frowns deeper. 'Yes. She had a visitor two weeks ago.'

'When? Which date?'

'I remember it now.' Excitement is gleaming in her eyes. 'Two weeks ago. On a Friday. She was rather disappointed about Mrs Bingwell's condition. I suppose that was why she stayed for only ten minutes.'

'She? A woman?'

She checks the list again. 'Yes, a woman. Here it is. Penhallow. No initials. I was sorry for her. She said she had come a long way to see Mrs Bingwell. I gathered she meant abroad. I said she'd just missed Mrs Bingwell's daughter, who had been here the previous day.'

I look around the entrance hall. There are cameras in almost every corner.

'Do you have CCTV here?'

She smiles as if she's dealing with a young child. 'Of course we do. We lock the wards here, but our residents can be very inventive finding ways to sneak out. We have a security system in place 24/7.'

'How long are the images kept?'

She grins conspiratorially. 'I suppose you would like to see them?'

Three hours later I drive out of Clevedon. Dusk is setting in early, and with it arrives a gloomy, fine mizzle. Beside me on the passenger seat is a blurred picture of a woman's face with short dark hair. The photograph is from the moment she looked up at the camera and she's staring straight into my face. It feels like I've seen her before.

33

Although they have picked up some fresh leads to carry on with the investigation, the afternoon briefing seems to have a sombre atmosphere to it. Everyone is slumped in their chairs, talking about the latest fashion, about football matches and plans for the weekend; anything else but the investigation.

'All right, boys and girls!' Maloney slams his hand down on the table.

Someone bravely mutters an objection: whether serious or not, it is probably a reference to the new legislation that we're not allowed to differentiate gender anymore. My neighbour Mr Curtis has an outspoken opinion about this issue. He blames do-gooders with no sense of reality, he blames politicians who try to court voters, he blames the general public for voting for a man who has a beard and dresses like a woman to win the Eurovision Song contest. He says that we aren't ladies and gentlemen, or boys and girls anymore: we are now persons, individuals, human beings. When and why has a 'black woman' suddenly become a 'coloured person'? Why are black people called coloured and white people aren't? If black is a colour, then white should be too.

'Let's get started, shall we?'

Maloney looks like he spent the day asleep behind his desk. His suit is creased. There is curry stain on his tie. Eyebrows furrowed sombrely, he takes us through the list of suspects, alibis and motives. Alibis have to be checked and re-checked. Suspects are to be interviewed, and, in most cases, interviewed again.

Iris's solicitor has reluctantly supplied names and addresses of the beneficiaries in Iris's will, which doesn't appear to be helpful in all cases. For instance, according to the solicitor, Iris Spencer's mother Anna Bingwell is still living at her former address in Crantock.

'Questions?' Maloney stretches his lips over his front teeth and looks at the assembled officers, daring someone to say something.

No questions.

A rumble of low voices. Chairs scrape on the floor. Papers are picked up, footsteps and voices disappear.

Returning to my desk, Penrose is already on the phone, trying to locate Bryan Connolly. He is in Iris Spencer's will as the beneficiary of shares in a company called Coniris. As soon as the call comes through, she puts it on speaker. A clipped female voice is telling us that Mr Connolly is on a business trip to China. He has been away for the past three weeks. He's due back in twelve days. If required, she can give us a full list of his whereabouts. Clients. Hotels. Dates. Penrose duly gives the woman our email address, miming to me that it'll be a waste of time.

'As his secretary, do you know how Mr Connolly knew Mrs Iris Spencer?' she asks.

'Ah. Tragic. Very tragic.' A brief silence. 'Well, I suppose it's isn't a secret. Mr Connolly knew her quite well. They had several mutual business interests. They used to work together.'

'What does Mr Connolly's company do?'

'We supply to construction companies. Building materials, in general, but we're now specialising in sustainable materials. His trip to the Far East is mainly to find suppliers for a new type of solar panel. Lighter and cheaper.'

'How was Mrs Spencer involved in Mr Connolly's business?'

'Coniris. They started the company together. Iris was still a member of the board of Coniris.' She hesitates. 'I'm sure Mr Connolly can tell you more about that. Would you like me to ask him to call you? Looking at his diary, he is currently travelling between places, but I'm sure he'll be able to find a quiet moment for you.'

Thanking her politely, Penrose finishes the conversation.

'That's a dead end,' she says grumpily.

'Who's next?' I say optimistically.

'Ashton.'

'Right. Ashton. First name? Initials? Gender?'

'We only have Ashton.'

Ashton's address is in London. When Penrose finally gets through to someone, we're kindly informed that it's just a mailing address. They don't know Mr or Mrs Ashton personally, but they can tell us that their mail is forwarded each month to an address in Sydney, Australia. The voice reads out an Australian phone number as if he thinks we're suffering with dyscalculia.

I press buttons. Wait. The phone rings eight times and is answered by a sleepy voice. 'Hello?'

'I would like to talk to Mr or Ms Ashton if that's possible.'

'Who?'

'Mr or Mrs Ashton. My name is ...'

'Do you know what time it is?'

'Ehm...'

He answers his own question. 'It's nearly three o'clock. At night.'

'I'm sorry. We're calling from the UK. I didn't realise...'

'Okay. I understand.' The man seems to be recovering quickly. 'No worries. What can I do for you?'

I introduce myself, not yet disclosing the reason why Ashton is a person of interest.

'Mrs Ashton? You'll need to speak to Mr Andrew Dunne. I'm Liam, his son. We're solicitors. My father is dealing with the Clarke estate.'

'The Clarke estate?'

'Isn't that why you're calling?' He lets out a long sigh. 'Okay, since I'm awake anyway, I might as well help you. Just bear with me a sec. I'm not going to wake my father. If you prefer to speak to him, you'll have to wait. But for now, I can check his files.'

'Mr Dunne, I'm not sure …'

He's gone. I hear doors and drawers opening and closing. Papers are rustling. He hums. He's surprisingly cheerful for someone whose sleep has been interrupted.

'Right. Found it.' He's back. Slightly out of breath. 'Peter Clarke. Ehm, it's complicated, because he and his wife died in a road accident and it wasn't exactly clear who died first. Or last. Legally, if Peter died first, the estate would go to his wife, and after her death, to her daughter. If she had died first, everything would go to Peter, and after his death, to his relatives. In this case, to his only brother.'

Penrose taps my shoulder, pointing at her watch. Calls to the other side of the world aren't cheap.

'So who died first?' I ask.

'It was inconclusive.'

'Meaning?'

'I will spare you the details, Mr Tregunna, but the bottom line is that we've found their will. Mrs Ashton and Mr Clarke, Peter's brother, are both inheriting.'

'That's odd.'

'Is it? Well, clearly the pair made a will between them and I can assure you that they had it all done properly. We checked, there's nothing illegal about it.'

I clear my throat. 'I don't doubt your professionalism, Mr Dunne. I don't know anything about your case. The reason for our call is that we have come across the name of Ashton in relation to our current investigation. Did you say this Ashton is a woman?'

'Yes. Cecilia. Ehm, may I ask the nature of your investigation?'

'She appears to be one of the beneficiaries in the will of a murder victim.'

'A murder?'

'Mrs Ashton is mentioned in the will of someone called Mrs Iris Spencer. Do you happen to know the name?'

'Spencer? No, don't think so. Sorry.' Liam Dunne doesn't need time to think about it. 'I have a note here from my father about the young lady. She is currently travelling in the UK. Bear with me a sec and I'll give you her mobile number and the address of her relatives in your country. If that helps.'

A click and this time we are offered classical music. Soft and smooth. Penrose frowns in disapproval. She's of the opinion that it is never a good sign when you get music on the line: it usually means there will be a long delay.

A rather sombre sounding pianist is interrupted abruptly. Liam Dunne is back quicker than expected. I repeat what he says and Penrose writes down phone numbers and an address in Bournemouth.

'What else can you tell us about this Cecilia Ashton, Mr Dunne?'

'Nothing much, I'm afraid. As I said, my father is dealing with the case. I have met her, though. Only once. Beautiful woman. Very sad that her mother and stepfather died so soon after her husband.'

Liam Dunne ends the call with a cheerful 'goodnight-sleep-tight' and the promise that his father will call us to answer the questions he couldn't.

I put the phone down. Penrose clicks her tongue. 'I wonder if it is a coincidence that Mrs Ashton is involved in more inheritances than one.'

Imogen Gallagher is Cecilia Ashton's aunt. As soon as we ask for her, she bursts into tears. Her niece has been staying with her in Bournemouth since she arrived in the UK two or three weeks ago, but she's been traveling to the South West to meet other family and friends from her teenage years.

'Teenage years?'

'She was born in Cornwall. She grew up there until she and her mother moved to Australia.'

'We would like to talk to her, Mrs Gallagher.'

'Yes, well.' More tears. 'She told me she had booked a room in a hotel for a few days, but that she would be back this weekend. But I haven't seen her or heard from her since she left.' She pauses, searching for words. 'I'm getting concerned now. You are police, you said?'

'Yes, but we are only trying to locate her because she's mentioned in a will,' I reply diplomatically.

'A will?' A trace of excitement. 'Whose will? Oh I see, is this about her stepfather and her mother?'

'No, this is about something else.' I pause briefly. 'Mrs Gallagher, do you know Iris Spencer?'

'Iris Spencer?' A short silence. 'No, I don't think I've heard that name before.'

'Hugh Kelly?'

'I'm sorry.'

'Lester Boyd?'

'No, I … why are you asking me all these questions?'

'We are investigating a murder.'

'Oh! But you can't possibly think that my niece has something to do with … a murder?'

'I'm not saying she has, Mrs Gallagher. We would like to ask her a few questions in relation to our investigation. If she contacts you, could you ask her to call me?'

'I suppose.'

Penrose is pulling at my sleeve. Mouthing something inaudibly.

'Does your niece still have family or friends in Cornwall, Mrs Gallagher?'

'Oh yes, of course. That's where she went when she left here last week. My brother used to live in Cornwall when he and his wife were still living together. In Newquay.'

I see excitement appearing in Penrose's eyes.

'Do you have any names and addresses?'

'No, I haven't. If I had, I'd have called them already to find out where she is. She only mentioned a few first names. Amelia. Gabby. Zoe.' Another deep sigh. 'I can give you the address of her hotel, but they couldn't help me either when I called them. She said she was staying there for three nights and she'd be back here on Friday night.'

'Last Friday? And you haven't heard from her at all?'

'Well, I don't know her that well.' She sounds as if she's making an excuse for her niece's inconsiderate behaviour. 'I suppose she's been staying with a friend down there. I only wish she'd have called and told me.'

I promise to let her know as soon as we've found her niece and end the call.

'That places Cecilia Ashton in the area,' I say thoughtfully. 'But what is the connection? Could she be Iris Spencer's murderer?'

Penrose opens her mouth but when I think she might say something constructive, she closes her mouth and just shrugs. Distractedly, she glances at her watch.

'Time for a pint?' I joke. She isn't a pub goer. Neither am I.

'No, I have to go home.' Her shoulders hunch. The few euphoric moments from before, when she realised we've made a little bit of progress in the case, have gone completely.

'What's wrong, Jennette?'

She shrugs, eyes down. I know she feels responsible for her father's condition. Ashamed also. 'I've had a call from one of the neighbours. My father had turned off all the heaters at home.' She swallows. 'The sun was shining. He thought it was summer.'

'Is he all right now?'

'I hope so.' She stands in front of me, shoulders tight, hands balled into fists at her side. 'He's with a neighbour.'

'So he isn't sitting in the cold?'

'No.' She shakes her head violently. 'It is my fault! If I hadn't forgotten to switch on a plug in the corner behind a cabinet …'

'What plug? For the heating?'

'No! The cameras. If I hadn't forgotten to turn them on, I'd have been able to keep an eye on him and I'd have noticed …'

She stops abruptly. Her face turns red.

'You've lost me, Jennette. How can you keep an eye on your father when you're working?'

She looks down. Shrugs. Then the explanation comes as is often her way like an explosion. Loud and unstoppable. I listen as mixed feelings flash across her face. She feels guilty. Embarrassed. The bottom line is, I understand eventually, that she's installed webcams in their home and that, basically, she's spying on her own father. She shouldn't do it, she knows it is a breach of privacy, but it is for his own good.

I put my hand on her shoulder. 'Go home, Jennette. Make sure he's alright.'

She isn't finished. 'I'd have noticed that he was shivering. I'd have known he needed my help.'

'Stop torturing yourself with feelings of guilt. This isn't your fault.'

'But I ...'

'Go home, Jennette, for what it's worth, it is an order.' Gently I push her towards the doorway.

'But shouldn't we go to that hotel and talk to Cecilia Ashton?'

'Tomorrow. Besides, I have a meeting with someone else.'

She's in the doorway, tucking her handbag under her arm, checking her mobile phone. She turns with an expression I fail to read. 'A date?'

I shake my head. 'It's to do with the suicide in Hayle. Ed Lynham. It was on the same night that Iris was killed.'

'Any connection?'

'Not that I'm aware of, but we can't rule it out. They both had that letter.'

'Who are you going to see then?'

'A woman who claimed that Ed Lynham raped her.'

'But I can come ...'

'Go home, Jen.' I grin encouragingly. 'That's an order.'

34

Sylvia Grant is the woman who made a formal complaint against Edward Lynham for sexual assault. She has agreed to meet me, choosing the neutral environment of a supermarket cafe.

It is an echoing space with voices and laughter, clunks and clattering of plates and cutlery and music that is too loud to call it background music. It is late afternoon and I can see from here that the supermarket is beginning to fill with customers rushing in all directions as if they have forgotten something or only come in for quick microwave meal.

A woman in her late forties is hovering around the newspaper rack. She's dressed in a dark grey coat, a knitted woollen hat and black leather boots and gloves, clutching a tatty brown handbag as if it holds all her valuables. A young woman appears with two shopping bags, handing one to the woman. The automatic doors swoosh open and they hurry out into the cold.

'Ahum.'

I turn to find a woman in her twenties looking at me suspiciously. 'Andy?'

'That's right.'

Sylvia Grant smells of tobacco and there is a trace of gin on her breath. Her eyes register me with a mixture of surprise and disappointment.

'Can I see your ID?' she asks rather aggressively.

'Of course.'

I show it to her, but she barely looks at it. 'I thought you would let me down.'

A rather odd thing to say when you are meeting a policeman at his request, not hers. She was, in fact, reluctant to meet me and only agreed if it was here, in a public place. She feels safe here.

Carefully, she chooses one of the easy-wipe tables in the middle of the cafe area, away from the entrance, the till and the windows. At the self-service counter, I order a black filter coffee and a small pot of tea with extra milk.

'What is it you want to talk about?' she asks, as soon as I put the tray on the table and sit opposite her on one of those hard plastic chairs that make everyone's bottom numb after two minutes.

'Ed Lynham.'

She almost jerks to her feet, her face red, and fury in her eyes. 'I don't ... you said ...'

'I said it was about a job.'

'You lied to me.' She hasn't made another movement to get up and leave.

'I wanted to talk to you about your job.'

'I'm not working at the moment.' Her voice is thick with anger, or perhaps it is suppressed tears. 'I'm between jobs.' She hesitates. Anger is quickly replaced by curiosity. 'I thought you might have a job for me. That's why I came. But as that's not the case ...' Gesturing vaguely, she now rises to her feet and starts gathering her hat and gloves from the seat beside her.

'Please drink your tea, Miss Grant. I am a policeman. You can trust me.'

'I can trust no man.'

I motion towards the other customers. 'I'm sure you're safe here. Nothing will happen to you.'

'What do you want?'

'To talk about the charity night.'

'What night?' she asks, but I see she knows perfectly well what I'm talking about. She sits back down, pours tea and adds milk, stirring in one spoon of sugar.

'Ed Lynham.'

Her shoulders drop. The hand holding the teaspoon trembles.

'What about him?'

'You used to work for him, didn't you, Sylvia?'

'For a while, yes. Not for him especially though. I was assisting the department's secretary. Monica.'

'How was your relationship with Monica?'

She shrugs. 'I suppose we got on reasonably well, but she was much older than me. Why do you ask?'

'And how did you get on with Ed Lynham?'

'Oh.' Her eyes narrow. 'That was different.'

'How was that different?'

'He's ... he was a man.'

'And Aubrey Sinclair?'

'I didn't like him.'

'Did you ever meet Ed Lynham after work?'

'He drove me home a few times. Mostly when something was going on and I had to work late.'

'Did it happen often?'

'Can't remember. A few times. Five times, maybe.'

'And it was always Ed who took you home?'

'It wasn't a detour for him. It would have been for Monica or Mr Sinclair.'

I retrieve my mobile and scroll through my notes. 'You live at Greenville Terrace?'

'Yes.'

'How was it convenient for Ed Lynham to take you home?

He would have to drive all the way around the town to get to your house.'

'It must have been when I was staying at my mum's.'

'Where does she live?'

'Amberley Court.'

'Did you invite him in?'

'Yes.'

'Was your mother present when you asked Ed Lynham in?'

'Ehm, no, I remember. Mum was on holiday and I had to look after the cats. She's got two.'

'So your mother wasn't there?'

'I suppose not, I'm not sure.'

'The first time you asked Ed to come into the house was because you were afraid there was someone in the house?'

'How do you know all this?' She pushes her half-full teacup away with a gesture of disgust. 'I will not answer your questions! What is it for anyway?'

'I told you, it is about Ed Lynham.'

'Has he assaulted more women? Like he did to me? Was that why he did it?'

'Did what?'

'Take his own life.'

'Miss Grant, you made a formal complaint against Ed Lynham. You said he had sexually assaulted you.'

'Yes.'

'When was that?'

'At that charity-do. It was in the papers.'

'What did he do to you?'

'He was all over me. I must admit that I had a bit of a crush on him in the beginning, but that was over once I realised what he was really like.'

'You fancied him?'

'For a short period, yes. I thought he was handsome and nice. And I'm not the only one. Even Monica Gibb wouldn't have minded spending a night with him.'

'Ed Lynham was happily married.'

She shrugs and says cynically, 'Men are never happily married, Mr Tregunna. If they say so, they're lying. I've seen what happens.'

I wait until her angry outburst subsides. I show her a copy of the letter with the newspaper cuttings stuck onto it that Ed Lynham had received.

'Did you send him this letter?'

She barely looks at it. 'No.'

'Please look at it carefully, Miss Grant.'

'I don't need to. I never sent him a letter.'

'You tried to blackmail him.'

She looks down. Stares. Reads. 'I've never seen that letter before.'

'Do you know Mrs Iris Spencer?'

'The woman who was murdered?'

'Did you know her?'

'No. I've seen her in newspapers and on local TV, but that's all.'

'You didn't send this letter to her?'

Confusion on her face. 'I thought you meant I'd sent it to Ed?'

I take the letter back and turn it face down. 'The charity night. How did you get in?'

'Get in where?'

'The charity night. It was for men only.'

'There were lots of other girls.'

'They were from an agency.'

'Yes, well, maybe I was working for them too.'

'No, Miss Grant, you were not on their list.'

'How do you know?'

'I have checked. In fact, I have seen several videos of that evening. Ed was there with three other men, talking. There wasn't a woman or a girl anywhere near them. Ed and one of his friends left at about ten.'

'I … I don't know what you are on about, Mr Tregunna.'

'Ed and his friend shared a taxi. You said he sexually harassed you in his car one hour later.'

'That was true. I went to the police. My clothes were ripped apart. Ask the police. They have photos of me.'

'I did ask the police, Miss Grant. And as I already told you, I am the police.'

'You checked up on me?'

'Why did you lie?'

'I didn't lie! He … he tried it on … he really did … but …'

'Wasn't it the other way round, Miss Grant? Wasn't it you who tried to seduce Ed Lynham?'

She's in tears, hiding her face behind tissues and paper napkins. 'Why doesn't anyone believe me?'

'Perhaps you didn't lie about being assaulted in the car park, but it definitely wasn't Ed Lynham.'

'He said he liked me! A lot!'

'He was a married man.'

'He said … I thought he would leave his wife!'

'For you?'

'Yes. Why not? Don't you believe me?'

'I think you believe your own story, Miss Grant, but that is not what happened.'

'But I … how do you know all this?'

'I have spoken to his friend and to the taxi company they used. They left the charity evening early because they didn't like the fact that there were escort girls. They shared a cab and drove to Ed's friends house, where they had a few drinks and played a computer game. Ed took a taxi home from there after midnight.'

'But I … I was assaulted! I went to the police! I told them it was Ed Lynham who did that to me.'

'Miss Grant, there is no point in lying.'

'What do you want from me?' Suddenly, she stretches her neck and sits straight up. Her smile lights up her face and she even looks quite pretty. 'Do you fancy me, Mr Tregunna?'

'That is not what we're here for, Miss Grant.'

She leans forward. 'I asked you several times, what do you want from me?'

'It's quite simple, actually, Miss Grant. I would like you to write a statement that you made a mistake when you told the police that you were assaulted by Ed Lynham. I want you to apologise in a letter to his wife, or rather to his widow.'

'And if I don't?'

'Then I'm afraid I will have to charge you for lying to the police, wasting police time and filing a false complaint, obstructing the course of justice.'

'You can't do that.'

I shrug and say coldly, 'Watch me.'

35

At night, problems always seem more complex and unsolvable. Penrose had been awake until the small hours, tossing and turning, until she finally decided that nothing could be resolved in the night anyway. Then she dreamt. About travellers with mobile homes and cars with big caravans invading their village, being directed by Nathan Cawley with a shotgun under his arm. In the field across the road, migrant workers were cutting cauliflowers and daffodils and talking to each other in languages nobody seems to understand. They are supervised by Boris Cawley, who is trying to push a wheelchair with Iris Spencer in it. She's clutching a bunch of red roses in her hand. At the church gates stands a lone figure, staring through frosted glasses, stretching his arms out in front of him like he's trying to find a door in a pitch black room. He looks like Nigel Sparks, but when Penrose comes closer, she recognises Caleb Boyd. Children are running around, yelling and jumping over hedges and gates. All of a sudden, Maloney is there at the heels of Guthrie who is dressed in camouflage shorts, holding a toy lion cub under one arm. He opens his mouth, calling for Tregunna, but nobody seems to know where he is.

She wakes with a start, her mouth dry, heart pounding in her chest. She opens her eyes, seeing darkness. The dream, still clear and close, is slowly ebbing away. She tries to remember it but knows it will be gone if she concentrates too hard.

Squeezing her eyes shut again, she tries to go back to the dream. Guthrie was about to say something important.

Something about his son. She opens her eyes again, blinking into the darkness. She doesn't think Guthrie has a son, but what does she know about him anyway? She shivers and pulls the duvet up to her chin, but she can't get warm anymore. Reaching for her mobile phone, she is almost relieved when it tells her that it is twenty past six.

The floor is cold under her bare feet. She pulls open one of the curtains and looks out of the window. A carpet of frost covers the world outside and a mist blurs the street lights. Somewhere in the distance, an orange street lamp blinks at regular intervals.

Quietly, she showers, hoping her father won't wake up yet. She pulls on her dark trousers and goes looking for a clean shirt. Finding none, she grunts, retrieving yesterday's shirt from the laundry basket. She closes the kitchen door behind her before turning on the tube light, and the kettle. She puts slices of bread in the toaster, cursing under her breath when she finds the jar of marmalade almost empty. She places her tea mug on the kitchen table and eats the remains of a box of cornflakes, adding a large spoonful of honey. The cornflakes are stale, the milk too cold.

She's almost starting to feel sorry for herself, when it suddenly dawns on her.

Not the dream. A memory. Words she had read. Re-read, yet they didn't sink in. A report. She grabs her head with both hands, willing her brain to remember.

Pushing her half-full tea mug and the barely touched bowl of cornflakes to the centre of the table, she gets up, taking deep breaths. Her phone almost slips from her hand as she punches in the numbers.

'Are you awake, Louisa?'

Penrose presses the phone to her face, speaking softly to the woman from across the road.

'I am always awake, Jen, you know that.' Louisa Blake lets out a low rumble that ends with a rasping cough that must hurt her lungs. 'What's up, Jen? Why are you up so early? Something wrong with your father?'

'No. It's work. I … ehm I need to go to the station, Louisa. Can you …?'

'Can I keep and eye on your father again? Of course I can, love. What are neighbours for? Turn on that system of yours and everything will be alright.' She chuckles ironically, coughing again. 'No worries, love, I'll be here all day.'

'You don't mind? So early?'

'Of course I don't mind, Jen, I can't sleep anyway. But that's what I'm here for, isn't it? It is the only way I can pay you back for everything you do for me, love. You and a lot of other people in our community.'

'Thanks a lot, Louisa. Dad's still asleep. He won't wake up until …'

'I'll look after him, love. You go to work.'

Penrose sighs, suppressing a pang of guilt. She hasn't lied exactly, she's only chosen her words carefully. There won't be anybody in her team at the station yet. She hasn't been called in for an emergency. She just wants to be there before the rest of the team. Something is niggling her. She needs to go through some statements and find what it is. Or hope she'll remember it soon.

Reassured by the calm competence of Mrs Blake, Penrose switches on a plug in the corner behind a kitchen cabinet. She can hear it ping when the system starts operating. She hasn't told anyone about this. Not even Tregunna until she had inadvertently mentioned it when she was feeling guilty about her father. Only Roger Bamfield knows. He helped her set up the system after her father got lost, emerging the following day in the centre of Plymouth, dishevelled, confused and disorientated and with his wallet missing. Three small webcams are now keeping an eye on him when she's away, that she switches on when she leaves. One in the kitchen, facing the hob and the back door, one in the living room, and one in the hallway covering the bottom of the staircase and the front door. She has access to the webcams from her phone and her computer at work. Sometimes she feels like she's spying on her own father, but she knows it is for his own good. In the future, his condition will probably get worse but it is okay for now and she has learned to take every day as it comes.

With a quick wave to Louisa and a thumbs-up in return to the other woman's nod, she digs her car keys out of her pocket and walks to her car, wiping a thin layer of frost off the windscreen with her elbow.

At this hour, the roads are deserted. No sign of tourists or coaches. Not even delivery vans. It is only when she drives past the airport that she notices some human activity. The lights on the landing strip at Newquay Airport are on, awaiting the arrival of the first plane of the day.

As she drives along the coast road, she feels her shoulders relax. In the east, a thin line of pale light appears above the hills. Below the cliffs, the beaches of Mawgan Porth, Watergate Bay and Porth are still in darkness. There are a few lights on the horizon. Ships on which there are always people on watch.

The police station is quiet. Matt Morrison, the duty officer, frowns as she comes in.

'You're early,' he says grumpily, as though she has just interrupted a stolen nap. Perhaps she had.

'But you aren't the first,' he continues triumphantly.

'Oh.' She nods briefly, not wanting to be drawn into a

conversation so early. The fact that she is awake, doesn't necessarily mean that she is up for an intelligent conversation.

'Tregunna is already in.'

'Is he?' She punches the code in and opens the door before the duty officer can say more. Maybe he'll think she's rude, but so be it.

Most of the offices are still locked up and in darkness. A cleaner moves though the corridor, emptying bins and wiping door handles with a yellow cloth, hands in yellow rubber gloves. Earplugs attached to thin wires that disappear inside his breast pocket.

Tregunna is sitting behind his desk with his legs stretched out in front of him, hands folded behind his neck, eyes closed. Penrose takes a moment to look at him: his lean shape in loose clothing. He's lost weight, she notices, he looks old. Silver specks in his dark hair and the lines around his mouth and eyes seem deeper. Briefly, she considers asking him about his appointment at the hospital, if he has had bad news. Perhaps his cancer has come back, perhaps the malignant cells have migrated somewhere else in his body.

Trying to dodge a wastepaper bin, she bangs her toes on the corner of a desk. Ouch.

He opens his eyes with a start.

'Sorry,' she blushes with embarrassment. 'I didn't mean to disturb you.'

The rich smell of strong coffee hangs in the air. His takeaway cup beside his keyboard is half-full, which means he's only just arrived.

'You are early too.'

He nods. 'I couldn't sleep.'

'Me neither.' She feels the rush of excitement again. Words she can't remember, but that seem to get more and more important in her mind. Important information that can, hopefully, turn the whole investigation around.

She takes a deep breath. Silly to feel so nervous, like a schoolgirl going in for an exam, afraid to disappoint the teacher who has made so much effort to help her. 'I have remembered something,' she starts. 'Sort of.'

He picks up his coffee and turns it round in his fingers, staring into it thoughtfully.

'I saw Sylvia Grant yesterday,' he says, appearing not to have heard her.

'Oh.' She sits down opposite him, wondering who Sylvia Grant is. Clearly, he's been on the war path again. Alone. On his own. Not telling anyone, not telling her.

'Then I saw Chaz Lynham again. You know. Ed Lynham's widow.'

Penrose nods, strangely relieved. The suicide. She didn't know he was still working on the case. She'd assumed the case was already closed.

'I told her about Sylvia Grant. Basically, it was the same old story. Ed had been friendly towards Sylvia when she worked in the office. A few smiles, a wink maybe, and she thought he was in love with her. She tried to let him know what she felt for him, but he seemed not to notice. Or, as she thought, he was trying to fight against his feelings for her. She knew he was married and she could understand his dilemma. There was a charity event. She thought it would be the first of many nights together. She sneaked in and tried to lure him to one of the hotel rooms. He rejected her. Hurt her feelings, and embarrassment and humiliation made way for hatred and revenge. She cried rape.'

'Classic story,' Penrose mutters absently. 'Did she have anything to do with his suicide?'

He nods gravely. 'We will never know what was on his mind

when he ended his own life, but the fact is that, because of the accusations, he was politely asked by his superior to leave his position.' He sighs. 'I think it's wrong that people like him, who are such easy prey, are accused before there is any proof. They can't even defend themselves.'

'No smoke without fire.'

'Yes, but sometimes, it isn't even obvious which fire the smoke is coming from.'

'And what happens now?'

'She has now withdrawn the rape charges against him. She has also written a letter to Aubrey Sinclair with an apology.'

'That's good.'

'Yes, but that doesn't bring him back.'

'No. Of course not.'

'Perhaps it had nothing to do with it,' Tregunna continues thoughtfully. 'Chaz told me that Ed had a little sister who drowned at the age of three. Although he wasn't even there, in his darker moods, Ed blamed himself for her death and he's made several suicide attempts before. Once when he was a teenager and then two years ago, when his father died. He was on medication for depression.'

Penrose frowns. 'I can't remember if there were traces of drugs found in his body.'

'He had stopped using them. Apparently, people like him can get into the situation where they think medication isn't good for them. They stop taking them, the depression comes back and … sometimes with disastrous results. Like in the case of Ed Lynham.'

'So this Sylvia, or his colleagues at his political party aren't to blame?'

'It triggered something, clearly, but Chaz has realised that he probably was a walking time bomb. She blames herself that she didn't see the signs.'

'That's why suicides are so difficult to cope with for the family.' Avoiding his eyes, she turns on her computer. 'Guilt. Regret.'

'Hm.' He sips the rest of his coffee and drops the cup in the bin. 'And you? Why are you so early?'

'I ... I thought of something and I wanted to check it.'

'About Iris Spencer's death? So did I.' He grins sheepishly. 'I have the feeling that I have missed something.'

She looks at him. Confused. Uncertain. How on earth is it possible that he has been thinking along the same lines?

'My memory isn't what it used to be, sadly,' he continues with a regretful smile. 'It's somewhere in my head, but I can't remember what it is. What were you thinking of?'

'Caleb Boyd,' she replies, almost without thinking first. 'There is something weird about him.'

'He's got Asperger's Syndrome.'

'I know. I keep thinking about their kitchen. Everything is in its place. There isn't any logic to it, but, clearly, the family keeps everything in the way Caleb wants it. Otherwise he'll be upset.'

Tregunna nods, getting up and stretching his arms above his head.

'Like when he was so angry at his father because he had moved Caleb's scooter two or three inches. I mean, what was the point?'

'There isn't any. It only makes sense to Caleb, Jennette. In the same way as they keep the tea bags in one cupboard and sugar and coffee in another.'

36

We drive to the edge of Roche Industrial Estate, where a hotel is housed in a long stretched-out building that looks like it has formerly been a row of detached homes. The gravelled car park has designated spaces, divided by concrete blocks that only look as if they had a coat of white paint when they were laid years ago. A porch with neglected plants in dusty flowerpots leads to an area with two old leather sofas side by side against the wall, situated opposite the reception desk. A woman peers over the edge of the wood panelled desk.

'Hi. Have you already booked your room with us?' she asks cheerily.

Her name badge says her name is Madeleine. She is in her late fifties with dyed hair that makes her skin look pale and unhealthy. Bulging grey eyes, the whites jaundiced, thick black eyeliner and mascara. Her lips are beetroot-red and matching plastic hoops dangle from her earlobes, touching her shoulders as she talks.

Penrose produces her ID card and explains the reason for our visit. The woman's cheerfulness dissipates and she settles for an attitude of competence.

'We've already had an enquiry about one of our guests. A police woman. Champion, if I'm right.'

'PC Danielle Champion?'

She nods. 'I think so, yes. Quite young, I thought. Anyway, I was meant to call the officer back but it's been manic all day and I completely forgot. I'm so sorry.'

'That's why we are here.'

'She … the other officer, asked if I remembered a woman from Australia, who stayed in the hotel at the beginning of March. I said no, I didn't but, actually, I think I do, because it was so odd.'

'Odd?'

'She came in the morning and booked a room for herself for three nights. I told her it would be room 11 but, as it was rather early, she couldn't access the room before three o'clock. She said it was fine because she was meeting some people.'

'Some people?'

'Her words exactly. It made me wonder whether she meant friends or family or business.' She shrugs. For a moment, the earrings balance on her collarbones, then they drop. Hang. 'She paid upfront. In cash.' She pauses, looking as though she's going to pull a rabbit from a hat. 'The room was never used.'

'Was she with someone? Sleeping in another room?'

'Oh no, she was definitely alone. She demanded to know why the room price is the same when only one person is using it. She wanted a discount, which, sadly, we don't offer.'

'Are you saying she was never there?'

'Well.' She looks over her shoulder and lowers her voice: there are colleagues or guests in her vicinity. 'That was why I remember it. She didn't show up, but there was another couple from Australia and they booked in the same day. I thought what a coincidence it was that we had two bookings for people from Australia on the same day. Mr and Mrs Nelson.' She shrugs again, the earrings get momentarily stuck between the folds in her neck. 'She, Mrs Nelson, was swathed in a coat with a big fur collar, pressing paper tissues against her nose and sneezing all the time. She complained about the British weather that gave her that nasty cold but I thought she might have been allergic to the fur. Which was fake, you see. I offered her some anti-flu pills, but she didn't want them.' She stops for breath. Inhales. 'They paid in cash as well. He was saying they hadn't known we had the new £5 and £10 notes, suggesting they hadn't been in the UK for a while.'

Penrose stirs beside me and I interrupt the woman before she's completely lost her train of thought. 'Going back to Mrs Ashton, did she eventually talk to the Australian couple?'

'Oh no, of course not. Didn't I tell you? She … what did you just call her?'

'Ashton. Cecilia.'

'Oh. I'm sure her name wasn't Ashton. I'd remember that, because my daughter-in-law is called Ashton.'

'What was her name?'

She replies without hesitation. 'Clarke. Cecilia Clarke. She had booked for three nights, but never used the room she'd paid for. Her bed was unused. All three mornings.'

'And what about the Australian couple?' I feel as though I've been running a race but took a wrong turning and missed the finish line.

She blinks so heavily I fear her eyes will drop out of their sockets. 'What about them?'

'Did they meet?' Penrose asks.

Madeleine grins with superiority. 'Of course not. Do you make friends with British people when you're on holiday abroad? I certainly don't.'

Penrose is getting annoyed. 'Does the hotel make copies of passports?'

'No. We used to but we don't do that anymore for privacy reasons. We have our guests's booking references and payment details.'

'Can you then give us a copy of the payment you took off Ms Clarke?'

'Didn't I tell you? She paid cash.'

Disappointed, Penrose turns, examining the leather sofas as if she's considering a nap.

'Can you describe her?' I ask.

'She had short dark hair. About thirty years old, maybe thirty-five. A bit taller than your colleague here. Tattoo on her neck. A little dragon, I thought it was.'

'Anything else that might help us with our enquiry?'

'Well, we had CCTV. Of course we have that. I suppose you would like to have a look?' She reaches for an old-fashioned phone. Hesitates. 'Wait, I'll tell you exactly when she was here.' She flicks through a guest book. 'Right. Tuesday the 6th. 11.45. That'll make it easier for you if you're looking at the CCTV. I will now introduce you to the hotel manager.'

Samira Annalh is originally from Iraq. She's wearing a black headscarf, but seems confident enough to show an edge of her dark hair on her forehead. Her skin is slightly tinted and she has huge brown eyes. A wide smile reveals a row of white teeth. Her English is perfect, though with an almost indiscernible accent.

She barely inspects our ID cards and doesn't request any other papers before she allows us to see the potentially private information about their guests. We are taken to a small office with windows that overlook the car park and hedges that separate the hotel grounds from the industrial estate behind it. We sit at a computer screen which she brings to life with a tap on one button. Images flash up with the speed of light until the screen freezes again. Two cameras, different angles, show a woman with dark hair. She's dressed in a denim skirt and jacket, thick black tights and boots that reach up to her knees. A black scarf with printed blue flowers and black fringes is loosely draped over her shoulders.

'Is this her?' Penrose asks, sounding disappointed already. From what is visible of the woman, there is no useful view of her face and she's already half-convinced we are wasting our time.

Samira Annalh calls Madeleine in.

'Is this her, Madeleine?'

'Definitely.'

Once more the hotel manager scrolls through the video until she has found several sets of images. Cecilia Clarke waiting in the empty foyer, getting up as Madeleine appears from a small kitchen behind the reception, carrying a steaming mug and a small plate with apple slices. Cecilia Clarke, rising to her feet, leaning on the top of the desk, checking in, briefly showing her passport, paying with crispy £10 notes. People who are unaware of cameras, especially in an environment they're not familiar with, like a hotel, generally look around with a certain degree of curiosity and interest. There is nearly always a moment when they show their full face to one of the cameras. But Cecilia Clarke keeps her head down nearly all the time. Until she walks out and we see her in the car park, walking towards a small white Ford Ka. Just before opening the car door, she half-turns as if someone has called her. For a single moment she stares almost straight into the camera. Then she shrugs, gets in the car, checks her phone and drives away. The licence plate remains obscured by the concrete edge of the parking bay, but Samira Annalh taps the screen with the tip of a long nail.

'A hire car. You'll want to contact Becks Car Hire. Madeleine will give you their contact details.'

I thank Samira Annalh for her cooperation. She smiles with her perfect teeth. I smile back, sensing Penrose's disapproval.

'What?' she asks, getting in the car and looking at me suspiciously. 'You look like the cat who's just helped himself to the cream.'

'It looks like we've made some progress, Jennette,' I say slowly. She starts the engine. Black gravel crunches under the tyres. 'Because Cecilia Clarke who was married to Mr Ashton and Cathryn Penhallow are one and the same person.'

37

DI Maloney stands with his back to the wall, eyes darting from side to side as if he expects to be ambushed. I sit in the corner furthest away from the whiteboard that is dotted with sheets of paper, post-it notes, printouts and pictures, all held on by coloured magnets. In front of me is PC Champion. She's pulled her hair up with a clip which makes her look at least ten years older. As we wait for Maloney to make a start, she spends the time bent over, inspecting her tights, running her fingers along the rim of her skirt. I see PC Scott Massey follow her movements. As though he feels my gaze resting on him, he looks up suddenly, catching my eye. He blushes.

'Okay.' Maloney folds his arms across his chest. In his creased suit, he looks more like a deflated bouncy castle than a police officer in charge of a murder investigation.

'Tregunna. Let's start with you.' He sounds bored, like he wants the less important information out of the way sooner rather than later. 'Do you have an update on your visit to Anna Bingwell, Iris Spencer's mother?'

I clear my throat and rise to my feet. 'There isn't much to know about Anna Bingwell. The only thing I'm certain of is that we can rule her out as a suspect. She's eighty-two and suffering from Alzheimer's. She's living in a secure ward in a care home in Clevedon, Somerset.' I pause briefly. 'Background: Anna Bingwell's marriage to William Spencer lasted less than three years. They had one daughter: Iris. The father left when the girl was two years old. Anna never married again. She raised Iris on her own. When she divorced, she took on her maiden name again and, occasionally, Iris used this name too.'

'So your trip to Clevedon was a waste of time.' Clearly, Maloney is thinking about his budget.

I ignore the interruption. 'Apparently, Iris was a faithful and loyal daughter. She visited her mother every week on Thursday mornings. Although, she never stayed long. Staff in the nursing home told me that she deals with her mother's finances. Nothing wrong with that, but Mrs Bingwell seems to receive a lot of mail. I'm quite keen on investigating what it is.'

'I don't think we should spend more time on an old woman, Tregunna,' Maloney says affably.

'There is more. Horizon View, the care home where Mrs Bingwell, Iris Spencer's mother, lives, keeps a record of every visitor. Iris Spencer seems to have been the only visitor since her mother moved in there three-and-a-half years ago. But interestingly, she had another visitor recently.' I pause for effect. 'Ten days before Iris died.'

'Do we know who this visitor is?' Maloney is doubtful. He can't see the significance.

'We haven't spoken to the woman yet. She seems to have disappeared. I think we need to find this woman as a priority.'

Generally, Maloney is quite easy-going. He's open to all suggestions and at least takes everything into consideration. The one thing he doesn't like is being told what to do.

'May I remind you that I am in charge of this investigation, Tregunna?' he barks.

'I'm only ...'

'And do you honestly believe that we must interview every visitor of a demented old woman?' he asks rhetorically, looking around as if waiting for applause.

'Actually, I do,' I say slowly. 'Because this is the same woman who went to see Hugh Kelly in his office. In the same week as she visited Anna Bingwell.'

A hint of enthusiasm. 'Who is she?'

'Cecilia Cathryn Penhallow. She happens to be the daughter of the man who was the third partner in Hugh and Iris's business when they started twenty years ago.' Again, pausing for effect. I wait. Look around at faces that expressed scepticism and boredom before I started, but I see growing hope and expectation now.

'The same woman who is mentioned in Iris Spencer's will, by the name of C.C. Ashton.'

Maloney nods, trying to hide his cautious excitement. 'What do we know about this woman?'

'She's the daughter of Arthur Penhallow. He started the business with Iris and Mr Kelly, but he sold his shares to them after his divorce. He moved out of Cornwall to live in Bournemouth with his sister. He died of cancer twenty months ago.' I move a couple of printouts to the corner of the whiteboard and pick up a marker pen, drawing a blue arrow to connect Iris's and Hugh Kelly's company to this new information.

'Arthur's ex-wife, Rosie Penhallow and their daughter Cecilia moved to Australia, where her sister lived. She married Peter Clarke and Cecilia changed her name to Clarke, occasionally using both her first names Cecilia and Cathryn on several different occasions. She married Samuel Ashton when she was twenty-eight. He was widowed, thirty years older than Cecilia and he already had two grown-up daughters. Samuel Ashton died of a heart attack about a year ago.'

I write the details on the whiteboard as I speak, aware that I have the full attention of everyone present. Maloney hasn't moved, but his face is slowly going a pink colour and his eyes are shining.

'Five months later, Peter and Rosie Clarke were involved

in a road accident and they died. There was an issue with the inheritance which seems to have been resolved a few weeks ago. That is when Cecilia Cathryn Ashton, aka Clarke, aka Penhallow decided to travel to the UK to visit family and old friends.'

'Why did she go to see Anna Bingwell and Hugh Kelly?'

'I don't know why she went to see Anna Bingwell. But she met Hugh Kelly because she had inherited the remaining two per cent shares of the original company her father had with Iris and Hugh Kelly. But Hugh Kelly declined the offer to buy them off her and suggested she kept them and continued to get a yearly dividend.'

'Did she offer her shares to Iris?'

'Not to my knowledge. That day, Iris wasn't in her office. She did try to make an appointment with her, but I don't know if she saw Iris or not. Her secretary didn't actually make an appointment and Tilda Disley has never heard of her.'

'She must have met Iris and killed her,' Scott Massey says. 'That's why she did a runner.'

Maloney frowns. 'So we don't know where this young lady is at the moment?' he asks as if he is getting ready to make arrangements to charge her with murder.

I shrug. 'We know that when she first arrived from Australia she stayed with an aunt in Bournemouth. Then she booked a single room last Tuesday in a hotel in Roche for three nights. Cleaners were still preparing her room and she told the receptionist that it wasn't a problem because she was going to meet someone and she would come back later that day. But she never used the room and we don't know who she was going to meet. Her aunt mentioned some first names, but none of them has come up before in our investigation. Unfortunately, even her aunt doesn't seem to know what Cecilia's plans were. She was supposed to go back to her aunt's house in Bournemouth on Friday but she seems to have disappeared.'

The door opens and DC Penrose slips in, pressing a stack of A4 papers against her chest as if she fears they'll be stolen from her.

'When was she last seen?' Maloney asks, giving Penrose an angry stare for being late.

I attach a couple of photos under a red plastic magnet: a grainy enlargement of one of the camera images from the hotel, the best we could get. 'These are images of her leaving the reception of the hotel after she booked the room and paid for it.' I tap the other photo. 'And we have her on camera again when she visited the care home where Iris's mother lives. But that is as much as we've got.'

'Well, at least we have a new lead,' Maloney says, not wanting to show his enthusiasm in case it all goes up in smoke.

'Penrose?' I nod and she blushes as she comes forward. She gestures to hand me her papers, but I shake my head and sit down on the edge of the nearest table. 'What have you got?'

Penrose is shy and uncomfortable in front of an audience, however small, even if it consists only of colleagues. Reluctantly, she takes my marker pen and stares at her notes, gathering her thoughts and trying to find the courage to address the team.

Her voice trembles when she starts.

'We were able to locate the hire car company she used. Becks Car Hire. They have an office in Newquay. She hired the car for a week from their Bournemouth depot. A white Ford Ka. She drove to Cornwall on Tuesday and booked a room in Roche Budget Hotel for 3 nights, to check out on Friday. She was due to take the car back to Becks Car Hire to their depot in Bournemouth on Monday.'

She writes down the dates in her neat handwriting. Papers

rustle and pens click and scratch in notebooks as the team are scribbling down the relevant information. One or two tap on their mobile phones to enter their notes into a computer cloud.

Penrose continues, her voice growing more certain and businesslike. There isn't a single trace of a tremble in it.

'Cecilia never showed up again at the Roche Budget Hotel. She didn't arrive at her aunt's on Friday and she didn't take her car back to Becks in Bournemouth on Monday.'

'A disappearance and a murder in the same week?' someone mutters.

'Sounds like we've got our murderer,' Scott Massey states.

He's a new recruit. Young and bright, but inexperienced enough to seriously believe that he can change the world and that he is already a valuable asset to our team. In the three weeks since he was added to the team, he's managed to annoy Penrose and get a warning for his tasteless remarks that border on sexual harassment and disrespect for the professional abilities of his female colleagues. I've heard rumours that he is sheltering under DCI Guthrie's protective wings, but I'm not sure if that will last long. You might accuse Guthrie of many things, but he isn't stupid and he wouldn't risk a day of his career to protect someone.

Champion glances at Scott Massey, her face stern. 'It does indeed sound as if we have a serious lead to a new suspect, but we'll have to find her first.'

'That can't be too difficult,' Massey replies self-consciously, looking at Champion as if he doubts there is more to her than a pretty face and a perfectly shaped body.

Someone tuts, but Champion shakes her head and Scott Massey folds his arms across his chest. I wonder if there might be some tension in their relationship already, making a mental note to find out before things escalate.

Penrose continues. 'Becks in Bournemouth tried to contact Cecilia to enquire about the car but she didn't answer.' She stops a moment. A wide grin breaks through, lighting up her face. 'The good news is that Becks depot makes copies of passports and driving licences when customers collect their car. Initially, they were not so worried about the car. They have her credit card details and according to their terms and conditions, they are legally allowed to take the daily fees off the account until she takes the car back. There is also a daily fine in place. They've sent us a copy of her passport and we know which car she is using. We have already issued a warning to Devon and Cornwall Police to locate her car. And her, obviously.'

Maloney takes over, tapping the whiteboard with his knuckles. 'This is the car. A white Ford Ka.'

'Is there a tracker in the car?' Scott Massey asks.

Maloney frowns. He looks as though he's taken the lawn mower out of his shed to find his lawn has already been mowed. He doesn't look comfortable when he asks Penrose to answer.

Penrose nods. 'There is.'

'If they have trackers, why are they so keen on getting the car back?' Scott Massey continues, triumphantly. 'When the customer is paying for it anyway?'

Penrose shrugs. A knight in shining armour, Maloney comes to her rescue. 'Let's not dwell on how and why, shall we? Let's concentrate on what we have. Go on, DC Penrose.'

'Becks Car Hire can track exactly where Ms Clarke has been, or rather where the car has been but, under their rules and regulations, we need a warrant to get our hands on that information.'

Maloney nods. 'I'll take care of it.'

'Is Ms Clarke a suspect?' someone asks hopefully.

'Everyone is a suspect until we have the right man or woman

behind bars!'

Maloney finally moves away from his corner spot and springs into action. 'Right. Obviously, we need to find this woman. We are treating her as a person who we want to talk to. For now. We'll wait until we have the information from the car's GPS tracker and we'll take it from there. Meanwhile, we'll need to focus on her whereabouts since she arrived in Cornwall, perhaps even since she arrived in the UK.'

'I think we'll need to speak to Ms Disley again,' I say slowly. 'It is likely that Cecilia knew Iris. After all, her father was Iris's and Hugh Kelly's business partner. She visited Hugh Kelly to offer him the shares in their business, the shares she inherited from her father. When he declined the offer, she may have tried Iris and Tilda Disley might know something about that.'

'The lady certainly must have inherited quite a bit,' Scott Massey says. 'Her father died, then her husband, and her mother and stepfather. A lot of bodies in her wake, if you ask me.'

'Nobody is asking you, Massey,' Maloney says curtly. 'And I hope it is clear that we are investigating the murder of Iris Spencer. If there is anything suspicious about the death of every member of Ms Clarke's family, then I'm sure the local police will have dealt with that already.'

'Perhaps they don't know about the others, sir.'

Maloney fumbles in his pockets, not finding what he's looking for. I can see he's annoyed, but he understands very well that Massey has a point. Only he doesn't want to admit it.

38

There are less than a dozen cars in the supermarket's car park. A banner announcing even more price cuts flutters in the wind. A man with a yellow fluorescent sleeveless jacket over his coat, is gathering shopping trolleys. There are three sizes. He arranges them in three lines. To one side are other trolleys for wheelchair users and for mothers with small babies.

Penrose shivers. Outside, the temperature is two degrees Celsius. It can't be much warmer in her car. Her nose is cold, her fingers are numb and she can barely feel her toes through her socks and shoes.

She parks close to the shop entrance. A blue car that has been following her through town, keeping an irritably short distance behind her, parks opposite her. A woman gets out, pulling the long strap of her handbag over her head, adjusting it on her shoulder. Her face is flushed and angry. The passenger door opens. Slowly, a man gets out. The woman speaks to him. Her voice is raised but just not enough for Penrose to hear. The man replies with a grin and a shrug, clearly annoying the woman even more. Shaking her head, she tramps off to the trolley bay, pulling out one of the largest trolleys.

Penrose turns on her phone to check if there are any new messages. Brilliant. No signal. The government promises faster broadband everywhere, but they're still struggling to erect enough masts to cover the whole country.

Angrily, she grabs her small notebook. The air feels much colder than on the coast. Her breath forms small clouds, dissolving as the wind takes them away.

The man whose wife is entering the shop, casting a quick, furious glance over her shoulder, leans against their car. Although she doesn't know what the dispute was about, Penrose feels sympathy for the woman. She gives the man a cold stare. He closes one eye, cocks his head to light a cigarette, cupping the lighter in his hands, still staring at her.

Penrose purses her lips. Locks her car and feels the blast of heat as she enters the supermarket.

'You're not allowed.'

Penrose turns. 'Pardon?'

'You haven't got any children.' The woman behind the supermarket's customer desk looks over a pair of reading glasses. She is short and square, with thinning grey hair and fleshy cheeks that have a strange, orange colour, clearly applied from a make-up bottle. Deep furrows run down along her nose, connecting the corners of her eyes to the corners of her mouth, giving her face a constant expression of dissatisfaction and disappointment in life.

'I know, but …' Penrose stops abruptly, sensing that the woman has taken an instant dislike to her. The feeling is mutual.

'You can't park in that bay.' The badge on her voluptuous bosom says she is Shirley, shop assistant.

'There are no customers with children,' Penrose says, trying to sound reasonable. 'There are at least eight bays for parents with young children. There are at least eight bays for disabled people. None of these bays is currently taken by a mother or a disabled person.'

'That is not the point.'

'It is my point.'

Shirley shakes her head. The cheeks seem to follow in slow motion. 'Those special bays need to be available for the targeted customer at all times.'

Penrose is aware that she shouldn't allow herself to be drawn into the argument. Yet, she can't help herself. 'Are you expecting sixteen young families and people in wheelchairs or on crutches within the next half hour?'

'No, I don't think that will happen but, nevertheless, we have to be prepared for the possibility.'

'What happens if all the bays are occupied and some other so-called targeted customer appears?'

The woman stares back at her. 'To my knowledge, that has never happened before.'

'I'm a police officer. I'm here to investigate ...' Penrose starts, placing her ID card on the counter. The woman doesn't flinch. 'Police or not, you aren't with children.'

Penrose purses her lips. Facing a woman who seems to obey the most ridiculous rules mankind has invented just for the sake of it, her mood swings to a point somewhere below the baseline.

A phone rings. Reluctantly, the woman at the desk turns. Penrose clenches her fists. Clearly, the woman at the customer desk won't help her until she's removed her car. Which she isn't going to do. Definitely not. The woman is talking on the phone, half turning and staring at Penrose, whose face is turning pink with anger and frustration. Briefly, she wonders what Tregunna would do in this situation, then dismisses the thought. He would never be in a situation like this in the first place. He wouldn't park in the wrong bay, and if he did, nobody would stop him.

On the far side are two doors. One is marked '*Staff only*' the other '*Manager*'. There is a keypad next to the door handle. Safety regulations, no doubt. Only the door is ajar. Someone has wedged something on the floor to keep the door open. Penrose grabs her ID card. In three steps she is behind the counter, knocking on the door with one hand, pushing it fully open with the other.

'What the …?' Shirley's reaction is too slow.

Penrose steps into a small corridor. At the end is a door marked 'Fire Exit.' To the right is a small kitchen. A set of lockers opposite the kitchen counter. The table in the middle and the floor are littered with women's handbags and plastic shopping bags. Coats and jackets are thrown over a three-legged coat stand in the corner. There is a smell of coffee and burnt toast.

A woman sits behind a desk in a room to the left, typing with an enviable speed. Her nails are long and pink with sparkling spots on them. Her dark hair is pulled back and fastened at the back of her neck with a pink plastic clip making her look so young that she will be questioned about her age at every checkout till to stop her buying a can of beer.

'Are you the manager?'

'Who is asking?'

'DC Penrose, Devon and Cornwall Police. Are you the …?'

'Deputy shop manager. I'm Libby. And you're here … why?'

'I'm investigating a murder.'

Two plucked eyebrows rise. 'Here?'

Shirley has followed Penrose, her hand stretched out as if to pull Penrose out of the building, with force if necessary. Instead, her hand covers her mouth, eyes wide in horror. She gasps, then retreats quickly, probably to tell her colleagues.

Penrose can't help smirking.

'What can I do for you, DC Penrose?' the deputy manager asks.

'We've received a message that there was a white Ford Ka parked for several days at the end of the car park.'

The woman cocks her head to one side, a smug look on her

face. 'That was me.'

'Where is your manager?' Penrose demands.

The woman scowls. 'Our manager, Mrs Blackwell is off today. And tomorrow. I'm in charge. I'm the deputy shop manager.'

'So you said.'

'Ehm …what is the nature of your interest in that white car?'

'The car may be related to our investigation.'

'A murder, you said?'

'Hmm.'

'What about it?' Libby pushes her keyboard away and swings the screen to the side, placing her hands flat on the desk as if she's inspecting her nail polish. It wouldn't surprise Penrose if she pulled the nail polish out from the desk drawer.

'I suppose you have a camera system in place?'

'We have. Ehm … What was your name again?'

'Penrose. And what's your full name?'

'Sorry. Libby Browne.' She opens a drawer and finds a badge. Pins it onto the lapel of her suit jacket. E.M.M.A. Browne, Deputy Manager.

'We do have several surveillance cameras, of course. Most of them are in the shop, but there are a couple outside also. We have a different system in place for the car park. Licence plates, for instance, are picked up by cameras at the entrance and the exit. If a vehicle exceeds the maximum free parking time of 90 minutes, we receive an electronic alert from the cameras and our warden writes out a fine.' She sounds like she's reading from an instruction leaflet.

Penrose smiles tightly. 'I'm only interested in the white Ford Ka.'

Libby Browne smiles tightly back. She leans forward as

though she's preparing to share her best-kept secret. 'I made the call to the police. Our warden had already written out a fine. But nothing happened. Nobody seemed to be interested in the car. He contacted me and he showed me the car. It was parked at the very end of the car park. Beside the gate next to the footpath, used by customers coming from the other side of the town. The warden had made a note. He told me that the car had been there since last Thursday.'

Penrose looks at her notes. Nods.

'We looked inside the car. The warden tried the doors and the boot. He wanted someone else present when he did so. Just for security reasons. You know.'

'Was the car locked?'

'Yes. We just looked in.' She giggles briefly. 'The warden was a bit funny. He loves ghost and horror stories. He got me nervous by saying we might find a body in the car. Or something horrible. That's why I remember it so well.' She pauses briefly. 'There was a red-checked scarf on the floor of the passenger seat. On the passenger seat was a pair of foldable binoculars, a small notebook with a pen clipped on it. A newspaper, dated the 4th March. And a USB lead to charge a mobile phone. That car was well over the 90 minutes. In fact, it came to more than a week.'

'A week?'

Libby Browne nods seriously. 'We used to close the car park overnight when we had an employee checking the number plates all the time, but we don't bother now we have the cameras. People who live in this area park here sometimes, but we've never had an issue with that. They're not supposed to, but we do allow them to park here when the shop is closed, as long as they leave in the morning. But this car didn't. I'm not sure exactly when it arrived, although the warden said it had been there since Thursday when he was complaining about it to me. He said the fine he'd written was still under the windscreen wiper the next day. Sometimes teenagers use a car for joyriding and leave it somewhere, but it wasn't registered as stolen. I checked when I rang the police. But then I saw someone drive it away'.

'You said you saw it drive off the car park?'

'I did.'

'Can you remember when it was?'

'Of course. It was just after I called the police.'

Penrose inhales, starting to feel excited. 'Did you happen to see the woman who drove it away?'

'I did, but, it wasn't a woman. It was a man.'

39

As a young boy, I was intrigued by glow-worms. They're beetles, not worms. My imagination worked overtime when I learned that they kill slugs and snails by delivering a series of toxic bites that paralyse and eventually dissolve the slimy bodies of the creatures that invaded my mother's vegetable patch on summer nights. I used to look out for the greeny-orange lights that the females used to attract the males, hoping to catch them and keep them in a jar. It was frustrating and disappointing that the lights disappeared on my approach.

I feel like that young boy again when I try to grab a snippet of knowledge in the peripheral vision in my head. I know it is there, but it's gone as soon as I reach out for it.

Three young women are standing on the pavement. Laughing, gesturing. Happy. One has long curly red hair. As I drive past them, the sun catches her freckled face. She reminds me of Lauren and for a moment, I feel a pang of regret.

The display on the dashboard lights up and my phone starts ringing. I press a button and stare at the screen, half hoping that Lauren's name will appear on it but there is only a notification that the number is withheld.

'Hello?'

'Hello? Who is this?' I don't recognise the voice.

'I'm …' The line crackles. The voice is inaudible. Male.

'Have you heard …?'

'Heard what?' I ask, involuntarily raising my voice. Like people do when they are talking to a deaf or foreign person. The line goes dead.

I stop the car in a lay-by and return the call.

'Hello?' I recognise the voice. And all of s sudden, I realise what has been haunting me all the time since we found out that Iris mentioned Caleb in her will.

'Mr Boyd. You called me a few minutes ago.'

A long silence. 'Yes. I did, but I didn't … it was a mistake. I didn't mean to call you. I was calling my wife but I pressed the wrong button. I'm sorry. He sounds nervous and agitated.

'Is something wrong, Mr Boyd?'

'What? No, of course not. I just … I just …' He breaks down. 'It's Caleb. He's gone. I can't find him.'

'What happened?'

'I don't know. Ehm ... there was something on Twitter. About Iris.'

I hesitate. 'Does he know? About Iris?'

A short silence. 'No. We were going to but ... It's all in the news now, isn't it? Papers, TV, Facebook, Twitter. He's not stupid, Inspector. He must have guessed ...'

'Okay, please calm down, Mr Boyd. Everything will be alright.'

I don't know much about Asperger's Syndrome, let alone what goes on in the mind of a teenage boy, with a form of obsessive-compulsive disorder, who may have just found out that his mother isn't his real mother. It would be devastating news for anyone, but more traumatic, I guess, for someone like Caleb. He would have the feeling that his life is totally out of control, that his life has turned into complete chaos.

'Alright? Everything will be alright? How can you say that? You don't understand ...'

'I'm on my way, Mr Boyd, I can help ...'

'No! I will deal with it. There is no need for the police ...'

I disconnect before he can make any more objections.

Twenty minutes later, I park on their drive behind a blue Vauxhall Estate. Caleb's scooter isn't there. The paving slabs where he normally parks it are dotted with fresh oil stains.

Lester Boyd is standing in the doorway, hands on his hips.

'Mr Boyd ...'

His pale face gets even paler and he looks at me with a mixture of fear and horror.

'What happened?' His voice is hoarse with suppressed tears.

'Why do you ask, Mr Boyd?'

'Caleb. Is he alright?'

'He hasn't come home yet?'

'No. He is ...he has ...I am worried about him.'

He's dressed in baggy corduroy trousers and a dark, washed-out Old Guys Rule T-shirt that says '*The older I get,the better I was*'. Goose-bumps on his bare arms. He is too worried to feel the cold.

'Mr Boyd, shall we go inside? It's cold and it is starting to rain.'

He looks up at the sky as if he doesn't understand the meaning of the word rain. Then he inclines his head and turns, looking over his shoulder as if to make sure I'm following.

'He left the house about an hour ago. He was in a terrible state.'

'Did you have a fight or an argument?'

'No. No, I'm sure it wasn't that.' He shakes his head defensively. 'He was ... different ... this morning. Usually, he's up before the rest of us. But he didn't come out of his room till late. Not even before my wife left for work and the girls went to school. But when I was getting dressed myself, I heard him talking to someone. First I thought there was someone in his room but, when I asked him about it, he said he was chatting with someone.' He pauses, the present situation forgotten for a moment. 'Caleb has a lot of friends all over the world.'

'Like many of his age.'

'Yeah. Anyway, all of a sudden, he was angry. He said I was a liar and I had lied to him all his life. He was very angry with me and to be honest, he scared me a bit. I'd never seen him like that. Obviously, I asked him what he meant but he wouldn't tell me. In fact, from that moment, he refused to talk to me at all. It was like I didn't exist for him anymore.'

I nod understandingly, holding back my questions. However frustrating it is, they will have to wait.

Lester Boyd continues. 'He had his cornflakes and then he went back up to his room. He has a part-time job at a delivery depot, sorting out packages. He called in sick. He said he wasn't feeling very well. Which made me annoyed because there seemed to be nothing wrong with him. I said he couldn't do that. I said it was wrong to let his boss and his colleagues down at such short notice, especially as it wasn't true. He wasn't sick. The only reaction I got was cursing and swearing which I'd never heard him doing before either. Not like that. But I know very well that it's best to leave him alone when he is in a state like that. He won't listen to reason. He needs time to sort his thoughts out first. Get his head around things. So I left him in his room. I went out to get some milk and my paper. When I came back he was just coming down from his room. I'd never seen him like that before. He was dressed as if he'd just grabbed some clothes from his wardrobe. Jeans and a jumper he uses when he works on his scooter. I asked him what was wrong but he just pushed me away. I don't think he knew what he was doing. I nearly fell from the stairs. He was shouting and raging and telling me again that I was a liar, that everyone had lied to him and that he was about to find out the truth. The real truth.'

'Did you know what he meant by that?'

He looks down at his hands, shocked as he sees how they tremble. 'I'm not sure,' he says lamely. 'We've tried to explain to him that Rachel and I wanted him to live with us. We've never said a word about Iris, that she didn't want him. But … perhaps he was wondering why he never saw her.'

'Mr Boyd,' I say carefully. 'We are investigating the death of your ex-wife. I'm not sure if it is relevant, but we have to take into consideration that the relationship between Iris and Caleb is part of our investigation.'

'We were going to tell him the truth, honestly, but … somehow, it never happened. There was never the right time to do it and later, we thought, what was the point anyway?'

I look at him, hesitating. 'Were you present when Caleb was born?'

Shaking his head, he doesn't seem surprised by my question. 'No. It was a different time, I suppose. I wanted to, but … well, Iris wasn't around anyway. It was a difficult time for both of us. She had never wanted children and she blamed me that she was forced to have one.'

'Forced?'

'That was what she said. I remember thinking it was a strange way of expressing her feelings, but she said that was how she felt.' He shakes his head again. 'She suffered severe morning sickness in the beginning. Later, she had pains, aches and cramps. She hated being pregnant. Couldn't wait till the baby was born. We slept in separate rooms. But it got better eventually and she was just over her 36th week when she went up to Scotland with her mother, to visit a relative. I believe her mother had a brother there, but I've never met them. But in Scotland, she had a nasty fall and the baby was born prematurely. I went there straight away, but, sadly, I was too late for the birth. We were unable to come back home together because Caleb had to stay in hospital for a while. Iris decided to stay with him. When Caleb was eventually released from hospital, and they were back home, Iris went back to work almost immediately. We had a nanny for a while but that didn't work out. Then her mother came to live with us and she more or less looked after our son.'

'You both worked full time?'

'Yes. As I told you before, I was a teacher. It wasn't possible for me to work part time.' He pauses. 'Iris could have stopped working altogether, or worked part time, but she didn't want to. After Caleb was born, I hoped she'd start to have motherly feelings for him, but she didn't. It seemed she didn't have any interest in the boy.'

'Not all mothers have motherly feelings.'

'I guess not, but she didn't have any feelings for him at all! When we split up and we divorced, it was obvious immediately that there wouldn't be a fight over Caleb. She didn't want him. She was happy with me having full custody. She paid for him, though, still does, but that's all. She never sees him, she never sends him a birthday card. Nothing. It is as though he's never existed for her.'

'And Rachel became his mother, as it were?'

'She did. It was never a problem for her to stay at home with him. She got pregnant soon after we got together and then we had Emily. Our first daughter.'

'How old was Caleb then?'

'He was three years old. A lovely, cute little boy. But Iris saw him as a burden. She said he was better off with me and my wife. By then I knew she was gay. And we thought it was better for Caleb to grow up in a normal family, if you know what I mean. It sounds old-fashioned and prejudiced, I know, but that is the way I feel about it. I am not against same-sex marriages or anything. But I do think it is better for children to grow up in a normal family rather than with two mothers or two fathers.'

'Some same-sex couples do a wonderful job.'

'Yes. Maybe.' He scratches his head, steels a glance at his watch and frowns.

'Maybe we should start looking for Caleb.'

'How old is he?'

'Eighteen.'

'Then he isn't a child anymore. He'll be able to look after himself.'

'He's got Asperger's.'

'Is he on medication?'

'No.'

'Is he a danger to the public or to himself?'

'I don't think so, but ...'

'He'll be back, Mr Boyd. Young people can overreact, sometimes about nothing, but most of them will come home.'

He cocks his head. 'Do you have children, Detective Inspector?'

'I haven't, no.'

'Then how can you understand how worried I am?'

'I can't possibly imagine how you feel as a father, Mr Boyd, but I do know that there is no point in the police looking for him yet. He isn't a child. He's an adult.'

'With a condition.'

I sigh. 'He looked perfectly normal to me.'

His shoulders shake, then he looks up suddenly. 'Why have you come here today, Inspector?'

I hesitate. I dread having to tell him what I know. After his words about parenthood, I can't fathom out what his reaction will be when he finds out the truth.

As though he's aware that I'm going to tell him something he doesn't want to hear, he continues with his story.

'Rachel and I decided not to tell Caleb until he was older. He was always a difficult child and when he grew up we were afraid that he would want to live with his mother. Which would have been a disaster for all of us, especially for him.'

'Some mothers just don't like babies. Sometimes the relationship gets better when the child grows up.'

'Not with Iris, Inspector. When we discovered that he had Asperger's Syndrome, which explained a lot about his behaviour, Iris was even more adamant to ignore his existence, so it was more reason for us not to tell him that Rachel was not his biological mother.'

'Did he never ask questions?'

'He did, when he was six and our Lydia was born. Obviously, Rachel and I got married after he was born, but I explained that it was not so unusual, certainly not in those days.'

'He accepted it.' It isn't a question, but he nods quietly.

'Why was he so angry today, Mr Boyd?'

Unwilling to answer, he shudders his shoulder.

'Mr Boyd, do you read a newspaper?'

'I do. I collect my paper every morning from the shop, but I haven't had time to read today's properly.'

'Does Caleb read them too?'

He shrugs, stares at his feet. 'Youngsters nowadays don't read newspapers, Inspector. All they are interested in is FaceBook, Twitter and Instagram, or is there a new one and am I out of touch already?'

'There are newspapers with news on their websites,' I say gently. 'Is Caleb likely to read news items on his computer? Does he watch the news on TV?'

He takes a moment before he answers. 'I'd think so yes.

He always seems to know everything. When he was younger, he used to look up everything that he didn't know or didn't understand in a dictionary or an encyclopaedia, or equivalent material on the Internet. He is particularly interested in the sky and the planets and the weather, which is often the case with people who have the same condition.'

'So,' I say slowly, 'it is possible that he has found out, in the news or on social media, why he is one of the beneficiaries of Iris's will?'

He looks at his feet again, close to tears all of a sudden. 'I think so,' he says almost inaudibly.

'Is that why he was upset?'

'I was going to tell him about his mother but I did not get the chance. He was in such a state that I couldn't talk to him or make him talk to me. I tried, but he ran out. He jumped on his scooter not even bothering to put on his coat and he drove off.'

'Do you have any idea where he might have gone?'

He shrugs. Points with his head. 'I have tried several options. First I thought he'd gone to work, but he wasn't there. His boss was quite annoyed. He …' He is silent for about a minute. 'I should have told him years ago.'

I don't need to tell him that I totally agree with that.

'Mr Boyd, has Caleb ever harmed himself?'

'Harmed himself?'

'Has he ever cut his arms? Made deliberate burns on his skin?'

'No. Never. Not that I know of anyway.' He shakes his head. Uncertain. 'I think I'd have noticed, don't you?'

'People who do that, are very good at hiding it.'

He looks down. As a teacher, I don't doubt he has come across self-harming teenagers. Even if he hasn't, he must be aware of it.

'Does Caleb have a friend he would confide in?'

'He hasn't got many friends, Inspector, sadly. He was bullied at school, as you may have gathered. He's always been an outsider, although it got better as he grew older and it became easier for him to have contact with people with the same level of intelligence. Older people. He's never had what we call a proper childhood. School and children of his own age were boring to him.'

'Isn't there anyone he would turn to when he's got problems?'

He smiles wryly. 'I'd like to think he would turn to me. Or to Rachel. But in this case ... I don't know. He seems to have locked himself in himself, if you know what I mean. He ...' He stops. Frowns. Then, reluctantly, he adds, 'there was someone. When he was thirteen, as with other kids of that age, he was very difficult to handle. I asked a psychologist who was sometimes consulted when we had issues with a pupil at the school where I worked. He recommended to introduce Caleb to therapy. That would help him relax and learn how to control his anger and frustration. There was a woman, an artist. Sculptures, she did. Still does. Caleb works with clay with her. He seems to be able to concentrate when he's using his hands and make something that reflects the thoughts in his mind at that moment.'

'Do you think he might have gone to see this woman?'

He scratches his head. Flecks of dandruff drift around him like the first flakes of a snowstorm. His face brightens. 'I didn't think of her, but it's worth a try.'

40

Everyone seems to be focusing on the disappearance of Ms Clarke-Ashton-Penhallow, but Penrose is convinced they're all wrong. The Australian woman has nothing to do with Iris's death. The truth lies in something she's heard, seen or read, only she can't remember what it is. Sometimes she feels it is dangling above her head, and all she has to do is grab it, but it's gone before she can focus on it.

Perhaps if she could talk about it with someone. With Tregunna. His views and opinions are often so different from hers, but a discussion with him could offer her a clearer view on the situation. Until she remembers ... Pending decisions from their superiors and the HR department, he is currently balancing on a knife edge. One slip and he will fall. Out of grace, out of a job. If there is anything that can keep him in the team, it will be a serious breakthrough. A result. A praise and an applause which she would happily share with him.

She shivers. There must be a hole somewhere in her car. There is a constant draft swirling around her feet and over one side of her face. Turning the heater on full blast, she presses the buttons on her mobile. No answer. She calls again. Still no answer. She frowns. Where is he?

She calls the station. To her annoyance, Scott Massey answers.

His attitude towards women in general has caused friction between them. Rather than holding back and thinking before he makes another tasteless remark or joke at the expense of females or other minority groups, he seems to enjoy trying to get her to take the bait.

'Ah, Jenny-Penny.' He speaks her new nickname slowly, as if sucking something up from his throat.

'Is Tregunna there?'

'Haven't seen him.'

'Ollie?'

'Nope.'

'Champion?'

'Our lovely Danielle? No, you can't possibly know how much I would love it if she were here.'

In the background she can hear the sound of someone tapping on a keyboard. 'Anyone else from the team?'

'I'm here.'

'Yes, I've gathered that.'

'Have you?' He chuckles mockingly.

'Do you know where Tregunna is?'

'Do I look like I'm his keeper?'

Penrose opens her mouth but she knows better than to reply.

'Why do you need him, anyway?' he continues bluntly.

'None of your business.'

Massey chuckles. 'We are a team, remember?'

She doesn't reply and he continues, 'Clearly, you don't see me as your colleague?'

'Did I say that?'

'No, but I can tell by your voice.'

'You've got a lot to learn, Massey.'

For a moment he is quiet. 'Politics, Penrose. Always good to know who your friends are.'

'You'd know, wouldn't you? Being Guthrie's protégé?'

'You have to take the chances when you can,' he replies flatly.

'You are …' Penrose stops. Seething but she won't give him

the opportunity of accusing her of bad language or offensive remarks.

'I bet Tregunna isn't returning his calls to you?' he continues, adding fuel to the fire.

'Why wouldn't he?'

'He's had a call from that reporter-woman. The one with the blonde hair and big … ehm … blue eyes.'

She grinds her teeth. She can almost see his stupid grin.

'Kim Naylor.'

'That's the one. She called, Tregunna answered and then he ran off like a bull seeing the open gate to a field of cows.'

Penrose clenches her fists. 'Did he say anything?'

'Like where he was going? Ah! I thought you knew Tregunna better than any of us. Telling us where he's going or what he's doing? No way, not our precious Detective Inspector Tregunna! He was on his own planet as usual!'

Penrose feels her heartbeat quicken with anger and frustration. What a shame that the guy seems to be the DCI's little pet. Otherwise, he would have had his first official reprimand in his first week.

'Anyway, Jenny-Penny, I'm sure you have enough imagination to get an idea what Tregunna and the blonde are doing at this very moment?'

'You are disgusting, Scott Massey!' She kills the connection and takes a deep breath. She shouldn't let him get under her skin. He'd only laugh at her, mock her in front of their colleagues.

Her phone rings as soon as she puts it down. Frustrated, she answers without looking at the screen. 'Listen, Scott Massey, you'd better be careful what you're saying, otherwise you'll be in serious trouble.'

'Not made friends with Snotty Scotty?' a female voice says

flippantly.

Penrose sighs. Smiles reluctantly. She didn't know about Massey's nickname. 'Certainly not. Have you?'

'Not my type,' Andrea Burke says wryly. 'I'm trying to get hold of Tregunna, but he's either in hiding or he's somewhere out of reach of modern technology.'

'Probably the latter.'

Andrea Burke rustles through her papers before she continues seriously. 'I'll be in a meeting for the next few hours. Can you pass my message on as soon as you see him?'

'Of course.'

'First of all, I have a name for the fingerprints we found on the two letters that were found in the possession of Iris Spencer and Edward Lynham.'

Penrose straightens her back. The investigation seems to be moving in the right direction. 'Anyone we know?'

'Crystal Jones. 32 years old. She's on our database because she had some encounters with the police a few years ago. Nothing really major in the sense of what we're investigating in relation to a murder, but nevertheless she's done shoplifting and she's been charged with abuse several times. Seems to be a short-fused girl, by the looks of it. Anyway, I will send you the details and I will copy Maloney in for good measure. Right?'

'Who is Crystal Jones?'

'That's not my business, Penrose. I'm just giving you the facts,' Burke replies crisply.

'Okay. Sorry. Thanks. I'll tell Tregunna.'

'There is more. I've managed to get a set of fingerprints from police in Bournemouth. Our colleagues have been to Mrs Gallagher's over there and they've just sent through the prints that they got from possessions in the room her niece had been using. We also managed to get a few hairs from a hairbrush, but the results of that will take a bit longer than the fingerprints.'

'And?'

'We had the letter that Iris received. It had the prints of Crystal Jones all over it, and a few of Nigel Sparks, Iris's secretary, but there was also a partial print we hadn't been able to identify. Tregunna suggested we compare the print against Ms Clarke's. Now, as certain as we can be with partial prints, I think it is safe to say that this print matches Ms Penhallow's thumb.

'So it was Penhallow who sent this letter to Iris Spencer?'

'I don't know who sent the letter to Iris. All I know is that she at least touched it. Either she did send it to Iris, or she touched it after it arrived on Iris's desk, or after whoever opened the letter.'

'Weren't Iris's prints on it?'

'Nope. That's up to you lot to investigate, Penrose.'

Penrose puts down the phone. A sense of dread creeps up on her. A sense of urgency, but she can't grasp what or who or why. The fingerprint means that there is now a good chance that Ms Penhallow murdered Iris, which means that she was wrong dismissing her as a suspect. But she still can't stop thinking that there is something else, something that is still hidden in the depths of her memory, something that will surface sooner or later.

41

Tintagel has inspired artists and historians who have associated it with the legend of King Arthur and the Round Table. The ruins of a castle, said to be the birthplace of King Arthur, tower above the beach littered with caves, one of which is rumoured to be the home of Merlin. Set high on the cliffs, Tintagel offers dramatic sea views as well as emanating an atmosphere of magic and mystery.

Today, devoid of the tourists, the streets of the town are bare and quiet. The tearooms and pasty shops aren't open for trade yet. The shop doors are closed to keep out the cold wind.

I park behind an old school building that has recently been refurbished to make a light and spacious room that is now used for temporary art displays by local art groups. A sign on the road tells me there is currently an exhibition of works from Arthur's Art Group. I doubt if the founder's name was really Arthur. A man is attaching a banner to the wall. Despite the cold, he is wearing shorts, as if to convince the odd tourist that the summer season is near. He looks up and grins so apologetically that I'm half inclined to have a look at their exhibition. I might even buy a small painting for Mr Curtis. Every time I see my neighbour, he reminds me of his birthday at the end of the month, and his invitation to have lunch with him and his niece. Since he is still convinced that I need a woman in my life, I'm not sure what's more important to him: the lunch or introducing me to the niece.

Ruth Holborn lives above a tiny shop tucked between two pasty shops in Tintagel's main street. Unlike in most other shops in Tintagel, there isn't a single item to be found that refers to pixies, Arthur's Castle, Merlin or the Old Post Office. Nor is there anything that is remotely connected to witchcraft or the mystical world. A versatile artist, she has a stylish display of 'Ruthan' pottery on the shelves and embroidery on the walls, mostly in grey, blue and brown.

Lester Boyd had called her and, after he explained the situation, she had admitted reluctantly that she had seen Caleb earlier that day and that he'd told her where he was going. To Lester's frustration, she had refused to tell him where his son was. She said she would go and fetch him or at least let him know that his family is worried about him, but she's housebound with a twisted ankle. She did agree, cautiously, to talk to me.

From what Lester Boyd told me about her, I expect to see a flamboyant hippie with long black hair with tinted streaks in it, wearing a multi-coloured cotton dress with beads and little mirrors sewn on it, layers necklaces of coloured beads and rows of silver rings and bracelets, and bare feet in cotton espadrilles.

Instead, she is in her late forties with thin brown hair that hangs straight and lifelessly on her shoulders. Dressed in blue denim jeans and a grey sweater with its hood tied at the neck, she looks like someone who could easily make herself invisible in a room with less than six people. Dull and boring.

She's sitting sideways behind a small counter in the corner of her shop with one leg stretched out in front of her, a foot in a surgical sandal resting on a footstool.

'You are Andy?' Her voice is bright and clear. 'Police?'

'Yes.' I reach in my pocket for my ID card but she shakes her head. 'No need. I can tell that you are a policeman.'

I know better than to ask her what she means exactly. 'Thank you for seeing me, Ms Holborn.'

'Ruth,' she says brusquely. 'What's up with Caleb? Is he in trouble?'

'Not that I'm aware of. I went to see his father who was very concerned about his son. I believe they'd had an argument and Caleb drove away on his scooter, without his coat.'

'I gave him one.'

'He's been here?'

'Yes. I live upstairs. I had just managed to come down the stairs. A friend was doing my shopping and when she came back, Caleb emerged. He was in quite a state, I must say. I asked him what was wrong, but he was too cold to talk. My friend took him upstairs and made him a cup of tea.'

'Did he tell you why?'

'Something to do with his father, I guess, but he wouldn't tell me. He was too upset. I wanted him to call his home, tell them that he was safe, but he muttered that only his father was at home and he was the last person he wanted to talk to. I said I'd make the call, but he didn't give me the number and, to be honest, I couldn't be bothered climbing up the stairs again to find it. Caleb is an adult and I presumed his father would know that he'd be back sooner or later.'

'Where is he now?'

She frowns and all of a sudden a smile crosses over her face and I find myself staring at her, fascinated by the transformation. She seemed dull and lifeless, but with that smile, she comes alive and pretty.

'How do I know you won't tell his father?'

'I can promise.'

'Perhaps you can make us a coffee upstairs and bring a chair when you come down. Then we can talk.'

I park my car in a lay-by on the road between Boscastle and

Tintagel. There is one other car and a scooter. Caleb's. Across the road is a sign that points to a path that leads to the South West Coast Path. And, according to Ruth Holborn, to a hidden gem.

Following her instructions, I follow the narrow path, climbing over worn slate steps and crossing several small bridges over a river that, in places, trickles gently down the wooded valley or gurgles powerfully between the rocks. The air is crisp and cold, but there is a pleasant feeling of silence and belonging. I pass the inevitable holiday lets and finally descend to a decaying mill building. I slow down, not wanting to frighten Caleb.

On one side is an exposed rock face of dark shale, shaded by the still bare branches of overhanging trees. Here, Ruth Holborn told me, is a pair of mysterious labyrinth symbols carved in the rock surface. Very little is known about the origin of these petroglyphs, which is perhaps why they have attracted large numbers of pagan visitors.

There are ribbons hanging from the trees, some weathered, some new and colourful. Little objects hanging off them, the significance of which is probably known only to those who left them here. On the edges on the slate wall are pebbles and small pieces of slate, names and dates written on some, signs and simple drawings on others.

Caleb is hunched with his back against the wall staring at the two carvings opposite him. Holding his helmet against his chest. He doesn't seem to be aware of me, not even when I stand still a few yards away, debating what to say to him.

Following his eyes, I decide not to say anything. I look at the carvings, that seem to be smaller than I expected. To my limited knowledge about mythology, they represent what I imagine is the tree of life, but I can also see the logic of why people call them labyrinths.

I don't think Caleb has looked at me, but he seems to know I'm there anyway.

'They're labyrinths.'

'The carvings?'

'Do you know the origin of a labyrinth?'

'Do you?'

He nods seriously. 'In Greek mythology it was a maze-like structure that was built for King Minos of Crete to hold the Minotaur in.'

'Did the Minotaur manage to escape?'

He stares at me, perplexed by my question.

'The labyrinth also represents a journey to your inner self and then back again, into the real world.'

'Symbolic.'

He doesn't seem to be listening. 'I live in a labyrinth.'

'Why?'

'I am trapped in a labyrinth of lies and deceit.'

'What makes you say that?'

'There is a monster in its centre.'

'You can get out.'

'You have to find the centre before you are allowed to go back. The monster swallows you before you can go back.'

'You can't beat the monster?'

'No.

'Why not?

'The monster lives inside me.'

I have no response to that. I don't understand his logic.

He changes the subject. 'Do you hear the silence?'

I hesitate. 'I don't know. I can hear the river. And the birds.'

'I can hear the silence.' He pauses. 'It helps me to relax when I can't get out of the spiral of my anger.'

'It is peaceful here.'

'Isn't it?' He turns his head, his eyes scrutinising my face for signs of mockery. 'Do you think it is peaceful here?'

'I understand why your anger dissipates here.'

He nods.

'Do you come here often, Caleb?'

'Ruth used to bring me here. She tells me stories about this place. I like the idea that other people came here so many years ago.'

'Thousands of years.'

'Yes. Do you feel that they are still here?'

'Not everyone can feel the same.'

'You don't feel this place is magical?'

'I don't feel the magic, but I can understand it if you do.' I pause, waiting for his reaction, but he just nods as if I have passed a test.

'Would you like to tell me why you were so angry?'

He shrugs. 'I don't want to talk about it, otherwise it comes back.'

'You left without your coat. It is cold, still wintry. Your father is worried.' I see a flash of frustration on his face and remember that initially, his anger was caused by his father. I add quickly, 'And your mother also, of course.'

'They lied to me.'

'They didn't want to upset you.'

'They lied to me.' He gets up and stretches his legs. 'They should have told me.'

'I think they were going to but they couldn't find the right moment.'

'They lied to me.' He is stuck in his own thoughts. I need to find a way to break into his mind.

'Did you know Iris?'

'Iris? The woman who is dead?'

'Have you never met her?'

'I can't remember.'

'I can get you a proper photo of her, if you like. Better than the one in the newspaper.' I'm pretty sure Tilda will kindly supply one if I explain who he is.

He shrugs indifferently. I'm losing his attention again. His mind is drifting off to places unknown to me. I feel sorry for him, for losing his faith in the two people he's known and trusted all his life, for what he feels as their betrayal. His condition means he can't understand the nuances of their feelings for him, nor his feelings for them. Let alone his feelings for a woman, his mother, he never knew. He misses something he never knew.

'Shall we find a place where it is warmer, Caleb?'

'No, I have … there is something I need to do.'

'How about a cup of tea and something to eat?'

He shakes his head, repeating, 'They lied to me.'

'Let's go, Caleb.'

He shakes his head again, but he follows me on the path back to the road. Younger and fitter than me, he overtakes me and then has to stop several times to wait for me to catch up.

'I'm going home.' He tucks Ruth's coat around him and adjusts his helmet under his chin.

'Is there anything I can do for you, Caleb? Are you alright?'

'No. Yes. Never ask two questions at the same time.'

I smile. 'You are right. It can be confusing. Sorry.'

'They say I can't cope when I'm confused.' It sounds like he doesn't expect a response and I just nod quietly. I wait until he starts his scooter and disappears round the sharp bend in the road.

42

Crystal Jones is accompanied by a couple in their early seventies. As soon as I enter the interview room where they've been taken by the desk officer, I know it has been a mistake to invite them here. They are nervous and scared for no other reason than that they're with the police. Some people feel instantly guilty when they're talking to a policeman, searching frantically in their memory to see if they have something to hide.

The fact that Penrose is with me, isn't helping either. The Jones family seem overwhelmed, awkward. Intimidated. Sitting opposite two police officers in a nasty, smelly interview room is more than they can handle.

'Why are we here?' Dorothy Jones demands. Small and skinny with lavender-grey permed hair, she takes the lead, voice clear, angry and defensive because she feels an injustice has been done.

Penrose doesn't seem to feel sorry for them. 'We have some questions for Crystal in relation to another investigation.' Credit where it is due, she just holds back the word 'murder'.

'Just questions? This feels more like the Spanish Inquisition.'

'I'm sorry if we've made you feel like that, Mrs Jones.' I lean forward and smile reassuringly. She's not impressed. 'As my colleague has explained, we hope that you'll help us with our enquiry.'

'You haven't even told us what you are investigating.'

With piercing brown eyes and a high-pitched voice, Dorothy Jones appears to be the spokesperson of the family. Mr Jones has all his attention focused on turning his hat round between his fingers without dropping it on the floor. Their daughter seems in a total state of denial. She's staring at Penrose as though she's been overtaken by a terrible lethargy. The reason why she's accompanied by her elderly parents is down to a warning remark on her file about her low IQ, instability and sudden outbursts of anger and aggressiveness.

Crystal Jones is thirty-two, dark, short and plump. She has a small mouth but her lower lip seems fuller than the upper one, which gives her face an expression as though she is constantly sulking. She's also suffering from a condition that is commonly associated with male hormones and results in excessive hair growth. A fine layer of dark hair surrounds her mouth and her cheeks, as though she needs a shave.

Crystal's fingerprints were known to us because of previous encounters with the police, ranging from causing damage to other people's properties, mostly cars, verbal abuse and shoplifting. Her age, and maybe her job with 'Print-Out', a copy and print company in the centre of Newquay, have calmed her down; she hasn't been in contact with the police for the past six years.

'Crystal,' I start gently, trying to make eye contact with her.

Beside me, Penrose clears her throat. She is used to my silences which are primarily to wait for the other person to speak, but clearly she is already of the opinion that Crystal is guilty and she thinks I'm too soft in my approach.

'We have found a letter that has your fingerprints on it, Crystal.'

No reaction. Her expression is blank and unresponsive. The father examines the rim of his hat.

'We would like you to explain to us how they got there, Crystal.'

She doesn't appear to have heard me. Only Dorothy Jones stirs, lifting her shoulders in a failed attempt to look bigger than she really is.

'This letter.' I retrieve the copied letter Chaz Lynham found in her husband's papers, which is now in a clear evidence bag with smudges where forensics identified the fingerprints. The original letter with the stuck-on paper cuttings is still being examined.

'Crystal,' I repeat, 'Can you explain how your fingerprints got on this letter?'

'Crystal!' Her mother says loudly, almost screaming. 'Listen and answer!'

For the first time, the young woman stirs, as if waking up from a dose, looking around and trying to remember where she is. Blinking behind her pink-rimmed glasses, she mutters, 'what?'

Penrose points her finger at the sealed letter. 'We're talking about this letter, Crystal.'

The young woman doesn't move. Not once do her eyes move to the object on the table. 'I've never seen it before.'

'We have found your fingerprints on it. Which means that you have held it in your hands,' Penrose says curtly. 'Why did you send this letter to Mr. Lynham? And to Mrs Spencer?'

'I don't know. I didn't send letters.' She hesitates, uncertain. 'Sometimes I send cards. For Christmas. Or birthdays. Or when someone has a baby. Or a wedding.'

Penrose taps her index finger on the letter. 'You cut these words and letters out from a newspaper. You glued them on a sheet of paper. You made a copy. You sent a copy to a man who is now dead. You sent the original letter to a woman who is also dead. Murdered.' Penrose is losing her patience.

The young woman has only heard the last few words. 'Dead?

Who is dead?' Crystal looks at her mother for support, her face pale. The father, looking down between his knees, doesn't offer any.

Eyes wide in confusion or panic, Dorothy Jones has registered only one word. 'Who was murdered?' She speaks almost in a whisper. Her husband looks up but says nothing. They seem to stare at each other in an unspoken conversation.

'This is a murder investigation,' Penrose says firmly. 'You've probably heard it on the news or read about it in the papers. It's …'

'We don't read papers,' Crystal announces in a low loud voice. Her tone is clipped, although with a hint of triumph in it. 'We don't watch the news.'

'It upsets her,' Mrs Jones says. 'We watch Coronation Street, EastEnders and Emmerdale.'

'And 'I'm a celebrity get me out of here',' Crystal adds, eyes gleaming. 'I like ….'

'Your fingerprints are on this letter, Crystal,' Penrose insists. 'You'd better tell us why you …'

'I didn't …'

'… why you sent the letter to …'

'I didn't send it.'

'We found it in the possession of Mr Lynham and Mrs Spencer. How did you know Mr Lynham, Crystal?'

'L-lynham? I don't know anyone called Lynham.'

'Then do you know Mrs Spencer?'

A sense of relief and she relaxes visibly.

'I talk to Mrs Spencer,' Crystal says, no emotion in her tone. 'She's always very nice to me.'

'When did you last speak to her, Crystal?'

'I can't remember.' Her eyes drift to the ceiling, eyebrows furrowed in concentration. 'Maybe it was this week. Tuesday.

Or Monday.'

Penrose leans forward, planting her elbows on the table and smiling triumphantly. Clearly, she thinks we're getting somewhere.

'Where did you meet?'

'At the supermarket.'

'Where?'

'At Sainsbury's. It's very close to my work.' She looks sideways at her mother. 'I go there sometimes in my lunch break.'

'Did you see her inside the shop or outside?' Penrose presses on.

I shake my head. It doesn't make sense. Iris Spencer had been in Redruth and Camborne that last day. How could she have been in Newquay at lunchtime?

'We were at the same till. She was in front of me but she let me go first because I only had a bottle of Coke and a sandwich.'

'Crystal!' Her mother interrupts, looking horrified. 'I made you your lunch and you had it with you. There was no need to buy something else.'

'I told you I don't like it when you put lettuce on my sandwich.'

'But it is good for you. You have to eat your vegetables and …'

'Crystal,' I interrupt gently, 'How do you know Mrs Spencer?'

Her eyes widen in genuine surprise.

'Oh, we've known her for years, haven't we, Crystal?' Mrs Jones replies innocently. 'She lives in our street. Oliver, her husband, used to work with my Stan.'

Penrose stirs angrily, missing the point. Then, in the void after Mrs Jones' words, the Mrs Spencer mix-up becomes clear. 'We are talking about Mrs Iris Spencer. The councillor.'

Crystal shakes her head vigorously. 'Oh no, her name is

Cordelia. Cordelia Spencer,' she says, not blinking an eye. 'I think it is a beautiful name. I wish you had called me Cordelia, mum. We can ...'

'Crystal, I think the police officer means someone else who is also called Spencer,' Mr Jones says softly, taking her hand and patting it softly.

Crystal frowns. 'She bought a loaf of bread, Kipling lemon tarts, milk, tea bags, a bag of potatoes, a tin of beans, a bottle of washing up liquid.' She pauses. 'And a tin of Quality Street.' She hesitates, suddenly there are tears in her eyes. 'Are you not angry?'

'You could have told us from the beginning that you don't know Iris Spencer,' Penrose starts, annoyed.

'No Crystal, we're not angry,' I say.

'Mr Baretti will be.'

'Mr Baretti is her boss.'

'Why would Mr Baretti be angry with you, Crystal?'

She drops her head, her eyes drift to the letter still on the table. 'Is it about the letter?'

A small nod.

'We still don't know why you sent it ...' Penrose starts, but I motion her to keep quiet.

'We're not angry, Crystal, and we won't tell Mr Baretti about it. We would like you to tell us about the letter. But it will be a secret. Our secret.'

Tears wriggle their way down her chubby face. Her mother quietly thrusts a cotton handkerchief in her hands. A whiff of roses and lavender. Crystal doesn't react to it.

'I copied it.'

'You copied it?'

Again, a small nod.

'Crystal has a job with *Print-Out,*' her mother explains

proudly. 'A full-time job.'

'It was with other papers,' Crystal says now, appearing not to have heard her mother. 'I didn't see it until I sorted the copies.' She looks down at her hands, clasping them as if in prayer. 'There were sixty of them.'

'Sixty? But how …?'

'Print-Out copies and prints for other companies,' Mr Jones explains, suddenly alert. 'That is our Crystal's job. To make copies for their customers.'

'Do you know who these customers are, Crystal?'

An indifferent shrug. 'I make copies and put them in the boxes. Then Jeremy comes to collect the boxes.' Clearly, Jeremy makes her blush.

'Come on Crystal, you can't deny that you read those papers.'

Crystal blinks at Penrose. 'No … I don't do that. I … I don't understand them.'

'But this one? With the paper cuttings? I'm sure you saw it?'

'I did.' The young woman bows her head, hiding her eyes behind trembling hands. Penrose casts me a triumphant grin.

'There were letters from the council,' Crystal says softly. 'This one was in-between them but I hadn't seen it until it got stuck in the machine. Because of the cuttings. I had to open the machine to get it out. I was worried that Mr Baretti would be angry with me. They are good customers, he tells me.'

'What happened, Crystal?'

'I took the sheet with the cuttings out. There was one copy of it already and I put that in the pile that had yet to be copied. But I was worried, because the sheet with the paper cuttings was a bit damaged. I put it aside to put new glue on, to make it look right, but then Mr Baretti came by and I dropped everything on the floor and he asked if everything was alright.' She blushes, keeping her eyes down. 'I said everything was alright and he went. I was scared that he would come back. I picked up the papers and took everything with me to sort it out with Jeremy. But Jeremy wasn't there.' Her face darkens and her bottom lip trembles. 'I think Jeremy fancies Abbie. He … she … he was in our little kitchen and Abbie went in there too.' A shrug, trying to pretend that she doesn't mind. 'I think Abbie fancies Jeremy too. I see them look at each other all the time.'

'What happened to the papers, Crystal?'

'I … oh … I don't know. Mr Baretti came in. He was angry because I was on my own and Jeremy wasn't there and he asked me if I knew where Jeremy was and I couldn't tell him that he was in the kitchen with Abbie. Mr Baretti … said I looked pale and asked if I was ill and I said I wasn't feeling very well and he said, put the papers down and if I wasn't feeling very well, I could go home and … and I put the papers in a tray and I went home and the papers weren't there anymore the next day and Jeremy said that he had sorted the papers out for me.' She stops, breathless.

'Okay. Thank you, Crystal, Mr and Mrs Jones,' I say, gathering the papers into a neat pile. 'I'm sorry to have put you through the ordeal of having to come to the police station.'

'That's it?' her mother asks, incredulously.

'We have no further questions for Crystal at this moment, Mrs Jones. Sorry for the inconvenience.'

'You're not angry with me?' Crystal asks, pulling at the sleeve of my jacket as she rises to her feet.

'You won't tell Mr Baretti?'

'No, Crystal, I won't tell Mr Baretti.'

Clearly Penrose doesn't agree with the whole situation but she has the decency to keep her outburst at bay until the Jones's have left, Mr Jones promising his daughter that they'll go to MacDonald's on the way home.

'Why did you let her go? Her fingerprints are on the letter that was sent to Iris Spencer! She was trying to blackmail her.'

'All Crystal has done was make a mistake, Jennette. And it wasn't even her fault, I think.'

'What do you mean?'

'I think it was a very unfortunate coincidence. The original letter must have been in a pile of papers that Iris or her secretary had sent to Print-Out to make copies. We'll have to ask *Print-Out* for a list of their customers, but I'm pretty sure that we will find that Iris's office is on that list. And so is Ed Lynham's office.'

'Ed Lynham?'

'The suicide.'

'Yes, but …'

I shake my head. 'I'm not sure yet what happened, Jennette, but it looks like that letter disappeared in a pile that was sent to Print-Out. Crystal accidentally made a copy. I don't know who received the original letter in the first place, but the fact is that the original was found in Iris Spencer's office and the copy was on Ed Lynham's desk.'

'What has Lynham's suicide got to do with Iris Spencer's murder?'

'I think it was just a coincidence, Jennette.'

'I thought you didn't believe in coincidences.'

He smiles tightly. 'Let's ask Massey to investigate this, shall we?'

'Scott Massey? He'll …'

'I think we know what happened, but we need to be certain. It'll be a nice task for Guthrie's protégé, don't you agree? We'll ask him to get his hands on a list of Print-Out's customers.'

The penny drops. Penrose grins. 'Perfect.'

43

In Bodmin, the Town Council came up with an extravagant plan to make the centre of Bodmin a 'traffic-friendly' environment. Although the plans were highly controversial, the work went ahead and, after several years of disruption and chaos, at a cost of millions of pounds to local ratepayers, and loss of revenue to local businesses, the construction works have finished and project 'Building a Better Bodmin' is now in place. The goal was a series of highway improvements which aimed to improve traffic flows, make it safer for people walking and cycling in the area and provide a catalyst for the regeneration of the town centre. Since the completion of the system, the reality is general confusion. There are no road signs and nobody seems to know who has right of way. Drivers are either very impatient or very annoyed and several incidents have been used as arguments by opponents to prove the point that it was a ridiculous idea in the first place. To no avail.

Penrose drums her fingers on the steering wheel as she stops for pedestrians randomly crossing the road. If her brain wasn't working overtime, she would have been annoyed by the hesitating drivers and pedestrians and probably caused a collision with the cyclist who appears from nowhere and launches his bike in front of her.

But at that moment, Penrose has other things on her mind.

She pulls into a car park in the town centre and checks the signal on her phone. There are several missed calls. Maloney. Tregunna. Louisa, her neighbour. Kim Naylor. Tregunna again. And again.

She presses the button to return his calls when her phone rings. Without looking at the screen, she presses the green button.

'Tregunna?'

'Who is this?' The female voice is slightly breathless.

'DC Jennette Penrose. I am …'

'Is Tregunna there?'

'No, he isn't.' Penrose gathers herself. She shouldn't be so impatient with Kim Naylor. After all, for a reporter she can sometimes be useful. 'Listen Kim, this isn't about Iris Spencer's case, I hope?'

A silence. Penrose thinks she can hear the guilt in it. Although Iris Spencer had left strict instructions to her solicitor not to reveal the names of the other beneficiaries in her will, part of the list is now in the papers. Though, she has to admit, not in all of them. From the newspapers she has seen this morning, *The Cornish Gazette*, Kim Naylor's paper, has not published the essential parts of Iris Spencer's will. And not only that, a reporter from another newspaper has been digging deeper into Iris's past and her business affairs, speculating about how she made her fortune. To be continued tomorrow.

Penrose has her suspicions that Kim is annoyed that she's missed the opportunity to attract the attention of the editors of the national press. She wants to spread her wings. Cornwall is getting too small for her ambitions. Which is why she's now trying to get ahead of her colleagues. Possibly, she's after information to blacken Iris's name, to ruthlessly reveal the secrets in her past. In Penrose's opinion, everyone has some secrets in their past. Not all of them need to be revealed.

'Hello? I need to speak to Tregunna. It's urgent.' Kim Naylor's voice is clipped.

'Why?'

For a moment, Penrose's suspicions are redirected towards Tregunna. Is he the one leaking information to the press? No, he can't be. Or … maybe he's let slip something in a cozy tête-à-tête with Kim Naylor? She shakes her head. No. Not Tregunna. Definitely not him…

'Why?' Kim repeats angrily. 'Are you his minder? What I want to discuss with Tregunna is strictly between him and me, Ms Penrose!'

'Oh.' Penrose feels like a deflated balloon. 'Anyway, spare your breath, Ms Naylor. He isn't here.'

'He doesn't answer his mobile.'

'He's probably meeting someone,' Penrose replies carefully. 'Perhaps he is out of reach. You know what it is like with mobile reception down here in Cornwall.'

'It is urgent, Jennette. Really urgent. Where can I find him?'

Penrose hesitates. 'I don't know, is the honest answer.'

'Look, my phone's battery is running out. I prefer not to have it run out completely.'

'Talk to me then.'

'Okay, okay.' Kim Naylor takes a deep breath. 'I have no doubt you've read the papers. You've seen the list of people mentioned in Iris Spencer's will. Whatever you think about me, Jennette, it wasn't me. Honestly.' She stops for breath. 'But that is not so important at the moment.'

She stops to catch her breath. Penrose can hear the other woman puffing and panting as she speaks, as though she's running somewhere.

'What are you doing?' Penrose asks, curiously.

'I had a message on my phone. It was about Iris Spencer's death. Someone wants to meet me and exchange information. This person will …'

Penrose interrupts with a scoff. 'Exchange information?

Isn't that what the police …'

'No! Listen! Please.'

'Okay.' Hearing the urgency in Kim's voice, Penrose stops. 'I'm listening.'

'I have a meeting with Caleb. Iris Spencer's son, if the papers are right.' She doesn't wait for confirmation.

Penrose takes a deep breath. 'Caleb Boyd?'

'He says he has important information for me.'

Penrose shifts in her seat. 'I'm not sure if that is a good idea, Kim.'

'Why not?' Challenging.

Penrose hesitates. If possible, it would be better to keep Caleb Boyd's medical condition out of the papers. 'He's … I'm not sure how old he is, Kim. Perhaps you'll need the presence of one of his parents. An appropriate adult.'

'My information says he's eighteen.'

'Yes, but he isn't …'

'I have no time to argue about this, Penrose. What matters to me is that he has agreed to meet me. In private. No photographers, no nothing.'

'Sounds like you'll get a nice story.'

'He says he knows … who killed …' The connection crackles. ' … his mother.'

'Caleb knows what?'

'He claims that he knows who the murderer of his mother is.'

'And he is going to tell you? You?'

'I hope so. But … listen, Jennette. I would rather talk to Tregunna about this. He'll know what to do.'

'What's that supposed to mean?'

'You know Tregunna … or maybe you don't.' A short silence. 'Jennette, I hate to say this to you, but I am kind of … scared.

This Caleb sounds a bit volatile and I'm rather regretting agreeing to see him.'

Penrose laughs. Loud. Unnerved. 'Is that why you're calling? You want our back-up? You? The press?'

'This isn't the right time to be cynical, Jennette. I am very serious now.'

'Okay.' Penrose gathers herself. Tries to focus. 'Where are you meeting him?'

A brief hesitation. 'Caleb asked me to meet him where his mother was killed.'

'What?'

'You heard me, Penrose.'

'I meant, isn't that a bit suspicious?'

'Is it?'

'I think it is weird, Kim.'

'Exactly, but you know me. I will be recording everything. Ehm … all I want to know before I see him is … if he is one of your suspects?'

'Oh no! You must do better than this, Kim! I am not saying anything.'

'Okay,' Kim says, clearly annoyed. 'This conversation is a waste of time. Just tell Tregunna that he is … My battery is running out now, Jennette. I can't …'

'I'm sure you're efficient enough to have a battery charger with you.'

A deep sigh. 'Can you make sure that Tregunna knows? I want him to be there when Caleb confesses to the murder of Iris Spencer.'

'So you really think it was Caleb?' Penrose has to suppress a chuckle. She has a clear opinion about reporters in general: they have too much imagination and not enough common sense. 'Tell me, was it Caleb who suggested to meet you at Goss

Moor, or you?'

'He did. In fact, he said the deal was off if I suggested somewhere else.'

'You'd better be very careful. There aren't many people about on Goss Moor and I don't think there will be a phone signal, if you need it.'

'I want his story, Penrose, I need it.'

'But you need to be careful, Kim, you can't just …'

She stares at the blank screen. Taps buttons to redial. But Kim has switched off.

44

Traffic speeds under me as I cross the A30 on the flyover. For a moment, I can vaguely see the red roof of a car in the distance. Then it is obscured by the trees. A car pulling a long and heavy caravan pulls over in front of me. Slowing traffic down. I clench my fists around the steering wheel, telling myself that there is no need to hurry. Kim isn't in danger. She won't get hurt. She's meeting someone who is going to tell her, a reporter, something he has found out. Perhaps that is what makes me nervous about it. What he can have found out. Or what he has done.

Kim Naylor's red and white Mini is parked a few metres past the cattle-grid gate. It's parked askew. It looks like it has lost one of the front wheels. Wearing black jeans tucked in shiny purple wellies and a black leather jacket, a yellow scarf wound around her neck, Kim is standing beside her car clutching a crowbar in both her hands. For one long second I have the idea that she's going to attack someone.

She's with her back to me. Staring down at something I can't see. Something in a muddy ditch, shards of thin ice at the edges, cracked where the wheel of her car sank into it.

The quietness is intense. There isn't a single bird chirping or an insect buzzing. No plane taking off, no helicopter flying to the coast to rescue a heedless tourist trapped in a cove. Even traffic on the A30 is reduced to a low rumble in the distance. I can't register what Kim is doing. I jump out almost before my car has come to a complete stop.

'Kim!' I shout. 'Wait!'

She turns. Startled. Her face losing its colour. Then she laughs nervously. 'You scared the hell out of me!'

'I'm sorry. I didn't mean ...' I stop. Point at the crowbar. 'What are you doing?'

She smiles, embarrassed. 'Classic example of a woman driving a car.'

'I don't understand.'

'You know what they say about women parking their cars?' She gestures with her head, dropping the crowbar in the mud. 'See? You've got proof now.'

'You drove into a ditch while you were parking?'

'Not exactly.' Her face darkens. 'I was supposed to meet someone here. I'd been waiting for nearly half an hour,' she says with a mixture of frustration and disappointment. 'Then I realised he isn't coming. Perhaps he thought it was a joke.' She pauses. 'I started my car but I was so angry, also with myself, that I hit the accelerator a bit too hard when I drove backwards to turn.' She pauses. Shrugs. 'I hadn't seen the ditch.'

I point at the crowbar she's still holding in her hands. 'And what about that?'

She grins sheepishly. 'I couldn't think what else to try. The battery in my phone is flat and I couldn't call for help. It was either trying something myself or taking a long walk to the road and hope some helpful person would stop.'

I smile, but I know better than to remind her that women generally aren't as physically strong as men. It isn't discrimination or denying equality. It's just a fact.

I look around. 'Who were you meeting?'

She shrugs. 'It doesn't matter.'

'I think it does.'

'He didn't show up.'

'Kim! Who?' I repeat, more urgently.

'Didn't Penrose give you my message?'

'I haven't spoken to her.'

'Oh. I'm meeting Caleb Boyd.'

'What? Here?'

'He said he wanted to meet me where his mother was killed. He thought there was some symbolism in telling the truth on the spot where it happened.'

I realise I'm holding my breath. An alarm bell is ringing somewhere in my head. There they are again: the glow-worms that shut off their lights and hide in the dark at my approach.

'Were those his words? Exactly?'

'I can't remember what he said exactly. But it is what he meant.' She pauses. 'What I thought he meant. He called me. He wanted to see me. He said he had information about his mother. Something nobody knows about. Not even the police.'

'You should have called the police.'

'I did. I told Penrose.'

'And she probably warned you but you decided to ignore it?'

She shrugs, suddenly with a hint of guilt in her eyes.

'I realised I couldn't stop. I saw the opportunity. This is my job, Tregunna. I didn't want to stop before it got exciting.'

'But you didn't see Caleb? At all? Or anyone else?' I look around, expecting him to emerge suddenly from behind the bushes.

'No. Nobody, except cows.' Sombrely, she points at the ground where flies are having a feast on blobs of cow dung. Fat black flies, some have a shiny, greenish back. They buzz and zoom. They …

I stop thinking. I can't concentrate. Something is still lurking at the back of my mind. Something that is so obvious that I can't see it. I think of Caleb, who asked a reporter to meet him at the very spot where his mother was killed. Symbolism of the truth, he'd said. He didn't show up. Because it isn't the right spot. He knows it. And it can only mean one thing: that's what's been dangling in my face all the time.

'Get your bag, Kim. We'll call someone to get your car later.'

I take her arm. She shrugs free.

'Where are we going?'

'I thought you wanted to know the truth?'

She blinks. 'You know the truth?'

'I think I do, yes.'

'What? Who?'

'Later.' We go back to my car. She gets in, immediately fumbling with a battery charging cable and puts the end in the cigarette lighter. Charging her phone, turning it on.

'No recordings, Kim.'

'But …'

'No Kim. And come to that, I hope we can agree that you will let me read and approve your piece for the newspaper before it goes out?

She shrugs. 'It's my job, Andy.'

'If you can't promise, I'm afraid I'll have to leave you here and I will call someone to pick you up.'

'You can't do that.'

'Promise me.'

'Okay, okay. I promise, alright? But I want a good story not one that is censored to death by you.'

I grin. 'We'll see.'

45

When Penrose gets in her car, the sky opens and a mixture of hail and sleet sweeps across the road. As if she hasn't had enough cold to endure. The heater in her car seems to have given up too. There is only cold air blowing in her face, on her legs and feet. She hunches over the steering wheel, peering out. Switching on the wipers, she curses inwardly at the hailstones that dance on the bonnet and make an eerie sound on the roof.

By contrast, the heating is on full blast at the police station. The desk officer has red cheeks and wet stains under his armpits. 'Always too hot or too cold,' Matt Morrison grunts. 'They can never get it right.'

Penrose briefly considers telling him about her father's latest stunt. That he'd turned off the heating at home because he thought it was summer. She'd better not tell anyone if she doesn't want to become the subject of mockery.

'Any news?' she asks instead.

'Apart from the fact that the cells are full because Newquay's homeless were freezing to death? Nothing.'

She goes up to the incident room, making herself a cup of tea and sits down at her desk, staring at the blank screen of her computer. Accidentally she touches the mouse and the screen comes to life with her 'In' box. A whole list of unread messages.

With a sigh, she opens the top one. Reads, but not concentrating.

They still haven't a clue who killed Iris Spencer. They don't even have a suspect with an alibi they can pick to pieces. Nothing. Only blanks and dead ends.

Her phone rings. She stares blankly at it, numb with cold and lack of sleep. One minute later and her mobile rings again. Matt Morrison's name fills the screen.

'Forgot to tell you something, Penny.' Annoyingly, he's adopted her new nickname. The one Scott Massey gave her. She thinks it's worse than Jenny, but has constrained herself from commenting, thinking Tregunna would tell her to leave it and let it die down.

'What?' she snaps, looking around, but there is nobody within earshot.

'Tregunna called, just before you came in. He's on his way to … Boyd. Is that right?'

'Lester Boyd?'

'Think so. Anyway, he wants you to meet him there. It's urgent.'

She sighs. Takes a sip of her tea. Too hot. Grabbing her handbag and putting on her coat again, she leaves the tea on her desk.

Traffic is slow. The verges are speckled white with melting hail and snow. Rock salt crunches underneath her car. Penrose hunches forward, hands gripping the cold steering wheel as she drives to Bodmin, cursing and swearing as she gets stuck behind a tractor. The driver is either not aware of the traffic behind him, or he has decided to ignore it; he doesn't even pull over when he passes several suitable lay-bys. The decision to take a B-road, doesn't improve her mood, as she comes across a flocks of sheep on the road. The beasts are staring at her, hopeful that she can lead them back into the field. Gazing around with growing impatience, she only sees hedges and walls on both sides; no entrance to a field. Drumming her fingertips on the steering wheel, she dials a number, hoping someone will come to sort out the sheep.

It takes her a few minutes to realise that the number of sheep is growing. They must be coming from somewhere behind her. Reluctantly, she climbs out of her car. The chill of the easterly wind hits her. She shivers, bracing herself against the cold. Her thoughts briefly wander to Guthrie, whose escapade to Bodmin Moor following sightings of an escaped lion made him a laughing stock over the cuddly toy he brought back instead. She'd better not tell anyone back at the station about how she managed to get surrounded by a flock of sheep, otherwise she'll be nicknamed 'shepherd' for ever after.

She finds the gate one hundred yards behind her. Looking over her shoulder to check that there aren't any other people about to take the Mickey, and putting her faith in the idiom that sheep follow each other, she manages to herd two sheep back into the field, but the rest of them are standing their ground, staring at her blankly or even ignoring her while they chew monotonously at the dirty grass on the verge.

'They're scared of you.' A voice suddenly makes her jump with a start. From behind the gate of an adjacent field, a young man has appeared. His face red from the cold, he grins almost from ear to ear. 'If you can step back a bit and go to the middle of the road, I will chase them back.'

'Is that all you need to do?' She feels flushed, embarrassed.

'Well, it isn't always as easy as it sounds.' He grins jovially and walks in the direction of her car, where most of the sheep have gathered peering in at its contents.

He spreads his arms, waving them away and the sheep jump, their hooves clattering on the tarmac. To her horror, Penrose sees them all charging towards her, as though they've just decided she's their target.

'Spread your arms as wide as you can!' the man yells at her.

She stares at him. Is he taking the Mickey?

'Come on!'

Easier said than done. Clumsily, she opens her arms, waves them frantically as she's seen him doing. It seems to work. Only one of the lambs escapes past her, while the rest of the flock are running into the field.

'Thanks.' He grins at her again, closing the gate and sliding the bolt in its place. Then he catches the nervously waiting lamb and holds it in his arms, cuddling it for a moment. Penrose swallows, emotion tightening in her throat for a second as she observes the man's tenderness.

'I'm not used to doing this,' she says.

'You've done very well.' He looks down. 'Your shoes are dirty.'

She follows his eyes. Sheep droppings cling to her soles, sticking out round the edges.

'You can come to my house and clean yourself up if you like,' he offers.

'I don't know.' She feels oddly drawn to this man. His smile thaws her chill like a warm log fire on a cold day. His sparkling eyes light up her whole body, injecting her with life and joy. 'Ehm, I'm on my way to ...'

She stops abruptly. For some reason she doesn't want to tell him that she is a police officer, working on a murder case.

'Bodmin?'

'Yes.' At least it isn't a lie.

'It'll take only five minutes to clean your shoes.' He gestures towards a group of trees further along the road. 'My house is over there. I'm Dan.'

'Okay.' She hesitates, before adding stiffly, 'Jennette Penrose.'

Three minutes later, she has removed her socks, temporarily putting on a pair of thick woollen ones he has given her, while he is wiping her shoes clean with a hard brush. The room is a combined living room, dining room and study. Earth colours. Four armchairs in a semi-circle facing the fire, no sofa. A dining table with stacks of folders, papers and magazines, one corner cleared to make space for a folded tablecloth, dusted with breadcrumbs. In the corner of the room, a desk with a computer and printer. But most impressive is the bookcase that covers the longest wall. Filled with books. Fiction and autobiographies.

'I don't suppose you'll have time for a cuppa?'

She hesitates, then asks cautiously, 'Are you having one?'

He grins again. 'I am.'

She can hear him in the kitchen. Humming. Producing a generous piece of chocolate cake. 'Donated by a neighbour,' he confesses. 'I can't eat everything she gives to me. I put it in the freezer.'

'How many sheep do you have?'

'At this moment? I'm not sure. It's lambing season at the moment.'

'And each ewe has a lamb?'

'More than one, hopefully.'

'Twins?'

'Or triplets, but that can be a bit tricky. There is often one of them which gets pushed away.'

'How sad.'

'I keep an eye on them and if necessary, I feed them with a bottle. Or I try fostering them.'

'Fostering? Sheep?'

'Why not? If it works, it's easier than using a bottle.'

'How does that fostering work?'

'There are several methods, but there's one which, in my opinion, seems to work best. When a single bearing ewe starts lambing, we assist with the birth. We remove her own lamb immediately and replace it with the lamb that we intend to foster. Once the ewe has accepted the foster lamb, we bring back her own lamb. And the ewe thinks she's got two. Not exactly like foster parents and foster children.'

'I don't know anything about sheep,' she says, feeling as if she should have done.

'We can change that.'

'Can we?'

'Of course. In my view, anything is possible.'

He makes more tea. He talks about his sheep as if he knows them like they're his children. Penrose listens and asks questions, thinking she could stay here the rest of her life. No father to worry about at home, no work, no murder investigations. Not even Tregunna.

Tregunna. She has forgotten all about him. Startled, she looks at her watch. 'I … I have to go. I didn't realise what time it is.'

'I have to go too,' he says regretfully, rising to his feet and reaching out for her hand to help her get up from the chair. 'I think we've both forgotten the time.'

'I'm sorry.'

He smiles. 'Sorry for what? It was good meeting you, Jennette Penrose.'

'Thanks for the tea. And the cake. And sharing your knowledge about sheep.'

'I love them,' he says simply.

She stares at him. She knows she should say something, but all of a sudden, her mind is blank. One word blinks in her head like a huge neon advert on the side of a skyscraper. Foster. Fostering.

It is as though someone is waving a sheet of paper in front

of her eyes. She knows she needs to reach for it. Read it, but she can't move. The post-mortem examination report. Name: Iris Spencer. Date …

Caleb.

He'll be confused. Troubled. For him, it must feel like someone has taken the fundamentals away from his whole being. He has found out that Rachel Boyd, the woman he's known all his life, isn't his mother. Not his biological mother. He had to read in the paper who his real mother is: Iris Spencer. A woman he'd hardly met, who died before he was given the chance to meet her and get to know her.

Iris. Who didn't want a child. Who was forced to have it. Who could have had an abortion, but didn't. Yet, the autopsy report said that she had an abortion. Once. They haven't followed that up. They haven't checked if that was before Caleb's birth or after.

Before or after.

Penrose almost stops breathing. She's aware that Dan is looking at her with curiosity and confusion. She can't speak. She has to concentrate. It isn't a question of when Iris had an abortion. Whether it was before or after she gave birth. Because she didn't.

The autopsy report said that Iris Spencer had never given birth.

All of a sudden, everything is so clear that she can't understand why she didn't realise the significance of it before. She or anyone else in the team.

None of them had looked properly at the report. They thought they knew the situation, but they didn't look closer at the one line in the autopsy report that should have alerted them from the very beginning. Iris Spencer named Caleb in her will as her son. A will is an official document. You don't doubt an official document. But a post-mortem examination is conclusive. It deals with facts, not assumptions.

'Is something wrong?' Dan asks.

She stares at his face. Not seeing him.

'Jennette? Are you okay?'

'Yes. Yes I am. I'm sorry, but I have to go.'

'I hope you'll come back, Jennette.'

She doesn't reply. 'Do you have an internet connection?'

'Yes, of course. Why?'

'Can I use it?' She opens her phone. 'I need to call someone. My work. I need …'

She stops. It'll take too long to explain everything to him.

'No, forget it. Thanks. For everything.'

She runs to her car, feeling Dan's eyes on her back. Her mind is a whirlwind. A roller coaster. A tsunami.

If Iris had never given birth, then why did she leave the bulk of her money to Caleb Boyd, who she called her son?

46

There is a black scooter parked on the drive, a fresh patch of oil underneath it. Caleb's. No cars. Not Rachel's green Citroen or Lester's blue Vauxhall.

'Are you sure about this?' Kim asks in a low voice.

The silence is eerie. Even the birds in the trees and hedges alongside the road are holding their breath. Kim feels it too. She is close to me when we go to the front door and ring the bell. A faint ding-dong is heard inside. We wait. Nothing happens. I ring again.

'There's no one here?' Kim is disappointed.

'Maybe he is in the barn, behind the greenhouse. Caleb has a workplace there for his scooters. His father told me that he likes to take the whole thing apart and rebuild it.'

We walk back to the drive and go through a small gate, entering a garden. A grass oval in the middle, surrounded by smallish shrubs. Some of them already have small leaves, others only buds. A handful of camellias, colours varying from pale pink to almost red. The cold winter has delayed their blooming, but it looks like they're trying hard to catch up. A small flagstone path leads to another gate, behind which we find a neat and tidy vegetable garden. Bare canes where beans will be growing later, the seedlings probably still in the greenhouse. The path continues between the greenhouse and a shed, leading to an open, gravelled yard in front of a much bigger barn. Wondering briefly if Caleb has to take his scooter through the vegetable garden to the road, I notice a gate in the wall, leading to a track to the main road. The doors of the barn are wide open. Lester Boyd's car is parked in front of it. The back door is open.

There is a strange sound, like a wounded animal, squirming and moaning. I don't know the reason, but I stop in my tracks, grabbing Kim's arm to shield her behind me, ducking between shrubs and a big black water butt. Water drips in it from the gutter on the greenhouse.

Something feels wrong.

I hear a voice, muttering and sniffing. Feet shuffle on the dusty floor.

'Help me, boy, I can't do this on my own.' The voice comes from inside the barn. It is followed by a scraping sound. A figure appears in my vision. Lester. Then Caleb.

'Who is that?' Kim is tugging at my sleeve, her voice low. I shake my head gesturing to her to keep quiet.

Shoulder to shoulder, we hunch behind the shrubs. 'Lester. Caleb's father,' I whisper.

Someone is sobbing. Caleb.

'Is that Caleb?' Kim hisses, taking her mobile phone from her pocket. For a moment I stare at her, incredulously. She can't seriously consider recording this, can she? At this moment? In these circumstances? But I see from the expression on her face that it is exactly what she is planning to do. She is a reporter. It is in her blood. In her genes. She can't help it.

I push a few branches away, making a gap between them for a better view. A pigeon flies up from beneath it, startling us. My pulse quickens. I see Kim breathing rapidly, as if she's been running a marathon without practising.

'What was that?' Caleb stops sobbing abruptly.

Lester peers out. Shrugs. 'Just one of those pigeons.'

'Dad, I can't ... do this!' He is sobbing again.

'Oh, for God's sake, man, stop crying like a baby! Get up

and give me a hand with this!'

From the doorway, Lester looks out again. He's dressed in the same grubby corduroy jeans, and a grey long-sleeved Old Guys Rule jumper with a logo and the words *Aged to Perfection* on his chest. His green Wellington boots are covered with mud. I expect him to see us straightaway, but he wipes his hands on his hips, looking down at something I can't see.

'Pick up that end, Cal.' He bends, picking up the end of what looks like a roll of green plastic sheet. Only it is heavy. Too heavy to lift for him. 'Cal!'

'I … I can't, dad, I can't.' Anger. Despair.

Lester stands, hands on his hips. Cursing. Swearing. 'Fuck, Cal. You need to help me!'

'You're saying a bad word.'

'Oh, for fucks sake, Caleb, stop it!'

On the road a car drives past. Rock music pounding loudly from open windows.

'You are swearing, dad. Mum says you must not do that.'

Carefully, I push aside different branches. I can see Caleb now. He is slumped on the floor just inside the barn, with his back to a green wheelie bin, his legs spread out in front of him in a weird pose of innocence. His head hanging low, snot drips from his chin and nose. Every now and then he wipes his sleeve over his face.

'The police are coming for you, dad,' he says flatly. He looks up all of a sudden. I freeze. He has seen me. Us. He seems to be staring straight in my face, lips moving, making no sound.

'That is why we need to act quickly son.' Lester is trying to reason with his son. Frustration colours his face as he knows that it'll take a lot of patience and persuasion. Caleb isn't the easiest person to convince and make him change his mind.

'Caleb, please, get up. I can't lift this on my own.'

'What are you doing, dad?' It is as though Caleb hasn't yet realised what his father wants of him.

'We need to get her out of here, boy.'

'Police are coming, dad,' Caleb repeats, the tone of his voice sulking.

'Shut up, boy, help me with this.'

Eventually, Caleb slowly rises to his feet, running his hands through his hair, a picture of despair and sorrow.

'What is in it, dad?' His voice is laden with suspicion.

'What?'

'This sheet. What is in it? Why is it so heavy?'

Kim is frantically pulling at the rim of my jacket. 'Is that what I think it is?'

'Shh.'

'Andy! Is it a body?

'I'm not sure,' I reply grimly.

But I am.

47

'Just stop talking, boy. Get the other end and lift it up. We will put it in the boot of my car. That'll be all. I will take it away.'

Caleb stands, unmoving, the package hanging between them. 'Where?'

Lester sighs with a mixture of fear and despair. I can almost feel his frustration, as his son keeps holding him up. 'I'll take it away. Somewhere safe.'

He pulls, but Caleb isn't yet moving. The tip of one corner slips from his hand. A dull thud.

As if the green sheet somehow has caught fire, Caleb drops it. Screams.

'No! No! No!'

'Be quiet, boy. Don't be stupid. You'll alert the neighbours.'

'But I can see a foot, dad. There is a shoe on the floor.'

Kim is shaking. I can feel her body beside me, even though we are not touching. Her breath is light and shallow and her eyes are wide open. She licks her dry lips. Swallows. Closes her eyes and opens them, hoping to find a completely different view. There isn't.

'You killed my mother.' Caleb's voice is strong and loud. Accusatory. Repeating, 'You killed my mother.'

'Shut up, boy. Rachel is your mother. You know that. She loves you. We both love you very much. You know that, don't you?'

'You killed my mother.'

The constant repeating is finally getting to Lester.

'She wasn't your mother! Do you hear me? Iris wasn't your mother. She didn't even want you!'

Caleb drops his head and stumbles, leaning against the door frame for support. He stares at the shoe again and screams in horror.

'It is her shoe! It is her! I know! She was wearing these shoes when I saw her. You … you killed her. You killed my mother.'

'Cal … son, listen to me …'

Lester stops abruptly. A phone is ringing. He looks around. Startled. Shocked. Aware that they aren't alone. 'What the … ?'

'Bugger.' Kim hisses beside me. 'It is me. It is my phone. I forgot to turn off the sound.'

Lester has seen us. He's coming in our direction with a face that tells me we're in trouble.

'Kim, call the police. Now! It is urgent.'

But before she can dial a number, Lester has reached us and he's holding a knife in his hand.

'Put the phone down.'

She hiccups. Frantically, she punches in numbers, but Lester is faster. He rips the phone from her hand and chucks it away with a wide swing of his arm. Leaves rustle as it lands somewhere on the overgrown wall.

Caleb has recognised me, but stares at Kim. 'Who are you?'

'Kim Naylor.'

He nods seriously. 'I have been waiting for you,' he says accusingly. 'You didn't come in time.'

She shakes her head. 'You told me to come to where your mother died.' She hesitates, sensing that something is wrong. 'I was in time.'

'Iris wasn't your mother, Caleb,' I say slowly. 'You knew that, didn't you?'

He looks from us to his father. And back. Confused. 'Ehm

… I don't know. I think Rachel is my mother.'

'Rachel isn't your biological mother, Caleb. She is …'

'Shut up you!' Lester grabs the collar of Kim's black leather jacket and pulls her in front of him, holding the knife dangerously close to her face. 'You, Tregunna, go into the barn. No tricks. One wrong movement and I will kill her.'

'You killed my mother.' Caleb sounds like an old gramophone where the needle has got stuck in a groove and the end of the song is repeated again and again.

'Shut up!' Lester's face is very white, then it turns red, then white again. His mind is working overtime but he can't concentrate. He can't improvise. Beads of perspiration are gathering on his forehead and on his upper lip.

'You can't get away with this, Lester,' I say evenly.

'You shut up!' To express how serious he is, he presses the point of the knife on Kim's cheek. I see a small red dot appearing, just one inch below her left eye. Her eyes are wide with panic and horror.

'Let her go, Lester. She has nothing to do with this. She is a reporter. She is just doing her job.'

'Exposing people's lives in the papers, that's what she does!'

'She hasn't done anything to wreck your life, Lester,' I say brusquely. 'You've done that all by yourself.'

He shakes his head. Confused. He is worried that he can't keep control over the situation.

'I said, shut up and go into the barn. Caleb, find a piece of rope or something and tie his arms behind his back. Then tie him to one of the chains.'

The chains he's talking about, I notice, are dangling from the ceiling. They're for hanging Caleb's scooter when he's cleaning or repairing it. We step from the pale sunlight into a gloomy barn that is full of racks, tools and junk. Caleb is steering me to one side, Lester following with Kim. She is bleeding, but her eyes are wide and bright. She's recovered from her shock and is trying to think about how to get out of this situation safely.

Caleb is rummaging in a box that contains all sorts of rubbish, finding a piece of bent electric wire. As he straightens it, I put my hand in my pocket as casually as I can and find my mobile phone. Press the button to unlock. 999. Think. Where is the nine button on the screen?

'You! Stop that! Take your hands out of your pockets! Caleb, check him.'

Trying to remember the exact location on the screen, I slip my thumb over it. Press. Press again. No sounds. Again. Then Caleb pulls my hand out, finding my phone. I can see the screen. I have pressed four nines.

'He's dialled 999,' Caleb says slowly. 'He was calling the police.'

'Give me the phone!' Lester grabs it and without looking, chucks it in the water butt just outside the barn.

'You must help us, Caleb.' I say, trying not to beg but to sound patient and reasoning. He is our best option to release us before Lester can do us any harm. 'He is a murderer. He's killed your mother.'

'Rachel is my mother.'

'Your mother is Cecilia, but you know that already, don't you?'

'Who is Cecilia?' Kim. Always the reporter.

I don't take my eyes off Caleb. 'Lester has killed Cecilia. He has wrapped her in that plastic sheet. He is taking her away. You know I'm telling you the truth, Caleb.'

Kim's eyes are shining, sparkling. Despite our precarious situation, she is thinking of her next article, what to write in her article for the papers, to which paper to sell it.

Lester turns around, his knife pointing in my direction. 'Caleb, tie the woman to the other chain.'

But Caleb's mood swings yet again. 'It is all your fault!' He cries out, jabbing his fist towards Kim.

'The only person who lied to you was Lester, Caleb. He told you that Rachel is your mother. That was a lie. Your real mother is Cecilia.'

'No! No! No! Stop lying to me! All of you!' He presses his hands to his ears, squeezing his eyes shut as well.

'Cecilia?' Lester says slowly. 'What are you saying about Cecilia?'

But his eyes betray him. He's already worked it out, probably when he spoke to Cecilia and she told him the truth. He killed her to keep her quiet. I'm not sure whether is was the hurt or the humiliation, knowing, after almost twenty years, that the difficult boy he'd raised as his son, wasn't his. A young cuckoo egg, laid in the nest of his family. A lie that lasted as long as one generation.

'No, no.'

I shake my head, but I look at Caleb, not at the man who has always been a loving and caring father for him. 'It's true. Iris has never given birth.'

Then everything happens very fast. Like a sudden burst of a pipe, unstoppable, gaining in strength. Caleb jumps towards his father. Fighting with his fists. Hitting him hard. Kicking with his toes. Screaming. Calling him a liar, a murderer.

Almost in the path of his rage, Kim pulls back, pulling at the chain. Hers is shorter than mine. I can see that her shoulders are already aching. She looks at the ceiling, then grabs my chain and gives a sharp pull. The chain drops on the floor.

I am free but my hands are still tied. As if on cue, Lester and Caleb stop fighting. Caleb stumbles to his feet. Lester is one step slower.

An eerie silence settles in. Kim is crying softly, aware of how vulnerable she is, tied with her hands above her head, unable to run away. I hear sirens in the distance.

'Police are arriving,' I say. 'Give yourself up, Lester.'

Caleb runs out. Lester shouts after him. A warning. 'Come back, boy. I can sort this. I promise.'

His shoulders sag when we hear the scooter on the drive starting, revving loudly.

Fear is dawning in Lester's eyes. He lifts his hand. The blade of his knife is long. Dirty, but the sharp edge is clear. He has recently sharpened it. Dried blood at the tip. Kim's blood.

He looks at her. At me. Weighing up his options. Kim is still tied to the chain to the ceiling. I can run. He tries to read my expression, wonders if I will leave her behind.

He grins. Madness in his eyes. I try to yell, but it comes out as a groan. He is only a few paces away from Kim. He looks at her briefly, lifting his arm. For a moment I fear he is going to stab her in front of my eyes. I can kick him, but I can't take his knife.

Instead he has other plans. Stumbling forward, he's closing the gap between us. Horror takes over when I realise I am within reach of his knife. It is too late to run. I won't even be able to open the gates in his garden.

Eyes mad, open so wide I can see the whites, he comes forward, aiming to drive the blade into me, aiming for my heart. At that moment, we hear footsteps. Coming closer. Lester spins on one heel, slipping on the dusty floor, losing his balance.

I take a step forward. Shouting a warning to whoever is coming towards the barn.

Lester regains his balance. He stabs. Just in time, I step back.

The knife slides through the sleeve of my jacket but not into my flesh. Kim screams, eyes wide open, terrified. Lester takes one more step and I am within his reach again. My back against a work table with empty plastic flowerpots, trays in which he recently planted seeds. He growls, lips pulled over his teeth. I can see pure hatred in his eyes. This time, I know, he aims for my belly.

My arms tied behind my back, I can only turn away from the knife to defend myself, but I'm too late.

I drop to my knees, bent double, sticking out my elbows in a vague attempt to cover the front of my stomach.

I can hear a scream. It is not Kim. It is me. I can feel the warmth of something liquid on my thighs. The smell is disgusting. My stoma bag is ripped open. The smell penetrates the air. It seems to stick inside my nostrils. I'm embarrassed. Humiliated. I want to be able to get up to change my bag. There should be an emergency kit in my car.

I stumble to my feet, staggering, falling back to my knees, frantically trying to keep my upper body upright. I look down. The stains on the floor are red. Brown. Mixing.

With the realisation that I'm bleeding, the pain arrives. Throbbing, growing in intensity. It is as if someone has driven a heated metal rod into my belly and is jerking it from side to side to cause more pain and damage. I know I need to get away. Away from the knife, away from those mad eyes telling me I'm going to die.

He stands upright in front of me, looking down. Breathing hard. White spit is gathering in the corners of his mouth. He licks his lips. His bloodshot eyes shoot from one corner to the other. He doesn't know what to do. He watches me as I manage to hoist myself onto one knee, bending over to defend what has become the most vulnerable part of my body. My shirt is sodden, sticking to my body. I look down, frightened I see the stains. Red and brown liquid spreading over the concrete floor.

Kim starts screaming again. Lester turns away from me, lashing out. Her screaming stops. She's begging now. Begging him not to hurt her. Begging to stay alive. To keep me alive.

I am cold. I'm shivering. The world around me is shaking. It feels like cotton wool is blocking my ears. Footsteps are running. Grunts and groans. Cursing and swearing.

Someone shouts. 'Caleb!'

Light is fading. I don't know what time it is but I don't think it is already getting dark. Beside me a woman is sobbing, whispering my name, telling me to hold on. Hold on to what? I want to lie down and close my eyes. I'm falling onto my side. I don't want to feel the pain, I don't want to think about the damage the knife has done to me.

Then suddenly the sun appears, shining brightly in my eyes. It is white, pure white. I hear a distant voice. In the light is a figure, coming forward, arms stretched out as if she's going to embrace me. It takes me a while to recognise her. It is Becca. I don't understand. Becca is lying comatose in a bed.

'No!' She screams at me. Or perhaps it isn't her. Penrose? Lauren? Kim? 'Go back, Andy. Go back.'

'Come.'

'Go back.' The pain in my stomach is overtaking all other senses. My fingers are cold, my skin clammy. Becca is gone. The light is fading now.

I am so cold.

48

What should have been a lovely sunny mid-March morning, has become a nightmare. People are standing beside the road, neighbours, passers-by, delivery van drivers. A cyclist in yellow and green Lycra. Two police cars are parked on the road, blocking all traffic coming through. At the entrance of the drive to Boyd's house, a uniformed officer is standing with his legs spread, hands folded in front of him, shoulders made wide, a warning for people not to come closer. His face serious, his eyes are staring over everyone's head. The blue light on the ambulance is still silently flashing.

Penrose stands on the drive beside Caleb's scooter, a blanket over her shoulders, head dizzy, gulping for breath, trying hard not to faint. Her eyes are wide, unseeing, in shock. She's refused to sit down and the paramedic is keeping a close eye on her.

'Alright, love,' the paramedic says for no other reason than to make sure that Penrose focuses. She is a short and stocky built woman, with piercing blue eyes and a sharp pointy nose. She is wearing a green uniform that looks at least two sizes too small and her dark hair is pulled back from her face so tight it makes her look like a Chinese wrestler. Her name tag reads Mo.

'You're doing very well, love. Breathe in through your nose, hold it for a moment, then breathe out slowly through your mouth. Right. That's it. Good girl.'

Obediently, Penrose follows the instructions, not even thinking about objecting. A chubby hand pats on her shoulder encouragingly.

Penrose nods. She will do or say anything just to get away from here.

Voices appear behind her. She turns, but nobody emerges in her vision.

She shivers. Tregunna … 'What's happening?'

In the field opposite the house is the red shape of the air ambulance helicopter. Doors closed. Rotor blades still and silent.

'You were unconscious, love.' Automatically, the paramedic reaches for her hand, to check her pulse, but then pushes up her sleeves, rummaging in a paramedic bag with the other hand.

'I'm not asking what has happened to me,' Penrose snaps. 'I know perfectly well what happened. But I want to know what happened … to Tregunna.'

Mo nods seriously. 'Tell me what happened to you first, love,' she insists. 'Tell me how you became unconscious.'

Penrose hesitates. She has a vague recollection of voices. Urgent. Distraught. Blow on the head. Lost a lot of blood. Concussion. Hospital. Pulse. Emergency. She can't remember what they were talking about. She doesn't want to remember who they were talking about…

'I was hit,' she says, realising that she's got more chance to get away when she gives some answers. Sensible answers.

'Where?' The paramedic is not convinced.

'Where? Down there of course. At the barn.'

'I meant, where on your body were you hit?'

Penrose swallows, confused. She can't think. Her neck feels like it is wrapped in cotton bandages. She has a terrible headache. Every so often, light flashes in her eyes, but she is not sure if it is the blue ambulance light.

'My head,' she says, reaching up with a shaking hand, almost relieved when she feels a bandage on her forehead.

'Do you know who did it? What were you hit with?'

'Why do you ask? You can see for yourself that …' She stops abruptly. A flash of memory. 'Kim. Where is Kim?'

'The reporter?'

Reporter? The world around her is slanting awkwardly. Like she's on a ship being thrashed from one side to the other by huge waves. There are coloured lights. Shapes. Colours. Bright neon lights, like big advertisements on skyscrapers.

'Yes,' she says. Her voice is slurred. 'Where is Kim?'

'She's in the ambulance.'

Penrose stares over Mo's shoulder. The ambulance looks abandoned, the back doors open. The stretcher has gone. A blank monitor screen. A foldable seat. Equipment bags. One of the fluorescent coats is lying on the floor. Nobody. Only those damn flashing lights.

'Why aren't they taking Kim to the hospital?'

More memories are emerging. They are too scary. She does not want to think about them. Behind her, the police officer guarding the entrance to the house half-turns and stares at her with a mixture of pity and compassion. Opens his mouth. Closes it.

'They've taken her to the hospital already,' Mo says crisply. 'She'll be alright.'

Penrose swallows and clears her throat. Her lips are dry. 'And … Tregunna? Where is he?'

There is no reply. The police officer turns his back to her, fumbling with something in his breast pocket. The paramedic just shrugs.

'What is wrong with him?' Penrose grabs the paramedic with both hands, almost shaking her.

'Where is Tregunna? I need to see him.'

'Best not, love.' The paramedic, Mo, smiles sympathetically. 'He was your partner, right?'

'Yes, we were always …' she stops. Something locks in her throat. Was. The paramedic has said he was her partner. Was.

'W-what … what happened?' she asks, realising at the same time that she does not want to hear the answer. She'll be better of being kept in the dark for as long as possible.

Blood, she remembers it now, there was so much blood. On the ground, all over the flagstones on the garden path. Dripping from the knife.

A car stops behind the police crime scene tape. Doors open, bang shut. Footsteps. Quick. Urgent.

'Penrose! Jennette!'

Maloney. His face ashen, his eyelids suspiciously pink. Flashing his ID card in front of the police officer on guard.

'My god, Jennette, what happened?'

His hand lands on her shoulder, shaking her. The paramedic pushes him back. 'Please sir, she is in shock.'

'Why aren't you taking her to the hospital?' Maloney barks.

'Because we're not sure if we will need the ambulance, sir.' She makes a gesture towards Penrose, clearly sending out a warning to him not to say too much.

'What about the air ambulance?'

The paramedic takes a deep breath. 'Too many casualties, sir.'

The police officer steps closer, lowering his voice to make sure the growing number of onlookers can't hear him. 'Three as we speak, sir.'

Maloney turns on his heels so abruptly he almost loses his balance. 'Tregunna?' he asks hoarsely.

'I'm sorry sir.' The paramedic has a sad smile. 'They're trying to get him back sir, but ...' she finishes with a gesture of her shoulders that says more than words.

49

Ten days ago.

The doorbell rang.

Caleb looked up from the chessboard. 'Who is that?'

'I don't know until I open the door, do I?' Lester said, not wanting to show that the interruption was annoying him. He had a terrible headache. Being on his own with Caleb was often so stressful and demanding that he knew it would only get worse. All he wanted was to find a quiet place and close his eyes.

'Don't open it, dad.'

'Why not?' Lester has risen to his feet. The words were pleading with him.

Caleb shrugged. 'This is your home, dad. Whoever is at the door, is invading your space. Our space. This person has chosen this moment to come here and ring the bell and do whatever he or she has set out to do. Right?'

'I don't know what you mean.'

'I'm saying, that everyone has a choice. Always.'

'A choice?'

'This person has made the decision to ring your doorbell. It is your choice to decide whether you open the door or not.'

'Not opening it would be rude, Caleb.'

'Maybe it is also rude to ring the bell.'

'This is ridiculous, Caleb.'

'No dad, it is logic. Simple logic.'

'You want me to stay here and carry on as if we haven't

heard the bell?'

'Why not? We are playing a game.'

'That can wait.'

'The visitor can wait. Or come back later. It is his decision. Or hers.'

'Whatever you say, Caleb, I can't leave anyone waiting on the doorstep and not open it, while they can see that we're here.'

Caleb shrugged, rose to his feet and, as he ran to the hallway, he kicked the chessboard over with his knee. Then he ran up the stairs and closed the door of his bedroom with a loud bang.

Lester shook his head, put the chessboard back on the small coffee table but left the pieces on the floor to pick them up later. Then he went to the front door and opened it just as the visitor pressed the bell again.

'Hi.'

It was a woman in her mid-thirties with dark, short-cropped hair. Three studs in one ear, a big silver ring dangling from the other earlobe. Lester had to force himself not to tell her that she'd lost one of her earrings.

'Mr Boyd? Are you Lester Boyd?'

'I am, yes.'

She nodded briefly. 'I'm looking for Iris Boyd.'

'Iris?' He looked into the street, weary. For some silly reason, he was half-expecting someone else to pop up, giggling and shouting 'surprise!'

'There is no Iris living here.'

'I didn't ask if she lived here,' she corrected. 'I said I am looking for Iris Boyd.'

'She's now called Iris Spencer.'

He could hear footsteps on the landing. A door opened. Caleb, going to the bathroom. Or listening in a dark corner. Despite his reluctance to let his father open the door, curious *about their visitor.*

'Oh. Spencer? And why is that?'

'We divorced.'

'You had a son.'

'I have a son, yes.'

'You and Iris had a son.'

The woman's voice was flat, almost without emotion. He stared at her, his discomfort growing. There was something unnerving about her.

'Do I know you?' he asked slowly.

'I don't think we've ever met.'

'No, but …' He thought of Caleb. His logic. Quite often there seemed to be sense in his reasoning. It makes him wonder how Caleb would react in this situation. 'I don't think so either, but … should I know you?'

He could almost hear Caleb saying this. Absurd.

'My name is Cecilia Cathryn Clarke.'

He shook his head with a weird sense of relief. 'I've never heard …'

'My father was Penhallow. Arthur Penhallow.'

'I don't … Iris's business partner? Who left the country?'

'No, he moved to Bournemouth'

'And you are his daughter? Is that why you are here? To see Iris and Hugh and what has become of the company they started with your father? Bear with me and I'll get you the address of the company.' It's in Truro in …'

'I'm not interested in a company. I want to speak to Iris.'

'She doesn't live here. I told you.'

Upstairs, the toilet flushed. A door was closed and Lester knew that Caleb was on the landing. Listening and waiting until the visitor disappeared. Caleb couldn't handle unexpected situations. Like the arrival of an unexpected visitor. It made him nervous and twitchy. He wouldn't know how to behave, what to say.

'You and Iris had a son.'

'Ehm.' Lester wiped a clammy hand through his hair. 'Rachel and I have a son, yes.'

'Who is Rachel?'

'My wife.' He was uneasily aware of Caleb's presence. Knew that the boy was listening. No doubt trying to make sense of the conversation.

It would be a disaster if he found out.

'Listen, Miss, I can't help you. You can find Iris in her office in Truro. Otherwise, she lives in Newquay. It won't be that difficult to find her. She's a public figure nowadays. She'll be in the phone book, Yellow Pages. Facebook, maybe. Whatever.'

He moved backwards, pulling at the door to close it.

'I want to see your son.'

'What?'

'Caleb, that's his name, isn't it?'

'Yes, but …' He was so surprised he didn't fully register that Caleb was moving towards the top of the stairs.

'I need to see him.' The woman's voice was trembling now. Tears in her eyes. He noticed, all of a sudden, that those eyes looked strangely familiar.

'Who are you?' he asked, his heart in his mouth.

'I'm Caleb's mother.'

'That's ridiculous.'

He could hear Caleb smothering a sound behind his hand.

'Listen, lady, I don't know what you want, but I have nothing to do with Iris anymore. We divorced years ago. Please leave me and my family alone.'

'I have travelled from Australia to see him.'

'Dad?'

'It's okay son. This lady is leaving. I'll make us a fresh cup of tea and we'll play chess again. Okay?' As he was talking to his son, Lester closed the door. Almost closed it, because the young woman put her foot on the doorstep.

'Leave us alone, please?' he hissed, shocked and panicking. He didn't know the woman, but he knew intuitively that she was about to cause trouble. A lot of trouble.

'No,' she said firmly.

'Listen.' He lowered his voice. 'I don't want my children to get upset.'

'You listen to me, Mr Boyd.'

'Alright, alright. Let's go to my conservatory. We can talk there, in private.' Without waiting for her reaction, he stepped outside and took her arm, ushering her to the back of the house.

'Listen,' he said urgently. 'Caleb is different from other children. He doesn't know Iris. He doesn't know Rachel is his real mother.'

'I am his mother.'

'That's ridiculous. Iris is his mother. She ...'

'No. Ask her.'

'I have no intention of asking her things like that.'

'Were you there when the boy was born?'

'Yes. Well, not really. He was born too early. She was visiting family in Scotland with her mother. He was born in Glasgow.'

'That's true,' she nodded seriously. 'But it wasn't Iris who gave birth to him. It was me.'

'This is ridiculous. I'm his father. I don't even know you.'

'I'm sorry. It's the truth.'

'No. I have never ... we have never ...'

She saw his distress, but despite saying she was sorry, she smiled at him. 'We never made love, Lester.'

'But how can you ...? Who ...?' He stopped. Swallowed.

'Who is his father?'

He stared at her. However unbelievable and farfetched it all sounded, in his heart he knew that it was true. It explained so much …

'I don't know who his father was, Mr Boyd. I was fifteen. I had a little job at my father's company. I worked for him, for Iris and Hugh. That night, there was a party. Iris invited me. It was only afterwards that I realised that she had plans for me. Oh, she was very kind, offering to take me home in her car before the end of the party. Then she drove to a dark road. We stopped. She touched me. Tried to kiss me. It was … awful. Disgusting. I couldn't believe what was happening to me. I was upset, I told her I wanted to go home. She started the car again and we drove back to the main road, but she still tried. She told me she was in love with me. She said she knew I felt the same. I had looked at her … in that way. I didn't know what she meant. I was scared. And when I got the chance, I got out and I ran into the woods.'

She was crying now. Lester stared at her in disbelief, knowing she wasn't lying.

'I ran and ran. I got lost. Then I found a petrol station. There was a van parked there. I was so cold and the van was warm. I sat there for a while. And I fell asleep. Then the driver got in. I asked him to take me to Newquay. I thought he would do that. But he stopped and raped me.' She let out a high-pitched laugh. 'Can you believe that? I ran away from a woman and ended up with a man. It was much worse with that man, I can tell you that.'

'I'm …'

'I couldn't tell anyone. I couldn't tell anyone that it was Iris who had caused me to run away from her. Who would believe me? And I couldn't tell anyone that a strange man had raped *me.'*

'But ...'

'Three months later, I found out that I was pregnant.' Her tears dried, her voice was devoid of any emotion. *'It was Iris's fault. I had to make her pay for it. I knew she didn't want children. So I blackmailed her. I forced her to accept the boy as her child.'*

'That was Caleb?'

He looked at her incredulously. Shock and disbelief on his face, but slowly those feelings were overtaken by anger. Rage.

'Are you saying,' he said slowly, his voice hoarse and low. 'Are you saying that the boy I raised as my son, is not my son at all? He is the son of a rapist and ... you?'

'I'm sorry.'

He opened his mouth to say something, he didn't even know what. But there was a movement in the corner of his eyes. Caleb. His face white and eyes like charcoal.

Blindly, Caleb grabbed something. A spade. Pieces of dried mud dropped on the floor as he lifted the spade above his head, stepping towards the man he'd always known as his father.

'You lied to me.'

'Caleb, I swear ...'

'You aren't my parents. You and Rachel are liars. You are ...'

'I didn't ...'

Lester stopped abruptly, astounded when Caleb dropped the spade and turned away. He ran. Lester made a gesture to follow him, but then froze as he heard an engine revving. It wasn't safe. Caleb couldn't drive now, not in this state ...

'I didn't mean ...' Cecilia Cathryn Clarke said. ' I never ...'

'No?' Lester picked up the spade and swung it. He heard her skull crack. He wasn't sorry at all. All he knew was that this woman wasn't the only one who had to pay for this betrayal, this agony. There was Iris too.

50

There is no laughter, no banter. No triumph or celebration. The team is silent. Only the most important thing is being said. Everyone is still shocked about what happened to Tregunna.

Penrose sits at her desk, staring blankly at the window. Her dark blonde hair is shaven where they stitched the wound and it is standing upright around the edges. Her lips are almost as white as the knuckles of her hands, as she sits and holds the edge of the desk.

'Penrose! What are you doing here?' Maloney comes in. His voice is as dark as his face, his eyebrows furrowed.

'I can't stay at home, sir. Sorry. I just can't.'

That morning, when he arrived at Lester Boyd's house, he had asked her to tell them what happened. She started crying and said it was all her fault. Because she arrived too late at the crime scene. Because of the sheep on the road. Because they had black heads and pale eyes and they stared at her accusingly. Even they seemed to know that she was to blame. Because she'd been drinking tea. Milky tea. Because she was warming her feet by the fire place and listening to the voice of Dan, the shepherd.

At that point Maloney had interrupted and ordered Champion to take Penrose home. 'She isn't fit for work.'

Penrose had resisted. She knew he was right, though, but the prospect of being at home all day with her father and with nothing else to do than relive that day and think what she could, what she should have done differently, was worse than anything else.

'Bollocks.' he snaps. 'I gave you an order.'

Penrose lifts her chin, tears welling up, but she swallows them away. 'I want to work.' She almost shouts. 'I need to work! I can't sit at home and do nothing.'

Maloney opens his mouth. She knows he's going to tell her that she needs counselling, that he won't want to see her coming back before she's been declared fit for work again. If ever. But the phone rings and Maloney is immediately distracted.

DS Ollie Reed picks it up, his face flushing with anticipation. As he listens, his shoulders sag and his curt 'thank you' comes as an afterthought. He puts the receiver back and looks around, his eyes wandering across their faces.

'That was Boris Cawley,' he says flatly. 'The referendum is off. His brother Nathan has withdrawn the application for the development of the plot.'

'I bet he didn't have any other option,' Penrose interjects. 'He won't get anywhere without the support of his corrupt councillor.'

'Penrose,' Maloney starts, but she shakes her head and continues. 'If that woman had been a considerate human being like us, this would never have happened.'

'Her death had nothing to do with that.'

'Iris Spencer was a corrupt councillor. She'd been doing it for years. Hiding her corrupt activities using her old mother. Who would have suspected anything? The poor old soul didn't have a clue! She was suffering from dementia and her daughter managed to get power of attorney over her. There was nobody, nothing to stop her concealing her illicit financial dealings in her mother's name.'

'Let's not forget that Iris was also the victim of a ruthless murderer,' Champion says softly.

'She's only got herself to blame!'

'Jennette, you're not fit for work,' Maloney repeats, pity on his face and in his sad tired eyes.

But Penrose shakes her head. She can't let it go. 'We need to prepare this case for court. We need to make sure that there are no loose ends and that the murderer gets convicted, and that Iris Spencer and the likes of her are publicly nailed to the pillory.'

'That is enough, Penrose. We are the police. We make sure that justice is done. Our job was finding Spencer's murderer and we did that. Our next job, as you say, is to make sure that we have all the evidence sorted so that the prosecutor can make his case. But we are not here to malign Spencer, or her business, however ill-founded that was.'

Penrose feels her cheeks burning. She swallows heavily and it takes all her strength to hold her tongue. If she wants to keep working with the team, she'd better be careful about her comments and behaviour.

'Jennette, please rest assured that we will do everything to make sure that every crime in this case will get our attention,' Maloney says diplomatically.

Ollie steps forward and before anyone else can say something, he interrupts quickly

'Anyway, this call from Boris Cawley is a step in the right direction. Boris just told me that Nathan has sold half of the piece of land to him, so that he can widen the lane and make access to the farm easier. The other half will be used to build affordable homes for the locals.'

'That's at least one good thing that's come out of this,' Champion says.

'But it won't bring the victims back.'

At these words from Penrose, the atmosphere changes

again. Silence fills the room. They are all staring at their feet, hands, the ceiling, avoiding each other's eyes. Penrose turns to her blank computer screen and swallows, taking deep breaths to control her breathing. Maloney is right. She isn't fit for work. She will do as she's told. Accept the fact that she really needs counselling. But not from someone Maloney or his superiors will assign her to.

She won't go home, though. She'll take the B-road, the same road she took when she went to Bodmin. With a bit of luck Dan will make more tea for her. He will talk about his sheep. His lambs. Grin at her again. He doesn't know what happened. He won't look at her with pity or accusations in his eyes. She will tell him, though, but later, not today. Somehow she needs to create some distance between her personal and professional life.

'Okay,' she says.

'Let Champion take you home,' Maloney says, suppressing his relief. 'And Penrose, I don't want to see you here before next week.'

'Okay,' Penrose says again. There is no point in arguing and in all honesty, she knows she needs to get away from all this. 'But I can drive myself. It isn't necessary for Danielle to drive me.'

Maloney stares at her. Eventually he nods. Penrose gets up and tucks her handbag under her arm. As she walks out of the room, her fingers stroke Tregunna's empty desk.

It feels like a farewell.

Carla Vermaat

TREGUNNA

In a farmhouse on the Camel Estuary in Cornwall, a 5-year-old girl finds her parents brutally murdered.

Fifteen years later, the house is deserted and the killing still remains a mystery.

Then the body of a 50-year-old woman is found on a cliff edge in Newquay. DI Andy Tregunna is faced with the task of leading the investigation, but soon personal matters force him to step back.
On compassionate leave and with little else to do than fight his own demons, the unsolved case becomes more and more an obsession to him. As he is draw deeper into a dark world of secrets, lies and revenge, his private investigation collides with his personal life.

The truth is even more sinister than can be imagined ...

WHAT EVERY BODY IS SAYING

A warm sunny day in August. Cyclists pass on the Camel Trail near Padstow. For a young couple, their happy life comes to a sudden halt with an horrific find in the mud on the river bank.

Six weeks later, Tregunna delves into the case of missing schoolgirl Leanne. He is still on compassionate leave and with little else to do than fight his own demons, the case can't be more welcome for him.

Then a shoe with a foot still in it, is found at Pendennis Point and when more body parts wash up along the Cornish coast, it soon becomes clear that they all belonged to the same person.

As he is drawn deeper into a world of violence and revenge, Tregunna comes face-to-face with an old adversary to haunt him and it seems that the past can never be buried ...

COVER THE LIES

Two women enjoy a night out in Newquay. Only one of them comes home.

A man who shares the care of his demented father with his sister, doesn't come home from an early morning meeting.

As the investigating team focus on the disappearance of one of the suspects, Tregunna approaches both murder cases from a totally different point of view.

Notoriously stubborn and uncooperative, he work in his own unorthodox way when a picture of a young girl leads him to someone with a secret so incredible that even he can't believe it.